The Devil's Eyes

Jennifer Loren

ISBN: 0984733604
ISBN-13: 9780984733606

DEDICATION

This book is dedicated to everyone who gave me a smile when I needed it, made me laugh to keep me from crying and cried with me, when words just weren't enough.

PROLOGUE

The last time I saw him, I didn't breathe again until he had dressed himself completely. From the crack in my sister's door, I saw him get out of her bed and inhale, as if he had accomplished his mission for the day. I had seen many of my sister's boyfriends before, but none were ever like him. Athletes, academic-All Americans, and the prom king, attractive as they may have been none came close to comparing to him. You could recognize him from any angle: lean tall stature, deep black hair, and a walk that had an air of authority - like no one could possibly have anything to say that was of any importance to him. Biting my mouth closed, I struggled to keep from blinking as I watched him, taking in his entire body with a long, single breath. I knew his body would be incredible, but the blackened tattoo blazing up his right side reminded me that despite his designer clothes, his background was all but respectable. It was his eyes, though. Ooh his eyes … Adjusting himself comfortably as he dresses, he only glances at my sister's naked body draped across her bed, still gasping for more from him, until she faints from exhaustion. Without even a single word, without even a gentle kiss on the lips, or even a wave of good-bye, he walks out the door making eye contact with me for only a second. It was at that moment that he lured me in. I was captivated by him and, for the first time, I understood his power. Nicholas Jayzon commanded attention when he walked into a room. If you were ever damned enough to make eye contact with him, you would know what it is like to be lured in by *The Devil's Eyes*.

~1~
KAYLA

*T*oday is the anniversary. After picking up some flowers I catch the noon train to the Bleaker Street bus stop and ride it all the way to the cemetery. I walk solemnly to the modest grave marker and crouch down to lay her favorite flowers next to her name. "Hi Bray. I know it has been awhile but I have had a lot going on lately. A lot of work to do you might say, but it has finally paid off. I have worked real hard learning everything I can about him and how to get his attention."

"Those are beautiful flowers, dear." Stunned, I turn around to see an unassuming, older woman walking towards me. "Oh, I am sorry I startled you. My manners aren't the best sometimes."

Standing, I brush myself off with a gracious smile. "It's perfectly alright, I guess I wasn't paying attention."

The old woman grips my arm and struggles to read my sister's name. "Braylin Patrick ... someone special to you?"

"My sister." I said with a shaky breath.

"Oh, she was so young." The woman said with a tragic expression.

"Yes. Too young."

"Excuse me for being nosy, but how did she die? I have always wondered what happened. My husband is right over there and I pass her grave all the time."

"It is a long story." I tell her, hoping to end our conversation.

"Well, I don't have anywhere to be. My son isn't due to pick me up for a while now. So, if you don't mind, I would love to hear about her. My name is Dorothy." She responds with a friendly face.

"Kayla. Nice to meet you." I give her my hand with a weary smile.

"You were close to your sister, weren't you?" Dorothy asked and I nod simply. The woman seems to sense my hesitation, "It may help you to talk about her, I know I always feel better remembering

2

my dear Charles."

Faking a smile, "I don't want you to think she was always like the way she was at the end, because she wasn't."

"So, start where you feel comfortable." Dorothy pushes with a little more persistence.

Taking a deep breath, I look down as the breeze blows the dirt across her name. "Braylin wasn't just my sister, she looked after me once she was old enough to get her own place. She was optimistic, responsible, and motherly. She wouldn't let me work so I could concentrate on school. I could take classes during the school year and in the summers so I finished high school in less than three years. I loved living with her, even though I worried about her all the time. I always tried to pretend I had been asleep for hours when she would come home from work only because she would worry if I waited up for her so late. Except for Fridays. On Friday, Bray would buy me a used book with what she had left over after paying the bills. I couldn't wait to read it. I would rush to the restaurant where she worked to see her just so I could start reading it right away. When she would get home we would lie against each other and I would read it again to her."

"She sounds like a wonderful sister." Dorothy says with a smile.

"Bray was beautiful, she had every man she met with eating out of her hands." I smiled at the woman before recalling the reason she is here. "Except for one, he had her spinning for him. When we escaped my mother's house, Bray promised to take care of me. *"Take care of us,"* she said. And then one day she came home on top of the world. She had met the perfect man and he was going to take us away from the run down shack we were living in, buy us a new car, and even help pay my way through college. I was already sneaking into the college and taking classes on my own. The prospect of being a student became all I could think about and Bray knew it and tried even harder to please him. I should have known better, I shouldn't have been so excited and encouraging of the relationship. No man is that wonderful." Bending down, I reset the flowers against the marker and brush the dirt away from her name. "The first time I met him, not even a meeting really, he came over to see Bray and he didn't notice me at all. I was so nervous around him I would hide whenever he would come over. I don't know why, but I was jealous of her. I never thought anything about her other boyfriends. But Nick … Nick was amazing. He would buy her some beautiful things and treated her like a queen. I began dreaming about him, pretending he was my boyfriend. It all seemed perfect for a time and then suddenly he stopped coming around. I never knew why, but I assumed it was because of me. Bray suddenly would stay away from home for days and would forget to pay the bills. I was afraid she was staying with him because he didn't like me. When she did come home, she was lost- absent of any life. She would carelessly throw money at me and tell me to deal with the household bills. "She didn't have time," she said. She would be gone all-night and sleep all-day, if she slept at all, most of the time she cried. I asked her so many times if it was Nick and she would say "No ... no, Nick's perfect." I tried to ignore the signs, hoping that she would pull herself back up but she was doing whatever she could to please him or what she thought would please him. It didn't take me long to realize what she had become, what he had turned her into. Drugs, prostitution, whatever he needed she did until he finally agreed to meet with her and discuss getting back together. She was overjoyed to see him again. She had spent all-day getting ready, even bought a new dress." I smile remembering her spin joyfully in front of her mirror. Taking a deep breath, I continue. "But ... he dismissed her like she was nothing. She came home devastated and nothing I said or did would bring her out of it. After days of sitting up with her, I finally fell asleep. The next morning I found her ..." Tensing my lips, I fight back my tears. "She had hung herself from the showerhead." Sighing, I wipe the tears from my cheek and refocus on my mission.

As I crouch down and hold my face, the old woman takes my head in her hands, "Oh dear, that is terrible." She pats my head searching for the right words to say. "How did you get by after that?" She asks surprisingly. I didn't expect her to ask any more questions. *Was that not enough to know about a total stranger? Nosey old woman.*

Standing, I clear the lump in my throat, "I was still under age so they sent me back to my mother and her new husband. He was the worst of them all. He hid all my books from me one night. He promised to give them back to me, depending on the deeds I would do for him. Each deed was worth so many books. Give him a blowjob? I got one. Let him screw me? I got two. If I entertained his friends, I could get three back. I told him to go ..." I look over at the old woman's horrified expression. "Well, I said no." The woman snickers some as I try to clean my language for her.

"Good for you. I am sure you earned some respect from him

then." She said with an encouraging smile.

"Not exactly. He took all my books outside and started to burn them. I was in a rage and I went at him to try to save my beloved books. I tried kicking him and hitting him to get him to stop. I don't know what I was thinking, he was so much bigger than me. He had me down on the ground in an instant, telling me the dirty things he was going to do to me. I screamed and I kicked and I screamed some more."

"He didn't …?"

"No, actually, a crazy thing happened. A man came out of nowhere and started yelling at him. While he was distracted, I ran and hid. The next thing I remember is hearing my stepfather scream. Whoever the stranger was, he stabbed my stepfather to death. Probably some out of his mind drug addict looking for money. There were plenty of them around. I stayed hidden for a couple of days. When I returned my mother was passed out drunk and my books were gone. So I gathered what I could and ran away for good."

"Well at least you were able to get away from him. I am sure your sister would be proud of you now."

"I hope so." I said.

"Well, dear, I have to go. My son is here and he gets impatient quickly." Cradling my face she looks up at me fondly, "He is single by the way." She said pointing to the nearly bald, squirrelly man sitting behind the wheel of a giant old Lincoln. Looking back up at me with her eyebrows raised, she seems hopeful.

After what I told her and she still wants me to date her son? He must be a perfectly wonderful catch. "Well, I don't know. If he wants to visit me at work sometime, I will talk to him and see if we have anything in common. I start tonight at Pigalle Place." Without another breath passing between us, she is gone- waving good-bye as she double steps towards her son's car. I watch her leave with a slight smile. *I guess I am not right for her son after all.* Pigalle is well-known in this city, even among the elders who wouldn't dare step foot in such a place no matter how upscale it is. I turn back towards Braylin's grave and take in a deep breath. "Don't worry, Bray. I know what I am doing and I am prepared for him. Unlike the others, I know what to expect from him. I know how to gain his interest and beat him at his own game. I have nothing to lose now and he has everything for me to take."

~2~
KAYLA

*H*e walked out of our lives, making us feel privileged that he even bothered to make the trip across town for us. I am not even sure he knew her last name, or cared to know, let alone remember me. There was no reason for him to remember me. I was awkward and shy the last time I saw him. We never spoke and he only looked at me the one time. I have changed a lot since then and I am not a shy, awkward girl anymore. Now I am a woman who is standing outside his club working up the courage to go in and perform well enough to gain his attention. Stripping was never my intent, but it is money and more than I can possibly make working at the same diner my mother worked at until her pained legs gave way. *Oh hell, why do I even bother to think of her at this moment?* She was no saint and certainly no mother to Braylin and me. The men she brought home were no saints either. I think she drank so she wouldn't have to realize what was going on around her. It was Braylin that got us out of there. Bray's on a rare occasion, successfully, gambling father was kind enough to give us enough money to get us started. We didn't dare bother to ask for much more. And, of course, my father, whoever he may be was useless to us. Walking in the, for the moment, brightly lit room, I gaze over the stage that I performed on to get this job. "Great ass and certainly great tits," the judges said as they admired my every move. I know I have the body- they didn't have to tell me that- or that I am innocent looking enough to drive the men crazy, but I blushed when they called me pretty. "Really pretty," they said, twice. No one has ever said that to me. They have commented on my body before, or my long brown hair, or my bright green eyes, but I never have been called pretty.

"Kayla, come with me and I will show you your locker and your area. It's your responsibility to keep it clean and make sure you have all your valuables locked up. I'm not policing every girl in this club,"

Kyler, the manager of the club, tells me as he walks me through to the back of the club. "You did bring a lock with you, didn't you?"

"I did. And I picked up some new costumes and makeup from the supplier you suggested." *Suggested?* It wasn't much of a suggestion. This is no ordinary gentleman's club. The women have to be perfect, expensive, and, yet, unattainable. The women don't strip nude, they leave a well designed and expensive g-string bikini on, not that it covers much. Between the somewhat respectable line of the barely there bikini and the money, it is enough to draw in some of the most beautiful dancers. The place is so clean and so upscale that even women come here to watch the shows, some come for the atmosphere of rich men and others hoping to meet Nick. Nick has a reputation and every woman in the city is aware of it, if not from word of mouth, then simply by catching a glimpse of him. He has come a long way since dating my sister. He is no longer the bagman for Harvey Rice. In fact, he took over most of what Harvey used to own and now nearly owns the city. And yet, he is only a few years older than me.

Kyler opens the door in front of me and points to an area with a makeup table and a small, open closet. "Well, here you are. It's not a bad spot but make sure you keep your things on your side of the closet. You're sharing with Meagan. She is not too good about sharing and I am not too good with having to listen to her complain. So, please stay away from her." Kyler's stern look gives me pause but it is not enough to scare me.

"So! You're the new girl." I turn towards the lanky, dark figure coming at me, full of attitude and swagger. "I'm Exie and despite what you may hear I am the best dancer here. No one else compares. So, don't even think you're going to come in here and take my time slots."

With a slight smile, "Well, if you're that good then you shouldn't have to worry about it, should you?" I said.

Exie's bright smile forms smoothly across her face, "I like you, so a piece of advice from me to you: most of these bitches are backstabbers, but as long as you understand that pretty much whatever you're told is a lie, you will be fine." From the moment Exie eyed me up and down, I knew we were going to be good friends.

"Thanks, I will keep that in mind." I said.

"No problem. Now, I hope your little white ass can dance because, if you can't, you will not make it here. They are constantly bringing in new girls to keep the atmosphere fresh. The same goes for your outfits and your routines. Otherwise, you will be replaced quickly." Exie said admiring all my makeup. "Can I borrow this? I will give it back."

I snatch the tube of lipstick out of her hand as she tries to disappear with it, "I don't think so! Get your own."

Exie smiles, putting her hands on her hips, "You may last after all."

The night goes as I would have expected: a little nervous the first round, but eventually I learn to focus outside my surroundings, and put myself in a place that eases my nerves. This isn't my first time on stage, but this place is a little more intimidating because of its upscale clientele. During my down time, I watch from the side as each dancer performs, waiting, and wondering if he will ever show. Towards the end of the night, walking in like she owns the place is Meagan. Looking me up and down, she spaces herself around me as if I have a disease she doesn't want to catch. Her superior attitude is understandable, the gorgeous blond dresses to kill and a single piece of her jewelry would pay my rent for a year. I'm impressed despite her loathing of me. Not far behind her, Nick swaggers in with his entourage of men, all dressed in designer, tailor-made suits. As always, he commands attention from the moment he enters and is already causing my knees to shake and my heart to race. I have prepared for this numerous times in my head, but standing near him again is almost enough to send me running out the door in fear of failure.

"Hot as hell, isn't he?" Exie questioned from over my shoulder.

"Yea, I guess he is."

"You guess? Are you blind? Girl, he is so fine it's scary. I nearly had an orgasm the other day when he asked me for a cup of tea. But don't stare too hard, Meagan will scratch your eyes out if she catches you staring at her man." Exie said with a high eyebrow warning.

"He is seeing Meagan? Why?"

"That's Nicholas Jayzon, the man that owns this club and the sole reason that Meagan thinks her shit don't stink. And why the Bitch is getting the prime time slots. Not only is Nick sexy as hell but he also takes care of his women, which isn't only Meagan no matter what she may say. Although she seems to be the main one or at least the one he flaunts in front of his associates over there. The worst part is the scrawny white girl can't dance for shit. If it wasn't for her big tits and blond hair no one would look twice at her." Exie sighs and walks away with an air of disgust and jealousy. Laughing as Exie does a mock impression of Meagan's dancing, I find a good spot and eagerly wait until Meagan enters the stage. She gives a weak performance, just as Exie said she would. It doesn't matter to me though because I mostly watch Nick: how he moves, how he watches her, how he responds to every twist and turn that she makes. When she finishes he gets up to leave, catching sight of me with interest. Holding my ground, I take his intimidating stare head on. Nick pauses briefly before a slight smile tugs at the corners of his lips. He turns away from me and after a second glance over his shoulder, I know he is interested.

~3~
KAYLA

*A*fter my first week at the club, Exie invites me to have breakfast with her and to shop for some new costumes, since I only have a couple that are worth showing at the club. "So how was your first week?" Exie asked barely bothering to look my way between her admirations for the passing men.

"Do you come here because you actually like the food?" I asked her.

Smiling with a wink, "Well, I do like their sausage." She said taking a bite of her food. "Seriously, how are you doing?"

"Fine." Her expression seems to question my response. "I'm fine. Really. Why are you looking at me that way?"

"I don't know, but something about you doesn't fit."

"What about me doesn't fit?" I laugh.

"I'm not sure yet, but all the girls, well, except for Meagan, come in, do their job, and are just as eager to leave as they are to get in and make that money. You, however, hover and stick around like you never want to leave."

"I don't know what you are talking about," leaning back in my chair, I pretend to check out the passing runner.

"Do you have a place to stay? Is that why you shower at the club? Why you stick around long after your shift is over?"

"I, uhhh, I am between places right now." I said dismissing her concentrated stare.

"Where did you stay last night?" She leans in closer to me as she continues her interrogation.

"Motel. It's not bad. It is clean, quiet, and easy to get to." Exie's head cocks in a caring position. "What?" I said as she rolls her eyes.

"Don't think this is an invitation because I like you, but I could use the help on rent and I do have an extra room ... if you're interested."

"Can I borrow your shoes too?" I laugh as her expression instantly changes to disgust.

"Don't push it! And there are some rules you have to follow. No men, no drugs, and no alcohol in my house. My little boy is only five and I don't want him around that if I can help it."

"That won't be a problem."

"Oh, and he is not good with boundaries- so make sure you lock the bathroom door. He has caught me a few times but I am his mother. Seeing your white ass might scar him for life."

Laughing, "Got it."

"Any kids of your own?" She asked with a sincere curiosity.

"No, I like kids but me as mother is ... well, it's best that I don't." I replied.

"Details, please." She pressed, leaning towards me again with a growing interest.

"My sister was the motherly one. I have always been the selfish one, too selfish to warrant having children."

"Well, at least you are honest about it. I can't say Jerran was part of my plan, but I wouldn't give him up for the world. And as far as stripping goes, it is only a means to an end. As soon as I finish my degree, I am packing up Jerran and moving far enough away from here to start over."

"You're going to school?" I asked, scooting to the edge of my seat.

"Wow, girl! That got you perked up. Do you want to enroll? If so, I know this great counselor who can help you with grants and ...."

"No. School ... that's not for me." I say, easing back in my seat with a disinterested, wandering eye.

"Really? Hmmm, that's what I thought too. I hated high school so I thought, why bother suffering any further? But college is different. You might like it. I actually thought you were in school when I met you. You talk differently than everyone else, more sophisticated. That's why I thought you took the job- to help pay for classes or something like that."

"No, but I do read a lot. I love to read. I could read for days and never stop. I use to be such a bookworm. I would barely look up to notice much of anything."

"So, why not go to school?" Exie asked concentrating on my reaction suddenly.

"Because that dream died a longtime ago and ..." Pausing, I know there is no comfortable way out of this one, so I change the topic. "I think now I would like to see my new place."

"Okay, but I am not done talking to you about this." Exie retorts, picking up her bag to leave.

"Wonderful, so excited to be moving in then," I said as I walk back to Exie's car.

"Oh my! Did you see him?" Exie stops abruptly and turns to watch a man who smiles at her. "Ooh yea, he is fine."

"You're not going to stop to talk to him?"

"Why ruin what we have by getting to know him?" She said with a wink.

СЗВО

*T*he club is especially insane on Saturday nights. The clientele doubles since this is the night women come in. At the end of my shift, I get comfortable in a dark corner and watch them all chatting with one another like they don't have a worry in the world. I imagine their lives outside this place to be dull and routine. The women, with their bachelorette party gear and high-pitched squawking, are the easiest to distinguish- with their Beamer key chains and Jimmy Chu shoes, preparing to marry Mr. Perfect, live in their perfect house with their perfect kids, and ignoring it all to pamper themselves with pricey treats and useless tea dates. To say I dislike them would be wrong. Jealous of them? Maybe, but I have a hard time believing they are any happier than anyone else. Tonight's future bride dons a huge plastic penis around her neck, hanging absurdly in front of her precious summer dress. Why this is supposed to be funny, I will never know. It is more like wearing your true desire openly between your tits. When Nick walks in, I know I couldn't be more right. Daddy's sweet little girl's eyes widened as soon as she spots him walking across the room. As always he has a group with him: business associates he brought out to impress and his usual accompanying suspects of Luke and Dwayne. Luke Norton bounces in as he always does with energy like no one person could ever contain. Dwayne Dobbins couldn't be more opposite. His size is enormous and he never smiles, no matter how much Luke tries to get him to. But they both follow Nick- always. When Nick comes in and sits down, he doesn't even bother to look towards the table of debutantes, causing the squawking Country Club Barbies to become louder, in their futile attempt to get as much attention as possible. The men sitting with Nick take notice, but not Nick. They don't interest him a bit. Time and again they make spectacles of themselves, but only succeed in gaining the attention of the college boys sitting next to them. Chuckling to myself quietly, I squeeze tighter into the dark, enjoying the show. I assume they will eventually give up. *I don't understand the point. Do you have to have every man's attention?* Apparently they do. Whispering among themselves, one lucky woman finally stands up and straightens herself to perfection before walking away. The bride scoots her chair slightly away from the table primping until receiving nods from her cheerleaders. The lone brave woman walks up to Nick's side and waits for him to look her way. Obviously annoyed, he sits back casually and looks her up and down before meeting her eyes direct. He doesn't say a word, but simply watches her begin to fidget and tremble.

"Ummm. Hi!" She squeals. "I don't mean to bother you but my friend over there is getting married next Saturday and we are playing a kind of scavenger hunt game for her bachelorette party." She pauses as if she expects him to finally speak. "Well, anyway, she has to get certain items on her list in order to get all her points and one of those items is to get a kiss from a handsome stranger. On the cheek, of course." She giggles pleasantly.

Nick almost breaks a full smile when the men around him laugh aloud. "I don't kiss on the cheek." He said smoothly giving her the opportunity to end it there, but instead, she drags the bride over to him and asks again.

"Please? Just once?" She said laying her head on the bride's shoulder.

Nick looks the bride over from the corner of his eyes, "You're getting married?" Blushing she nods. "Why?" He follows up, in a condescending tone.

"Because, he is sweet and can provide for me and I love him."

"And you think he loves you?" Nick asked shaking his head at Luke who is vibrating from holding his laughter inside.

Taken aback, she pauses to answer with a firm voice, "Yes, I do. I have a lot to offer and most men would kill to have me for their wife." Nick's obvious disinterest angers her even more. "You know, you're not all that and you sure as hell would be lucky to have me." She said proudly, walking off arm in arm with her friend.

Nick excuses himself and walks up behind her, catching her eyes perfectly when she turns. "If you want a kiss, Sweetheart, come with me." The bride gives a quick smile to her crew and nearly has to run to catch up to Nick.

Curiously, I watch him direct her into his office and shut the door. They are gone long enough to cause her crew to become uncomfortable. They are hoping for the best, but it is unlikely. When his office door opens, the bride stumbles out, straightening her sweet dress before she gets out into the open. She sits with an awkward smile at her all-girl table, minus the plastic showpiece that was previously around her neck. She is a mess, her dress once pressed perfectly is now twisted and wrinkled. Her hair once pulled together long and fresh, now drooping and awkwardly weighted to one side of her head. "What happened? Are you okay?" The women clamor around her.

Nick walks out in perfect order, and perfect swagger, passing her with a downward glance. "You forgot your panties." He said tossing her underwear onto the table in front of her. After being embarrassingly ignored by the group of debutants, the nearby college boys feel justified by the turn of events and break out into hysterics. Slinking out the side door, the mortified women exit without another word. Nick sits down and goes back to business as usual. I wonder if Meagan will ever find out or care. Nothing seems to ever be said between them, but the gossip increases by the day. I can only imagine what excitement this will start.

As I wait for Exie to pack up, I stand outside talking to Dawson who, from what he says, is Nick's new punching bag. He is trying to move up and get more responsibility from Nick but doesn't seem to be getting anywhere with him, or so I understand from his nonstop complaining.

"Oh, baby, can I get some more money?" Meagan asks as she exits the club with Nick.

"What for now?" Nick responds with a sigh.

"I want to do some shopping and pick up a few things that I am sure will make you happy. It's all for you, baby." Meagan said with her baby voice.

"No. I am not giving you cash. Tell me what you want and I will get it."

"Nick, please. I want to surprise you." She says with a whine.

"No, Meagan. Get in the car." Meagan plops down in the car with her bottom lip protruding. Nick glances at his driver Tanner and the two seem to share some knowledge no one else is privy to. He sighs, but before he gets in the car he looks my way and, again, the two share a look. Tanner watches me closely as he walks towards the front of the car, nothing that would alarm me but almost as if he is worried about me. *Strange man.*

Luke walks out soon after, checking out Exie as she walks in front of him, and motioning for Dawson to follow him without taking his eyes off Exie's ass. "You ready to go?" Exie said running out with her keys in hand.

"Very much so. Can we pick up something to eat on the way?" I asked, jumping into the car eagerly.

"We can go to the store on the next corner. I need to pick up some cereal for Jerran, too. That boy is eating like crazy this summer."

"He's not eating it, Exie. He's hiding it so he can get to the toys quicker." I said, not realizing my mistake.

"Are you shitting me?" She yells at me.

"I thought you knew that!"

"No! Where is he putting it?" She exclaims in exasperation.

"If you don't know, then I am afraid to tell you!" I laugh.

"Oh, that boy is in so much trouble." Exie screeches out of the parking lot as if Jerran can hear her.

೧೩೮೦

*I*t has been several weeks since Nick humiliated the bride-to-be and I had almost forgotten about her until one Friday night. As I sit in my usual corner admiring the crowd, a man comes steaming in with a group of friends. "YOU! I want to talk to you!" He yelled pointing at Nick.

"Don't yell in my club." Nick calmly replies.

"I will do whatever I want to, and YOU are advised to step outside if you don't want your club destroyed."

"Sir, I think you should leave." One of the bouncers suggested strongly.

"Oh! So this loser can't take care of himself? He has to get one of his goons to do it?" The man proclaims, playing proudly to the crowd.

Nick waves the bouncer back, "What is your problem?" Nick asked eyeing the man with darkened eyes.

"You forced yourself on my wife and I am going to give you the ass-kicking you deserve!" The man yells. Nick begins shaking his head as he takes a drink from his glass. "My beautiful girl! And you just couldn't handle her turning you down." The man pulls out a picture and shoves it in Nick's face. During the escalating events, I glimpse Kyler ready to have a heart attack. "Look at her! Look at her, Scumbag! She is too good for you and you know it. You are never going to touch her or anyone else again." Nick snatches the picture from the man's hand and laughs. "This is funny to you, Asshole?"

Nick tosses the picture back behind him. "No. No, it's not. What is funny is that you believe your whore of a wife."

"Stand up you spineless punk!" The man yells in sheer rage.

Nick takes out his phone and scrolls through it calmly before standing up and putting it in the man's face, "Is this your whore? The girl with her legs spread on my desk?" He asked as the moans from the video echo in the room. "I didn't fuck her. She wasn't worth my time. She wanted a kiss so I gave her one- between her legs. It's not my fault she begged for more. The only penis that fucked her was the plastic one she wore around her neck. She said it gave her more pleasure than you ever have." Nick smiled deviously, pressing his cell closer and closer to the man's face as he punches him in the side of his head, pulling him back by his hair to shove the phone in his face again. "Look at her! Look at her sucking my dick. Your girl's a fucking pro. Do you still see your sweet girl now?" Nick yelled slamming the man's face into the table once, twice, and yet again, all the while forcing him to listen to his wife's orgasmic moans. Nick stops once the man begins to cry and plead for mercy. Only then is the man allowed to be picked up and carried out by his accompanying friends. Nick takes a single deep breath, cleans the blood from his hand, and sits back down, taking a drink before gesturing to get the club going again.

Few approach Nick the rest of the night, I am the only one brave enough to take him his specially made tea. "Thank you," he said barely glancing up at me.

"You're welcome," I said waiting for him to look up at me but he won't. I have to force myself to say something before the doubt takes me over. "That guy was wrong, but you should have ignored her to begin with. She would have been humiliated enough by that alone. Your ego got in the way of your judgment." I said before walking away proudly.

The following night Nick comes in earlier than usual and in time for me to take the stage. He sits alone as my music begins and displays nothing but disinterest in me. I become unnerved and begin to force my usually flawless show. Nick finishes his drink and begins to twirl his glass impatiently. I try to refocus and get back into what I know I can do. The small crowd of businessmen seems more than appreciative, yet Nick sits back and yawns. I finish smiling, exiting the stage while holding back my fervent anger.

"Are you okay?" Exie asked, seeing the look on my face.

"NO! He is such a fucking asshole. He sat out there on purpose." I yell throwing my things on my table.

"I know he did. But, did you really think you were going to get away with what you said to him? That he was going to let it go? Or maybe thank you for pointing out his flaws? You know better than that, Kayla. You need to let it go and move on." Exie lectured, standing over me like a mother.

"Not sure I can do that." I said looking away from her judging eyes.

"Oh God. Please, Kayla, let it go. You can't win against him." Exie finishes, leaving me to deal with my anger.

"No. He can't win." I mumble to myself.

"Well, there she is." Meagan said with a most annoying expression. "You know, you bored my boyfriend so much with your little routine that I had to beg him not to fire you."

"Really? You did that for me? I'm so sure." I said rolling my eyes.

"Sweet little Kayla, while I can barely stand to look at you, if he fires you, then I have to get to know some other poor slob and deal with her. I already know how to deal with you, I don't want to have to break in someone new." Meagan said as Exie huffs.

Ignoring Meagan's smirks and mumblings, I change and prepare to tuck into my dark corner but on my way there, I see Nick laughing and enjoying himself and I want nothing more than to ruin it. I take the first opportunity to sit at the table next to him and take out my book to read. I go out of my way to ignore him. When Meagan comes out, I sit up straight in front of him and block his view waiting for him to say something but he never does.

"I think somebody is trying to ignore you, Nick." Luke comments.

"I think somebody better fix her attitude or she is going to be fired." Nick replies.

I turn around quickly, catching his eyes briefly before he turns from me. Defiant still, I whisper directly in his ear, "Fire me then. But you know damn well I am the best you have here. Don't let your ego get in the way again … Nick. Give me a chance, you might like it." I said grabbing my bag and heading to my dark corner. Tensely sitting at the edge of my seat, I wait all-night for him to either, fire me, yell at me, or do something to vent his anger but I get no reaction. He goes on like I never existed. Every night I wait outside for Exie but watch Nick leave before us, not even giving me a glance. If not for Dawson, I would feel as if I were invisible. Desperate, I try something new and begin flirting with Dawson who is more than receptive. As if I had arranged it myself, Nick walks out as Dawson whispers a compliment in my ear and I kiss his cheek in appreciation. I agree openly to go on a date with him and finally I get a glance from Nick but not much more.

The next night Dawson is missing from outside the door. His replacement tells me that he was reassigned. Afterwards, I get scolded from Kyler for conducting myself in an inappropriate manner on business property. *Chicken shit couldn't even confront me himself.* The next time I see Dawson is when I accidentally run into him at a nearby coffee shop. I try to say hello but he avoids me like the plague. Frustrated, I watch for any opening to force my way into Nick's view. Luckily, my opportunity arises when Meagan begins to take a downward slide. She is rarely on time these days and seems to be pushing Nick to the edge. The last few nights he has sent her home by herself.

Tonight is no different, Meagan is nearly forty minutes late when she shows up in a state of delusion. "Where is my lipstick? Who the hell took my lipstick? It was you, wasn't it?" Meagan yells pointing her crooked finger in my face. "You better give it back and I hope for your sake you didn't touch it with your nasty lips. I will make damn sure you never see the light of day again. Nick hates you, you know that? I am the only reason you still have a job!" She yells at me.

I get up and Exie quickly pushes me back in my seat. "Calm the fuck down. Your lipstick is on the floor behind your chair, Slut,"

Exie yells back at her with disgust. Meagan turns noticing the diamond encrusted tube on the floor. She reaches down to pick it up, stumbles into her table, and then falls flat on her ass. Exie bursts into laughter, "Hey, Graceful, you think you could look for my earring? I mean, since you're down there already?" Exie walks away still chuckling to herself. I would laugh to if the scene didn't look all too familiar to me.

After watching Meagan struggle to get her makeup on properly, her shoes on at all, and finally giving up on trying to do anything with her hair, she stumbles out to perform. *This is going to be a disaster.* I'm not sure I even want to watch but my curiosity gets the best of me. I walk out just in time to see her take two steps and fall right off the stage- into some exceedingly shocked man's lap. Everyone's first response is to rush to Meagan and help her up. Mine is to watch Nick's reaction. The anger in his eyes is clear and I know this night is about to get interesting. Scrambling, the DJ, Mickey, comes out making jokes and offering free drinks to everyone while they wait for the next show, except no one else is prepared to go on. Seeing my opportunity in front of me, I quickly make my presence known to Kyler. As Kyler vibrates nervously, I smile happily, waiting.

"Fine Kayla! You're up, get dressed ...QUICKLY!" Kyler yells at me.

I look up at Exie, ask her to give my music to Mickey, and change quickly to an outfit I have been saving just for Nick. Before taking the stage, I grab Meagan's signature hat and put it on my head. Nodding in Mickey's direction, I take my mark meeting Nick's eyes as a surge rushes through me. Concentrating on him, I perform- for only him. I barely notice the time pass or the money coming my way until Nick sends one of his cronies over with five hundreds from his own pocket. The man happily walks over to the stage calling out to me and waving his prize. Eager to make him hungry, I lock-down the edge of the stage, teasing each hundred away from the overtly blissful man. Upon receiving the last hundred, I kiss him gently on the cheek, enjoying the man's heart attack act that he performs for the applauding crowd. Running my hand up between my legs, I wet my mouth, eyeing Nick until the music ends.

"Damn, Girl! Where did that come from?" Exie asks as I pass. I shrug and smile.

"Kayla, Nick wants to see you," Kyler says with harsh breaths, "In his office."

I look back at Exie and she looks more nervous than I. "Change first. And put on two pairs of underwear just in case. Oh and let's tape them on!" She yells running at me with duck tape. I laugh and decide to go in my new, jeweled bikini. *I'm not scared of him.*

I make my way slowly down the dark corridor stopping at the edge of the light coming from his office. "I don't have all-night. Get in here." He yells from inside. Rounding the corner I ease my eyes up to his, as he sits at the edge of his desk waiting for me. "Shut the door."

"You know, I would prefer it open I have a slight case of claustrophobia." I said ignoring his request.

"Close the damn door!" He watches me hard until I complete the task as told. "Thank you."

"Did I do something wrong?" I asked innocently.

"No, on the contrary, you made my clients very happy. And after Meagan's … incident, I didn't think that was going to be possible." Nick gets up and walks around me, "You seem to want to get in my face and challenge me every chance you get. Your attitude stinks. I should have fired you by now."

"Then why haven't you?" I challenged.

"Do not talk right now." He demands as I stare directly into the devil's eyes.

"Why? Can't I ask you questions? Tell you how I feel?"

"You are the most exhausting woman I have ever met. Fine, what do you want to say? What are you trying to prove to me, Kayla?" He said shocking me that he even knows my name.

"I want to do more, I want to prove I can be even more valuable for you."

"Do I dare ask? Fine. Like how?"

"What do you need?" I asked, standing up straight as he looks me over.

"What do I need? What are you after? Tell me something. Why did you start working here, Kayla?"

"I needed a job."

"Kayla, you're beautiful and you could get a job anywhere. Why here? Why my club?" He pressed, looking down on me. I am not even sure how to answer that, at least not without giving up my true intentions. "Now you're quiet?"

"What do you want me to say, Nick, that I came here specifically to work for you? It's not true there are other places I can go, but I thought I might learn the business better from you. Contrary to what you may think, not every woman is after you for sex." He smirks and rolls his eyes. "Maybe I should go work for someone else. This is clearly a mistake on my part. I thought you could help me get somewhere better." I turn to leave as he takes hold of my arm.

"Where are you going to go?"

"I have had other offers. A man, just yesterday, told me he had something that was more suited for me."

"What man?" Nick asked eyeing me closely.

"I don't know. I wasn't interested at the time."

"Kayla, there are men that come in here that are not after dancers."

"I know how to do other things as well ... Nick." I said eyeing him.

"You put on quite the show of such strength and defiance."

"It's not a show." I challenge.

"We will see, I guess." He said sighing and seeming to decide on something significant. "There's a party tomorrow night. I would like for you to go with me."

"Me? But I thought you are Meagan's ..."

"I don't belong to anybody. Besides, I am asking you to go as a favor to me. Not as a girlfriend."

I step up to him meeting his black eyes strongly, "I don't have anything to wear to a party."

"I'll take care of it."

"My car is not ..."

"I said you're going with me. You don't need a car."

"What about shoes?"

"Kayla!" He tensed.

Smiling, "No reason to yell, I just wanted to make sure to ask all the important questions before I say yes."

Nick laughs harshly, jerking me close to him by the back of the neck, "I don't like games. Got it?"

"Got it," I said taking notice of his scent as I press my hands against his firm chest. His eyes gaze over me as I try to stand strong against them.

Luckily, Meagan interrupts our silent standoff with an abrupt opening of the door, "Nick?"

"Fuck," Nick lets go of me and walks away to pour himself a drink. "What do you want? And before you say a word, know that you're on thin ice with me right now."

Meagan takes a stand in front of me, "You fucking Bitch, you steal MY lipstick, take MY hat, take MY stage, and now you're trying to steal MY boyfriend? Get the fuck out of here, you gold digging whore!"

"Maybe if you weren't so strung out and drunk, I wouldn't have had to save your ass. You have never been that great of a dancer, Meagan, but well done on the dive. Perfect ten from all the judges." I smile harshly back at her. Screaming, Meagan comes at me in full rage, while still unstable on her feet, making it easy for me to dodge her. Nick walks around me and helps her off the floor, before turning to face me.

"Apologize." He said calmly. Meagan laughs at me, waiting to hear me grovel for her forgiveness. "Not her, you."

"But, Nick?" She asked looking up at him in shock.

"You know I don't like to repeat myself ... Do it NOW!" Meagan starts to speak, "On your knees." Meagan looks up at him and slowly tries to get down on her knees but falls on her face first. Watching her struggle makes me nauseous.

"I ... am ... sorry." She said.

"For what?" Nick asked watching me closely.

"I'm sorry for accusing you and yelling at you and everything." Meagan cries.

"Get up and get out. I don't want to see you the rest of the night. Make sure you're here early tomorrow, you have the lunch shift from now on." Meagan, crying, stumbles for the door. "And shut the door on your way out." Once the door is securely shut, Nick steps to me, coming in close, and nosing my hair out of the way as he breathes in my ear, "Did that bother you?"

"No, she was wrong."

"Should I punish you too for stealing?" He whispered.

"I didn't steal anything." I said facing forward and trying to control my unstable legs.

"We both know you are," he said, stroking my cheek.

With a clear defiance, I turn to him and look in his black eyes, "It is not stealing if it doesn't belong to anybody."

With a slight smile he steps away from me, "Tomorrow at 7:00. Be ready." He said motioning for me to leave.

I walk off smiling and run into Exie, who looks as if she is ready to explode. "What happened?"

"Nothing." I said calmly.

"Nothing?" She snapped. I shrug, not understanding her worry. "No one goes into Nick's office alone and has nothing happen. At least tell me that you didn't remove any clothes while you were in there. And, if you did, I want details- very specific details."

"He just invited me to go to a party with him."

"And you said no right?"

"Oh yea. That's what I did. Are you kidding?"

"Kayla, I know he is extremely good looking, but I don't think you understand how dangerous he is. He is ..."

"Exie, I understand exactly who he is. Don't worry about me, I can handle him."

~4~
KAYLA

$\mathcal{N}$ick makes sure I have the day off and sends a driver to escort me to a specialist that has been given the task of making me perfect enough to stand beside him. I returned home to find my outfit for the night waiting for me with a note from Nick saying he picked out the dress himself especially for me. As charming as that seems, I'm not swayed in the least. However, the dress slides on like silk and the shoes feel heavenly. I stand in front of my mirror admiring the stranger in front of me and for a second, I allow myself to enjoy living in this dream.

"Wow, you look amazing." Exie said leaning against my doorframe. "That dress must be at least … what? A thousand dollars?"

"Nearly three, actually. He said he picked it out himself." I whisper in amazement.

"Of course he did." Exie remarks with a harsh tone. "I still don't understand why you are doing this."

"And I assure you it's best that you don't." I reply, with an encouraging smile. As soon as the doorbell rings, I grab my new handbag and rush to the door.

Tanner greets me with a simple nod before escorting me to the car where he opens the car door for me and nods once again. I peer inside to see the edges of him and my butterflies instantly take flight. Sitting down slowly, I avoid looking in his direction. "You forgot something," Nick said opening a flawlessly adorned box and taking out a beautiful diamond necklace that he carefully wraps around my neck. "Now, you're perfect." Touching the heavy jewel dangling against my chest, I breathe in deeply as he takes my hand to help me out of the car. My comfort level doesn't improve as I began to feel as if I am only here for the view, nothing more. When a man approaches my side, it takes me a second to realize that he is actually speaking to me. Introducing myself, he kisses my hand looking me over like he is inspecting me. And that's when I realize what my purpose is at this party. I'm not here to be viewed, but to be judged, and sold to the highest bidder. Nick hands me a hotel key with a number on it, before walking away. Standing across the room watching, waiting, and almost certainly upping the price with every second passing, Nick eyes me with a knowing expression. The anger that builds up inside me overshadows any leftover butterflies. I smile at Nick as he enjoys his secret. Eyeing him the entire distance between us, I ease my way to his side and glide my hand up his chest releasing a soft moan against his earlobe. "How am I doing? The bids coming in high enough for your approval?" I eye him with an edge of disgust. "Nice of you to let me know what I am really here for."

"You said you knew how to do other things. I wanted to explore how far those other things might go. Have I gone too far in my expectations? Because I am more than willing to pull you out of here and take you back home where you belong." Nick smiles giving me a quick glance as he admires the other women working the room.

"No, I'm fine. Keep counting your money, Gigolo. So do I just take them in the backroom or ..."

Nick laughs, "This is just a party Kayla. However, if someone happens to receive the same hotel room key then ..."

"Then it's all up to me." I said, strutting away with purpose. Leaving Nick to ponder over his new prize, I walk over to a group of men and introduce myself, making sure to smile sweetly, touch them innocently, and blush at their compliments. Once I have their full attention, I excuse myself politely and move on to the next group and then the next, working my way through the room effortlessly. Expecting to leave with someone other than Nick, I'm shocked when he takes me by the hand before the night is over and escorts me back into his car. "Where are we going?"

"My house." He said looking straight ahead.

"No one bid on me?"

Nick laughs, "They all did. In fact, Luke could barely keep up with all the offers coming in."

"So then why? ..." I asked catching him licking his lips. "Nick! Who won the bid?" He ignores my question, turning to me and trailing his finger along the delicate line of my necklace. "Who, Nick?"

Sliding my matching hotel key into my hand, "I did," he said simply, locking me in with the devil's eyes. "I misjudged your value,

Kayla. None of those men can afford you." Nick plays with the edges of my dress until we pull up to his vast estate. Quietly I follow him not knowing if I should take my clothes off now or wait for him to do it for me or if I should stay dressed just in case he decides to kill me.

It was only a few years ago a female agent went undercover to get the information needed to arrest Nick. She didn't get far before Nick coaxed her out of her clothes and left her naked in a hotel room. Assured she would be killed before she could get two steps out of the hotel, she called for backup and was escorted out by police in nothing but a bedsheet and a fellow officer's jacket. She was forced to excuse herself from the investigation and asked to transfer immediately. The next agent to try, assured she would not fall for the same. Her name was Claire and we quickly became friends. She was the first to investigate Nick deeper than most and found me visiting my sister's grave. It took little persuading to convince me to clue her in on everything I knew about Nick. I was sure she was the one that was going to get him. The investigation took a positive turn when he invited her back to his home, she felt as if she was making progress getting him to trust her. However, Nick lured her into bed and fucked her every way possible before sending her home confused. To make matters worse, a video somehow surfaced of the rendezvous and Clair was laughed out of her job and rejected by her fiancé. The next agent ... well they still haven't found her. No one else will volunteer and no man can get any closer than the previous women. Nick has been untouchable. And now here I am being led into his bedroom in a similar fashion, where I will await my fate. I prepared myself for this, I just didn't anticipate it so soon. *I hope he doesn't know who I am.*

The plush room is amazing and when Nick walks in with wine for us both, I am still wary of his intentions. I take my glass from his hand and welcome the warmth coating my throat. "So, tell me. What is your plan for me tonight?" He says nearly stripping me naked with one look.

"Tell me what you like and I will do it," I respond placing my glass down and giving him my full attention.

"Why don't you start by dancing for me like you did last night? I enjoyed that." He said looking down on me with suspicious eyes. I agree and Nick makes himself comfortable, pulling out a remote and turning on the music he prefers. It's slow and erotic so I move the same using everything around me, including him. Down to my underwear I crawl up his legs feeling his erection through his pants and ease into his lap. I lean in to kiss his neck but am pulled away before I can reach him. Nick grips the back of my head studying me for a second before taking in my lips with his. He grips my ass with a single hand and picks me up, carrying me to his bed. Holding me still, he presses against me, kissing me hard from my thighs to my butt, caressing my body with heated hands, as he turns me to face him. Running his fingers gently down my face he watches me with an emerging smile. I reach down for his belt and get it half undone when he abruptly pushes me away. Shocked, I search the room for someone, something that would cause him to stop.

"Damn! I forgot I have a meeting I have to get to." He said with a glimmer of disappointment.

"Right now?"

"Sorry, but I think this is going to have to wait. Feel free to get naked and in bed. I'll wake you up when I get back." Nick grabs his jacket, smiling as he leaves me dumbfounded and alone.

"What the fuck?" Unsure what to do next, I try to wait up for him but hours go by and I can barely keep my eyes open. Exhausted, I can't help but crawl into his incredible bed and sigh as I sink into it. I am already nearly asleep when I remember he said get naked but I am too comfortable to move. *He'll just have to get over it.*

∞

*D*eeply dreaming, I begin to feel hands, lips and then the fumbling and jerking at my underwear. This is not what I expected from him. I open my eyes to the lit up window and to a blurry figure sitting in front of me. Clearing my focus, I sit up and stare horrified at Nick sitting in a chair watching me while another man continues tugging at my underwear. I reach back and smack the shit out of him until he stops, "Get the fuck away from me! Who the hell are you?" I yell turning to a humored Nick, "Who the hell is he?"

"I met him last night, I thought you might like him so I brought him home for you." Nick smiles proudly.

"Well, I don't! And I don't appreciate being fondled by some stranger while I sleep!"

"No? Mea culpa." He says calmly.

"Mea culpa? That's all you have to say to me? Fuck you, Nick!" I wrap myself up and race to get my dress so I can leave.

"Where are you going? Ummm … I'm sorry what was your name?" Nick asked pointing to the confused man.

"Tony."

"Ah. Tony here I think was just getting going, you barely gave him much of a chance." Nick smiles wide when I turn to say something.

"Then you fuck him! I'm sure you will both enjoy it!" I yell scrambling to get the dress straightened out to get it back on.

"Get out." Nick says motioning to Tony to head for the door.

"But you said …" Tony holds out his hands in confusion.

"Did I ask you to speak? No. I said leave." Tony huffs out the door in his oversized boxers, carrying the rest of his clothes under his arm. I get the dress almost on when Nick rips it right back off. "What are you doing Princess? I thought you wanted to fuck?"

"No that was you and only you!" The words barely leave my lips before I feel his taut chest against my back. Nick's powerful arms surround me and suddenly his scent takes hold of me. His erection begins pressing proudly into me while he takes his time fondling my body closer to him. "I want to … ohhh … I want to leave … Nick."

"What?" He whispers. "You don't want me? You know you do." Nick pushes his hands underneath my bra, taking hold of my breasts fully with a sigh. "Beg me … beg me, Kayla."

"No." I whispered into the air.

His hand runs through my hair while his lips chase up my neck to my ear. "Beg me to fuck you."

I gasp as his hand feels down under my panties, "No. I won't ever beg you for anything."

"Are you sure?" He asked pressing his hand down between my legs, pushing his fingers inside me and fondling me into a heated ecstasy. "Feels good, doesn't it?" Rendered silent, I grip the back of his neck, and lean into him more and more. "Just imagine what my dick would feel like."

"No … no. I don't want you." I gasp feeling my body tense and betray me with waves of pleasure. Nick watches me, gleefully. Regaining enough strength, I push away from him, "Damn you!"

"Damn me? Princess, you're the one that had the orgasm, not me. Although I am hard as a boulder after watching you. Do you think you can take care of it for me?" He laughs, looking me over.

"Is that what you want? For me to suck your dick?" I asked.

Laughing still, he steps back away from me, "No, I would rather

rub it out myself than take a chance sticking it anywhere near you."
He smiles.

Furious, I forget who he is and smack him with all I have. "You
are a demon!"

Nick's smile erases instantly as he grips my wrists tight. "Do you
know how close you are to dying? You're lucky I didn't kill you last
night after the money you cost me."

"If I cost you so much money, then why didn't you take the
highest bid? Why save me for … for this?"

"You don't get it! Did you not notice the other girls at all? Not
one of them secured a bid last night because of you. Those men only
wanted you and if they couldn't have you they weren't interested.
NOT one fucking bid, Kayla! Taking even the highest bid for you
wasn't going to make up for all the ones lost. You didn't just cost me
money you cost every girl in there her money too."

"So instead you bring me here and have some troll try to rape
me in front of you?"

"Don't overdramatize the situation. It wouldn't have gotten that
far. I would have sent him packing before it got to that, unless you
liked him." He smirked.

"How noble of you."

Gripping my face he pulls me forward, "Kayla, this is not for
you. Go home and stay out of my business."

The sudden realization that I might be failing in my goal surges
to the forefront. "Nick! No, I can do it. I can do whatever you need
me to."

"You nearly knocked what's his name's head off!"

"That's different and you know it! Give me another chance and
I promise I will make up for the money I cost you last night."

"Go home, Kayla. And I would appreciate it if you would leave
my club and go find a more suitable job for yourself. Go find Romeo
and get married, be the little homemaker it suits you better."

"You're firing me?" I ask chasing after him before he can leave.

"Yes, and I am advising you to stay as far away from me as
possible. Now get dressed, my driver will take you home."

"I'm not giving up, Nick. I refuse to go work at a diner for the
rest of my life and slave for some man that doesn't give a shit about
me. This is who I am, I have no one else … I mean there isn't
anyone I need to prove myself to so I might as well live my life to get
whatever I can."

Nick stares at me with a tense mouth, "Kayla … figure out another way, Princess, because this isn't the one for you."

"Why not? Why won't you let me work for you? What do you care? Are you afraid I will mess up again? Because I won't! I understand how it works now, I can do what I am supposed to." I beg, heading him off before he can reach the door.

"Go home, Kayla, before I have you dragged out of here." He replies slowly, showing no sign of backing down.

Fighting my anger and frustration, "Fine! I will go work for your competition then and if you think you lost money last night … you wait, I will personally put you out of business. Or maybe I will just let the cops know how your business works." I stomp away from him, gasping when he takes hold of my neck and forces me to turn towards him.

"Are you threatening me?" Trembling to the point of pain, I wait for him to kill me. Staring at him with more fear than I have ever felt in my life, I grip his wrist touching the ground from the tips of my toes. The silence makes my breathing sound more forced and desperate. "You have nothing on me, trust me it would only cause you more pain than me if you ever decide to go to the cops." I nod continuing to barely brush the floor with my toes. "Look at me!" I feebly raise my eyes up to his and watch as the darkness suddenly fades from the devil and he loosens his grip allowing me to stand firmly on the ground again. "You can continue working at the club, but I am not convinced that you are capable of much more. Give me time to think about it." He releases his grip and turns his back to me, "And Kayla, if you get any more job offers, I expect for you to let me know."

"Okay." I say meekly, holding up my dress that is now torn and hardly worth trying to put on. I lower my head and hold my breath to keep from crying. *Death has never felt so real.*

Taking a deep breath, I look up at him and realize he is watching me. I throw the dress to the floor, drop the jeweled necklace on the table without a single tear from my eyes, and give him one last look before walking towards the door with my head held high. Nick chases after me, taking hold of my waist, he guides me back into the room. "My closet is over there. Take whatever you need." He said with half a smile and a shake of his head, before he walks out the door.

Leaving his house smelling of him, wearing his clothes, and

feeling strangely more aware of him than ever before, I can't help wonder …. *Why didn't he kill me?*

~5~
KAYLA

*A*s I work at the club I continue watching and waiting for him to speak to me, but every night he sticks to his routine and ignores me. I have tried everything to get his attention, to remind him what I want, but no matter what I do, he finds a way to shut me out. *There doesn't seem to be any hope at this point but I am not about to give up.* Tonight I watch him with a new gentleman who Nick is discussing intense matters with. He hasn't taken his eyes off the man and I can only imagine how important this man is to him. When the gentleman goes outside to make a call, I get an idea and follow him. Standing outside as if I am waiting for someone, I watch him, biting my bottom lip and tugging at my shirt until he notices me. Casually flipping from one foot to the next, I sigh in distress.

"Are you waiting for someone?" The man asks sliding his phone into his pocket.

"Yes, but obviously they aren't going to show."

"Boyfriend troubles?"

"Nothing but. Typical huh?" I said shyly looking up at him.

"I can't imagine any man would leave you standing alone."

Walking towards him, I toy with his tie and lick my lips. "What would you do … with me? I mean would you leave me standing here or …"

"No. I would have come to get you." He said with an interested grin.

Smiling up at him, "Well, I better go back in and call someone to come get me. Nick doesn't like his girls standing out here by themselves. He is very protective, you know?"

"So I have heard."

I walk slowly away, "Have a good night." I said feeling confident in my efforts and even more so when I see the man sitting back down with Nick and gesture my way. For the first time in weeks Nick makes eye contact with me.

Happily, I go and wait for Exie as she changes. Sitting back against the wall, I run through the highlights of my expert skills when suddenly I am jerked out of my seat, "Come with me." Nick said dragging me into his office. "You are either really stupid or suicidal."

"I don't believe I am either, just determined."

"What were you thinking? Do you even know who that was?" He asked breathing his fire into my face.

"No, but you brought him here I assume to entertain him, so I entertained him." I said backing away from him.

Nick laughs, "You entertained him alright. He could barely keep his dick in his pants after he spoke to you. I was trying to talk business and all he wanted to discuss was fucking you."

I look at him with a mocking expression, "That's good, right?"

Nick throws his hands up in the air, "You really have no idea what you are getting into."

"What is the problem, Nick? Let me soften him up for you- make him happy."

"NO! Duke Durham is sick and twisted in public. There is no telling what he is like behind closed doors." Nick paces the room huffing and shaking his head at me. "You are not to ever go near him again! Not that he will have much to do with you now anyway. I told him that you put on a good show but that's about all there is to you. I directed him to where he can find someone more suited to his needs." I start to speak, but he stops me. "You want another chance?"

"Yes, I do." I said, standing up to him.

"If I let you do this, you have to do it my way. You approach no one on your own or without my or Luke's approval. Got it?" I nod and he sighs walking away from me. "Tomorrow night, there are some gentlemen that have budgets that will suit you better."

"What time are you picking me up?" I asked joyfully.

"Oh no, Princess, you are on your own. Luke will make sure you make it to the right place and he will let you know who your ride is at the end of the night. Still interested?"

"Yes!"

❦

*T*he night is slow, the men here are tightfisted and too scared to even make eye contact with me, forget about talking. Nick's idea of another joke I'm sure, no one could get these men to loosen up.

They're content to simply admire from afar, too far. Grabbing a drink, I give up my pursuit and escape to the balcony.

"Bored with the blue bloods too?" A man says as he approaches me with a warm smile. Taking a deep breath, he holds his hand out to me, "Daniel Bonner."

Shaking his hand, I give him the name Nick has chosen for me and relax, hoping to make him feel more comfortable with me. Daniel is out of shape and older I would say considering the gray at his temples but still handsome and seemingly respectable other than the ring on his left hand. We talk easily and I feel confident that I have him hooked, but at the end of the party I check in with Luke and he introduces me to an entirely different man: bald, uncomfortable, and at least three inches shorter than me. Not my ideal, but I take his nearly dripping wet arm and tell myself this is what I should have expected. The man is nervous but respectful, opening the door for me as he escorts me with honor to our hotel room. I enter ahead of him and turn to say something only to be waved in as he leaves.

"Come in," Daniel said rounding the corner to take my hand. "Not real sure of what etiquette is suitable for something like this, so forgive me if I seem ... awkward."

"No it's ... fine. It is my first time too."

With an amiable smile, "Well, we can learn together then." Daniel leans in and kisses me gently. "Your lips are so soft." I take his face in my hands and kiss him back, easing him back on the bed, I stand up and slip my dress off to his instant delight. With a slight hesitation, he holds out his hands to touch me.

"It's okay, I'm all yours." I say taking his hands and rubbing them over my body. Excitedly, he presses his lips between my breasts and eases off my bra, rubbing his face over my bare breasts with a slow groan. I coax him out of his shirt and pants while he leisurely pulls my panties down my legs. Suddenly his nervousness disappears and he takes the lead. Showing his erection fully, he lets me stroke him and help prepare him. Taking hold of my body, he penetrates me with a gasping groan. He never ventures outside the normal and never asks me to do anything outside simply being here with him. He seems to have been trained to appreciate simply the presence of a woman. I like him, I like being with him, and I don't want this to be the last time for us. Urging him to roll on his back, I sit up on him and dance along his erection, letting him enjoy my entire body on him.

"You are so beautiful." Leaning deeper into the bed, Daniel lets go of his inhibitions. "Don't stop."

I bring him to the brink and then slow my pace, before bringing him right back to the edge again. I enjoy controlling him, giving him the pleasure he seems to need so desperately. He releases holding me tight against him, throwing me off my game. Kissing the side of my head and rubbing my back as if he has just made love to his wife. I lie against his chest and feel his exhale. He holds me through the night running his fingers through my hair. I leave him the next morning with a defined smile across his face. He says that he wishes to see me again and I encourage him, he is so respectful and warm, something I have never experienced with any man.

I ignore my strange feelings for Daniel believing it has to be because of the newness of it all for the both of us. With my next client my feelings are easy to distinguish, the man is much older and oddly excited by simply seeing my bare breasts. He wants nothing more than to watch me fondle my breasts until he comes. Easy money for me but I can't leave the man fast enough. A few days later, I meet Mr. Nick-Want-To-Be. He wears similar suits, wears his hair the same, even as tall as Nick, but that is where the likenesses end. His smile is too cocky and not suave and hypnotizing. His eyes are desperate and feeble, his hands are rough and clumsy, but most of all he fails miserably in comparison to Nick. Nick's body doesn't lack muscles and he doesn't lack anywhere else either. You can try to be whoever you want to be, but unless you're honest with yourself about it, you're only going to disappoint and this man does nothing but. The end comes quickly and even though he is appreciative and kinder than Nick, I have no trouble leaving him as soon as we are done.

Within a few weeks attending the parties aren't necessary for me because my calendar is fully booked- mostly by Daniel. Seeing him so often makes it even more difficult to separate business from pleasure. Even as I stand outside his door, I am tempted to call in for someone else to take over. Daniel is too comforting when we are together and his demands to have me with him all-night are overwhelming. I barely have a chance to knock before the door flies open.

"There's my girl," He says taking me in his arms immediately. "I have missed you."

"That's sweet but ..."

"But what? Don't tell me I am making you feel uncomfortable?"

"Well Daniel I am here to do a job not ..."

I feel horrible when his entire body sinks. "I know, but I was hoping that maybe you were feeling the same way I was. I guess I am being one of those insane clients who want to believe I have someone incredible to add to my life."

"Daniel, you treat me well but I don't know how to deal with this? I have never been treated like this before."

"So, you do feel it to?" His hope returns in an awe inspiring smile. I can't help smile back. "I knew it."

"It doesn't matter what I feel. I am still a prostitute and you're still married."

"Well, one of those might be true but the other not so much anymore. I guess I shouldn't be wearing this ring anymore but it is hard to let go of her. My wife died a few years ago, I haven't cared about anyone since ... until you."

"Daniel, I am sorry, but are you sure you're not trying to replace her with me?"

"Sweetheart, I have had plenty of dates and plenty of women since her. Trust me. You're not my rebound girl. You're my girl." He said pulling me back into his arms. "I am falling head over heels for you. Do you have any idea how amazing you are?" Daniel takes my hand and walks me over to the window and points outside. "Do you see anything out there you want?"

"What are you talking about?" I asked uncomfortably.

"Tell me what you want and I will buy it for you. I will find it for you. I will make sure it is made specifically for you just tell me what it is. All I ask is that you take down your walls and let me love you." Daniel said with loving eyes. As much as I may want to jump into his arms right now, my past holds me back. I manage to put Daniel's expectations off for a little while, calming him back down into our usual routine. Even though I will lie next to him tonight, I won't be sleeping.

CB&EO

*T*he club is busy as usual and after a long night with Daniel the night before, I am ready to crash. As soon as I finish my last set, I get dressed and head for the door but before I can reach Exie, and my ride home, Nick's car pulls up in front of me. Tanner doesn't even bother to get out. Nick simply rolls down his window and barks, "get in."

"I am tired, Nick."

"Did I ask you a question?" He said opening the door for me.

"Ass," I whispered in the wind. I wave Exie on, hiding my laugh as she huffs blatantly, falling into her car, and driving off.

"I don't have all-night, Kayla." *Uggghhhh* I sit down next to him ignoring his eyes on me. "You've done well these last few weeks. And it looks like you have impressed one client so much that he would like to see you exclusively. He is paying big bucks to keep you to himself." I glance over at him and quickly look back down at my hands. "I'm impressed. Intrigued even, as to what you did to make this man so in love with you?"

"Who said he was in love? It's just sex!" I snap back at him.

"Easy, wrong choice of words. Anyway … what's his name?" Nick said thumbing through his phone for the answer.

"Daniel." I said.

"Daniel? That doesn't sound right. No, it's Lawrence Jennings." Nick looks over at me with a curious expression. "What made you think his name was Daniel?"

Unsure why Daniel is keeping his name private, I panic on what to tell Nick. "Oh, I thought it was one of the other guys. Lawrence, yea … we hit it off too." I said quickly before pretending to notice something out the window.

"Right. Well, I would like for you to get with Luke tomorrow and give him details about each of your clients."

I spin my head towards him, "Why? It is none of your damn business what I do with them."

"You know I'm getting sick of your attitude with me. I don't know why you think you can talk to me like that, but it better change … quickly." Nick leans around to catch my eyes. "Kayla?"

"I got it. I will be more respectful to my pimp."

Rolling his eyes, "That's much better. I am in too good of mood to deal with you tonight but I wanted to tell you that I don't want you working the club and dealing with clients too. It is too much. So put in enough time at the club for Kyler to find someone to replace you and then concentrate on keeping yourself pleasing for your client. These new gentlemen you have brought in are paying more for one night with you than the other girls are making in two weeks. I don't know what kinky, screwed up shit you are doing, but keep it up Princess and you will be buying your own Mercedes. Luke has the new address for your meeting with this Lawrence guy tomorrow."

Nick casually looks me over with obvious doubt, "Man must be insane." I glare at him as he laughs in the opposite direction.

When the car stops, I get ready to jump out but realize we are not at my house, "Nick, what are we doing here? I want to go home."

"Hold on. We are only picking someone up and then we will drop you off." I slump down in the corner. When the car door opens, a tall blond gets in with a smile a mile wide. "There isn't much room in here right now but we will be able to move around better when we drop her off." Nick said smirking at me.

"Oh, it's okay! I am just so excited to see you!" She squeals jumping into his lap and nearly screwing him right beside me.

"Could you not do that until after I get out, please?" I said repulsed.

Nick looks over at me with enjoyment, "Don't worry about her, she's just jealous." I ignore his comment and pray for green lights.

"If you like, Nick, I could play with her while you watch." The blond gushes over him.

"You would do that for me?" He asked handling her overtly in front of me.

"I would do anything for you, Nick." She moans.

"Even share me?" She nods shaking the air out of her ears even faster. Nick turns to me, "I guess I might be able to stomach you for tonight. What do you say, Princess?" I look over at his obnoxious smile.

"REALLY just want to go home! And slam my head into a wall until I get these images out of my head." I expressed clearly.

"So that's a no?" He laughs, fondling the woman. The blond takes his fingers and puts them into her mouth, sucking each of them one at a time. "Be careful, sweetheart, some women like what I can do with those. Don't they, Kayla?"

"This is a fucking nightmare," I huff as Nick laughs next to me. I barely wait for the car to stop before I jump out and run into the house.

CustomEndmark

*M*y next rendezvous with Daniel, I decide to stay distant and stick to the task at hand. However, he greets me with such warmth, hugging and kissing me deeply. "I missed you," he exhaled against my cheek.

"It has only been a few days."

"It seems like forever." He said before I can push away from him. "Did I do something to upset you?"

"I honestly don't understand what your intentions are, Daniel."

"My intentions are to spend as much time with you as possible." He said with his usual shocked expression during this conversation.

"I don't understand why you're pretending that this is anything other than sex or why you think it can be anything but?"

"It doesn't have to be. I told you that I can take care of you. You don't need to work for Nick anymore." He said confusing me how he would know anything about Nick. Nick doesn't handle any of the business personally, only Luke knows for sure of his involvement.

"Nick? You mean Luke?" I asked.

Daniel smiles with a slight laugh, "I guess I assumed. Nick Jayzon is well-known and suspected of such ventures. Luke, then. Tell him you're done and stay here with me. I bought this place for us."

"Daniel, I don't think that's a good idea."

"I know what you think but you're my only escape. The nights I spend with you I come alive again. So forgive me if I can't wait to see you, to touch you, to hold you, and especially to kiss you. I rush through every day until I can get to that moment you fall asleep in my arms. I want to know your real name so when I dream about you I can whisper the right one." His eyes smile and comfort me like no other, "Let me take care of you?"

"Daniel ..."

Lifting my chin he looks into my eyes, "Don't speak ... think about it. Now come here, Beautiful, and let me make love to you like a man should." He picks me up, carrying me to his bed and laying me down in sheets made of clouds.

Looking into his smiling eyes, "my name is Kayla," I whispered against his lips.

"Kayla. And what's your last name, Kayla?" He smiles teasing me, "I know! It's Kayla Heartbreaker." I laugh shaking my head. "No? Then it's Kayla Goddess?" He said laughing with me.

"It's Donovan."

"Oh, Donovan. Nice to finally meet you, Kayla Donovan." He said beginning his slow journey down my chest. His lips are so warm and soft against my skin and his hands handle me so gently and respectfully that I exhale and allow myself to enjoy him. *Maybe I have found the perfect man?*

~6~
KAYLA

My last night at the club and I should feel happy about it but I don't feel confident that it isn't a setback in my plans, especially when Nick is at the club several nights a week. I don't know how I am going to see him when I am with Daniel all the time. I am going to have to come up with something to get closer to Nick, something other than having to sleep with him like the rest of his female entourage. There has to be a way to get Nick to slip up and give me something to hold over him. Everyone has secrets and he has to have at least one that I can use. As the various ideas run through my head, Exie's car is cut off by another. I look over at Exie as she puts the car in reverse only to slam on the brakes to prevent a collision with a second car.

"Oh, this is not good." Exie said reaching under her seat and pulling out a gun.

Shocked I stare at the weapon in her hand, "What exactly are you thinking that's going to do?"

"I don't know, but I know I am not going anywhere with these guys. Whoever they are." Exie said gripping the gun.

Two men exit the car behind us and tap on my window, "Our boss would like to talk to you. Briefly." The large man said with a forced smile.

"Do you want my gun?" Exie asked.

"Why so I can accidentally shoot myself?" I said slowly getting out of the car. I follow the man to the car in front of us and hesitate as he opens the back door for me. I look into the dark car and I instantly recognize the cigar-smoking weasel, Harvey Rice. He's as dangerous as Nick, but even more so to me now. Nick and Harvey have been at odds for some time and now someone has let Harvey know about me. Someone has betrayed Nick and put me right in the middle.

"Hello, sweetheart. Do you know who I am?" Harvey said

looking me over with little to no interest as anyone would do to someone they know is not going to be around much longer.

"I do." I said sitting as small as possible so as not to get any closer to him than necessary.

"Very good, then I will get right to the point of my visit." *Visit? Well, I hope that means I am not going to die right now at least.* "I hear you are valuable to my old friend Nick." I glance over at him as he smiles. "I would like to make you an offer. Come work for me instead. I will make sure you have only the highest paying clients, some of the most respectable men in the city. I have a nice house you can live in rent free. A car. Everything you need. All you have to do is leave Nick and come work for me." Harvey said sticking his cigar back between his large chapped lips.

Of course, I leave Nick and then he will surely kill me himself but if I say no to Harvey he will kill me to get back at Nick. Talk about being stuck between a rock and the bottom of a grave. "As nice of an offer as that is, you don't mind if I think about it for a night at least, do you?" I asked, hoping it wouldn't cause my immediate death.

"Sure thing." He said flashing his crooked stained teeth at me. "Take all the time you need, honey."

I graciously take his card and pretend to consider his offer, but as soon as I get a chance, I seek Nick out, determined to get help- even it is from him. "Nick, I need to talk to you." I said ignoring Luke as I barge in on their conversation.

"I'm talking, Kayla. Maybe later." Nick said waving me off.

"NO! I need to talk to you now!" I demand standing straight and trying to control my trembling legs.

Nick's demon eyes meet mine immediately, "Talk and it better be damn good."

"Alone, please." I asked not giving a shit about Luke's evil glares.

"You have to be kidding me! Sweetheart, you better be glad you are still able to talk!" Luke said slamming his fist on the table.

"Please, Nick. I promise you are going to want to hear what I have to say."

"Fine. Let's go to my office." Nick said getting up and waving me in front of him.

"Nick?" Luke holds out his hands as Nick waves him off.

Nick impatiently grabs my arm and hurries me along. Once we enter his office, he begins searching for something seemingly uninterested in what I have to say. I am hoping it is not a gun to shoot me with. "I'm waiting. What is this huge news that you have for me?"

"Someone came to see me today."

Nick looks up at me ready to bite my head off, "Kayla, I swear!" I lay Harvey's card down in front of him and his temper eases instantly towards me. "What did he want?"

"For me to leave you and work for him."

"And what did you say?" He asks eyeing me directly.

"I said I would think about it. I'm not stupid. He would have killed me right then if I had said no, just as you will kill me if I leave you for him. So instead, I am asking for you to help me get out from in the middle of this feud you have with him." I said feeling better about my decision to come to him.

Nick sits back pondering my information, "Call him and tell him I offered you a better deal and you have decided to stay."

"He will kill me if I do that!" I yell back at him.

"No he won't. Do it and I will take care of the rest." Nick said confidently.

I leave Nick's office not feeling much better than I did. I spend the rest of the night listening to Luke huffing at me for shaking down Nick for more money. I don't understand what he is talking about at first but after Nick tells him that I have earned it, I play along nervously. I thought for sure Nick would tell him what I said and it worries me that he didn't. I drop off Exie at a close friend's house, who is already watching Jerran. Knowing they both are safely away from me, I head home alone becoming more nervous the closer I get. I run into the house, locking every door and window, and sit in a corner with Jerran's baseball bat. I barely breathe while I watch every movement in the yard. I know I am probably making myself go insane but when I hear a noise in the basement my heart stops. *It's footsteps, definitely footsteps coming up the stairs.* I stand up slowly and wait to take aim. When the door opens, I swing.

"Fuck, Kayla!" Nick yells catching me in midswing before taking the bat away from me.

"Nick, damn it! You scared the hell out of me!" I stomp and yell at him.

"Obviously! Calm down. I checked around, there is no one out there yet."

"What are you doing here?" I huff at him.

"I told you I would take care of everything."

"I thought that meant you would go find him somewhere *else* and take care of it."

"Oh, Princess, Harvey is not going to put himself in a position to be killed by me. But he will not miss a chance to get at me, especially if he thinks I am nowhere near."

"Tell me you brought some people to help." Nick smiles tapping my chin. "Nick, are you stupid? He will kill us both."

"Princess, just do what you normally do and leave the rest to me." I stand awkwardly looking around. "Seriously? That's what you do every night?"

"NO! I usually get ready for bed, but I am not going to do that now."

"Why not?"

"Why NOT!" I yell.

Nick shakes his head and turns me around, pushing me forward. "Go clean yourself up and go to bed. You don't have to go to sleep and you can go to bed with your bat, if you like, but the quicker you look vulnerable, the quicker they will try to kill you."

"Oh, well. Let me hurry then." I said faking my excitement.

"I know I'm excited." I glare at him as he smiles back. Getting cleaned up I find something to put on and start to change before noticing Nick sitting in a corner watching me.

"Do you mind?" I say to him hiding myself.

"Are you kidding?" He said before shaking his head at me. Exasperated I do my best to change and show him as little as possible. "Wow, I know I'm turned on."

"Shut up."

"Is that what you wear to bed?"

"Nick!"

"I think my dick shriveled up looking at it."

"Well, I am not trying to get you turned on right now. I am trying to not get killed."

"Okay, but I was hoping for better from you. You could put on something a little smaller and tighter, at least. Anything would be more appealing than that mess. I am here to save your life. Give me a little reason to want to." Even in the dark I can see his obnoxious smile.

"Ass! I swear..." I mumble climbing into bed.

Hours go by and I begin to fall asleep. When reality seeps back into my mind, I wake up quickly, "Nick?"

"It's okay, go back to sleep." He whispered from what seems closer than I remember him being. I reach out into the dark and he takes my hand. "Go to sleep, I'm here." I settle in and slowly fall right back into my dreams.

Suddenly I am startled awake. I gasp before realizing Nick is still holding my hand. "I'm right here and yes I heard it to. I'm going to drop back and give him space …" I nod understanding.

I get up to investigate the noise with my bat in hand. They come right through the front door, with little trouble. I swing and fight with everything I have, but am ultimately in their control. Harvey walks in at their signal and smiles at me. "I hope we didn't wake you," he says.

"You fucking son of a bitch!" I yell fighting my restraints.

"You are a fighter. I can see why Nick has taken such a shine to you. Now, Kayla, why are you here alone? You must think I am afraid of Nick. Why else would you feel so confident leaving yourself vulnerable this way? I will have you know honey despite the power you think Nicholas has, I promise you I have even more. I wish we could work together Kayla, but since you made the wrong decision I am going to have to take you out of the business. Unless you think you can convince me otherwise?" He laughs checking out our modest home.

"It must be hard to live up to Nick- what with all his manly assets compared to your glaring dysfunctions." I said proudly.

Harvey turns several shades of pissed off, "Leave us." I am released and Harvey approaches me quickly, knocking me backwards into a wall. He begins taking off his coat and shirt while I struggle to reach my bat. Harvey grabs my leg and laughs as he pulls me closer to him. "Let's see what you think about my assets once I am finished with you." Harvey pins me down and forces his smoked chapped lips towards mine.

"Hi, Harvey! What brings you to this neighborhood?" Nick said before nailing Harvey's shocked face in the jaw with his foot. I slide quickly out of Nick's way as he takes out a wire and wraps it around Harvey's neck. Nick's smile is bigger than I have ever seen as he continues pulling the wire against Harvey's throat tighter, "I was starting to wonder if you were going to show. You have always been disappointingly slow, Harvey."

"Nick? What a surprise. I hope you are not still holding a

grudge." Harvey grunts out of his burning throat.

"No. I am over you shooting me and trying to kill me. Although, I am not too happy about what you are trying to do to my girl and trying to steal her away from me, what is that about?"

"Oh, is she your girl? I didn't realize." Harvey chokes.

"Who told you about her?" Nick asks directly into Harvey's ear as he tightens the wire a little more.

Harvey harshly laughs, "Nick, you should know better. But I will tell you this: it is somebody you know well." Harvey tightens his lips as his breathing becomes labored.

"Ahhh, Duke." Nick guesses as he watches Harvey closely to confirm his suspensions. Laughing, Nick looks up at me, "I told you that man is sick and twisted."

"And I thought you told him that I wasn't worth his time?" I said back to his smirk.

"Did I?" Nick cocks head before smiling. "Well, maybe I actually told him to stay the hell away from you."

"Nick! Why would you lie about that? That is so stupid!" I yell.

"Kayla, please, if I had told you anything else you would have went after him just to spite me."

"I most certainly would not have." I said, crossing my arms.

"This coming from the girl who was determined to piss me off to win my favor." Nick huffed.

"I wasn't trying to piss you off. It just happens to be easy to do, you fucking Hothead." As I yell at Nick, I notice Harvey pulling something from his leg. "Nick!"

Nick takes hold of the wire with one hand, grabs his knife with the other, and quickly stabs Harvey in the leg. If he could breathe, he would have screamed out. Harvey refuses to say another word, but just smiles at Nick, pissing him off more. "One thing you should know, Harvey, before I kill you: it was me that cleaned your safes out." Nick said stabbing him in the neck and then stepping back to watch him gurgle words through the gushing blood. "Disgusting fucker! Next time don't distract me, Kayla. You could have gotten us both killed!"

"Distract you? You're the one that was too busy enjoying yourself instead of getting right to it."

"Trust me, I deserved to take my time, Princess." Nick kicks Harvey's lifeless body away from him. "You okay?" He asked reaching out for my hand to help me up.

"For now. But how are we going to get out of here?"

"Good question. I didn't expect him to bring so many men." Nick said taking a quick look out the window.

"Well, can't you call someone?"

Laughing, he replies "Who? The police?"

"No, your people."

"I don't think that's a good idea. Those boys out there will get suspicious and come running in here before I can have anyone get here." Looking around the room, he looks up at me with an emerging smile, "How are you at playing dead?" Nick begins to clean up the blood with a nearby towel, "Come here." I shake my head but he pulls me to him and spreads the blood over me. I am barely able to stand from my nausea. He covers me in a blanket and puts on Harvey's trench and hat before throwing me over his shoulder. I grip hold of him and release a shaky breath as the blood drips onto the ground. "Try not to breathe too much," he whispers. Nick walks out with a similar limp to Harvey's and surprisingly matches Harvey's coarse voice, "Let's go."

"How was she, sir?"

"A fine piece of ass boys. A fine piece of ass, I must say." Nick says smacking my ass.

"Where to next? Jayzon's club?"

"That's the plan, that's the plan." Nick says sliding me in the car ahead of him and following in quickly. Trying to remain still, I watch Nick take out his phone and rapidly type something. When we arrive at the deserted club, they open the car door for Nick and he gets out throwing me over his shoulder once again. Walking up to the door of the club, he shoots off the lock. "Wait here, boys, I want to leave a love letter for Mr. Jayzon." Nick walks us into the club and once the door shuts, he quickly pushes me under some tables, "Stay put." He said before running to meet Luke who throws him a gun. Now that I am free from my barrier I see all his boys running out the doors with guns. Cowering tight into the corner he put me in, I close my eyes and wait for it to be over. "Get rid of them all! I don't want any trace of any of them! And make sure to go to Exie's and clean up too!" Trembling and still clenching my eyes shut, I feel Nick's hand on mine. "Kayla, it's alright now." I look up at him shaking uncontrollably. "It's okay. Come on, let's get you into something less disgusting. Not that it was much better before." He says handing me some clothes from the club's gift shop.

"Shut up." I whimper and wobble forward on my shaky legs. Nick sighs as he helps me become a little more stable. Giving his men some final orders Nick escorts me into the back of his car and sits quietly next to me, calm and at ease. I crave that. *I wish Daniel was here. I wish Exie or someone other than him was here.* Wanting that comfort, I ease in next to Nick and wait to be smacked backwards. But with each inch I take, he gives up a little more until I am curled up under his arm. He's a little stiff but at least he's not being his usual self. When we pull up to his house, I am already half asleep- drifting in and out of consciousness. Nick nudges me to wake up, "Just leave me here, I'm good sleeping here." I said closing my eyes and leaning on him for support.

"Pushing it. She is so pushing it." He mutters as he carries me to a bedroom where he leaves me for the night.

At some point, I wake up and step into the adjoining bathroom where I take full advantage of the luxury shower. When I finish cleaning up, I dive back into the plush bed, letting the soft sheets comfort my now clean, bare skin, drifting back to sleep with no worries.

ᲝᲖᲒᲝ

"Kayla." I feel the low whisper in my ear. "Hey Princess, do you always sleep naked in other people's beds?" Nick says with a slight tug of my blankets.

Yawning and stretching fully, I look up at his humored face with little interest. "What do you want?" I spit out roughly.

"I want my bed back."

I quickly sit up and take in the room around me, "This isn't your bed, is it?" I asked.

"Well, it is my guest bed but still." He said smiling his stupid smile.

"Screw you, Nick, go away and leave me alone." I said lying back down and curling up within the cloud of pillows.

"Damn! I have had it with your attitude towards me." With my back turned towards him I feel the cover move from my body and instantaneously turn. "Just seeing how naked you are." He said with an easy smile.

Glaring up at him, I snatch the cover from his hands and tighten it around myself, "Do you not have other people you can bother?"

"You know I did save your life. You could be a little more grateful."

"If you hadn't of made such a big deal about Duke staying away from me, then you probably wouldn't have had to."

"Hmm ... maybe. But if I hadn't, Duke would have taken you himself. Then you would have surely been viciously raped and tortured to death." Nick leans down to look right into my now wide eyes, "Harvey would have just shot you ... that is, if you could have kept your mouth shut."

"Why were you associating with him in the first place, if he is so disgusting?"

"Well, it is not because of his charm. I needed some information and that's all you need to know. For now I suppose you can sleep here however long you want. But you should know your home has been ... well, let's say somewhat destroyed."

I sit up straight and look him in the eyes, "What?"

"Sorry, the boys got a little out of hand with Harvey and the others. So we had to set it on fire. But, the good news is that only the living room and most of the kitchen are missing. The rest is fine." My eyes widen and I can feel my face heat up. "Calm down. I set Exie and her son up in a nice place rent free for a while. She was forgiving."

"She may be but I ..." Nick covers my mouth and shakes head.

"Be quiet please. In the meantime, I want you to stay here until I can make sure no one else is out to kill you. You can have this room. Do what you want with it and whatever you can't salvage from your old place, I will pay to replace. For now, I guess you can stay in bed for as long as you want. At least you're dressed a little better than you were before." He laughs at his stupid joke before pausing, "Wait, what's wrong with you?"

"Nothing. Why?" I asked, confused by his question.

"Because I have rarely told you to do something without being met with attitude. Are you figuring out a way to defy me or are you sick and I need to get you a doctor or something?"

"No, I'm fine. I'm not arguing with you because I feel safe here and it will be safer for Exie and Jerran if I am not living with them. So, I am good with your decision." I smile at him only making him more suspicious, "Thank you ... Nick."

"Uh huh. Well, I am going to leave you before this feel-good moment gets any more disturbing." Nick said shaking his head as he leaves my now beautiful room.

I fall back into MY bed with a great feeling and exhale: "Yes!"

~7~
KAYLA

"Oh Daniel you should see it, my room is bigger than my last apartment and I have my own bathroom and a maid that has it cleaned up before I can even turn around to make another mess. It is the most amazing thing I have ever seen." I said, bouncing happily next to him.

"I don't think I have ever heard you this excited. It is too bad I'm not the reason for it. I can't stand the thought that it is that ... loser who is responsible for your beautiful smile." Daniel said.

Sitting up on him with a smile, "Why, Mr. Bonner, are you jealous?"

"I am jealous of anyone who gets to spend time with you." Daniel smiles as he pushes the strands of hair away from my face. "Do you spend much time with him?"

"No, not really." I shrug, not giving the question much thought.

"So, he doesn't try to do anything with you?"

"No, we can barely stand each other." I said, looking at him from the corners of my eyes.

"Oh, come on! Isn't it nice to have a man a little jealous over you? Especially one that is so in love with you and wants nothing more than for you to move in here and let him take care of you?"

"Daniel, I told you I don't like being taken care of."

"But it's okay for me to pay that punk to spend time with you? Kayla, I don't like you being there with him. The man is dangerous, he is into some things I don't think you know about."

"I know everything about Nick." I said ignoring his concern.

"Does he tell you things?" He asks with a smile as I shrug. "I love you." He said taking my hand and leading me into the steaming shower with him. Placing me against the wall, Daniel raises my hands over my head and begins rubbing my body, lathering me all over. "I was wondering if you could do me a favor."

Smiling with a low hum as he soothes my warm body, "Sure.

51

What?"

"I would like to send you some flowers but I don't want Nick around when I do it so I thought maybe you could call and let me know when he leaves."

"When tomorrow?"

Daniel kisses me sweetly, "Tomorrow and the next and the next, I want to surprise you so I don't want to tell you exactly when they are coming."

"You want me to spy on Nick for several days?" I ask feeling oddly exposed.

Daniel shrugs, "Days or a couple of weeks at the most. If he has a routine, then once I know what that is, I can send them safely. Unless you already know his routines, then maybe I can bring them to you myself and we can have some dirty sex in his bed!"

I try to laugh with him but I see something curious in his eyes. "Nick would kill me if he ever found out I was letting someone know his routines. Besides, he doesn't have any and I don't want you coming to his house."

"I guess you're right, but wouldn't that be a rush? Having sex in Nicholas Jayzon's bed?"

"Are you an adrenaline junky?"

"I think you are bringing out the worst in me." He laughs. "I was wondering though, what is your favorite flower?" His sweet smile warms me as it always does. Once we finish our shower, I say good-bye, which takes a little longer than usual. I leave Daniel daydreaming and smiling, but as soon as I get back to Nick's, I find him waiting for me impatiently.

"Where have you been?" Nick asked with a tense posture.

"I was with a client."

"I don't like not knowing where you are." Nick said, becoming disturbingly unglued.

"Luke knew ..."

"Luke is not in charge. I am! I didn't let you move in here so you can wander around freely without anyone there to protect you." Nick stands strong in front of me.

"Nick..."

"Don't you start with me! From now on, someone is to be with you at all times. You are to be escorted to everywhere you're going and you are to stay there until someone can pick you up. Do you understand me?" He asked eyeing me until I nod in acceptance. Nick leaves me standing silently like a punished child.

The house is huge but the silence makes it feel even bigger. Needing to hear a comforting voice, I call Daniel's cell, "Hi! Miss me already?"

"Of course. But I was also needing a little ..." I sigh heavily.

"What's wrong, baby?" Daniel asks sweetly.

"Nick. He was not happy that I got back so late, so now he wants me escorted everywhere I go."

"Well, that's going to make things interesting. I take it he isn't around since you are calling me to complain about him?"

"No, he left."

"He left you there alone?" He asked with a hopeful tone.

"Yes. I feel like Rapunzel isolated in her tower."

Daniel laughs, "Where did he go? You don't want him coming back and catching you talking to me."

"Oh, I doubt he comes back any time soon he ... well, who knows with Nick."

"What were you going to say? He- what?" Daniel's voice jumps with excitement suddenly.

"Nothing. I just had an impression that he might not be back soon." I said wishing I could take it back.

"He took something with him, didn't he?"

"I don't know. He just seemed like he was going to be gone awhile, but I ... Daniel, don't you dare even think about coming over here." I said.

Daniel laughs. "Okay, but just in case, I better let you go so he doesn't catch you doing something naughty again. I love you so much."Smiling, I hang up my phone and go to bed. Feeling better, I can fall asleep peacefully until I am awakened out of a dead sleep by Nick yelling. Getting up quietly, I go find out what he is so mad about and see Luke surprisingly calm and Dwayne blocking my view of Nick.

"Who let him get near me?" Nick yells again.

"I don't know, Nick. What I would like to know is how he knew you would be there?" Luke said.

"Fuck! That son of a bitch! I should have killed him when I had the chance!" Nick walks around Dwayne and I can see him holding his severely bleeding arm.

"Are you okay?" I yell at him without thinking.

The three of them turn and stare at me. "Kayla, go to bed!"

Nick yells back at me.

Running down the stairs, I reach out to him, "But your arm!" He pulls away from me before I can touch him.

"It's nothing. Go to bed." Nick said forcefully.

"It doesn't look like nothing! And you don't have to be such an ass I am only trying to help you. I can bandage it for you, if you want, or you can be your typical asshole self and let it get infected and …"

"Oh my God! Fine." Nick turns towards Luke, "Find out how Connor knew I was there and whoever let him near me …"

"I'll take care of it." Luke said glancing over at me with a cursing expression.

"I have no idea what you are talking about if that makes you feel any better?" I said.

Luke walks around me, "Not really."

Dwayne follows him out, "Kayla." He nods in my direction.

"So, where are your bandages?" I ask as Nick motions for me to follow him.

"I can do this myself you know." He sighs.

"Oh, I am sure. Because you can do everything, right?" I mock him. He shows me a storage closet where I pull out what I need and follow him into his bathroom. "Take your shirt off." Nick smiles and I roll my eyes. "Shut up." He slips his shirt off with a low grunt and a knowing look in my direction. His body is only half exposed and I already have bad thoughts. None of them include me killing him, unfortunately.

"Owe! Fuck! What the hell are you trying to do? Kill me?"

"Yes, Nick, I am trying to kill you with ointment." He looks the other direction trying to not make another sound as I clean him up. "It is a little deep, you might need stitches."

"I don't need stitches."

"It might scar …" I insist.

Nick stands up looking down at me. "It won't be my first, Princess."

"Don't you dare leave yet!"

"What now?" He yells.

"I have to bandage it unless you want it to bleed again." Nick huffs giving me back his arm so I can roll the gauze smoothly around his arm. "So, who did this to you? It looks like someone tried to stab you."

"Kayla, you need to stay out of my business. Luke almost shot you earlier for sneaking in on us like that."

"I wasn't sneaking. I heard you yelling."

"Next time you hear me yelling, put your headphones on and ignore it."

"Can't you at least tell me who did this to you?" I look up into his eyes.

"His name is Connor. This is a fun game for him."

"I guess he doesn't like you much."

"We have hated each other since birth." Nick looks at his arm after I am finished, "Looks good. Thank you, Princess."

"You're welcome."

Nick leans in close to my ear, "You know, even with one arm I can show you my appreciation."

Huffing, I walk away from him, "You were so close to being descent."

"Goodnight, Princess."

"Goodnight, Nick."

 CB8O

$\mathcal{R}$ushing out to the car that is waiting for me, I expect to take it to meet with Daniel, only I find Nick inside. "Get in. I am taking you out to dinner." He demands.

"Me? But I have a client to see."

"Yes you. And your client will get over it." I try to come up with a reason I need to see Daniel but nothing comes to mind before Nick becomes impatient with me. "Now that Harvey is out of the way, thanks to you, my business has become much easier and friendlier. So to thank you, I am treating you to a night out."

"You're not going to take me to the club, are you?"

Nick laughs, "No, I reserved at an actual restaurant."

"I'm not sure I am dressed properly."

"You look beautiful."

"Wow, I never thought I would hear a compliment from you." I said sitting down beside him.

"Don't get use to it."

"You look alright, too." I said trying to hold my smile back when he laughs.

Nick offers me his arm as we enter the restaurant and for the first time, I feel like a Princess as everyone turns to watch us walk in. Although it is hard to miss the women drooling as Nick passes them.

He does look incredible, I wish I didn't hate him so much. He holds out my chair for me and I begin to wonder who taught him such manners. Who took this deceptive thief under their wing and gave him the tools to destroy women's hearts?

"Wine?" He asks while already perusing the wine list.

"Sure. If you're buying, I will have one of each." I said earning his usual eye roll. He orders with perfect pronunciation, speaking fluent French with the waiter. Impatient and a little insulted that he thinks I can't understand what he is saying, I interrupt and ask my own questions before ordering.

"And where did you learn French?" He asked.

"Books." I said with a smile.

"Books?" He asked with disbelief.

"You can learn a lot from books." His questionable expression forces me to confess, "Okay fine, I used to sneak into classes at the college."

"You snuck in? Ever heard of signing up for a class like a normal person?"

"I couldn't. I was only sixteen and they wanted money- which I didn't have."

"And, at sixteen, you didn't have anything better to do than sit in on some boring French classes? No boyfriends or proms to worry about?" Nick asked with a sarcastic smile.

I huff, "I wasn't exactly noticed by any boys. Well, except for my mother's boyfriends, but they were the reason I stayed out of the house as much as possible."

"Ahhh... so, the troubled teenager grows up and rebels against the world because Mommy wasn't there for her?"

"I'm not making any excuses for what I am doing. Besides, I am doing better than most of the people in those college classes. I am living in a mansion and I have my own driver." I smile to Nick's immediate laughter.

"My mansion, my driver, and you're a temporary guest, Princess. Don't forget that."

"Okay, so how is it you know French? Prep school? Mommy and Daddy pay for the best tutors? Travel overseas to live for a while?"

"Not hardly." He smirks, taking down his first drink of our wine. "What's that look for?"

"So, is your life a big secret or are you just shy?"

"What is with the smart mouth all the time? No. No prep school. Harvey taught me a lot when I worked for him. I paid attention and used my spare time to learn more. Which, as it turned out, saved my life."

"How is that?" I asked.

"Because he thought I didn't understand when he ordered my death warrant. Dumb son of a bitch did it right in front of me. I flew out of his house shooting everything in sight. Luckily, Luke decided to get my back rather than stick it out with Harvey."

"But Harvey did shoot you?"

"He got off one shot before running and hiding like the coward he was. I think he was aiming for my head but was barely able to get me in the right side. Bullet went right through."

"Is that the reason for the tattoo? To cover up the scar?"

"Watching me undress, Princess? You know, if you want to see me naked just ask and I might let you."

Uggghhh "Tell me how you got involved with Harvey in the first place."

Sighing, Nick settles in comfortably with me. "Typical story, I was doing petty crimes, stealing cars, breaking into homes and taking whatever I could. Then I met Luke and he introduced me to Harvey, who taught me how to make real money."

"So, Mommy ignored you and Daddy ran out on you?"

"Since when did we become pen pals?" He said smartly.

"Come on Nick, did you have parents or did the devil just create you from some spare parts?"

Laughing out loud for the first time that I have ever seen, "Yes, I had parents. My mother worked three jobs to help pay the bills while my father stayed home with me. He didn't run out on us, unfortunately. And before you ask: yes, he was a mean son of a bitch at times, but his temper was short-lived. He preferred to have a good time. Whenever my mother got paid, he would send her back to work and then take me out to get him a prostitute. Fucked her right in front of me. Good memories."

"He took you with him? Why didn't he leave you at home?"

"He didn't want to leave me by myself. I was too young. Better to take me with him and learn something. Hell, it's because of the old man that I learned how to fuck, eat pussy, and ..."

"Nick!"

Laughing, "Well, anyway, he was good at teaching me what he

knew. After awhile, he found it easier to bring the girls home and do his thing while Mom would make us something to eat or clean the house. Whatever she could do to stay busy while he was occupied..."

"She knew and she stayed with him?"

"She was something. Never fazed her. She preferred to have him around no matter how big of a Dirtbag he was. He had some kind of control over her and every other woman he met." Nick said glancing around the room to avoid me.

"She loved him that much?"

"Love?" Nick chokes. "I wouldn't go that far. Scared to be alone, maybe too weak, and definitely too pathetic to stand up for herself. You know, I came home one day and found my Dad sitting in a chair with a full meal on a trey in front of him. She was in the kitchen cleaning and oblivious to the fact the man was dead." Nick said with a harsh laugh. "The old man dies of a heart attack and what does she do? Picks him up off the floor, sticks him in a chair, and feeds him. Insane." I can't help stare at him with a feeling of heaviness and sorrow for him. Nick senses my question before I can even ask. "I thought maybe once he was gone she would snap out of it and show some life... or I don't know, be a mother for once. Instead she hung herself two days later."

Without thinking, I reach over and grab his hand, "Nick, I'm so ..."

Nick pulls his hand away from me with a glare that sets me back in my chair. Leaning over the table towards me, "Tell me, Princess, did you lose that golden virtue to a pimpled faced boy from school or to one of your mother's boyfriends?"

He gets a kick out of pissing me off. "You know the answer to that." Sitting back with a nod, he seems proud of himself for making me angry. "And before you ask, no, I didn't go after him. And, no, she didn't care as long as he paid attention to her when she wanted it."

"Maybe we should change the subject?" He said.

"Maybe. So, Nick, with all your women, I assume one of them has given you at least one child?"

"After the stories we just shared, you think I am looking to be a Daddy? No, Princess, I haven't gotten anyone pregnant. Thank God. What about you? Are you waiting for the right Daddy-figure to get you barefoot and pregnant?"

"Why do you have to paint everything with such a sour disposition?" I reply with disgust.

"My personality, I guess." He retorts with a smirk.

"Well, you should try some yoga or something. Might loosen up some of those anger issues you have. You would think with all the sex you have you would be a touch more optimistic about things." I said sipping my wine.

Laughing, "I'm optimistic. For instance, I am positive that I am getting laid tonight."

The devil's eyes take hold of me and I stare right back without an ounce of give. "Not from me you're not."

Nick is seemingly satisfied for the time being but I know I started a contest between us and I am going to have to fight off any desires I have for him if I am going to win. Turning up the charm, Nick holds out his glass and toasts in French to me. The ride home is filled with tender touches and soft whispers. Battle for battle, I hold strong against him. I spent years studying him, preparing for him, and now Nick has finally met a woman that is not falling deep into his trap. Walking into the house, I step cautiously wondering what he is planning next. "Goodnight, Nick. Thank you for dinner. I enjoyed it very much." I said, kissing him on the cheek and turning to go upstairs. He takes hold of my wrist and pulls me back to him.

"Where are you going?"

Looking into his eyes, all I can see is his dizzying desire. My whole body begins to feel the draw, pulling me to him and making me both weak and wet at the same time. "I'm going to bed, Nick. I am really tired." I said unable to move away from him

Holding me tight to his chest, he pulls back my hair from my ear and breathes gently, "Are you sure? Just imagine what I can do when I use my whole body to satisfy you and not just my fingers?" His warm lips trail up my neck, making their way to my lips and heating them up with every touch. Enjoying the feel of his lips on mine, I ignore his wandering hand, intent on stripping me naked as it massages my body into submission. I feel myself giving in, wanting to surrender to him, and he knows it. He already believes he's won. Reaching down I feel for him and taking hold of his erection, I excite him even more. With one last kiss, I push away from him and enjoy the shock on his face. "Oh damn, I forgot … I have a meeting I have to go to. How about you get naked and wait for me in bed. I promise I will wake you when I get back." I said taking my bag and the keys to his car. I turn once to wink at him as I walk out the door. I believe he will surely chase after me or be waiting up for me when I get back, but he lets me go and he lets me fall peacefully to sleep … alone.

The next morning, I sit quietly watching the rain as I eat my breakfast. "You didn't wake me." Nick said, entering with a cup of coffee already in hand.

"Knowing you, I figured you had already found a replacement." I said, turning away from him.

"Nick, everyone is here. You ready?" Luke said, holding out his hands as if he is confused by having to wait for Nick.

"I'll be there in a second." Nick says, dismissing him. Luke huffs, stomping off like a child. Before I can look back at Nick, he is already reminding me of where we left off. "I did as you asked, Princess. All you had to do was wake me." He whispers with a quick kiss on the cheek and a smile as he leaves. Biting my lip hard, I fight my smile the best I can. *I won the battle for now, but can I win the war? I am so close I can't stop now.*

~8~
KAYLA

*N*ick is taking a new approach with me. I prepare for a sensual attack that I will not be able to resist but instead, he takes a step back and asks me to dinner, to dance, or to have a glass of wine with him in front of the fireplace. It is an attack I didn't expect and it blindsides me. He's patient and his charm is at all new high. Today, he left me flowers with no note. And, as if that isn't enough, my appointments have slowly disappeared, allowing me to have more than enough time to spend with him. It is not until Nick leaves for a few days that I am able to see Daniel again.

"I was beginning to think that you were avoiding me." Daniel said, holding me tight.

"No, it's Nick. He has been requiring much my time lately."

"Why? Why does he suddenly want you for himself?" Daniel laughs forcefully.

"I don't know. He is playing a game with me."

"Are you sleeping with him?" Daniel asked with a concerned expression.

"No."

"He wants you to though." He snaps.

"Maybe, but …" I said, noticing his angered expression.

"But what? You're enjoying it? You're enjoying his attention?" Daniel screams, outraged.

"Why are we talking about this? Nick has nothing to do with us. You're not even paying him for me anymore."

"If you're not working for him anymore, then leave him. Let me take care of you!" Daniel said, changing his tone and smiling deep into my eyes causing me to doubt my original plans with Nick. I don't want to lose Daniel because I am so determined to get back at Nick. "Kayla, if you stay here, then I can see you whenever I want and I will know you're safe from him."

"He will find me. If I leave him, it would have to be his

61

decision, which is not going to happen until he does get me into bed."

"Don't you fucking sleep with him!" Daniel rages at me. Wiping the anger from his lips, he steps back, and takes a drink of his bourbon. "Sorry, but the thought of you with him … makes me insane."

"I'm not going to be with him. I promise, I have been able to resist him so far, hell, it's easy for me. Fun even- to make him crazy."

"FUN! You call it fun? It is fun for you to tease a dangerous man? You are so fucking stupid. Why don't you wise up, Sweetheart? He doesn't give a shit about you. He just wants to fuck you. I'm not sure why you haven't fucked him already. What? Hasn't he paid you enough already?" He yells.

I jump out of bed and smack him. "You paid me. He at least is taking me out like he is proud to be seen with me."

"Is that what you want? You want me to take you out … date you? Oh, I know! How about I introduce you to my friends. I can introduce everyone to my personal whore." Feeling my heart sink deep into my chest, I swallow the lump in my throat and quickly get dressed. "Kayla, stop. I'm sorry. I didn't mean any of that."

"It sure sounded like it!" I yell, determined not to let him see me cry.

Taking my face into his hands, "Baby, I am so worried about you. I'm serious when I say it makes me insane that you are living with him. Please stay here and let me take care of you."

"So I can be your full-time personal whore?" Exasperated, he kisses me and tries to persuade me to stay. Stopping his advances, "And why do I have to stay here, Daniel? Why can't I stay with you? Why can't I stay in your house?"

"You know damn well that can't happen right now."

"And why not?" I ask, stepping away from his persuasive sweetness.

"Because the wounds are still fresh. If I am seen with anybody right now, there will be questions galore about whom she is and how we met. Now, once I start dating a few other women and get those initial curiosity questions out of the way, people will get used to seeing me with someone other than Nadia. Then it will be easier to bring you in and introduce you. I love you, Kayla. Do you love me?" He questions but doesn't give me a chance to answer before he is all over me again.

"Daniel!" I yell pushing him away from me. "I thought you said that you had been dating other women already. That I am not your rebound girl. Remember?"

"Now you don't trust me?" He yells pointing to himself. "You have some nerve." He said, waving me off with a brokenhearted expression.

"It just doesn't make sense to me, Daniel."

"It doesn't have to make sense. That's what love is sometimes. Alright, maybe I am too cautious. But my friends aren't always the nicest people and I fear putting you through their ridicule. I don't want you to ever feel like you're not worthy of me." He said, smiling at me as if I am some insecure, awkward child. Daniel grips me suddenly, kissing me hard and giving me what he thinks I want, but sex is far from what I am wanting right now. I leave Daniel while he is still asleep. Tonight, I prefer to be in my own bed at Nick's where I can sleep alone.

CRXD

*W*hile I ignore Daniel's constant calls I try to sort out my own feelings. "What's wrong with you today? You look sad." Nick asks before he walks out to one of his meetings.

"I'm fine. Bored, I guess. Maybe if I had a job I wouldn't be. And don't tell me no one wants to book me. I'm not stupid, Nick."

"I know you're not. But I also know that you're also too good for that kind of work- for those kinds of men. You want another job?" I turn to see if he is making a serious offer. "Help me run the club. I have so much going on these days, I don't have time to deal with it and I need someone checking on Kyler before he does something stupid." Nick sits down in front of me, "I'll show you everything about it and all you have to do is keep the reputation up, keep the girls in order, and keep the drugs out. I don't need the cops having any reason to get nosy about my business. Can you handle that?"

In shock, but wildly excited, I nod quickly, "Yes, I can do that."

"I will buy you a car so you don't have to borrow mine anymore. Anything in particular you prefer?" Smiling all over myself, all I can do is shake my head. Nick chuckles at me, "Alright, I will surprise you then. I have to go for now, but I will come back here to get you and we will go to the club together. Also, Kayla, you know from time to time I have special clients come in..."

I move to the edge of my seat, "I will make sure they are well-taken care of and I won't ask any questions- or get involved in any way other than what you ask me to do."

"Alright, then be ready when I get home, Princess."

"Nick?" I say waiting for him to look at me. "Can you not call me Princess when we are at the club? If I am going to be running your business …"

"I got it." He smiled.

Nick keeps his promise and returns to take me to the club. I am shocked at how much detail he gives me. It is only a small portion of what he owns but Pigalle is one of his more legitimate businesses, except for one small area which I'm not allowed to know, but I have a good idea. My job is to keep the club respectable so he can concentrate on keeping his other ventures running smoothly. My first week on the job I can barely think of anything else than work. I stay up late making notes: jotting down new ideas and figuring out how I'm going to look for new girls. Excited, I approach Nick one night with one of my ideas: to have open tryouts, a special contest on our slowest night. A contest will bring in the amateurs to strut their stuff for a spot in our lineup and a cash prize. It will also bring in the crowds to watch the spectacle. Surprisingly, Nick lets me run with it and promises to make an appearance which should bring the girls running to impress him. On the night of, I know it is going to be a good night. The list of girls wanting their chance is a mile long. The lines outside waiting to get in are beyond our capacity and Kyler is having his third drink before the doors even open. I hire Exie to assist with keeping everything running smoothly and she is more than helpful, especially with the new raise I was able to get for her. When Nick arrives, everything is in perfect order and he and his crew walk in amazed. Exie sits them at the table closest to the stage so the girls can see him. Once they are settled, I make my way to sit across from Nick and don't say a word as I enjoy his smile in my direction.

"Nick!" The blond that had once tried to molest Nick in his car, runs up to him and sits herself right in his lap. "Oh, baby, I have missed you. Where have you been?"

"Working." Nick says catching sight of my obvious displeasure with her. "I have been busy."

"Well maybe tonight, after I dance for you on stage, I can dance for you privately?" She says with her best sexy smile.

"I might like that." He said, laughing at me rolling my eyes as she touches him aggressively.

"You know, ummm …" I said.

"Amanda." She said continuing to play with Nick.

"Yea, right. Amanda. Uh … Nick is not the only judge here." I said making sure she understands that securing his vote doesn't secure her the win.

"That's right, Amanda. Bring your hot ass over here and work it for my vote." Luke yells out. Getting the point, Amanda walks her hot ass back to where she belongs.

Once the show starts, the crowd eats it up. The DJ, Mickey, is on fire tonight and enjoying himself immensely watching the auditions. The girls are trying so hard, some are successful, but most are terrible and I can't help wonder why they would embarrass themselves. However, the bad ones give the crowd more to cheer for. When it's Amanda's turn, I begin to cringe. From the moment she steps on stage, she eyes Nick and stays focused on him as she struts out in her absurd outfit. If the pink pleather isn't comical enough, her excessive use of licking her lips is. Holding on to the pole for dear life, she struggles to stay standing in her disastrous heels and nearly falls numerous times. Her skinny arms begin to give early, but she insists on ending with an aerial split that lands her on her face. Kyler rushes and helps the hysterically crying girl off the stage, while I cover my mouth to try to hold my jaw off the floor. I glance in Nick's direction, but he looks away from everyone.

"Damn, Nick, I am surprised your dick is still attached if that chick swung on it like that." Dwayne said, causing everyone to laugh.

"Laugh it up, Assholes." Nick said, shaking his head.

"Hey, Nick, what's it like to fuck a Pepto bottle?" Luke laughs with everyone else.

"I never fucked her alright. I was going to but …"

"But she slipped off and broke her face?" Luke yelled, laughing. Nick hid his face, trying to hold back his own laughter. I watch him having fun and don't even realize my own enjoyment until he sees it.

Nick leans across the table towards me, "I admit I enjoy making you angry, but I enjoy your smile more, Kayla." I watch him lean back with his devil eyes piercing right through me and I feel thankful that we are surrounded by people- to keep me from jumping across this table for him.

The night ends with a considerable profit, happy customers, and an extremely pleased owner. Nick greets me as soon as I get home with a glass of wine, waiting for me with a small wrapped box in hand. "What's this?" I asked.

"A toast to you and an appreciation gift. I'm impressed with your work, very impressed." I drink with him and welcome his kiss on the cheek, as I unwrap the key to my new car. "Keep it up, Princess, and enjoy the car. You earned it." He said respectfully, leaving the bottle of wine for me, and walking upstairs towards his room.

"What? You're not going to try to seduce me again tonight." I asked.

"Do you want me to?" Nick asked with an intoxicating gaze in my direction.

"No."

"Then what would be the point." He said, walking quietly to bed.

~9~
KAYLA

*M*y first few weeks at the club, I barely have time to do much else but work. Once I clearly understand the business and select people I can trust to help me, I am able to take a little more time for myself. I step out for a little while and meet Daniel once I open the club and make sure everyone is too busy handling their jobs to notice me being gone.

Daniel meets me at the door with open arms. "Oh, baby, I have missed you so much."

"Well, now that I am working at the club and have my own car, I have a little more freedom to come see you without Nick's watchdogs keeping track of my every move."

"What exactly are you doing at the club?" Daniel asked.

"Running the whole club, making sure everything runs smoothly."

"You?" He laughs.

"Yes. Me. Why does that shock you?" I ask feeling insulted.

"Don't get me wrong, Kayla, you are capable at some things, but running a business doesn't seem like a job for such a pretty girl. You don't have to pretend for me, Sweetheart. I'm sure you look real good behind that desk, but I doubt Nicholas gave you that kind of responsibility. It's too much for you to handle."

"Nick did give me the responsibility and I can handle it fine." I reply as the anger rises.

"Baby, you're way too pretty to be working. You should be shopping and pampering yourself. If you would let me take care of you, that's exactly what you would be doing."

"Daniel, sometimes you say the dumbest things."

"What? I am worried about you. I don't think you understand how dangerous Jayzon is!"

"I know damn well what Nick is into and I know he wouldn't hurt me." I said, shocking myself.

"Really? Why do say that?" Daniel approaches me in a way that makes me feel suddenly uneasy. "What's wrong? Why do look scared? Come here." As Daniel takes me in his arms, I stand stiffly and quickly realize that he is reaching into his pocket.

"What are you doing?" I yell, pushing away from him.

Daniel laughs as he pulls out a necklace with a dangling ruby heart. "I was only going to surprise you with a gift. You sure are jumpy today, Baby. I think this job is causing a little more stress than you realize." Daniel walks around me, draping the necklace around my neck, and lays a tender kiss below my ear.

"I love it but I don't think I can take this while I live with Nick. If he finds it ..."

"No buts. If he can give you gifts, then I want to give you something, too. Besides, you seem so positive of his intentions, I am sure he would never think to question you on where the necklace came from." I accept the necklace and tread lightly so that I can leave Daniel with no more arguments. After I get a couple of miles down the road, I take off the necklace and hide it in my bag. I can't help wonder if my past is causing me to push away from Daniel or if everything I have learned still holds true- even with Daniel. Returning to the club, I go about my night in a daze. There doesn't seem to be any real reason for my concern about Daniel other than fear. Exie, noticing my distance, volunteers to finish closing for the night so I can go home and get some rest. I put up a respectable fight before giving in and heading home. Before I reach my car, I get a text from Daniel asking to meet me at a nearby parking garage. It seems like an unusual place to meet, but I go anyway and find Daniel sitting in his car alone. He gets out immediately and greets me while holding his body awkwardly.

"Are you okay?" I ask him as he stumbles towards me. "Daniel, what happened?"

"He knows, Baby. I don't know how he found out about us but Nick knows about us." Daniel said, looking at me with pain filled eyes. I begin shaking, not knowing what to do or say. "You need to come with me. You can't go back there now that he knows. He beat me, Kayla. Beat me and threatened me. I can only imagine what he will do to you."

"I can't believe Nick would do this to you. I don't understand why he would threaten you over me?"

"He's psycho, Kayla! He thinks he owns you, and if he can't

have you then no one can." Daniel tries to open my car door, "Kayla, you have to come with me for your own safety."

"I can't. If he did this to you, I can only imagine what he will do if I don't go back."

"I can protect myself, Kayla, and you." Daniel pleads.

"I can't, Daniel. I have to talk to him and find out why he did this. I will pack and leave if I have to, but I am not going to run from him." *I have spent too much time trying to get to him.* "Go home and I will call you later after I handle this my way." I said as he becomes more frantic and tries to push his arm through the crack in my window.

"Kayla! Get out of that car! Are you insane?" Daniel yells at me as I jerk the car forward to keep him from sliding his arm through.

Daniel stands staring at me mystified by my actions. I drive away, watching Daniel in my mirror screaming at me. Pulling up to the house, I hesitate with trembling hands before getting out of my car. I don't know why I don't fear Nick more, I know what he is capable of. I have seen it in his eyes even. Nick sits back in his chair waiting for me when I enter. I walk towards him slowly, making sure to check every dark corner for Luke standing by to shoot me. "Nick …" Before I can finish, Nick jumps up, setting me back on my heels instantly.

"No! Don't even treat me like I'm stupid, Kayla. I have been watching you, hoping you were only trying to earn money behind my back, but it's even worse. You are damn lucky that it was me that figured it out and not Luke. I don't know what you think is going on between you and him, but it stops now."

"You can't tell me who I can see and who I can't!" I yell back at him.

"I can't? Then get out!" Stunned, I'm not sure what to say next. "He's using you, Kayla." He finishes.

Huffing at him in disbelief, "How could you attack him like that? You have no right to beat someone because you're jealous. You really hurt him!"

Nick laughs, "Is that what he told you? I beat him up? Wow. The story just gets better and better."

He stands stiff in front of me, shaking his head at me as if I am supposed to believe his silent denial. "Am I not allowed to be with anyone other than you? You own me? Is that it?"

Nick leans down into my face, "Kayla, I have given you plenty of chances to go. Plenty of chances to get away from me and yet you are still here. You made a point to be in my face, to be noticed. I gave you a chance and you have exceeded my expectations, but I will not have you jeopardize my business because you want to get laid."

"How am I jeopardizing anything? I don't talk about business with him."

"No, but you talk enough for him to stay interested. I am not arguing with you about this, Kayla. If you continue to see him, you will not be welcome in any place I own."

"Is it because I won't sleep with you? Are you that jealous?" I yell at him, fisting his shirt to keep him from leaving.

Nick throws up his hands, "This has nothing to do with us! I know you don't believe this, Kayla, but I am trying to protect you. If you want to leave, then leave. I'm not going to force you to be anywhere you don't want to be." Nick leaves me without another word. *His jealousy is unbelievable but I can't take a step back now. I will simply lay low for a little while longer until he trusts me again.*

∞

The next day is quiet and Nick never leaves the house. He stays around watching and waiting for me to say something to him. I am not sure what he is expecting, but after awhile he gives up waiting and invites me out to dinner. I accept, not feeling I have much of a choice. "How is the club?" He asked.

"Good. The new girl is working out well and Kyler is getting used to the new ideas."

"Good, I'm glad. And how are you?"

"Fine." I said, smiling forcefully at him.

"I fully expected you to be gone when I got up this morning." He said.

"He was just … he doesn't mean that much to me." Nick's expression is obvious and purposeful. *He doesn't believe me at all.* Luckily, he is willing to talk about other matters. Everything seems normal until Daniel walks into the restaurant. At first I become excited that he is alright, but then I see her. He walks her in as a gentleman would. I would have thought her to be a girlfriend if not for the giant diamond on her left hand. Feeling my hands begin to shake, I take a second before looking back at Nick's knowing expression. "Is that why you brought me here?"

"I thought he didn't mean that much to you." He states simply, sitting back in his chair with a superior attitude. "You didn't even know he was married?" Nick laughs harshly.

"Are you enjoying this, Nick?"

"No!" He said suddenly leaning across the table at me. "I find it ridiculous that I have to go to this length to get you to see what a mistake you're making."

"So what? He's married. That doesn't make him a bad person, just an unhappy one."

"Let's go." Nick said helping me out of my chair and escorting me right past Daniel, the two eyeing each other with evil intents. I manage to pull it together to work at the club later in the night but I am shocked to find Daniel waiting for me when I get out.

"Daniel? What are you doing here?" I rush over to him, trying to push him out of sight.

"I had to see you. You have to let me explain." Daniel said holding on to me desperately.

"Explain what? That you lied about your wife being dead?"

"Baby, please understand. My marriage has long since been over. She might as well be dead. You're all I have that keeps me going."

"Then leave her, Daniel."

"It's not that easy."

"It sounds easy to me." I said, folding my arms in front of me so he can't get near me.

"Kayla, I love you."

"I have to go. If Nick sees me talking to you …"

Daniel grabs my wrist and pulls me back to him, "I will leave her if you leave Nick. Let me take care of you." His sincere eyes give me pause. "We can get married if you leave with me right now, Kayla."

I stare into his determined eyes and feel strangely weak to him, "I can't leave. I …"

Daniel takes hold of my arm and begins to pull me towards his car, "You're mine! Not his, Kayla! I'm not letting him have you." I look up at him as he signals two men to approach us. I pull away from him which makes him angrier. He grabs me by the back of the neck and he pushes me forward, knocking me to the ground. "I'm not telling you again. Now-" Before he can get out another word, Nick's car pulls up in front of us. However, Nick approaches from the opposite direction of the car, causing Daniel to back away from me. "Nicholas? I should have known you would be watching her."

"Nick-"I try to stop him from pulling out his gun but gasp when I see the men Daniel directed pulling out their guns at Nick.

"Let go of me, Kayla." Nick said focusing on Daniel. Luke suddenly approaches with his gun held out from another direction. At that moment, Dwayne pulls up in a car from another and Dawson comes out of nowhere with five other men approaching from several more directions.

"He was just leaving." I said, continuing to try to hold Nick back, but he is too strong.

Nick takes hold of me and walks with me to his car. "Get in the car, Kayla."

"No, Nick, please let him go." I said but the intensity in his eyes scares me.

"It's okay, Kayla, if he wants to try to take me on, then let him." Daniel boasts like a fool. "You better kill me, Nicholas, because if you don't, I will surely kill you."

Nick laughs, "This guy?" He asked me. "Really, Kayla?"

"We love each other, Nick. No matter what you say, she will never be yours." Daniel said.

"Stay away from her!" Nick states with meaning that sends chills down my back.

"Sorry, but I can't do that." Daniel said, smiling wickedly at Nick.

"If I had known it was you, I would have never …" Nick said.

"Never what? Never let me steal her right out from under you? Oh wait, she turned you down cold so she never was *actually* under you. I guess there is a first time for everything."

"What is going on between you two?" I asked.

"Don't worry about it, Baby, I will explain it to you later when we get home." Daniel said reaching for me.

Nick nearly throws me in his car. "Kayla!" He says through his teeth. "Don't you move!" He yells at me.

"Are you going to kill me in your own parking lot, Nicholas? Not a wise move."Daniel says, backing up to his men.

"So help me God, if you ever come near her again, I will kill you. And this time, I will make damn sure you're dead and buried myself." When other cars begin to approach, Nick motions for Luke to get in the car with Dwayne and they speed off. Nick's other men hold strong against Daniel and his men as Nick gets in the car and orders Tanner to drive quickly. Too scared to speak, I sit quietly rubbing my arm that still shows the mark Nick left when he threw me in the car. When he makes a noise, I sit back unsure of what is coming next. "I'm not giving you a choice anymore, Kayla. You are not to talk to him or to see him again. I don't want you to even look his way. Until you prove that you understand this, you are going to be escorted to and from everywhere you go and you will be watched over until you get from one place to the next."

The anger quickly builds up within me, "Let me out of this car!" I yell.

"No."He said calmly.

"I don't want to be with you, Nick! I don't want to live with you and I don't want to work for you anymore!" I yell.

"I don't care what you want." He said tense but calm.

"Nick! I thought you said you would never force me to be somewhere I didn't want to be?"

"That's when I thought I could trust you to make the right decision."

"And how has that changed? Because I want to be with somebody you don't like?" I asked watching him ignore me.

I grab the door handle and start to open it when Nick pulls me back in and pins me down, "Kayla! Stop! I am not doing this to be mean to you, I am doing this for your own good. You have to trust me."

"Why? Tell me why and maybe I will." I asked, struggling against him.

Nick holds my face still, forcing me to look at him, "He doesn't care about you, he is only trying to get to me."

"That doesn't even make sense. He doesn't ask me about you or about anything you do. He doesn't care about you. He loves me!" I yell at him. "He loves me, Nick! No one has ever loved me before."

"No, he doesn't, Kayla." I push away from him, hiding my face into the corner. "I'm sorry ... I ... If you ... You're going to do as I say, Kayla, and that's all there is to it." Nick makes it known to his house guards that I am not to leave the house alone again. When I protest, Nick forces me into my room and locks me in for the night. Over the next few weeks, I am followed everywhere I go. I go to work and I am forced to return to Nick's at the end of the night. I'm miserable and I hate him even more than I did. I am desperate to leave the situation I have put myself in, but I don't know any other way out other than to kill Nick.

~10~
KAYLA

*T*onight is the night. I have to talk to Exie for hours before she finally agrees to help me. When she arrives at the club I rush her into my office and shut the door behind us. "You brought it right?"

"Are you sure you want to do this?" She asked hesitating.

"Exie, I am his prisoner now. I can't live like this."

"It's not like he doesn't let you go anywhere."

"Yea, I can go out as long as I have the two goons following me."

"Kayla, have you thought about what will happen after? If you do pull this off, Luke will hunt you down and kill you. Not to mention, Nick always has a gun himself. This is going to get you killed. Come on, it's Meagan. She is so dumb, she probably won't know to point the gun away from herself." Exie said. I giggle until she expresses her annoyance clearly.

"It will be fine. I will coax her into a rage and casually mention where the gun is. Then it will be up to her. I am sure she knows how to handle a gun. I can work up enough hysteria to make myself look innocent before anyone can get to us. Even Nick will assume I'm innocent if I do it right. Luke or Dwayne will take over and surely they will let us keep our jobs, at least. If not, well, you're finished with school now and I can go find something new that doesn't involve Nicholas Jayzon.

"You are going to die." She says as I take her gun and put it in my bag. "And please don't leave that gun anywhere. I really don't want to be connected to this crazy plan. In fact, I am a little worried about what they will do to me if they ever find out."

I didn't consider that they may go after her. Sighing, "Wait I thought you said this gun isn't traceable."

"Not traceable by cops, Nick's crew is a little more successful at getting information."

"So complain that Meagan came in to talk to you first, and while you were distracted, she stole your gun."

"What if she says she got the gun from you?" Exie asked.

"Who are they going to believe? Me or crazy Meagan? I think we both know that answer. Meagan is so drug induced these days, she can barely speak an entire sentence that makes sense. I will call to let you know when it is done." As I finish, Exie shakes her head in amazement. "Don't worry, I have thought about this for a long time and I am not going to fail." I said surely.

After I make a call to Meagan, I wait as long as I can, hoping to give her enough time. Becoming impatient to hear that I made it home Nick sends Dwayne to escort me home. When we pull to the gate of the house, a strange car suddenly cuts us off and maneuvers in front of us.

To my pleasant surprise, Meagan jumps out waving her hands in a tirade. "You stupid bitch! Get out of that car and face me!"

"Stay in the car, Kayla," Dwayne says getting out to calm the psycho down.

Watching her and listening to her complain, I feel good about my plan. I open the car door and wave Meagan over, "You want to talk to Nick yourself?"

"Yes. He needs to know what he's done." Meagan said.

"I agree that you have a right to be heard. Come in and I will make sure you get a chance to talk to him." Meagan eyes me closely as we walk into the house.

"Nick is going to be pissed at you for letting her in here." Dwayne said shaking his head.

"I didn't ask for your opinion." I said waving him away so I can be alone with Meagan.

"You want me to leave you alone with her?" Dwayne asked wide-eyed.

"I will be fine." I said as he walks away mumbling under his breath. "So, do you want something to drink?" I asked Meagan.

"You live here now?" I nod hoping to stir the anger more. "So, you are still working for him?"

"I help run the club, but that's it. He forces me to stay here even though I don't want to be."

"Why?" She asked staring at me in amazement.

"Because I love someone else. But you know Nick, what he wants goes." I pause and give her an innocent smile as I gaze over her tattered once expensive wears. Tell me something Meagan, how are you doing?"

"He won't let me work for him anymore. I don't know how he expects me to live without any money." She cries.

"Are you still using?"

"A little, but I told him I would quit if he would help me."

"He doesn't care about anyone. Once he is done with you … you're on your own. You use to be so beautiful when you two were together and then he left you without anything. Why did you let him do that?" I asked encouraging the thoughts in her head. "He's not going to let you back, no matter what you do."

"But he owes me."

"Exactly." I said.

"I did everything he asked of me and he owes me."

"I think that's his car now. You should tell him how you feel about what he has done to you." I get near her and whisper, "If you need any help convincing him, I have a gun in my bag that's on the table next to you. That should help drive your point home." She looks up at me suspiciously but nods seeming to understand.

Nick comes in and I turn to him with an innocent smile, "You have a guest."

"What are you doing, Kayla?" He asked frustrating me that he immediately assumes that I am up to something.

"Meagan here has something she would like to talk to you about."

"Well I don't want to talk to her. So you make sure she gets out of my house." Nick starts to leave the room and the nutcase rushes for my bag and pulls out the gun.

"Nick!" She yells after him. He turns and shakes head before eyeing me with a smile. "I want you back, Nick. Get rid of her." *What?*

Confused, I turn and see her aiming the gun at me, "Are you insane?" I yell at her.

"He's mine, not yours." Meagan said shaking the gun at me.

"He is not going to take you back, you moron!"

"Watch it, Kayla. You don't want to piss her off, she is the one with the gun." Nick said having way too much fun with this. "Okay, Meagan, what is it you want?"

"I want you! I want to be back in your bed. I want everything to be just the way it was- before her." She whimpers.

"Hmm. No, I don't think so." Nick said calmly.

"I will shoot her!" Meagan yelled at him.

"I guess you will have to shoot her then because I don't want you back. Not while I got her." I look back at his amused smile.

"I'm serious! I will shoot her!" She yells, shaking the gun at me.

"Do what you've got a do, but I like her too much, to even consider taking you back." Nick said obnoxiously.

"Nick," I cringe.

"What, Kayla? You want me to stop her? How could I possibly? She has a *gun*." He sarcastically trembles with fear. "Although, for the life of me, I can't imagine how she got the gun. You wouldn't know, would you?"

"She told me to get it out of her bag." Meagan, the dumbest person on the face of the earth, confessed.

"Really? Why do you have a gun, Kayla?" Nick eyes me as I begin to realize that I'm the dumbest person on the face of the earth.

"Shoot me then. Nick is going to kill me now anyway." I said sinking into my own failure.

Humored, Nick sits down relaxing, "Probably. So, I guess it does make sense to save time, go ahead ... shoot her." Confused, Meagan stands silently not knowing what to do. "Go ahead shoot her, it's okay I will have someone clean up the mess."

Meagan pulls the trigger. "It's stuck," she said, holding the gun out to Nick.

Nick glances in my direction, laughing, before getting up to take the gun. As he takes possession of it, he holds it against Meagan's head. "It's not stuck, the safety is on, Sweetheart. Now get out of my house."

"But, Nick?" Meagan pleads.

"Get out, Meagan. I gave you plenty of chances. I paid for rehab twice and yet you still think I owe you something. Get your life back together and maybe I will give you a job, but I can't have you working for me high all the time." Meagan falls to her knees and refuses to leave. Nick calls for Dwayne and he physically removes her with little effort. "Oh- and, Dwayne? Take this gun before Kayla hurts herself with it."

"No problem," Dwayne said shaking his head at me.

I sit down waiting for Nick to kill me or call someone to come back and do it for him, but instead he goes upstairs and goes to his room. Sitting at the edge of my seat, I wait as Nick turns out the lights on me and goes back to his room. *What the hell he is doing? Trying to make me crazy?* Angry, I run up the stairs and barge into his room. Undressing he barely looks at me as he removes his shirt. "Are you going to kill me while I sleep or something?" I asked him.

"I wasn't planning on it." He said amused.

"Then why are you getting ready for bed?"

"Because I'm tired, Kayla. That's what people do when they are tired."

"I just tried to kill you."

"You did? It looked more like you were trying to get yourself killed." He laughed.

"Ha-ha. You know I gave her the gun to kill you."

"I know." He said taking his shoes off.

"So, why aren't you yelling at me or ...?"

Nick comes at me quickly causing me to step back, "Do you want to kill me, Kayla?"

"Yes."

"Why because I won't let you see your boyfriend?"

"Yes."

"Or is it because of your sister?" My jaw drops. "I know who you are, Kayla. I knew the first day I saw you at the club. Did you think I wouldn't remember you?"

"You never paid attention to me when you came over." I said as a slight smile crosses his face.

"I paid attention to you more than you know. I didn't kill her, Kayla. Braylin was a sweet, beautiful girl, but she ..."

"She was nothing to you!" I yell at him. "She loved you and you just threw her away like she was nothing!"

Nick stays focused on me, "I didn't love her."

"I hate you!"

"I didn't love her, Kayla. She couldn't handle that and that's my fault?"

"I hate you!" I screamed even louder at him.

"Kayla, she did everything to get my attention focused back on her. She talked Luke into letting her get her own set of clients, hoping that she could impress me somehow. When I found out, I forced him to let her go." I try to turn away from him but he forces me to stay and look at him. "She became desperate to earn money to impress me and got caught up with the wrong people, Kayla. It was those people that messed her up so badly. And I'm sorry about that but by the time I found out it was too late. She was so far gone she wouldn't listen. All she wanted to do was take care of you and she thought the people she was working for could help her do that. She wanted so bad to send you to that college you kept sneaking into. She loved you so much but she wasn't strong enough to get out." Trembling with rage, I struggle to get away from him but he holds onto me tight. "I don't know for sure who killed her Kayla but I have an idea." I look up at him, "You thought she killed herself, didn't you?" He said. "No, she wouldn't have left you like that. Somebody got to her and they left you alive."

"I don't understand. She always talked about you."

"After I forced Luke to let her go, I assumed she would go back to that diner and work."

I push him away, "No! The way you treated her, the way you would fuck her and leave like she was nothing." I said fisting my hands.

"I was a stupid kid, Kayla. Yes, I wanted to fuck her but I didn't love her."

"Shut up! I hate you! I wish you were dead!" I scream hitting him.

Nick takes hold of my arms. "You hate me?" I nod. "Then kill me." I pause watching him take his knife out. "Here take it. Kill me if that's what you want." He hands me the knife and holds out his arms so I have easy access to his bare chest. I take the knife and go at him but he catches my hand, "Not like that Princess. That was too light. If you want to kill someone, you have to go at them with all the hate you have inside. Now try again." He pushes me back and I look at him unsure of myself for the first time in years. "Braylin was weak, easily manipulated. She was so easy to get into bed, too bad she was a horrible lay." I rage at him and he stops my hand again, "Much better." He pulls me closer. "You're not at all like her, your strength is amazing to me. I knew you wanted to kill me the moment I saw you watching me in the club. I wondered how long it would take you. What would finally push you over the edge, I begin to wonder if you even had the courage to do it at all." Nick pushes me away, "Try again."

"No, Nick." I said, trembling.

"Try again. Come at me and mean it!"

"I don't want to." I whimper.

"Come on, right here!" He says smacking the area over his heart. I step back and he comes after me, taking hold of my face,

"What's wrong? You hate me, remember? Stick it in my heart, Kayla. Teach me a lesson. You said yourself that I am going to kill you, you might as well get me first. Do it! Do it, Kayla!" He yells at me over and over until finally I come at him with everything I have reaching his chest and stopping myself just as the tip touches his skin. I look at the redness of his skin against the shiny blade and feel nothing: no hate, no anger, nothing at all until I look up into his eyes.

"Nick?"

"What, Princess?"

"I ... I." I manage to say before Nick takes the knife from my hand and throws it behind me pressing his lips to mine with a heavy breath. His eyes hold me hostage as he rips my shirt from my body. His strong hands hold me still as he kisses down to my breasts, taking each nipple into his mouth and sighing at the touch of them. He raises me up against the wall sucking on my lips as he pushes his erection between my legs. He feels so good, I can barely think. When he pulls back to look at me, the devil's eyes tease me, provoking me until I can take no more. "I want you, Nick. I want you so bad. Fuck me, Nick!" I moan. Nick pulls me fully into his arms and lays me on his bed. With one jerk, he pulls my skirt off and begins kissing his way up my legs, fingering me through my panties until he is satisfied with my want. Easing them down my legs, he slowly gazes over my naked body, his eyes burning with desire. I try to sit up and reach for his pants but he reaches underneath me and pulls me to the edge of the bed causing me to fall back. Nick spreads my legs out in front of him, with the feeling of his tongue he sends me gasping backwards. I fist his hair and beg for him to stop but within seconds I am begging for more. Holding a pillow against my mouth I mask my final pleasure filled screams. Pleased with himself, he steps back and removes his pants. Standing naked and erect, he watches me lick my lips with a slight chuckle. I haven't seen him fully since that day I watched him with Braylin, but I am just as in awe of him now as I was then. Gazing at his body, my eyes find their way to the menacing dark tattoo stretching from his ass to the side of his ribs, highlighting the edges of his muscles all the way up to his neck. I lay back waiting for him. With an irresistible turn at the corner of his lips, he eases over me, caressing my body to his. With a groan, he glides his lips down one of my arms and then up the other, kissing each finger as he takes hold of my hands. When I open my eyes, I see a different man staring back at me. I try to speak but the fervor in his eyes takes hold of me and relaxes every muscle in my body. Leaning down, he kisses me gently before he rises again and looks deep into my eyes, penetrating me tight and strong. I gasp his name as he whispers mine. He moves slowly and precisely, handling me with ease as he moves me around the bed, smiling and enjoying every push into me and every kiss I reward him with. Moving me on top of him, he grips my hips watching as I rise up and down on him. I lean back, moaning, trying to hold on, but it is no use, the feeling of him inside me, the scent of him, and the sight of him enjoying watching me makes me insane.

"Come on, Kayla, I'm all yours." Dizzy, I watch him close his eyes and moan, "Kayla ... oh you feel so good." With renewed energy, I slide down on him and ride him until I vibrate, until my body is so overwhelmed in pleasure that I am paralyzed by it. Nick follows, gripping me still, as he works his erection out inside me, moaning and groaning his enjoyment to the end. Taking comfort in his arms, I curl into him as my body begins to shiver. Nick sits up, pulling the covers over me, before he gets up. I watch him closely as he cleans up and turns off the lights before lying back down in bed next to me. *I am unsure how to act. Do I move to the edge away from him? Say something?* I look back at him and he rolls over against me, pulling my back to his chest. His arm wraps around me and I sink against him, listening to him breathe. The rhythm of the rise and fall of his chest against my bare back puts me right to sleep.

He wakes me up twice during the night, whispering to me until I wake up, rubbing his hands over my body as he begs to be inside me again. I surrender to him every time, letting him paralyze me all over again and again.

~11~
KAYLA

*W*aking up, I have to squint to see the time on the clock. "Twelve thirty? Fuck." I whisper until I realize Nick is nowhere in sight. Sitting up, I have to move slowly as my body rejects the abuse I put it through the night before. Once I am able to focus, I notice a large box across the room. Curious, I get up to see what it is and realize it's for me when I notice the note on top.

Kayla,
These are yours. I have saved them for some time. I would have given them to you sooner, but I wasn't sure how- without being accused of stealing them or trying to seduce you or whatever insane idea you would have come up with to paint my intentions horribly. I did the best I could to take care of them for you.
Open it, they are yours - Nick

Hesitating over the edges of the top, I take in a single deep breath and tear it open. My jaw drops and I gasp as I realize what is inside the box. *My books! He saved them.* I pick up each one of them, reading the notes Braylin left in them for me. When I get to the last, I have trouble recalling ever having this one. I pick it up, reading the French title and slowly open it to read the simple note left inside, *I thought this one seemed like something you might like, Nick.* Sitting back on my heels, I read the first few pages of the old French novel and cry with a smile.

沀沂

*N*ick is gone most of the day, and with me having to leave soon for work myself, I am becoming anxious to see him. Within an hour before I have to leave, I hear him coming through the door and I run at once to meet him. I come within a foot of him before I realize he is not alone. Coming to an abrupt stop, I bite my bottom lip as Nick, Luke, Dwayne and Dawson all stare at me with questioning expressions. "Hi," I managed to say in the most awkward way.

"You okay?" Nick asked, handing his paperwork to Luke and holding his hand out to me.

Suddenly, I feel like the fifteen year old girl trying to get the star quarterback's attention. "Ummm," *Oh crap. Nothing, I have absolutely nothing to say. Ummm, Nick, I … damn! They are all staring at me and so is he.* A soft smile forms at the corners of his lips and I forget about everyone else. Taking a step towards him, I wrap my hand around the back of his head, stand tall on my toes, and pull him to my lips kissing him gently, "Thank you." I said with a grateful smile before running off to get ready for work.

"Well, that's new," Dwayne remarked.

CR80

*T*he club is busy as usual but none of the usual problems are bothering me tonight. "I assume since you are still alive that you did not kill Nick?" Exie asks as she plops herself on my desk. "And where's my gun?"

With a sorrowful expression, "Oh, I'm sorry but Nick took it."

"Kayla! Oh wonderful! I'm dead. My son is going to be an orphan. I knew I shouldn't have given it to you. Oh God, please let him be merciful and kill me quickly." She goes on and on about her long desire to be buried at sea, by a ship full of crying naval men, or some other crazy scenario. I tune Exie out until she slams her hand down in front of me. "Wait. If he knows you were trying to kill him, why are you still alive? Why are you here without his henchmen standing over you?"

"Stupid Meagan! The dumbass blond tried to kill me instead." I said with a groan.

"That is a lesson for you, stay as far away from trouble as possible. I told you! I told you, but nooooo you didn't want to listen to me." She said shaking her head and fidgeting with her nails with a superior attitude.

"Are you busy?" Nick asked, walking into my office, looking as good as ever.

"No. We were talking about the club." I said.

"Nothing's wrong, is it?" He asked staying focused on me.

"No, everything is fine." I smiled at him.

"Hi, Nick, I am so glad to see you. You look so good tonight." Exie smiles wide at him.

"Dwayne has your gun. If you would like it back, you can have it but make sure not to give it to her again. She only gets herself into trouble with them." He says eyeing her briefly before returning his concentration on me. I stand up and wait for him to make his way towards me.

"You know, Nick, I had no idea she had taken that from me. If I had, I would have stopped her immediately. She gets excitable sometimes. She means well and I am sure she will never try anything like that again. I certainly will do everything I can to make sure she thinks things through before …" Exie steps back as Nick leans across my desk towards me. "Oh-kay, so I am going to go check on Kyler and I guess you two will … do whatever this is you are doing." Exie exits quickly eyeing me for an explanation as I wave her on.

"What are you doing here?" I asked.

"I wanted to see you. Sorry, I didn't get a chance to talk to you earlier, but I have a lot going on today." Nick said looking me over with an easy smile.

"It's okay. I only wanted to thank you for my books. It was …"

"You're welcome. I would have given them to you sooner, but you did hate me and I was enjoying that."

"I can try to kill you again if that will make you happy." I laugh.

Nick leans in taking my lips, "You can try, Princess." I give him a soft moan and he leaps across the desk startling me.

His hands wander intensively over my body as he kisses me with soft whispers. "I should be working. My boss is very strict."

"I'm sure he wouldn't mind if you took a break."

"I am afraid if I do, I won't want to stop." I try to hold him back and he reluctantly releases me.

"May I drive you home at least? I can have Dwayne drive your car home for you."

"You may." I smile kissing him again. "I have some questions for you anyway." I said to his immediate eye roll. "I think I am owed a few answers." I said with a determined tone.

"Fine, a few answers … maybe." He said holding me closer to him and obviously trying to change my focus with his wandering lips.

"Kayla! We have a rowdy group out here and it is getting nasty." Kyler interrupts.

I jump towards the door and Nick grabs my wrist, asking "You want me to handle this?"

"I can take care of it." I said confidently. He nods but doesn't seem to be convinced.

Racing out to the scene, I notice two men in each other's face with accompanying friends encouraging them on. I jump up on the table next to them and they instantly take notice.

"Hi, Sweetheart." One says looking up at me.

"You boys having a problem?" I asked eyeing them both to see which one is the real problem.

Both are intoxicated, but one, I believe, is beyond reasoning. He takes hold of my bare leg and becomes excited. "I think I am good now." His friends laugh as does the man he was previously arguing with.

I let him get so far and then free my leg from his grasp and stick my heel against his throat. "Get out of my club." He struggles to swallow as I press harder. "And if you come back, I will make sure this heel becomes a permanent accessory for you. As far as the rest of you, you can either sit and enjoy the show, like gentlemen, or you can leave too. Butts fall into their seats at once while my bouncer, Jake assists in removing the gasping gentleman from my heel. "Call him a taxi on the club."

"You got it." Jake responds.

I look down at Nick's hand held out for me respectively, "Thank you." I said taking it happily.

"I enjoyed that very much." He said letting go of my hand and walking to his table mouthing, "Very much."

CR&&BO

*W*hen we get home, I hesitate at the bottom of the stairs, wondering which room I should walk to. Even though Nick encourages me during the car ride home, I don't want to presume that I am to climb in his bed tonight. As I ponder the idea of being bold, "I decided something tonight," Nick said taking my hand and escorting me to his room.

"What's that?" I smile.

"I am going to make sure you have a whole house full of spiked heels." He laughed before capturing my lips within his. Out of the corner of my eyes, I see the box that contains all my books and I remember that I have several questions, which need to be answered.

Nick's hands begin to get control of my body, but I push him back, to his immediate huffing and eye rolling. "None of that, until we talk." I insist. Nick takes a step back, cursing under his breath. "I want to know about my books, Nick." As I wait impatiently, his posture changes ever so slightly and he slowly looks back my way with his devilish smile. His eyes begin to gaze over me with a look that I have learned to overcome, but something about it this time makes areas of my body tingle with an excitement that I am not sure I can control. "Nick we ..." I force out, before having to inhale deeply when I feel his heated breath linger down my neck, kissing me softly in all the right places. "Nick ..."

"You said that already, Princess." He breathes, removing his clothes blatantly in front of me.

"Talk ... we need to talk." I said pushing myself further away from him.

"No talking right now, I just want you to come here ..." He pulls me in tight and kisses my ear gently as he whispers, "Je veux avoir le sexe avec vous." His French request, causes me to overlook his hands moving up my dress. With a wisp, my dress falls and my body leans backwards, enjoying his kisses down my stomach. Standing back and showing his naked body proudly to me, he picks me up in his arms and tells me again, what he wants to do with me, with an encouraging moan I accept my defeat. Holding onto him, I let him move inside me, let him feel my body and let him grip my ass fully in his hands, as he lifts me and brings me back down on him. I reach for the nearby wall to hold onto, "No. Hold onto me." Nick smiles into my eyes. "I've got you." Sliding my hands up, over his muscles in his arms, and then reaching down his back and tasting his lips with my tongue, finding my way to his.

At the end, Nick lays me in his bed and runs his fingers down my cheek, "vous êtes si beau. So beautiful."

❧

I wake up in the middle of the night angry and look over at him sleeping soundly, "Damn him!" I shake him and finally punch him until he wakes up just as angry.

"What the fuck is wrong with you!" He yells.

"You tricked me." I said as he looks at me in bewilderment. "You were supposed to answer some questions and instead you ... well, you know what you did."

Nick falls back into bed laughing at me, "Sorry, I will try not to do that ever again." Frustrated, I move on top of him and look down at him with a fierce expression. "Princess, if you want me to fear you, you should try yelling at me with clothes on because this is only turning me on." He said handling me with a moan. "Where are your shoes? Those might work." He laughs.

"Nicholas Jayzon, you are not getting anything from me until you answer my questions. Now stop touching me."

"You're sitting on me!"

"How did you get my books, Nick?"

"I found them. Happy?" I cock my head, folding my arms in front of him with a determined huff. "Oh, fuck! Fine! I was there that night. I went looking for you after I found out about Braylin." He explained.

"What night?"

"The night you started screaming and that disgusting fuck climbed on top of you. As soon as I heard you scream, I ran after you and ..."

"You were the drug addict that killed my stepfather?"

"Well, I wasn't a drug addict, but yes ..." Nick glances around the room nervously avoiding the complete answer. "He started to run after you and I made sure he wouldn't. I don't care what you say, he deserved what he got." Nick said eyeing me unapologetically. "Anyway, I called out to you but I guess you had run too far away or were afraid. You didn't answer, so I gathered your books and put them in my car. I waited for you to come back, but you never did."

"And you kept them all this time? Why?" I asked softening towards him.

"I don't know. I forgot about them, I guess, at least until I saw you in the club. And like I said in the note, I was afraid to say something before because I know how overdramatic you can get." Nick sits up and moves away from me.

"Nick." I said trying to keep him from leaving. When he looks back at me, I move towards him and hold onto him. "Why did you come looking for me?"

"I don't know, Kayla! Damn! Why do you have to know everything? Can't you just accept it happened and maybe there is no real reason for it?"

No, I can't, but the look in his eyes means he isn't going to tell me no matter what I do. "Okay, it happened and I'm glad it did. I'm glad you were there. I'm happy that he died the way he did." I move closer and kiss his lips when he looks over at me. "I don't need to know anymore to be grateful for what you did for me." I said making use of my seductive skills to seduce him back into bed. Within seconds, I have control of him and feel good about making him come all on my own.

⟳

"**K**ayla ... Kaaaayla." Nick repeats softly in my ear as he nudges me back awake. Barely able to open my eyes, I roll over and smile at him before curling under his arm. Nick laughs, kissing the side of my head, "I need to ask you something."

"Now? I am so tired, Nick."

"You've been working a lot lately, huh?" I nod with my eyes closed and he laughs again. "You want some time off?" I sigh barely interested in what he is saying to me. "How about going away with me?" The words jumble around in my head for a few minutes before they straighten out and make sense to me. I sit straight up wide-eyed, hoping that I wasn't dreaming. "I was planning on taking a little trip to get away for a while and I was wondering if you would like to come with me?"

"Okay!" I said without thinking.

"Don't you want to know where?" He laughed.

"I don't care. Anywhere. Somewhere other than here is better than anywhere I have been."

"Well then, Princess ..." he pauses to kiss me, "Make sure everything is in order and get your passport rushed so we can go soon ..."

"My passport?" I yell with my mouth wide open. "Nick?" He nods enjoying my excitement. Biting my bottom lip, I jump on top of him and kiss him.

~12~
KAYLA

*W*e arrive in style, although I have no idea where I am. Nick has a helicopter waiting for us to fly somewhere else before getting into a car and driving another two hours. The whole thing is exhausting, but we arrive at a beautiful home that is settled next to the ocean, surrounded by trees and flowers, and home to brightly colored birds and curious monkeys. The place is like a scene from one of my books. Nick grabs our bags and we settle in for the night, but I wake up early the next morning eager to take advantage of the place. While the conscionable servants run around quietly trying to anticipate our needs, I lie back between the trees enjoying the warm breeze as it rocks my hammock. I could easily fall asleep if not for the sight of Nick swimming in the ocean. Extending my relaxed body over the edge, I sink my feet deep into the sand and make my way towards the water. Standing at the edge of the shore, I watch as the warm water floats up and around my feet, sinking me deeper into the soft sand. "Are you coming in?" Nick yells out to me.

A feeling of eagerness races up my legs but before I can think another thought, I am running through the water and into his arms. "The water is so warm. I can't believe how good it feels."

"So, are you having fun?" He asked.

"Very much so. Thank you!" I said laying my head against his.

"Thanks for coming with me." Nick said holding me tight to his chest and throwing us both into the oncoming wave. We play, kiss, and enjoy each other's laughter throughout the afternoon. When the sun begins to go down, we climb into the hammock together to enjoy the night.

"It is so beautiful. I could die here." I sigh peacefully.

"No dying. I would miss you."

"You would miss me? The woman that tried to kill you?"

"Yes, I guess you're kind of cute when you get all murderous on me." Nick said looking away from me uncomfortably. Rolling over on top of him, I take hold of his hands and push them above his head and lightly twist the hanging rope around each one. "What are you doing?" Without answering, I slip my top off and kiss him. "Mmm, seems good so far." Rubbing my hands over his muscles, I press my lips to his warm skin and make my way down. When I reach my goal, I pull him out and wrap my lips around the tip of him, enjoying his gasp. Moving further, I go deeper in and hum. He grows rapidly in my mouth and tenses with his moans. I take control of him and work him slowly to the edge and make use of my hands to encourage him further. Nick watches me with a heavy breath before dropping his head back and moaning out loud. "Oh damn … mmm … ewffuc …" Cleaning him up, I crawl over top of him and release his hands. "I am so glad you're here." He says pulling me in close. I find a comfortable place on his chest and close my eyes. "Let's go inside."

"Why?" I asked.

"Because I am going to fuck the hell out of you as soon as I get my strength back."

"And how long will that be?" I smile teasing him.

"How long will it take to get those bikini bottoms off?" I jump off him and run into the house, laughing once I catch sight of him running after me.

We spend days being lazy and relaxed, Nick assumes I am bored after awhile and volunteers to drive us into town. "I think this is the first time I have seen you without a group of huge men surrounding you. You're not worried here?" I asked nervously taking in the scenery that is passing by a little too quickly for me.

"No one knows or cares who I am here. That's why I come here. I don't do it often, but when I do, I take a few detours to get here to make sure no one- including Luke- knows where I am at. This is my place to find some peace for a little while." Nick said.

"But now I know about it. Why?" I asked as Nick glances at me but ignores my question. I am not sure if he doesn't want to tell me or if he doesn't know. Either way, I am having too much fun to ruin it with an argument.

"There is a great little place down here that we can eat at and then walk to the market." He suggests as I nod happily and follow him everywhere enjoying the environment but enjoying him holding my hand more. We eat some great food and talk about all the people and crazy animals running around. When we finish, Nick takes me to the market and tells me to pick out whatever I want. He buys me a cute dress but I can't help notice that he seems to be searching for something. When a small jewelry store appears off in the distance, Nick pulls me into it. "Kayla, what do you think of this?" I walk over to him and look at the beautiful emerald and diamond pendant necklace.

"It's beautiful." I say as Nick wraps it around my neck. "Nick, this is very expensive."

"Do you like it?" He asked

"Yes, but I can't." I replied as I try to unlatch it from my neck.

Ignoring me, Nick begins making the guy an offer for the necklace. I take one look at myself in the mirror and for the first time I see my own happiness. One of the workers assumes I am looking at something in the case and rushes over and takes out a diamond ring for me to look at. I put up my hand and shake my head, "Oh no! No, I ... no."

"You like it right?" He asked me.

"Yes, it's very beautiful, but no." I said while trying to back away.

"He will buy for you, if you like."

I laugh nervously, trying to hurry him up and put it back before Nick sees. "I don't think so, we aren't ... well, that's a little beyond what I think he is willing to get for me."

"Are you getting greedy over here?" Nick says from behind me, kissing me on the cheek before catching sight of the ring over my shoulder.

"I just glanced at it. I didn't ask him to take it out." I said quickly.

"We should probably go." He said and I nod, waving at the man with a nervous smile. I feel uneasy walking out, until Nick takes my hand again and seems unfazed by the event. "I think they are having a fair tonight. Do you want to go back and change for it?"

"That sounds like fun."

I put on my new dress, with my new necklace, and find Nick waiting for me. "You look beautiful." He said.

"You look incredible ... but I probably shouldn't tell you that." I blush as I take in his mouthwatering ensemble and consider my lame remark.

"Why is that?"

"I don't want you to think that I can't resist you." I said with a laugh.

Nick pulls me in close, "Can you?" Kissing me quickly, he leads me out before I even have a chance to answer. The fair is crowded but so much fun. We play games, watch people perform, and dance to the music. We give up trying to keep up with the locals and search for our own little corner to keep it simple. A drink or two in, I feel lightheaded and have to hold onto Nick. Not long after, I realize he is feeling it too. It is not surprising, the drinks are nearly pure alcohol.

"Nick, I don't think I can feel my feet."

"Me either which is probably a good thing because I think you are stepping all over me." He laughs.

"Oh, am I?" I pull away and look down at my feet but the motion instantly makes me dizzy. I look up at Nick and fall into his chest. He pulls my face back up to his and takes hold of my lips. Nick holds me so close and so tight, I can barely kiss him. I have never felt so wonderful and safe in my life. I thought I had that with Daniel, I thought I was in love with him but it is clear now that I was more in love with the idea of him. With Nick however, I feel different somehow, he is … different. Resting in his arms, I lay my head against his shoulder, "I love … you." I whisper into the wind.

ᚼᚱᚢ

I can feel the sun beating down on me but I am unsure where I am and I am too scared to open my eyes to find out. I stretch my arm out and immediately feel Nick, so I open my eyes and am surprised to see the house we have been staying in. Nick rolls over wrapping his arm around me. "What's wrong?" He says with a rugged voice.

"I don't remember how we got here." I said with a roughness of my own.

"I called for someone to drive us, I think. Most of the night is a blur." He says as I try to sit up.

My head immediately pounds, "Oh, my head!" I complain as I slide back into bed and try not to move.

"They brought us a hangover cure in a cup over there. I tried it, but it was not easy to get down." Nick said watching me ease slowly to the edge of the bed to reach out for the cup of odd sludge. I look in the cup and nearly faint from the smell. Nick laughs, "Hold your nose and swallow. It's worth it, I promise." I do as he says quickly. After I get it down, I lie back down and curl up next to him. "Did I forget to say brush your teeth before you got back into bed with me?" I ease up to look at him. He smiles and kisses me.

I smack him playfully, "Uh huh, you didn't brush yours either." Before I lie back down, I notice a shell ring on my finger. "When did I get this?"

"Oh, you married some local last night."

"I did what!"

"You are a horrible wife, too. Having sex with another man on your honeymoon night? That's not right at all." He teases.

"What's that on your finger?" Nick rolls over, laughing into his pillow. I pull up the side of his pillow as he pushes his hand deeper. "What are you hiding?" I say as I manage to uncover his hand showing a similar ring. "And who did you marry?"

"You ..."

"But I thought I married a local?" I asked feeling confused.

"You did. Well, you were set to, I had to bribe the guy to let me have you instead." I smile and kiss him. "Best five dollars I have ever spent." My jaw drops open and I smack him hard as he laughs.

"Real funny. Now how did we really get these?"

"I don't know. We were playing and then you decided you had to buy me something and for some reason that something had to be for the both of us, so you bought these. Then, I said I feel like I am married so you forced me to stand on the pier and say: "I might as well", over and over."

I laugh holding my pained head, "I might as well?"

"Because I refused to say I do." He laughs playing with my hair.

"Ah, well, that makes sense."

"Doesn't it?" Nick rolls over top me, taking in my lips one at a time. "You know those rings were only a couple of dollars, I think you owe me the difference for the necklace I bought you."

"How about I just bathe us both in the giant Jacuzzi outside?"

"Mmm. Okay, but you are going to brush your teeth first, right?" Before he can get too far away from me, I throw a pillow at him.

"You better, as well! I mean ... YOU MIGHT AS WELL!" I yell after him, smiling when I hear him laugh.

Sitting in his lap with the bubbles surrounding us, I massage his muscles, lathering them up, and washing them off before finding another place to clean him. It's quiet, apart from the waves, the birds, and the sound of our breathing. I take pleasure in the moment, feeling his body, touching him, and feeling his hands on me. I fight my urge to look up into his eyes but my curiosity gets the better of me. He is staring right at me with a crooked smile, sending a wave of exhilaration through my body. I lie against his chest and sigh deeply, wishing for the moment to never end. *I hate how I feel about him. I hate being this vulnerable to him. Now I know why Bray fell so hard for him. I hope when he is done with me, I can leave him easier than she.*

CECSEO

*B*eing back at work gives me the opportunity to tell Exie about all the details of my trip, but I would easily forgo that to have stayed alone with Nick. I had to promise to not talk about where we were, not that I even knew for sure. The maze of stops and detours he took before finally getting to some type of civilization would have confused anybody. I am pretty sure of the continent, but that is about it.

As far as the club, Kyler clearly did not have such an easy time running things while I was gone. There were several fights with the girls. If not for Exie threatening to cut the heels off their shoes, it might have gotten out of hand. My first night back is filled with complaining and exhausting conversations to get Kyler back at ease. Tonight, I am so tired I don't even consider waiting up for Nick. I am out before my head hits the pillow. After a few hours, my deep sleep is disturbed abruptly by Nick yelling. I put on my robe and walk out to the balcony to see Nick screaming at Luke.

"What do you want me to do, Nick?" Luke holds his hands out in defense.

"Who brought that FUCKER?" Nick screams.

"He's a friend of Jack's. Marcus was supposed …" Dawson yells back defensively.

"Supposed? He was supposed to be? Did no one check him out?" Nick yells again as they move to the other side of the house. Curious, I follow quietly to the back of the house and cower in the dark on the balcony above them.

"I checked him out myself and he was good." Dawson said.

"Well obviously not!" Nick yelled waving his hands and pacing. His normal perfect dress is in disarray. "Where is Jack?"

"Outside." Dwayne motioned.

"Bring him in here." Nick said. Luke motions to Dwayne and a man soon wanders in slowly ahead of Dwayne. As soon as Nick eyes him, the man drops to his knees with his trembling hands in the air. "You set me up!" Nick yells.

"I swear, Nick, I didn't. I don't know how they found out but I swear it wasn't me. Marcus swore to me he was …"

"Shut up!" Nick gives a nod to Luke and Luke takes out his gun.

"Nick, please! I swear I will take care of it." Nick jumps back towards the man pulling out his own gun and putting it against the man's head.

"Nick!" I yell, shaking and startling everyone. Nick puts his gun away and runs up to me, wrapping his arms around me and nearly carrying me back into the bedroom.

"Kayla, what are you doing up?"

"I heard you yelling." I said backing away from his menacing eyes.

"How much … how much did you hear?"

"Not much. I heard you yelling and then I saw you holding a gun to that man's head. You were going to shoot him." I said gripping his shirt and craving him to hold me rather than grip me like he is.

Nick grabs a hold of the back of my neck and pulls me in tight to him, "Go to bed. Put your headphones on and don't get up until I say so. Do you understand me?" With my entire body shaking uncontrollably and tears fighting their way free down my face, I nod. Nick presses his lips to my cheek, "Everything is going to be fine, I promise. That man is going to help me and I have to make sure he understands that he doesn't have a choice. That's all that is going to happen." After kissing me once again, he lets go of me and watches as I grab my headphones and climb into bed. I can feel his eyes on me as I try to settle my nerves and calm down. With every vibration and every slight noise I think I hear over my music, I cringe thinking it is a gun going off. I fear for Nick, I fear for the man crying for his life to be spared, and I fear for me hearing something that I shouldn't have. When I feel Nick pull the headphones from my ears and wrap his arms around me, I search over his body to prove to myself he is unharmed. He cradles me to him, playing with my hair, and rubbing my back until I fall asleep.

~13~
KAYLA

*N*ick has been overtly attentive since the other night: going out of his way to make sure I smile or at least smile at him. It's not easy. Tonight he got us tickets to the ballet, I have never been but am enjoying it immensely. At intermission, Nick suggests a glass of wine. I agree and walk with him hand in hand to the reception area where he buys us both a glass. "So, are you enjoying it so far?" He asked.

"Yes, thank you for bringing me. It's … I don't know what. I have never seen anything like it before." I say watching him smile back at me, with the darkness in his eyes faded into the background. "Are you staying with me all-night tonight?"

"Is that what you want?" I nod in response. "Then I will." He said as his eyes dart over my shoulder. I sink a little, assuming that he has to be noticing another woman, but he kisses me deeply instead. The display is comforting, but obviously meant for someone else to see. I smile appreciatively at him, but make sure to glance back when we walk back to our seats. Daniel nods in my direction with a scowl as Nick wraps his arm around me and guides us back to our seats. I try to enjoy the show, but it is difficult. I have a terrible feeling that Daniel isn't going to let it go. During the next intermission, I try to keep Nick with me in what I think is a safe corner. I am positive he knows what I am trying to do but he is being kind enough to oblige.

"You're not still seeing him, are you?" Nick asks suddenly.

"No, not since we … no." I said, feeling good that it seems to put him at ease.

"If you're finished, I will take your glass back." I hand him my glass, kissing him before he walks away. I begin to feel better about the night but then Daniel heads off Nick. The two meet like two bulls preparing to rage at each other. They speak tensely for several minutes before the clash suddenly ends. At the end of the ballet, Nick rushes us home and I assume the night is long over. "Kayla." Nick said stopping me from going up the stairs. I wait for him to speak again but instead he props me up on a nearby table and latches on to my lips, ripping my panties halfway down my legs.

I push him off me, "Nick! What are you trying to do to me? It is not my fault. It's not my fault, Nick. If you can't get over me being with Daniel, then you need to tell me so we can go our own ways. I haven't seen Daniel since that night you threw me into your car and I don't plan to. You can't treat me like you own me, Nick. If you want to talk to me about it, then talk. Don't fuck your way into my life." I head up the stairs to bed and hope he follows but almost an hour passes before he finally comes in to the room.

Walking to my side of the bed, he fights with himself over the words he wants to say to me. I look up at him and he groans like a child, "I don't know ... I hate that you were ever with him. It is my fault that you were. I should have ..." Nick sighs looking away. "I want you to want me more, but if you don't, I won't stop you from leaving. However, I also won't stop trying to protect you from him." Sighing deeply his shoulders sink, "So I guess I am trying to say ..." He looks down at me, groaning, "I'm sorry."

I reach up and pull him down on top of me, "You are forgiven!" Kissing him passionately, I rip his clothes off his body as fast as I can go but he gets impatient and finishes them off himself. "I do want you more, Nick. I never cared about him the way I care about you. I always felt like something was missing with him. You're different somehow." Nick suddenly finds his patient side and romances me with sweet kisses and soft touches before he finds his way inside me, moving his body like he dances to a rhythm that reaches down to my soul.

CR&U

*W*aking up this morning I cannot wipe the smile off my face. I bounce around the house greeting everyone blissfully and, to some, I nearly sing my cheery attitude in their direction. When I see Luke coming in, I try to share with him as I have with everyone else.

"I'm in no mood for your shit today, Kayla." Luke said with a glancing dark attitude.

"What did I do to you?" I asked stunned by his concentrated glare.

"Are you really asking me that? Are you that stupid?" Luke huffed in my face.

"I guess I am, because I have no idea what your problem is." I replied while my posture becomes rigid.

"My problem is that you are distracting my best friend. I can't believe he hasn't gotten rid of you or … done away with you yet? No, that's not Nick. I don't know what you're up to, but know this, I am watching you even if he isn't."

"I'm not up to anything, you paranoid jerk!"

"I'm paranoid, huh? Well maybe I am and maybe I'm not, but either way you're going to get him killed."

"And how exactly am I going to do that?"

Luke approaches leaning into my face. "That's easy to explain. Because he is so distracted by you, with protecting you, trying to make you happy, and making sure he plans his days so he can spend as much time with you, rather than worrying about what he should be."

"Nick knows what he's doing and I am sure he has had distractions before. I think you're just jealous that he isn't spending his free time with you."

Luke rolls his eyes and prances away like a schoolgirl. "Oh yes, that's it! I wish he would let me suck his dick too." *Idiot*. Luke turns around and points his finger in my direction, "Don't get too comfortable, Sweetheart, because it will be only a matter of time before Nick sends you packing. That! I'm sure of."

∞

*D*espite Luke, the day is perfect and couldn't be any more so. I have a special date planned with Nick tonight and I intend to find the perfect outfit and under garments for it. However, when I walk into my favorite store, I am immediately cornered by two men. "Ms. Donovan, can we talk to you please?" I try to step away from them but they flash badges at me.

"About what?" I asked.

"I think it would be best if you come down to the station and talk with us." Said the first officer.

"This is not a good time." I replied as I tried to step around them again.

"That's fine then we will follow you around until you have time." The same officer threatened. Frustrated, I reluctantly agree to go with them. Hours go by before they start their interrogation. "Ms. Donovan, what is your relationship with Nicholas Jayzon?"

Rolling my eyes but not surprised, "Nick is my boyfriend. Is that all you wanted to know?"

They toss a picture my way. "Do you know this man, Kayla?" I pick it up with no recollection at all.

"No. Should I?" I said, tossing it back to them.

"Look at it closely. Are you sure you have never seen him before?"

"I am looking at him. I don't know him and have never seen him before." I said with a long sigh.

"He works for your boyfriend or I should say worked for him." I shrug. "He was helping us and suddenly he went missing."

"I told you I have no idea who he is. I have never seen him and, more importantly, I have never seen him with Nick."

They become frustrated with me and one of them aims his finger down on the picture over and over. "Look at him! Marcus Knox, that's his name. Marcus Knox, Kayla! You don't know him? Are you sure?"

The name begins to take shape in my mind but I remain blank faced as they yell at me. "Can I go now? Or should I call a lawyer?" I asked pointedly.

"Do you need one?" Asks the smartass cop who is quickly wearing on my nerves.

"Maybe if you continue to hold me here against my will," I say with boldness that sits them both back in their chairs.

"You're pretty tough. Do you know who your boyfriend is, Kayla?" I ignore him. "I hope so because a lot of people have turned up missing around him. I would hate for a pretty young woman like you to go missing."

I cock my head to one side and pull out my cell phone and dial, "Nick, for some reason I am being held against my will by some cops…. Thank you. See you soon." One of them gets up and leaves in a huff and the other leans back in his chair, eyeing me with a smile, "What is your name again?" I asked.

"Detective Simone, but you can call me Brady." He winks.

"Brady, do you harass women often?"

"None as pretty as you." I stare at him hard before looking away. "Here's my card. Take it in case you need it- or just need someone to share a dinner with."

"Are you kidding?"

He stands over me, "No, and I am not kidding about your boyfriend being dangerous. I don't care if you have information to help us or not, I would prefer you get away from him before you get hurt." He walks out and within no time Nick's lawyer walks in to escort me out.

As soon as I enter the house, Nick approaches me with concern but looks even angrier than I am. Luke following him, however, fights a smile, "I told you." Luke said.

"Shut up and let me handle this. What did they want, Kayla?" Nick yells, as he leans in close to my face.

"Stop yelling at me." I said, pushing back on his chest.

"Tell me what happened, Kayla." Nick said only slightly calmer.

"They wanted to know if I knew some Marcus guy. If I had seen him before."

Luke laughs harshly and Nick eyes him to be quiet. "And what did you say?" Nick asked.

"I said I had never seen him before. Which I haven't. I have never seen him or heard of him before. And that's all I said before I called you."

"You were there for a long time." Luke said.

"They held me in a room and left me by myself for hours. And then, one of the detectives spent time flirting and asking me out."

Nick spins around, "Who?"

"Detective Simone, I think was his name."

"He's trying to get you to open up to him." Nick said.

"I am not stupid, Nick. But I don't have any information to give him, do I?"

Nick throws up his hands and cringes. "I don't like this at all."

"And I do?" I yell back at him.

Nick turns to face me, "See? This is why I don't get involved with anyone. Nothing but trouble." He walks away from me cursing under his breath. "Son of a bitch! I don't know what I was thinking."

"Well, I can make it easy for you and leave. Then your trouble is gone." I said watching him pace around like a wild man.

"That would be great. I would appreciate it." Nick said not looking at me.

I pause, watching him lean against the wall still cursing. "I'll pack then." Nick waves me off. "Nick?"

"What?" He yells sending me back on my heels. "What, Kayla?" He looks at me, his eyes cold. "You want me to cry and beg you to stay? Maybe get down on my knees and beg for your forgiveness? What? If you want to go, fucking go! No one's stopping you. Hell, at this point, I will help you pack!" He slams his fist into the wall and heads out the door. Luke follows with a smirk that I want to smack off his face.

I pack what I can, what I feel is fair to take, and leave him a note resigning from the club. I have Exie pick me up and leave the new car Nick bought for me parked where I left it. I am gone before he gets back. "Are you sure this is what you want to do?" Exie asks. I nod hiding my face from her in case I am not strong enough to hold back my tears. "He was angry. You know, people say things they don't mean when they are angry."

"Not in my world. People say exactly what they mean when they are angry. That's when they are the most free to do so. They may not mean to hurt you, but they always mean what they say."

~14~
KAYLA

I spend weeks searching for a job, but Nick made sure no other club would hire me. The best job I can get is as a waitress at a cheap restaurant- a place where I can take the bus to and from Exie's house. *I hate not having a car.* My boss is lazy, disgusting, and too dumb to be running his own business. *How this place stays open is beyond me. He must have someone helping him or God owes him one.* The restaurant is nearly empty this late at night, outside of an old truck driver, a couple of streetwalkers taking a break from their own business, and two teenagers that are high and intent on smoking an entire pack of cigarettes each. *I hate the smell of cigarettes, my mother rarely breathed without one. As if this place doesn't make you feel dirty enough with its barely passing inspection grade or the ridiculous schoolgirl outfits the owner is so determined to make me wear. Now I have to sit back and breathe in the smoky sludge the idiots in the corner are trying to surround themselves with, all so they can hide from the world.* All I can do is sit propped up on the counter kicking my heels waiting for my nightmare to end. With an hour to go someone comes in forcing me to get up and pretend to care again. I walk out to greet the customer and sigh as soon as I see his stupid smiling face, "Ms. Donovan, I am surprised to see you here." Detective Simone said.

"What do you want to eat." I asked trying to ignore him.

"I take it you and Jayzon aren't together anymore?"

"No, we are not- no thanks to you." I said.

"And here I thought bringing you in was a waste of time, but now I feel like it was well worth the effort."

"Glad you think so. Now, do you want something or are you only here to harass me?"

"Coffee. Coffee will be fine." He said easing back in his chair.

"Great." I said walking away in a huff. The detective makes every effort to continue to get my attention, staying all-night and even waiting until after we close to watch me wait for the bus.

"I could give you a ride home if you want." He asked after

forcing his frozen window down.

"What is your problem? Are you trying to piss me off?" I asked him.

"It's just a ride. Just ... a ... ride." He spelled out sarcastically.

"I am not telling you anything about Nick. I don't know anything that would help you ... with anything."

"Just ... a ... ride." He expresses again.

I take a second to look down the road to see if the bus is anywhere close. Of course it isn't. *Stupid bus.* With a sigh I get up and get into his car without looking at him. "I'm not talking to you, so don't bother asking me any questions."

"A quiet woman? Wow! I thought they only existed in fairy tales." He laughs as I eye him with a stern warning. "You know I am not a bad guy. If we had met each other under different circumstances, I might instead be driving you home after we had dinner together instead." He glances my way and I shift closer to the window. "A friend of mine gave me these tickets to the concert tomorrow night. Everyone I know is working and I would really like to go but I hate going to these things alone." *I know he is looking at me again.* "You don't know anyone that might like to go with me, do you?"

"I don't know anyone with that low of standards."

"Ha! I got you talk to me after all." He yells out, ridiculously proud of himself. *Ass* "Tell you what, if you go with me tomorrow night, then I will stop coming around and asking you out."

"All I have to do is put up with you for a couple of hours?"

"Dinner and the concert and then I promise straight home. I don't put out on the first date." He said laughing at his own joke. *Idiot.*

"Uggghhh, I ..."

"This is a onetime offer."

"I don't think I can put up with you for that long."

"Okay then, I guess we will be seeing each other tomorrow and the next day, and the next and the ..."

"FINE! But that's it and you leave me alone for good!" I yell at him.

"I swear. For good. Unless you have fun and want to do it again."

"I won't."

"You might."

"I definitely won't." I said rolling my eyes yet again.

"Oh, I think you definitely might. I am very charming."

"Thanks for the ride," I say halfheartedly as I jump out of the car and race up the drive to the front door.

CR80

*A*s promised, Detective Simone picks me up at seven and drives me to his supposed favorite restaurant, which is a bar that happens to serve food. He makes sure to introduce me to his friends as we enter, all of whom are also police officers. Every time I look up, the crowd whispers and gestures towards me. After a few times, I concentrate on my hands placed in my lap. Brady, as he asked me to call him, notices my uneasiness, quickly pays for our meal, and leads me out the door. The concert is fun but unfortunately Brady catches me smiling and smiles back. I erase my good time from my face as quickly as I can, but it's too late, he's obviously proud of himself. Brady takes me straight home, as promised, and leaves me alone, for a few days at least. One morning, I wake up to flowers asking me for another date.

"Exie, look at this." I said holding up the flowers Brady left on our doorstep.

"Wow. You must have made an impression on him. You didn't sleep with him, did you?" She laughs

"No, but thanks for the vote of confidence in my skills."

Exie smiles and points towards the door behind me, "Is that him coming up the walk?"

Turning, I see Daniel as he knocks on our door, "No, that's Daniel."

"Daniel? The guy Nick nearly locked you in a box over? Don't answer the door, Kayla." Sighing, I approach the door as Exie picks up Jerran and goes to the back of the house.

Opening the door I force a smile, "Daniel what are you doing here?"

"That's not the greeting I was hoping for." He said forcing an awkward smile.

"Well, what do you expect? The last time I saw you were …"

Daniel steps in and takes hold of me, "Baby, please. You don't understand how much I need you, how much I miss you." Daniel tries to get me to look at him. "I wish you would look at me. I'm proud of you though."

Pulling away from Daniel's grasp, "For what?"

"For finally getting away from that Dirtbag. I thought for sure you would eventually give in to him, but you are ..." Daniel glances at me awkwardly. "You ... you did give into him?"

"Daniel, yes I did and I don't regret it, so please just go."

"Are those flowers for you?" Daniel points to the vase with my name clearly displayed on the outside of the card. "Nick sends flowers now?" Before I can explain, Daniel throws the vase across the room into a wall. "I can't believe you would let him touch you!" Daniel approaches me with a dark cloud hovering around him. "You fucking whore!"

"Get out!" I screamed as Daniel closes in on me, "LEAVE!"

"Kayla, are you okay?" Exie said running in from the hall.

"Do you like the way he feels, Kayla? Do you think he feels better than me? Does he fuck you the way you like?"

"Get out, Daniel, and don't ever come back here!" I yell opening the door wide for him. Daniel eyes Exie briefly before walking out the door but pushes his way back through and throws me against a glass case causing it to break and the glass to cut up my arm. I slide down the wall gripping my arm when Daniel grabs hold of me and slams my head back into the floor.

"Give Nick a message for me," Daniel hits me hard across the face.

"Get out! You fucking son of a bitch! Get out before I call Nick!" Exie yells kicking at Daniel and beating him with whatever she can get. Daniel pushes her down but leaves. "Are you okay?" Exie asks while looking me over. "Oh, you are bleeding. Let me get Jerran and I will take you to the hospital.

"No, Exie, I'm fine. I will bandage it myself." I said grimacing as I try to get up.

"Kayla, your arm, your head ... no, I am taking you to the hospital."

"But, Exie, I can't afford that."

"We will figure it out together." Exie said grabbing Jerran and hustling me out the door to the hospital.

❧

*T*he emergency room is insane and I am becoming impatient while waiting to be released. Lying in this hospital bed makes me feel so vulnerable and stupid. "Now, this is no way to get out of a date." I open my eyes to see Brady smiling wide in front of me.

"What are you doing here?" I asked trying to sit up.

"I heard you were here and I wanted to see if you were okay." He said cringing at the mark on my face. "I hope you filed a report."

"I did but ..."

"Don't tell me you're not going to press charges against this bastard?" Brady asked helping me sit up comfortably.

"I don't want to deal with him anymore. Daniel is obviously crazy and, from my experience, crazy people are not intimidated by restraining orders or threats of jail. It only makes them crazier."

"Daniel? What's his name?" Brady asked looking at me with a puzzled expression.

"Daniel Bonner."

"And what was he so mad about?"

"He thought the flowers you sent me were from Nick." I said and immediately Brady laughs. "Am I missing something?"

"Apparently, because that man's name is not Daniel Bonner, I can guarantee you of that." I sit up with my head still spinning. Sticking his hands in his pockets, Brady looks at me with a peculiar expression. "Kayla, his name is actually Connor Daniels. He's Nick's brother. That's why he was so angry about you being with Nick."

"What? But ... neither of them said anything." I said looking up to see Nick at the nurses' station, but as soon as I see him, he tries to leave. "No, get him. Nick!" I yell trying to get up.

"Kayla, lie back. You have a concussion." Brady said helping me back into bed. "I will go get him but stay in bed." Brady races out the door after Nick.

"Where is he going so fast?" Exie said coming in with some food and water.

"Nick was here, but he left without saying anything." I look up at Exie, "Did you know Nick had a brother?" Exie shakes her head. "I didn't either, or that it was Daniel, or I guess his name is Connor Daniels."

"Whoa, seriously? Hmm... Well, that makes sense now. Connor Daniels has been battling Nick for some time. He's Nick's most hated rival."

"How do you know that?"

"I have been working at the club forever now. You hear things even when you're not supposed to. Connor managed to get in and confront Nick one night. I didn't see what happened, but I sure did hear about it. And you wonder why Kyler is so stressed all the time? The man knows things that would push the Pope to drink."

"How did Nick know I was here?" I asked recognizing her guilt immediately.

"Well, I know you can't afford it and I can only help you so much, but no matter what you say, I think Nick would do anything for you. So yes, I called him. And to prove my point, he was here in a heartbeat, paying for everything, and making sure you are well-taken care of."

"Why would you let him pay for everything? Exie, I cannot let him help me like that."

"Too late." She said proudly.

"I chased him down but he said he has a meeting to get to." Brady said as he comes into the room. I roll my eyes and sink deep back into the bed.

Exie left shortly after that for work, but Brady stayed with me until visiting hours were over. With my bill paid in advance, the doctors are more than accepting of me staying as long as needed, even to ridiculous measures so I'm forced to stay overnight and rest. After I was moved to a plush room by myself and given enough pain medicine to knock out an elephant, I don't feel the need to complain about anything anymore. At some point in the night though I feel something strange and force open my eyes. The blurry figure in front of me seems familiar. "Nick?"

"Go to sleep. You're dreaming."

"If I am dreaming, then I am already asleep." I said recognizing his huff immediately. "How did you get in here?"

"Money can get you in anywhere, Princess."

"I'm going to pay you back for everything." I promise him.

"No, you're not. It's my fault you're in here." Nick said sweeping my hair out of my face and grimacing at the site of my swollen eye.

"No, it was Brady's flowers that he didn't like. He thought they were from you."

"I wouldn't send flowers that cheap." He said making me laugh.

"Why didn't you tell me that he is your brother, Nick?"

"By blood only, we weren't raised in the same house or in the same way. My father left his mother when she got pregnant with him and married my mother. He didn't have anything to do with Connor, especially when his mother married his rich slime-ball stepfather. He thinks he's better than me because he had money to begin with. So, he did everything he could when I was younger to make my life a living hell. He was older and bigger, so I took several beatings from him. Eventually, I grew up and gained the upper hand to his ... bitter disappointment. I don't consider Connor my brother. I didn't tell you because I didn't want you in the middle of it if I could help it. You were already wrapped up in him when I found out he was the client you were seeing. I'm sorry. If I had known he was trying to steal girls from me, I would have protected you better."

"I don't need you to protect me."

Nick laughs, "Sure, that's why you're here." I try to roll my eyes but it only makes me dizzy. Nick caresses my face, "Go to sleep. I only wanted to make sure you were okay."

"Don't leave." I whisper, feeling him grip my hand. I struggle to stay awake, but my body gives in to the medication and I drift away only to wake up alone. Brady returns the next day to take me home. His charming ways convince me to go have dinner with him. He is sweet, generous with what little he has, and respectful every step of the way, but he is not Nick. The power of the devil's eyes still holds me hostage, but I am becoming hopeful that Brady can help me break free.

~15~
KAYLA

*B*rady manages to convince me to go to a ball game, then to a movie a few days later, and tonight he has brought me to a traveling carnival. Despite my still uneasy feelings about him, I do feel comfortable with him. As we walk among the laughing children, the colorful lights, and playful music, Brady has his arm around my shoulders and searching for every possible reason to make me laugh.

"You hungry?" Brady asked.

"Why? So you can try to make me sick and then talk me into getting on that death trap over there after I eat some disgusting carnival food?" I laughed.

"Okay. How about I win you a giant turtle?" He asked motioning towards a game.

"I prefer the big blue dog." I said as he winks and hands the dubious gentleman some money.

"Did I mention I was all state in baseball? I'm serious. I am really good."

"Just throw the ball." I said laughing at his overzealous attitude. Brady throws the ball and misses the target. "That's impressive."

"I just needed a warm up throw." He said throwing again and barely hitting the edge. With the final ball, he overthrows it. Frustrated and determined, he continues to throw ball after ball until he finally scores. "Yes! I told you."

"Here is your prize, sir." The man said handing him a red plastic squeaking ball. Brady looks at his prize and reluctantly hands it to me with a humble expression.

"It's ... the exact one I wanted." I smile as he hugs me tight and leads me away.

"I knew it was. So, are you ready to go?" I nod in response to his question. "Do you want me to take you home or are you interested in getting a drink at my place?"

No matter how hard I try, Nick remains in the back of mind. I feel like I see him everywhere I go or somehow feel him nearby. As much as I want to spend the night with Brady, I need more time and luckily I don't have to say the words. Brady nods with obvious frustration but takes me home and leaves with nothing more than an innocent kiss.

The next morning I wake up to find the stuffed big blue dog from the carnival on my doorstep. There is no note but I have a feeling Brady would have never gone back to get this for me. If he had, he would have left a note. My new dog is nicknamed The Devil's Dog and it sits proudly next to me as I sleep.

⊗

*T*he restaurant is dead and I have several hours left of my shift when two men come in. With an exhausted exhale, I jump off the counter and go to take their orders. "You gentleman in for a late night, huh?" They both look at me with side smiles and seemingly making odd notions towards each other. "So, what can I get you?"

"How about a blow job?" One said laughing with the other.

"No. How about a lap dance? Naked, of course." The other said.

"Sorry. I am only willing to give out food tonight." They both laugh and eventually order something but continue to make my night miserable. I try to talk my boss into handling them for me but the lazy son of a bitch refuses to leave his well-broken in chair to help me out. Mike, the cook, offers to spice up their food for me but he is powerless to do much else considering his small stature. Taking them their food, I fight off their hands and their obscene comments and wait out their stay from a distance. I have never been so happy to see people leave. I was ready to go from the moment they came in and am thankful the night moves along quickly soon after they leave. I grab my things and rush to the bus stop hoping that somehow it will be early. I sit up high on the back of the bench to catch the first glimpse of the expected bus. My seat also allows me to catch a glimpse of a dark maintenance van coming my way. As it slows in front of me, I quickly take in my surroundings for a quick getaway.

"Hey, sweetheart, you still serving?" The losers from earlier asked as they poke their drunken heads from the van. Watching them, I take notice of my boss leaving for home. I make my way towards him and he stops his car, rolling down his window with a cocky smile. The lesser of two evils I believe, I run towards him but before I can get to him he speeds off. I turn back to see the two losers stumbling towards me. Alone, I make my way back towards the restaurant as fast I can, fumbling with my keys trying to find the right one for the door. "Hey, where are you going?" They yell at me. While running, I notice a huge pipe used to hold open the back door of the restaurant and concentrate on reaching it. Within feet of it, one of the men jerks me backwards, grabbing, and fondling me as I try to get away from him. When the other one begins kissing me, I kick and scream, searching for anything to get away from them, when a car pulls up and startles them both. "What the fuck, man?" One of them yells as I am suddenly dropped in preparation to fight. I try to see over the men but I am guarded like a prize. "Oh, I see you must be looking for an ass whooping tonight, son." The larger of the two laughs but is slammed by something sending him to the ground fast. Unsure if I am being rescued or being traded for a worse situation, I run after the pipe and prepare as I watch my two abductors enter a brawl they are clearly overmatched for. The dark figure, beating the men into a crawling, begging position, has his own weapon of choice and is having no trouble using it. The long, black club is lifted high in the air before plummeting down on its intended victim. Blood is splattered and the men are screaming as I stand motionless watching them beg for their lives. As much as the world would be better off, I can't let someone I love do this for me.

"Nick! Stop! You are going to kill them!" I run back and grab hold of him. "Stop, Nick, please!"

"Get in the car, Kayla!" Nick yells at me.

"No, not until you do." His frustrated sigh lingers around me until he finally gives in and follows me into his car. "What are you doing here?"

"I was in the mood for some pancakes."

"Nick ..."

"Don't start with me, Kayla. You should not be walking to a bus stop this late by yourself." Huffing at me, he takes out a knife and hands it to me. "Take this at least. I would give you a gun but you don't have the best track record with those. Some cop you're dating! He lets you do these stupid things? I hope he is at least ..."

"I was only going to say thank you." I said staring at my fingers fumbling in my lap.

Calming some, Nick looks me over with a shake of his head. "You're hurt."

"I'm fine. Just a little scrape is all." Nick takes hold of my arm and lifts it off the gash in my leg. I try not to look at him, but his eyes, as always, have a drawing force about them. "You know I was about to handle it by myself. There was no need for you to butt in." I say boldly. "Now, if you will please take me home so I can clean up and go to bed." Nick shakes his head and continues driving away from my house. "Are you listening to me?"

"No." He said with half a smile to my growing frustration. "Kayla, what are you doing? I told you that you didn't have to quit the club. Why are you working at such a shit place? You are just asking for trouble." Facing my window, I raise my left shoulder to hide him from my view. Nick laughs at me, "You are the most frustrating woman."

Nick pulls into his drive way and waits for the gate, "Nick! Why are we here?"

"Because I need to change for a date tonight now that I got blood on my shirt and you need a car. There is no reason for that car to stay here. Whether you work for me or not, you earned the car. Now get out of the car and come in the house." Nick walks over and opens the car door for me.

"Take me home! I am not getting out of this car until I am at my own house!" I yell crossing my arms. I feel good about my defiance, until he suddenly throws me over his shoulder and takes me up to his room. "Nick! Nick! Put me down!" I yell until he sits me on his bathroom countertop. He takes out his first aid kit and glances over at my wound. Removing his shirt, he looks me over and begins pushing my schoolgirl thigh highs off my legs.

"This is a ridiculous outfit." Nick mumbles.

"I thought men had fantasies of women in schoolgirl uniforms." I said enjoying his hands caressing my legs.

Pulling off my last sock, he smiles leaning in towards me, "I don't."

"Whatever, liar. You know you like this." I said running my bare leg up between his with a smile until he glares at me.

"Kayla, if I wanted you looking like a vulnerable child, then I would have never had sex with you in the first place." He says rubbing my leg with medicine and blowing on it to ease the pain for me. "Take your shirt off." He said looking up at my shocked expression. "Your arm is cut too." I must have hesitated too long for him because he begins unbuttoning my shirt for me and easing it off my shoulders. My broken bra dangles to one side of my chest and I have to hold it up to my breasts. "They did that?" I nod and he looks away with a curl of his lips. Taking my hands, he removes them from my chest and grazes his fingers over the scratches on my chest. "Come with me." Nick takes my hand and leads me to his shower, turning it on, and removing my skirt with a flick of his fingers. "Take 'em off and get in." He said waiting for me to do as told. Turning away from him, I slide my panties down my legs and look up through my hair to see him watching me. Once I step into the luxurious double shower I cringe at the touch of the steaming water heating my wounds. "It only stings for a second." Nick said sliding in behind me, naked, and already washing me with a tender touch. His warm hands run soap over my arms, down my chest and cup my breasts as he gives off a soft sigh. I press my palms against the shower wall and try to remember to breathe as he moves down my stomach, between my legs and down over my calves, helping me lift my feet before returning to my neck and rinsing out my hair. "I think you're good now." He whispers in my ear before stepping back under the adjacent showerhead. "You don't mind if I take a shower myself, do you? I do have a date tonight."

I become mesmerized by the water running over his skin, his hands running through his wet black hair, down his chiseled stomach, while his eyes watch my every move. I reach out and take the cloth from his hand, "You should be at your best for your date." I say running my hands down his back, cradling his ass tight in my palms. His arms stiffen as I run my hands over them and press my fingers between his.

Sighing, Nick grips my hands but suddenly steps away from me. "You should go home now."

"No. No, I'm not and you're not going on that date either." I say smiling when he finally looks over at me. Shaking my head, I take a step towards him, finally knowing his weakness. Moving my hand up his chest and to the back of his neck, I pull him down towards my lips, "You can't say no to me and you know it." I whisper back to him, smiling wide when he takes hold of me and lifts me up against the shower wall.

"Kayla, we shouldn't be doing this." Nick says running his soft lips across mine.

"Nick …" I gasp, feeling him slide inside me. *He feels so good. His arms hold me so strong, his lips seem to know exactly what I need, and his dick grazes places inside me that exhilarate my entire body.* It all feels so incredible I can barely comprehend his own pleasurable moans.

Not a word is spoken when we finish, I dry off and reach for my clothes, but he stops me, taking hold of them. "You don't need these. I will be waiting in bed for you." He said, kissing me gently.

Smiling, I send Exie a quick message and let her know that I am staying with Nick tonight. I climb in bed with Nick, kissing him, and pulling him on top of me. I might regret all this tomorrow, but tonight it all just feels too good to stop.

~16~
KAYLA

*T*he morning sun radiates down on my cheek. I roll over, searching for him, but he is nowhere in sight. I get up and borrow his shirt before going downstairs to search for him. When I see Luke, I have to roll my eyes to match the roll of his. "Where is Nick?"

"Busy." Luke says harshly.

"Busy doing what?" I ask as Luke ignores me. "Can you at least tell him that I am up?"

"Oh, well, let me alert the world. Her highness is awake."

"Fuck you." I said walking towards Nick's office. Luke grabs hold of me and pushes me away. "What is your problem?"

"I told you he is busy. He asked me to tell you to take your fucking car and go." Luke said pressing his face fiercely towards mine.

"Nick! Nick!" I yell over and over, fighting with Luke's hand to hold my mouth shut. When Nick comes running out, I run to him instantly.

"What the fuck is going on out here? I asked you ..." Nick tenses towards Luke.

"I told her you were busy, but she ... well, you know how she is. Your own damn fault for bringing her here in the first place." Luke mumbles tossing his hands up in the air.

"Kayla, I don't have time for this right now. I need for you to go home."

"I will wait for you." I say taking his hand.

"Oh, you have to be kidding me! Kayla, get out. You got your fuck. Now go!" Luke yells. "Nick, what the hell are you doing- trying to make things worse than they already are?" Luke yells impatiently.

"Shut up, Luke, this has nothing to do with you." I say to him looking back at Nick.

"You know what you have to do, Nick. It is only going to be worse later if you don't, especially for her, and you know it."

"Kayla, go home."Nick said assuredly.

Staring into his unrelenting eyes, "Am I never going to be more important than your business?"

"What is wrong with you? You know who I am! You know what my life is!" Nick yells at me. "You need to grow up and realize that I can't be your boyfriend. I don't want to be your boyfriend, Kayla." He gulps, looking away from me. "I will fuck you anytime you want, but I am not doing this."

"I don't believe you. If you don't care about me then why were you there last night?" I cringe wanting to reach out for him.

"Curiosity, sweetheart, nothing more. I wanted to fuck you. What can I say? You're a great fuck." He says trying to look into my eyes but avoiding them somehow.

"Nick, you are such a liar. But, you know what? Have it your way. Last night was nothing. Good, I'm glad we have a clear understanding now. Now, I can move on with Brady and give him what he has been wanting from me."

"Good for you. About time you got it." Nick says staring at the floor.

"Oh, I got it! Enjoy your meeting I am going to go shop for something sexy and lacy for my date with Brady tonight. He is so sweet and goes out of his way to make me feel wanted. Why I ever …"

Nick rushes at me, "Yes, why did you ever? You should have known better. I am not your Prince Charming, Kayla!" Snarling he throws the keys to my car on the table next to me, "If it's still sitting there when I leave, I am going to blow it up. So, I would take it if I were you." He leaves me without another word. I chase after him, yelling at him to never come near me again. I want to make him as insane as I feel, so I make sure he understands clearly my intentions with Brady for our date tonight- not that he seems to care. He ignores me meeting with Luke and making jokes to drown me out. They both leave me laughing and dismissing my every attempt to get Nick to talk to me. The frustration only makes me angrier and more determined to rid him of my life.

∞

*I*t took most of the afternoon to get myself together, but I am determined to see Brady tonight and get Nick as far out of my mind as possible. However, when Brady picks me up he glares at me suspiciously. "So, there were two men brutally attacked less than a block from your restaurant last night." Brady asked knowingly.

"Really? That's terrible." I said pretending to be interested in what's outside my window.

"Uh huh, I don't suppose you know anything about that, do you?"

"No. They didn't know who attacked them?" I asked with a shrug of my shoulders but ignoring his awkward glare.

"They said a woman who works at the restaurant, coaxed them out of their car and then her and her boyfriend beat them up and stole their money. They are accusing you and Jayzon of it." I jump to say something but quickly catch myself and turn to stare out the window again. "You got something to say?" He asks and I shake my head in response. "Of course, you don't. Anyway they suddenly have disappeared. Their neighbors say they up and moved in the middle of the night, they said they do that often. Although I don't know how they would know that, since they could barely get their names right, or why two men would move and leave everything they own behind." Brady pauses glancing my way. "Jayzon says he never even saw you last night, is that true?" Taking a deep breath I realize the mess I am in and nod, "Okay, well I guess there is nothing to discuss then."

"Where are we going?" I asked to change the subject.

"I am making you dinner at my place." He says glancing my way out of the corners of his eyes.

"Oh ..." Tensing up, I walk into his place curling around myself protectively.

"Dance with me ..." Brady asked taking my hand. He begins kissing my neck and I tense up. "I'm not going to hurt you, so relax please. You have had sex before, right?"

"Once or twice." I smile as he cradles me closer and kisses me passionately. It all feels so urgent and not at all right. I push away from him and immediately feel guilty when I see his face.

"Can you give me a moment? Let me freshen up for a second?" I asked following his finger to the direction of the bathroom. The mirror does me no favors as I stare into it hoping to see someone other than myself. *You need to do this. He is better for you. He is good for you. Stop dwelling on who isn't and think about who he is.* Taking in a deep breath, I walk out and pass his bedroom. Taking a curious step inside, I look around. *It's certainly better than most men's bedrooms.*

Wandering my finger over the pillows on the bed, I fumble through the books on the backboard and pull out one that I know well. *I can't believe a man would read this. He must have had a serious girlfriend at one point.* I thumb through the pages and a picture falls out. I pick it up and as the image of the couple become clear, I feel the knife penetrating into my back.

"I was wondering where you were. Are you getting a head start on me?" Brady said walking up behind me.

"Who is this?" I asked holding the picture up in front of him.

He snatches the picture out of my hand, "None of your business." Brady turns back around with an apologetic expression, "Old girlfriend. I guess I am still sensitive about her, sorry."

"I have no doubt that you are, considering what Claire did." I eye Brady as he takes on a different demeanor. "I thought you were different, but you are no better than any of them. You are just trying to get back at him."

"I don't know what you are talking about." Brady said.

"I thought Nick had something to do with my sister's death, so I was checking in with Claire almost every day, hoping to hear something about the case against him. She promised she was going to get him, but she didn't quite make it. I knew she was engaged but I never knew to whom or I just didn't care to know. I was so focused on getting Nick that I lost myself in the mission. It is not my fault she let him fuck her the way he did. Nick has a way of getting women to do whatever he wants."

"Except for you. You left him. You said no and now he follows you around like a lost puppy dog. I don't know if that bastard has a heart, but if he does, then you're breaking it. So, yes, I wanted to help that along."

"By dating me? I don't think that bothers him as much as you think." I said.

"Oh it does- but simply dating you was not my ultimate goal." Brady uncovers a camera and looks back at me. "I had plans to record us and send it to him just like he did with Claire. I won't apologize for it. I hate him."

"And so you hate me? What did I do?" I asked as he tries to maintain his assured stature.

"You mean besides cheating on me with him." He eyes me with a sinister glare.

"I didn't know that we ..."

"Fuck you." He said shaking his head at me. "No matter what we are, you're not exactly an innocent victim. You volunteered yourself up to him, worked for him. Hell, you're the one that was sleeping with his brother- causing that whole mess. They are both dirty as hell and there is nothing you can say that will convince me you didn't know. You honestly expect me to believe that you are some sweet innocent thing who is going to come here after you fuck him?" Brady walks around me confidently as I realize my mistake was bigger than I had anticipated. "Hell, you are probably sleeping with Daniels, too. No wonder he freaked out about the flowers. You are something else, Lady. Trying to control the two biggest players in this city."

"I don't know what you are talking about. I don't know anything about either of them being into anything illegal. Neither of them has ever been arrested for anything or even brought in, that I am aware of."

Brady laughs, "Okay I will give you that Daniels has managed to stay out of jail but that dumbass is not nearly as clean as Jayzon. Daniels has left a mess everywhere, blatantly rubbing it in our face that we can't get to him. Hell, you even pulled your complaint against him." He eyes me harshly as he grasps his head with a heavy hand. "Ever since you came along, those two have gone toe to toe constantly. I'm not sure when it is going to end but I am sure one of them is going to be dead before it does. Yesterday was interesting. Whatever went down caused Daniel's to be in a real bad mood all-day. However, Jayzon was out celebrating with his boys so I assume he must have taken a huge upper hand on his brother." Brady turns to face me with a harsh laugh, "Yet despite everything they have going on, they both have been following you around like crazy men. I have never seen anything like it. We would sit outside the restaurant to watch you and we would get to watch both of them at the same time. I only wish we had been there last night." He says eyeing me suspiciously. "You are playing them both- and me for that matter- except I know what you're doing, so you can stop the act."

"Playing them? By working shit hours at a rundown restaurant? By letting Connor punch me in the face? What sense does that make?"

"Maybe because if you're not working for either, then they both have something to gain- bragging rights. You're their prize, Kayla. Hell, keep it up and they will probably kill each other off for you.

Then you will have both their operations to run." Brady said with pride.

"You know what, Brady, you have pinned up so much frustration and hate for Claire that it has blinded you to everything, or shall I say, anyone else. I can't believe I let myself care about you. You're too bitter for anyone to love." I said grabbing my purse.

"Where are you going? To find another fool to take advantage of?"

"Fuck you! You don't know anything about me!" I yell at him.

"I know that you are more devious than the two brothers. I suspect we will be after you one day, but maybe you can help change my mind about that. I was looking forward to knowing what makes you so good in bed that you have turned these two into your personal marionettes." Brady said relaxing into a chair. "We could make that video together. I'm sure it would drive Jayzon crazy enough to come after me. Hell, probably Daniels too and then I can take them both down and leave you with everything. Think about it, a much easier plan and way more rewarding. Not to add- a whole hell of lot more fun for both of us."

"Seek help, Brady. You really need it because now you have become worse than the man you hate." I said before storming out the door to get a cab, directing him to go to the club where I know Nick will be.

ᖇᔦ

"**E**xie, where is Nick?" I asked to her sudden shocked expression.

"What are you doing here? I thought you were on a date with that hot detective?"

"Where is Nick?" I asked again with a sharp tone.

"Okay. The over privileged co-eds over there have been battling one another for his attention for the last couple of hours. The winner just followed him into his office." Exie said shaking her head in disgust.

"Thanks," I said as I make my way quickly to the back.

"Kayla, ummm… Nick is in a meeting right now." Luke began explaining in his usual sarcastic way.

"Get out of my way, Luke. I know what kind of meeting he is in right now and I don't care." Luke laughs with a nod and kindly steps out of my way. Without even thinking, I barge into his office, interrupting the slut on her knees. "I want to talk to you."

"What the fuck? Kayla? I am a little busy right now." Nick pats the girls head and she continues blowing him, while he smiles at me. "If you want to join us …"

"I need to talk to you and I am not waiting another second." I demand.

"I thought you were busy getting laid by your new boyfriend. Is he here too?"

"Nick!" He finally looks at me and notices my anguish, "I need to talk to you." I said beginning to tear up.

Nick pushes the girl away from him, "Get dressed and get out." He says to her as he pulls away and puts his pants back in order.

"But …" The girl starts, but stops when Nick glances at her once. She frustratingly puts her clothes back on. "I will be here for another couple of hours." She said before huffing in my face and leaving.

"Sorry to interrupt." I said.

"Not a big deal. She wasn't that good anyway." He walks towards me and lifts my chin so he can see into my watery eyes. "Did he do something to you?"

"He was out to get you, Nick." His confusion is obvious. "You screwed his fiancé, the one that went undercover to try to get information. You remember, you made that video and sent it out to all his friends." Nick seems surprised that I know about it. "Yes, I know about it. I knew her. She promised to get you for me but she failed. So, because of that, her fiancé thought that it would be fun to return the favor …" Nick's eyes become hardened and black. "He was ready for me."

"You didn't …" Nick asked caressing my arm. I shake my head. "I'm sorry, if I had known I would have said something to you but at least you figured it out before."

"You don't get it! Every time I try to have something normal, it gets ruined by you. I am paying for all your bad deeds, Nick."

"What do you want me to do, Kayla?"

"Why have you been watching me?" I asked causing his expression to suddenly change.

Nick turns away from me, "I haven't."

"Yes you have and I want to know why." I demanded.

"I can't help you, sorry." Nick said making himself a drink.

"Damn it, Nick! Why won't you tell me why you feel you have to protect me? Do you feel guilty about Braylin?" I asked as he shakes his head with a smirk. "Then why? Why are you always there? Why do you watch me so closely? Why are you leaving stuffed animals on my door step?" I said as he laughs. "Why do you take me to a place you keep secret from everyone else?"

"What do you want from me, Kayla? You left me. I can't protect you and I am not trying to protect you anymore. I certainly can't keep you from dating every asshole out there that has a grudge against me." Nick turns towards me with a sarcastic smile, "You're dreaming, Princess, and as much as I enjoy fucking you, I am not going to go out of my way for you."

His coldness is obviously forced and I am quickly losing my will to fight him. "All I want to know is what you want from me." I plead, pressing my eyes closed tight to fight the tears that begin to trickle down my face.

Within seconds he has me in his arms and I rest easily against his chest feeling the warmth I have craved since I left him. "I want you to come home with me." He says cradling me and sighing as he leans his head against mine. "Come home with me, Kayla. I want you ... back in my bed, my house ... my life."

"Why? Why Nick?"

"I want you, I want to feel you next to me when I sleep. I sleep better ... I don't know."

"And Luke? What happened earlier today?"

"That was ... he was wrong. You could have easily told Simone everything tonight but you didn't, did you?" He asked knowing the answer to the question. "Luke wanted me to kill you."

"Why didn't you?" He ignores my questions with a cringing groan. I push away from him and focus in on his eyes, searching for the understanding I so desperately need. "You know Brady thinks that I am playing you and Connor both. That I am after your money. That somehow I have control over you two and am playing you against each other." Nick laughs. "He said things have heated up between you two since I have come into the picture. Now, I know I don't have control over either of you but I wonder if maybe Brady is right. Am I a bragging right?"

"That's ridiculous! Connor didn't care anything about you until ..."

"Until what? Until you did? That's it, Nick, that's all I am, is an interest? A hobby for you?" He shakes his head exhaling. "No, then what am I?"

"Why does it matter? I enjoy being with you! I want you to come home with me now. I want you right now. Hell, I was barely hard with that slut's mouth around my dick, until you walked into the room. I miss you. Do you need much more than that?"

"Yes! Yes I do. I deserve more than that." I take his face in my hands and look straight into his black eyes. "I love you, Nick." I said to his obvious shock. "I love you and I hate that I do. I am not sure I am ever going to be able to get over it but I can't live with you knowing that you don't feel the same way. It hurts way too much." Taking a deep breath I stand on my toes and reach up to kiss him on the lips. "Good-bye, Nick."

"Where are you going?"

"To find a new life." I replied over my shoulder, knowing better than to look at his face.

"Kayla! Kayla, come back here." Nick grabs hold of my arm as I leave his office. "Where are you going to go?"

"Somewhere where they don't know you and don't care who you are, so maybe I can forget you."

"Kayla, just … just spend tonight with me."

"I keep waiting for you to say it but you won't. That's all I want from you." I plead with him.

"What? What do you want me to say? That I messed up? That I was a jerk for yelling at you? I was. I didn't want you to leave in the first place. I listened to Luke telling me that you were going to cause problems. I didn't like them bringing you in and making you a part of what I do. I wanted you to be separated from that, protected somehow from that part of my life. I'm not sure how I fooled myself into thinking that you could be."

"And now you think that it can be different?" I asked knowing that it can't be.

"No, but now I know I can trust you."

"That's not what I meant, Nick." The tears flow rapidly and there is nothing I can do about it. "Good-bye." I pull my arm away from him and run out the door. I don't even stop for Exie. *I just want to go home and think and pack.*

"Kayla!" Nick yells running out the door after me. "Let me drive you home or at least … Tanner drive you. Please." I nod and

Nick waves over Tanner. "Don't leave tonight, that's all I ask. Sleep on it and then talk to me about it tomorrow. Give me a chance to think." Nick takes my hand and slips my shell ring from the island into my hand. "Please." His eyes saddened and pleading for the first time I have ever seen. "Please, Kayla."

"Okay. Tomorrow then." I said. He helps me into the car and kisses me gently on the lips holding my head against his with a heavy breath before shutting the door and sending me away.

CB80

*M*y eyes are still swollen as I sit on my bed thinking of him. I can't believe he had this ring. I assumed he threw it out. I didn't want to look at it ever again, that's why I left it. *Maybe I do mean something more to him. If he has that other ring ... I don't think I can wait until tomorrow. I need to see him now.* With a feeling of exhilaration, I jump into the shower and make myself up before stepping into an outfit that I am sure he will love. I throw on my coat, grab my shell ring and race out the door, while dialing Nick's cell. *Answer Nick. Answer.....*

As soon as I step out the door, someone takes my phone from my hand. "Where are you going, Kayla?"

"Dan ... Connor?"

"Hi, Baby." Connor said blocking my exit.

"I have to be somewhere. I don't have time to talk right now." I said trying to get around him.

"I think you have time for me."

"I don't have time right now. I am running late as it is. How about we get together tomorrow- for lunch or something?" I said as I take notice of his men scattering around my house.

"Nick's not here? Hmm, oh well. I assume you're running off to meet him? Tell me where and I will let you go."

"No, I have been seeing someone new and I ..." Connor grabs my arm and shoves me up against the wall.

"I saw him bring you home. I know you went to the club to see Nick. Your cop friend is on the other side of town with his buddies, flirting with some other girls. So, tell me- where are you going to meet him?"

"Let go of me, Connor. I know all about you and Nick and I don't want anything to do with either of you."

"Well, it's a little late for that now, isn't it?" Connor jerks me towards two of his men, I get out a single scream before they shut me up.

CRBO

I am locked in this room with no way out, while the voices outside decide my fate. When the door finally opens, Connor comes in with a smile. "I tell you what, since I have a soft spot for you, I will give you a choice. You can either work for me or you can die."

"Doing what?" I asked.

"Whom actually. You know the work well and you are good at it. I haven't had a good whore since your sister."

"Braylin worked for you?" I asked tensing up.

"She was sweet. Give her a little something to pump her up and she was a gold mine."

"You killed her?"

Connor laughs, "Kill her? Are you kidding? With as much money as she made me? The girl was the life of the party. She did everything that was asked of her. Gang bangs, video, hell, I even had her on a web cam for a few months until she left and killed herself. Stupid whore. If she wasn't dead already, I would have killed her. I didn't even know she had a sister until I read about her death. I tried to find you but Nicholas caused a bunch of problems for me at the time and my intentions became distracted ... I didn't think much about it until I saw you that night at the old blue bloods party. You look similar to your sister but better for some reason. I knew as soon as I saw you that Nick must have seen it too. I wasn't real sure how interested he was in you until I sent Harvey after you, and boy, did he come running." He said rubbing my bare leg. I jerk it away from him and he forms an honest expression. "I have a little movie I would like to make with you."

"Go to hell!"

"That's not the answer I am looking for. Now, I can help you get more in the mood. I have whatever you need." I shake my head as I back away from him. "I have the clothes that you will need to wear and I already have your costars setup." He becomes excited as he raises his hands up, "It is going to be great. An innocent young girl gets taken for a night of sex with a group of ... how you would describe them ... undesirable men."

"No! I prefer you kill me." I yell.

125

"Don't worry. You will probably die during."

"Because of Nick!"

"Just make sure you scream a lot … for Nick." He smiles huge.

"Connor, please. Nick and I have nothing to do with each other anymore. He doesn't care about me at all. He had some girl blowing him in his office when I went to see him." I begin to ramble whatever comes to my mind.

"You know how to save yourself?" I shake my head. "I want HIM!" He yells waiting for me to say something. "You have nothing to say? I know you can get him to come to you … alone even. Call him and tell him you want to see him. Give me him and I will set you free."

"You want to kill your own brother?"

Connor walks over to me and jerks me by my hair closer to him. "No, I want to torture him and then kill him."

"No. No, I won't help you. Do what you want to me, but I won't help you." Connor throws me to the ground.

"I have business to take care of tonight. I will see you tomorrow for your big debut." Connor leaves locking me in the room. I do everything I can to find a way out while he is gone. After hours of trying, I realize my only way out is the way I came in. I take apart the room to form some kind of weapon that I hope will allow me enough time to get to daylight. When I hear someone coming, I take hold of my weapon and start swinging as soon as the guard comes in with my food. I manage a few good hits and run. Unfortunately, I am only able to reach the next locked door before another man comes in and takes hold of me. I am quickly returned to my prison and forced to watch a needle pierce into my skin. Within minutes, I am falling-out of my own body and am subdued. They release my restraints and leave me alone again until Connor comes in screaming at me. "That fucking punk screwed me AGAIN! I should kill you and leave your dead body on his doorstep!" Connor yells stomping towards me and gripping me by the back of my neck, "I am sick of this! You are going to help me get him whether you want to or not. He cares for you, doesn't he?" I shake my head as a smile forms on his face. "Yes he does. I saw him. I thought he was worried you would turn on him at first, but no, he was looking out for you. I wonder how far he would go to save your life. I don't know. You tell me, Kayla, would he give his own life up for yours?" Connor lets go of me, letting me fall into the floor.

Shaking my head as best I can, I begin to cry exhaustively as I crawl to him, "No, no, Connor, please ..."

"You're in love with him too, aren't you? How beautiful. As long as I live I will never understand the hold he has over women. You know our father was much the same. My mother never got over him. Even after she married my stepfather, she continued to sneak out to him." Connor calls in some men, "Prepare her for our guests. Take some nice pictures and send out a notice to our poker participants that we will be offering up a new prize to the biggest winner." I am handled roughly as I fight the men sent in to take hold of me. "Be careful with our prize. Give her something more if you need to make her more receptive but don't damage her." Connor said with a callous tone.

As Connor begins to leave, I kick the man in front of me and force my way to Connor. Stretching up onto my toes, I lock eyes with him, "Nick is going to come for me and he is going to kill you." I said happily.

"Sweetheart, I am counting on him coming to get you but he is going to be the one that dies. Now, you won't mind if I turn the heat off, do you? The bill is becoming a bit too much these days. I will send in the boys for another dose of some relaxant for you in the meantime." Connor kisses me joyfully.

The room turns frigid. I have to resort to curling up in the one blanket in the room, while I battle the drug spreading though my veins.

~17~
NICK

*T*he slut that was sucking my dick earlier refuses to give up. She keeps coming at me and finally succeeds in breaking my cell when she grabs for it to get my attention. Dwayne removes her quickly from my sight before I do something I might regret. As soon as Tanner comes back, I intend to go home- by myself. I have to fight my urge to tell him to take me back to her house, but I know she needs some space right now. *She's upset, that's all. She will be better tomorrow.* Tomorrow I can talk to her and get her to come back. I don't know why she is so difficult for me to deal with, she drives me insane- not that she hasn't done that since the first day I saw her: that shy, young girl with the big ugly old glasses and oversized clothing. I don't even remember why I went into the diner that day. Luke was having a craving of some sort. Harvey had us running constantly for him at the time, we had just finished a long night and wanted to go somewhere out of sight of Harvey so we could discuss our plans to take over his business. I was barely in my twenties and already thinking I was too good to be working for someone else. *That's probably why he tried to kill me.* What I do remember is being deep into conversation and arguing about some small, irrelevant detail and looked away long enough to see her walk in and say hi to her sister. Nothing about the exchange was out of the ordinary, except her reaction to when her sister handed her a small package. She instantly beamed when she pulled out a book. I thought it must be some special edition or the latest craze for young girls, something to make her so excited. She sat down at the table next to us and I watched her, trying to read the cover to see what she was so interested in. It was nothing special. It barely even had a binding it was so old and beat up. I thought it strange but it didn't interest me much more than that, except she never even looked up and I waited for her to. Ego I guess but she never bothered to look at me. I even got up and borrowed the salt and then the pepper. She handed them over to me without a glance in my direction. I touched her hand in our last exchange, stroking it with my thumb but it seemed to give me more of a rush than it did her. I later figured out the waitress was her sister, Braylin and I talked to her hoping that maybe the book-girl would look up, but all it did was cause Braylin to gush over me. I couldn't get the book-girl out of my mind. I went back to the restaurant and watched her confidently read through her books with no attention to anyone, not even the jocks that were determined to try to make her cry. They teased her outdated and ill-fitted clothes and her horrible glasses, but not until they would try to take her book would she pay them any mind. Her reaction was not to cry or beg for her book back, she would do nothing more than pull out another and begin reading. She was fascinating to me. I found myself doing whatever I could to learn about her. I started dating Braylin because I enjoyed hearing about Kayla. I would visit Braylin to see Kayla, to be near her. Not that she paid attention to me at all. I was like a ghost in their house or so I thought. Kayla often screamed out from nightmares and Braylin would typically run to her, but some nights Braylin would sleep too deeply, worn out from long nights of sex. I always heard her though. Once I was sure Braylin was not getting up, I would go to her. I wouldn't wake her up like Braylin. I would simply adjust her fallen blankets back over her, remove some hair from her face, and go back to bed. It helped all the same, she would stop crying and be peaceful again. I thought nothing of it. She was never awake and it was nothing to me, until that one night I heard her whimpering and went to do the same routine. However, when I pulled the blanket back up over her, she moved. I thought she had woken up.

Staring at her, she rolled over and opened her beautiful green eyes to me, "I knew you would come." She said.

"What?" I whispered still unsure if she was talking to me.

"You always come and save me. Always." She smiled her beautiful smile, still dazed and rolled over taking my hand with her.

"Kayla." I whispered her name for the first time ever. It felt strange to do so. "Kayla, I need to go."

"Don't leave me. I need you." She said drifting off to some world I was unfamiliar with. *Maybe I will sit with her for a few minutes and wait until she is sound asleep before pulling my hand away from her.* However, she seemed to sense my desire to retreat and rolled over onto my chest. My emotions went into an immediate battle with each other. My legs quivered to run, my heart pounded out of my chest, and my hands trembled as I tried to remove her. She began to cry and held onto me tighter, "Help me. Help me." She pleaded over and over with me or whomever she was dreaming about.

"Help you from whom?" I asked brushing her hair from her face.

"The king." She said and I bit my tongue to keep from laughing.

"The king, huh? Well, he is evil. How can I help you?"

"I don't know. You're the Prince." She said with a huff.

I held my laugh in with my free hand until I regained my composure. "Oh, so I am. Well then, Princess, will you runaway with me? Far away from the evil king so we can be together? Happily ever after." I smiled watching her become excited by my proposal. I found myself making up a story of how we were going to fight the king off and how I was going to rescue her so we could be together forever. The more she smiled and rested closer against me, the more I wanted the story to go on. In the end I told her that we were going to get married and then out of nowhere she leaned up and kissed me lightly on the lips. The softest, sweetest lips I had ever tasted. All I could do was stare at her as she opened her beautiful green eyes to me.

"Do you love me?" She said gripping my hand.

"Yes." I said staring into her sleepy eyes as she smiled beautifully at me.

"I love you too." Kayla said making me weak all over. She laid back down on my chest and drifted further away. Within a few minutes, she was silent and peaceful again. I curled her safely back into her bed and kissed her cheek with a heaviness in my chest.

All I could think was how sweet and innocent she looked, just like a young princess. Too bad for her that I was far from being Prince Charming. I left Kayla and went back to bed with Braylin but didn't sleep at all. Early the next morning, I told Braylin that we couldn't see each other anymore. She cried and begged me to stay, doing everything she could to please me to make me change my mind. I eventually gave in and had sex with her for the last time, leaving her while she laid in her bed recovering. I walked out of her room quickly only to come face-to-face with Kayla. She was shyly waiting for us to finish in the hallway and looked me in the eyes for the first time ever, awake at least. It seemed like an eternity that we stood there but a second is all it could have been because I couldn't get out of there fast enough.

Such a fucked up thing to do. She was so young but I had some kind of fantasy that when she finished school, I could dump her sister and date her. Once I realized my mistake, I tried to stay as far away from Braylin as possible, hoping she would get it together and take care of Kayla. Kayla was almost seventeen, if Braylin could have only held out for another year, Kayla would have been off to college- or so I had hoped. *Damn I don't know what I was thinking!* When Luke told me what had happened, I did everything I could to find her again. I just wanted to make sure she was okay. I wanted ... I wanted to bring her home with me and take care of her like she deserved. Her stepfather deserved to die and I have no regrets for killing him. I only wish I could have stayed away from Braylin and maybe my brother would never have found her. He has an obsession of seeking out the women I become involved with. I think over the years he has learned my type even better than I have.

The first time I saw her in my club, I had to fight the urge to run to her. It only took a few seconds for me to realize why she was there and I had hoped she would kill me if that would help her. I didn't want her there but I also didn't want my brother to find her, so I did whatever possible to keep her from leaving. No matter how hard it was to give her what she wanted. I couldn't keep her away from the club and I couldn't scare her away from prostituting. And at the first chance I got to make her mine, I did. Then, I screwed it up and now I have no idea how to make it work or what to say to keep her here. I don't ever show feelings for anyone- it's dangerous for me and for them. It has already cost her so much.

I lie awake all-night, thinking of what I can say to her, what I can do to keep her without giving up too much of myself. She makes me work for it like no one else ever has. When morning comes, I get up still unsure of what I am going to say. I pass Tanner, grabbing my new cell from his hand, and eagerly jump into my own car to drive to Kayla's. Not something I should do, but I want to be alone with her. I want to make her feel comfortable enough to feel as if I am being as honest as possible with her and hopefully stay with me. Noticing her car, but not Exie's, I quickly scan the area and I feel comfortable to approach the house. I knock on the door but no answer. After checking the back of the house, I leave her a note and walk back to my car stopping when I take notice of the shell ring I gave her back last night. Bending down slowly, I pick it up and hope it isn't a sign that she is done listening to me. I get back into my car and call her cell but it goes straight to voicemail. After leaving her a message, I call her a few more times throughout the day, growing more anxious with each call. I fear that she has gone and there is nothing I can or will do about it. I'm not going to force her to stay and be with me, no matter how much I want her too.

CREO

"What's wrong with you today?" Luke asks with his usual lack of boundaries.

"Nothing." I said.

"Nothing ... right. Did you talk to Kayla?" He presses as I roll my eyes towards him but roll them quickly away. "Oh, so she skipped town on you, huh? Well, don't worry you will have ten others fighting to get your attention tonight."

"I don't want them." I mumble.

"What was that?" He asked but I shake my head dismissing the conversation. "You know there is a new girl at the club: young, blond, and hot. Your favorite."

"When did I ever say blond is my favorite?" I snap.

"Damn, you are in a shit mood today. Is there anything or anyone that can bring you out of it?" Luke snaps back.

"We have work to do." I said with a harsh tone.

"That's right. And that alone should put you in an excellent mood. We are about to take another piece of your brother's empire here. He doesn't have much left, the walls are closing in on him, and you're the one pushing them in. You can't tell me that you are not incredibly stoked about that." Luke jumps around in some form of a dance.

"I am happy about that." I try to say with some optimism.

"Wow, that was convincing. I think I will slit my wrists now." I eye him with a disgusted expression and the fool finally shuts up allowing us to work out the final details of taking Connor down. We are again getting help from his so-called wife who has wanted to leave him for years. At this point, she would rather die than live another second with him. She will get her wish if he ever finds out she is helping us take him down piece by piece.

CREO

Everything goes as planned and I should be on top of the world, but nothing lessons my thoughts of her. I plan on meeting the boys at the club after I stop by Kayla's one more time. I don't know why I did, the stop only depresses me more. No one is around and even though my note is missing, she is still not calling me. Tanner gives me a look of sympathy as we head to the club. I desperately crave a drink, something, or anything to take my mind off her.

"You should go find her." Tanner said.

"I can't do that and don't you dare ask me why." I said.

"You are a stubborn, young fool." Tanner mumbles.

"And you are an old fool."

"Two of a kind, aren't we?" Tanner said with his usual trouble-free smile. His blatant attempt to convince me not to make the mistakes he made growing up is ridiculous. Tanner's problems were more about his drinking not because of some woman that left him. She left him because he was a drunk and if he doesn't keep up with his AA meetings he will be out of a job too. I haven't been drunk since I was eighteen ... *damn, no the last time was with her.* I don't let myself become vulnerable, something Harvey always taught me. Drugs, drinking to excess only make you stupid and vulnerable to your own mistakes. I only felt safe enough to let go when I was away with her. Not that I was nearly as drunk as she was. I was at least sober enough to bribe the priest into marrying us that late at night. As the memories of her laugh and bright eyes cause me to smile, I pull out the ring she gave me and slip it on again while I play with hers. *I am still not sure if that paperwork was legal, but it felt perfect at the time. Feeling like a Prince, feeling like her Prince Charming, was the highlight of my time with her.*

The club is busy tonight and the new girl makes herself known to me as soon as I walk in the door. Hard to get she is not and she quickly gets on my nerves. I strongly encourage her to go bother someone else and then I down a couple of drinks to take the edge off. As I sit back and consider leaving so I can feel sorry for myself in the privacy and safety of my own home, I notice Exie inching her way slowly towards me through the bottom of my glass. *I am in no mood to talk to her tonight.* As hard as I try to ignore her, she continues moving closer. She is obviously intent on speaking with me about something. For her sake, I sure as hell hope it is not about Kayla. Exie inches towards my side and Dwayne takes hold of her before she can open her mouth.

"Now isn't a good time," Dwayne said.

"But ..." Exie said to him.

"It is not a good time." He stresses as he tries to drag her away from me.

Before I can relax, Exie makes a mad dash at me and grabs hold of my arm. "Nick, please! I just want to ask you about Kayla."

"I don't want to talk about her!" I seethe in her direction.

"Nick, please, at least tell her to call me or let me know somehow that she is okay ..." She cries as Dwayne begins to pull her away.

I hold up my hand to stop him as I stare daggers into her, "What are you talking about? I don't know where she is."

Exie's face pales, "Her text said she was going to see you." Exie cries reaching hysterics.

Taking hold of her, I guide her back to the office and try to calm her down. "When did she send a text, Exie? I haven't seen her since she left here the other night."

"The same night. I didn't get home until the next afternoon, so I didn't think anything about it. I wasn't surprised that she was with you again, but I called her that night to let her know I wouldn't be coming home. I left a message for her and even sent her a text. I was worried at first that she never called me back, but I just assumed she was too caught up in you. But then ..." Exie lifts out her hand and hands me Kayla's phone. "When I left for work tonight, I heard it beeping in the bushes."

Taking Kayla's phone, I search for her last outgoing call which was to me. "You haven't heard from her at all?" Exie shakes her head. "She said she was thinking about moving away. Maybe she left this behind to start fresh?"

Exie expression pains, "No, she wouldn't leave without saying good-bye and she certainly would not leave everything she owns behind. Even her books are still stacked up neatly on their shelves and her pictures of her sister are still on her nightstand. She wouldn't leave any of that, Nick."

"Go back to work and let me know if you hear anything." I said.

"You are going to do something ... you are going to look for her right? You have to find her." She pleads with me gripping my arms as if I am going to run away from her.

I wrap my arms around her to try to calm her down, "Don't worry. I am going to do whatever it takes to find her."

"What if someone has done something horrible to her?"

Tensing up, I feel the darkness taking me over, "I will rip their throat out."

~18~
NICK

I only know one person that might have some idea where Kayla is, but as we pull up to the bar even Luke looks nervous. I never thought I would willingly go into this place but I know he is here. Simone is always here. With a deep breath, I force myself through the doors. The place is disgusting and the people aren't much better by this time of night. *He wonders why his fiancé was excited by me. What woman in her right mind would want to come here?*

Suddenly the whole room turns our way and goes silent. "This is insane, Nick, let's go." Luke said tugging at my jacket.

"One second, I know he is in here." Standing tall and defiant I make my way around the stiff room searching for him. Nearing the back, I finally spot him showing some young women how to throw darts. *Darts? Ever heard of dinner and dancing, jackass?* I walk up behind him and wait as the girls turn and smile wide at me. Stunned by their sudden disinterest in him, Simone turns with an instant scowl on his face. "Simone." I acknowledge.

"What the hell are you doing here?" Simone asked while sending the girls away with money. I stop them both and give them each a hundred before sending them back on their way. "So, you're here to try to outdo me? Make me look bad? Pay me back for your little girlfriend? It's not like anything happened between us." He said taking a drink of his beer.

"I know that. She came to see me after." I said focusing on him as Luke continues to scan room.

"Then what's this visit about?" He asked watching Luke beside me.

"I want to know if you have seen her since. Has one of your people picked her up again?"

"One of my people? What are you asking me? Has she made some deal to talk about you and your friends?" Simone asks, tensing up.

135

"She doesn't know anything to talk about, but yes, I want to know if she has been picked up because you think she knows something."

"No, she wasn't to cooperative the first time and we aren't into wasting our time. So, unless she comes to us then …"

"But you have been watching her, right?" I asked.

Nodding reluctantly, "Okay, yes we have kept an eye on her. She is playing both sides."

"Both sides of what?" I ask, confused by his statement.

Simone laughs, "Oh, Jayzon, what makes me happy is that a woman has gotten the best of you. We watched her long enough to realize that you and your brother both have an interest in her."

"She has nothing to do with my brother. She didn't know who he was when she was involved with him. She knows better now."

"Really? Then why is it both you and your brother watch her leave work every night and get on the bus? Either one or both of you are worried about something she knows. Nonetheless, I think you both are being played by the same woman and are too caught up in her to notice."

"Connor was watching Kayla?" I asked feeling the sudden dread sink into my veins.

"Every night we were there, he was there and you, of course, were always there somewhere." Luke stares at me out of the corner of his eyes. "Oh, so no one knew you were there? Wow, Jayzon, at least your brother had people with him. I assumed you had people hiding somewhere. If we hadn't of been there, he could have taken you out easily. You must be out of your mind for her."

"Stupid son of a bitch," Luke mumbles under his breath.

"I need to know where she is." I asked ignoring Luke's grumbling.

Simone sits back with a contorted expression, "Where she is? You don't know?" I give him a look and he half smiles, "You ever consider that she is hiding from you? Maybe she wised up."

With my worst fears hitting me in the face, "She isn't hiding and she didn't run. She's missing and I need your help looking for her."

Simone stands up to look me in the eyes with his jaw dropped, "Excuse me? Did you just ask me to help YOU? Fuck you! Get the hell out of my bar."

"If you have been watching her, then your people might know what happened to her. She is in trouble, I know it." I said.

"Then get your boys together and find her on your own." Simone says, dismissing me.

"If you help us then we can find her that much quicker and possibly before anything happens to her."

"There is that word again. *Us.* I am not helping you do anything. Tell you what, if she turns up, I will tell her that you're looking for her. Now, get the hell out of here." He said directing me back to the door.

As his buddies surround us, Luke becomes anxious. "Nick, come on." He said tugging at my jacket, pulling me away as I eye Simone.

"If something happens to her." I threaten with a tense jaw.

"If something happens to her, then we are coming to arrest you." Simone yells.

Luke pushes me to the car and I fall in fisting my hands trying to push back the anger and frustration. At least now I know she didn't leave on her own because Simone would have been the first one alerted to her leaving on any plane or bus. Now that I have called his attention to her disappearance, I am positive that he is going to become curious.

"Dwayne said that no one saw her at the bus stations. Her neighbors said they heard a commotion early in the morning but they didn't see anything." Tanner says once we are safely away from the bar.

"Take me home." I said sitting back deep into the car seat.

"Nick, we still have business to take care of," Luke reminds me.

"Can you not handle it without me for once?" I snap at him. Calming myself, "I have some work I need to do on my own."

"No problem. Stop the car Tanner and let me out here." Luke snaps getting out of the car and slamming the door shut with force.

CX80

*P*acing for hours and making constant calls, I finally receive information about a woman that is being sold at a poker game. I have a terrible feeling about it and send Dwayne out to get more information. When he returns, his expression is telling as he shows me a large envelope. "This is what you asked for but I'm not sure you want to see it. It's what you expected." He said.

"What is it?" Luke jumps up to see as I take the envelope and pull out an invitation and photo. The photo is a picture of Kayla, who is being sold at a high stakes poker game. As my hands begin to shake, I read the invitation and realize I only have hours to decide what I am going to do. "Don't you dare consider going to that game!" Luke yells at me with a fierce expression.

"Is this address for the poker game Connor's clubhouse?" I asked knowing the answer.

"Yep." Dwayne said.

"That fucker is trying to set you up, Nick. He is going down and he knows it. He is using her to get to you. Don't let him do it, Nick." Luke said focusing on me as I pace. "She isn't worth it!"

"I need to make a call." I said walking into my study to have some privacy. After my call, I wait- nearly driving Luke to his breaking point as I make my plans carefully.

By the next morning my answer arrives at my front door. Simone stands humbly in front of me, "I guess you got my message." I said wondering why they are here without Kayla.

"I did and we found her." I stare back at the asshole as he watches me closely taking notes of my reaction. "Tell me what you know about her disappearance."

"Is she okay?" I asked ignoring his question.

"Answer my question," He insisted.

"NO! You answer mine." I yell back.

He stands up and I hold my ground, fighting every urge to throw him against the wall and beat his disgusting face off. "No, she's not." I turn away from him and begin texting Luke to search the hospitals. "She's dead." My hands start shaking so violently I drop my phone and have to ball them up into fists to keep from taking out my gun and shooting him. "I don't think I have to ask this, but just for the fun of it, you didn't have anything to do with killing her, did you?" If I turn around I may kill him, so I fist even tighter until my knuckles turn bright white. "She was beaten, possibly raped, tortured horribly, drugged, and then dumped into a gutter naked to freeze death. They must have gotten word that we were looking for her." Out of nowhere, tears form in my eyes and I don't know if it's from the anger or the pain that is suddenly ripping me apart. "I don't think you did it but I know it's because of you. Your brother did it in retaliation, didn't he? He wanted to get back at you for something. If you tell us what that is, maybe we can help you avenge her killer by bringing him up on murder charges."

Unbelievable. These fuckers must think I am stupid. Give myself up to them so they can screw up trying to get Connor. Hell no, the only justice Connor will get is from me. I remain silent trying to hold on until they finally give up and leave.

"Do you gentleman have any more questions because it's obvious we don't have anything that can help you. If we think of anything, we will be glad to give you a call." Dwayne said standing between me and them, shielding me from attacking them.

"This is your last chance to help her, Nick. She loved you and you are just going to stand there like she was nothing? I guess she was wrong about you or maybe I was wrong about her. She was stupid." I turn around and Dwayne grabs hold of me. With a smile, Simone stands up and walks closer to me, "I guess it is hard to care about a whore. I mean, who hasn't she been with? Maybe that's what happened. A John got a little out of hand with her? And a drug addict too?" Dwayne grips me tighter, his size outweighs me by more than a hundred pounds but he's beginning to give against me. "Oh well, I guess it's not a huge loss. Another drug addict whore gone from this world? We are all better off." He waits and his partner finally stands up and nudges him, whispering something. I assume to let him know the line he's crossing and that my attorneys will eat him up if I do not knock his teeth out first. "Fine, we will go. To be honest, I like her or I guess it is more that I *liked* her." I look up at him as he snickers to himself.

I try to climb over Dwayne, "You son of a bitch!" I scream.

"Nick, get a hold of yourself or you're going to end up in jail. He wants you to come at him." Dwayne said.

"Okay. Okay, so I checked in with some of our … well … our inside people and yes, Daniels has her. The good news though is that she is still alive."

My jaw tenses as the understanding becomes clear. *Son of a bitch.* "Why did you say she was dead?"

"Did I? Oh no, I was just joking with you. You can take a joke can't you, Jayzon?" Simone laughs as he foolishly sends his partner out the door.

Breathing heavily, I suck it up and refocus. "And I guess you're here because your so-called inside people won't do anything to get her out?" He turns with a solemn expression. "What the fuck kind of …"

Simone's expression changes dramatically once his partner is gone. Stepping closer to me, "Calm down, I can't help you, I wish I could. If I had known what he was up to, I would have kept an eye on her myself but I don't have control over these people. I am not even supposed to know they exist and I certainly shouldn't be telling you."

"Like I don't fucking know they exist!"

"Will you give me a second?" He yells back at me. "They are expecting to try to get her out once she is sold so they don't have to give up any of their inside people. But I know as well as you do there is no way they will find her again once she is bought. So while I can't help you get her out before that happens, what I can give you is a list of names."

"Names? That's helpful." I say sarcastically.

"Maybe, maybe not. But these are the names of all his men with their backgrounds, addresses, and everything we have on them. Maybe you can talk to a few of them and see if they can help you get her out. I am sure for a price one of them will find a way." He hands me the list. "This is the best I can do for now. All I ask is you don't make me regret giving you this. If there are suddenly a slew of bodies popping up, then I am coming after you."

"If it works out the way I want, then I will find a way to repay you properly." I said making a silent agreement with him.

"By the way, I'm sorry. Not for you, but for her. I was angry after I found out she went back to you and I said some horrible things to her. I was … well, I could see how someone could fall for her easily. Just make sure you get her out safely before you do anything stupid." I nod. "And this conversation never happened." Simone sighs and walks out the door. I call in Luke with Dwayne and begin to make our plans to which Luke reluctantly agrees. Connor is gambling that Kayla can be used to destroy me and I am gambling that I won't get us both killed before I can destroy Connor.

~19~
NICK

I would be kidding myself if I didn't admit that I'm a little nervous. However, this is how I got to where I am: talking people into giving me what I want. It may have taken me some time to perfect the skill, but I rarely have had anyone do something other than what I have asked of them. It is my business, finding out what someone wants and then talking to another to get it for them: a trade of favors, a concierge for the prominent and wealthy. If a senator needs a lady (or ladies) for the night I make sure he has one- or as many as he wishes, in exchange he makes sure my associate wins the bid for the new city project. If I have a friend who needs a certain amount of narcotics, I find out where the next shipment is coming from and either steal it or make a deal for it and sell it to my friend for a small profit. We both make money and neither has to deal with handling the merchandise across the border. I never handle anything directly, I only talk and offer up solutions to problems. In the process I make money for others and even more for myself. In return for my assistance, I expect my favors to be repaid as soon as I ask. Death is common in my business, I have gotten use to it. You have to make sure people understand that you own them and they have no other choice but to do as you ask. It is the beginning stages that are so tricky: before you own them, before they have taken a bite of what you offer them. This is where I have to be at my best, where I have to convince them that I can solve all their problems, all they have to do is ask and, in essence, sell me their soul.

These types of meetings don't happen as often as they used to. I don't need to approach anyone anymore to work for me, because they come to me. This time, I can't wait for them to come to me. My game with Connor has put me in a position that requires me to act fast and precise. I have to know exactly who to choose from the list Simone gave me. I have to find someone high enough, confident enough, and respected enough to pull off what I need him to. Once I have information on everyone on the list I study it until I am sure, and then I make my move personally. It is nothing to send one of my men, usually Luke or Dwayne, to talk to him. But for me to approach him and offer him what I know he wants, then there is no discussion or debate back and forth. It's done and we can move on quicker. I know this man, I have seen him at Connor's side many times and for a long time. Since he was a kid, he has backed Connor and yet Connor still has him picking up his dry cleaning. Connor's wife, Nadia, has all but confirmed that Reginald Blackstone is the man I need to speak too and she has made sure I can safely do that in her home when he brings her a monthly check from Connor. The meeting is unexpected and I know immediately that he is uncomfortable when he enters the room, but I know he is interested because he doesn't leave. I explain what I need from the start and then I ask him what it would take to get him to help me. He is shocked at my honesty and that I don't seem to be trying to double-talk him and coax him into something that he doesn't want to do. I reason that he can secure a better opportunity with me or take his chances with a falling Connor. I believe I am sitting in a powerful seat in Reginald's eyes, but if he knows how important Kayla is to me then I lose this negotiation. I make her a bragging right that I refuse to lose, a final order of business before squashing Connor for good. Looking him in the eyes, I hold out my hand to Reginald and with a nod of acceptance he shakes mine and agrees to my deal. There is much insecurity in trusting someone but trusting someone that owes you nothing is what most would call stupid. So I always make sure to find people I can help somehow, give them a favor with seemingly no expectations. Reginald needs a favor, he just didn't know it until I gave it. The opportunity to stop being someone's errand boy and finally be someone with a say is something a smart man like Reginald has been secretly aspiring too.

CRWD

*W*ith all my boys in place, I stroll into the building appearing to have no fear. As soon as I see him, I am ready to fight. He has no idea what awaits him- *I hope*. "Connor." I say with a subtle smile.

"Nicholas, what a surprise." Connor nods taking inventory of all the corners of the room, where his men stand guard.

With a sharp laugh, "I am sure it is."

"I guess I won't bother asking how you found out about my little game. Or how you got in here. But, I am curious as to where your men are." Connor comments with a smirk.

"They're nearby. I didn't think I needed them. I am only here to play a poker game."

"This is not exactly meant for recreational purposes, Nicholas."

"My money not good enough?" I said pulling out a roll of cash.

"Is that all we are playing for?"

"It doesn't have to be." I eye him waiting for it.

"You want Kayla?"

"Yes, I would like her back. You have stolen a great deal of money from me when you took her. There are some special clients that she handled personally for me."

"Oh please, Nicholas. This has nothing to do with business, although it is nice to see that you do have a heart after all, little brother. I was beginning to think you were too much like our father."

"He only hated you, Connor. You were his least favorite illegitimate child." I said as Connor raises his eyebrows but he quickly realizes that I am not going to divulge any more family secrets tonight.

"Lucky for me, my mother was smart enough to marry up." Connor said with his typical snobbish attitude.

"How is he by the way? Still the most popular one on his cell block? I heard he had a new boyfriend- or should I say boyfriends?" I said as someone brings me the tea I requested when I entered.

"The son of a bitch died, there was a misunderstanding among his friends." Connor said taking a glass of his favorite bourbon.

"Did the broomstick up his ass go too far?" I asked with a smile.

"Let's get to it, Nicholas, I assume since you are here you are willing to do just about anything to get her back. Let's talk about your book of secrets and the details of your operations. I can only imagine who owes you favors." Connor said boldly.

"If I know Kayla is safely set free, I am willing to negotiate a few details."

"Well, you are insane but I will take it. How about we make it a little more interesting though?" Connor waves his hand towards the table, "I will give you a chance to win it all back, including her."

"I am supposed to believe that?" I asked.

"Believe what you want, but we both know I need to make you look bad in front of my associates. So just destroying you is not enough. I need for them to see that I am able to outsmart you and gain the upper hand- despite recent events." He said eyeing me with a twitch that remains from the pain I last inflicted on him. "If I win, I get you kneeling in front of me- surrendering. And if you win, Dear Brother, what is it that you would like besides your precious sweetheart …?"

I get closer to him with a tensed jaw, "I want you. I want you on your knees, begging for me to kill you."

"You didn't come to the right place for that. This is my house, Nicholas. How in the world do you think you are going to get me here and walk out alive?"

"I told you. You're going to beg me to kill you- at least after I beat you in poker." I continue to smile as Connor reluctantly tries to match me.

"I can't wait to have you dead and buried in my backyard, little brother." Connor said eagerly.

While we wait, the other gentlemen arrive in awe, watching me as they whisper among themselves. They send out messages through their phones, presumably to locate my men and see if I am truly vulnerable. I am not convinced that he will give up Kayla, but I am still hopeful she will be able to escape before the action begins. After a few minutes pass, Reginald comes in nearly holding Kayla up. The jackass has dressed her like she is going to a big event in a fancy dress and heels, even going as far to do her hair and makeup. She is so drugged she is barely able to open her eyes. I approach her taking her feverish face in my hands, "Kayla?" I said.

Connor storms toward us and pulls her away from me. "I still own her. In fact, as far as I am concerned she is still part of the winnings. So take a good look, Gentlemen, and put in your bids. Trust me, she is worth the money." Connor said eyeing me with a smile. "This is my game, Nicholas. You want her? You have to win her." Connor places Kayla on display, antagonizing me even more by ripping her dress slit up past her thigh. "There. Now you can get a better idea of what we have to play for." Connor smiles and sits with the other men at the table as they all make jokes about what they would like to do to her.

It is all I can do to stay calm and not kill them all. "Let's play then." I said shedding my jacket and sitting down at the table with

Connor across from me while four other men sit down with us. As time passes, one man gets up to admire Kayla and boasts that she is his prize.

"Well, you know Jack, you're welcome to feel a little more up that dress- get to know her a little more, because I might be willing to take a cash offering for her instead." Connor smiles at me.

"Really? Well then maybe I would like to fold now and take her home so I can enjoy the rest of my night." Jack said as two other men get up to drool over her.

"I wouldn't touch her if I were you." I said without looking their way.

"Excuse me?" Jack said from behind me.

"It would be in your best interest to step away from her." I said as Connor tenses ever so slightly. "I mean unless you have a death wish." I sit back with a smile and the men slowly begin to sit back down silently. I know each of the men well and the sudden tension that is building between Connor and I is causing them to become uncomfortable. If I know them like I think I do, they won't stay in this game much longer. Confidence is my strategy, and it is the only card I need to win this game.

Checking the time, I lean back and smile wide at Connor as the first hour passes. And with that, two men fold and leave barely saying good-bye. Thirty minutes longer and I check my watch again and simply adjust my sleeve and the third throws in his cards and grabs his coat with a wave. Ten minutes passes and I cough and the fourth folds, leaving his coat and running out the door. The deal Connor was planning to make tonight just folded up and I didn't even have to get out of my seat. Walking in here with a boldness that put a fear into each of them makes them believe Connor doesn't have the power to protect them like they thought. If I can make it out of here alive, then I scored each of them as my own business partners and Connor knows that.

"Proud of yourself?" He asked.

"Pretty much." I said folding my cards down on the table.

"That was a lot of money you cost me, but you know that, don't you?"

"Costing you money, Connor, means I make money."

"Not if you're dead." Connor said with intensity.

"You haven't won yet."

"Neither have you, Nicholas."

145

"Oh, I think I have." I said turning over my cards. Connor eyes my royal flush and throws his cards across the room.

Pushing himself from the table, he stands up with a gun pointed at me. "I don't know what you think you have planned but you are going to die before you are able to see it through."

"Sit down, Connor, before you hurt yourself. Come on, let's play another game. I will give you a chance to win your life back."

"No fucking way, you son of a bitch! Get up and give me your gun. I know you have one. No way you walked in here without it."

Sitting back in my chair, I relax and fold my hands together. "No." I say calmly as I raise my eyes up to his, "you hand me yours," I growl with pleasure. Connor's stunned expression is priceless but none more so than when he realizes his own guards have just turned on him. "You should pay your people better or, at least, treat them better." Connor pulls the trigger of the gun pointed at my head, again and again until he finally realizes it's empty. Sighing with a smile, "You think I didn't think to take care of that? Oh, Connor, I guess being older hasn't made you the least bit wiser."

"Okay, Nick, what now? You going to kill me? Torture me? What?" Connor concedes eyeing his own men with disgust.

"We are going to take a ride." I let Connor's own men get control of him, while I pick up Kayla and carry her out with us. Tanner pulls up just in time. "Tanner take her home and get the doctor. She is burning up. Put her in my bed and make sure she has whatever she needs." I said placing her in the car. Covering her shivering body up with my jacket, I caress her face and kiss her before sending her off with Tanner. "Okay, let's go." I said as I get into the car next to Luke. Connor reluctantly leaves with us and it is all I can do to keep Luke calm. He is shaking the entire car, he is enjoying this so much. When we arrive at our destination, Connor seems shocked again. I simply smile and watch as Luke kicks him in the rear all the way inside.

"Move it, Chubby Nuts!" Luke yells with laughter.

My boys have already gotten control of things inside, tied up his men, and have his warehouse opened up for the visitors that are coming shortly. They restrain Connor while I look things over, praising my boys for their work.

"Okay, Nick, I am not sure what this is all going to accomplish for you, but I know I am going to eventually get out of it, and I will get you back. Not to mention, I am not begging for my life as you stated so dramatically earlier." Connor laughs.

"Oh, but, brother, have you not figured out what the real plan is? I mean, yes, the cops will be here soon to arrest you, but on top of that, you will be suspected of giving up some *very* important suppliers of yours. Now the cops will never be able to touch them because … well, I am sure they will take care of the only loose connection they have against them." Connor pales. "I don't know, how do you think they will do it?"

"I think they will start by cutting off his toes and then work up until there is nothing but a head left." Luke laughs.

"Nah, they will probably remove his eyes and then take turns stabbing him, like a Marco Polo fight." Dwayne remarks. I shiver and smile.

"Well, I got to go. My girl is waiting for me and I don't want to be away from her any more than I have to be on her first night back at home. The cops should be here any minute. Your list of shipments is laid out and that should help point some fingers clearly for you. Have a good night, Connor." I start to walk away, but before I can help myself, I storm back, sliding my gloves on as I take hold of a nearby screwdriver. "Just to make sure you don't go anywhere," I say, knocking his feet out from under him so he is on his knees. I force his hand against the bottom of the wall and send the screwdriver through his palm. His scream is gratifying, but the knowing in his eyes is what gives me pleasure.

Dwayne grabs hold of me, "We should go."

I walk out as Connor begins screaming for me to kill him, as my so-called only brother he says I should do him this one favor and shoot him. As we sit safely away, Simone pulls up with what seems to be every cop in the city. They cautiously sit outside yelling for everyone to come out. We laugh as they wait and no one comes. Finally they make a move inside and find what we left them. "Let's go home, boys." I said anxious to get back to her.

⋙⋘

"**K**ayla is real sick, Nick." Tanner says as I enter the house. "The doctor says she needs to be in the hospital."

"No! No hospitals, she is too vulnerable there." I say with a fire raging up into my throat. "Simone was appreciative for the help on Connor's arrest. He let me know the district attorney, Spencer Welch, has decided to come after me, now that they have Connor. The greedy son of a bitch is out to run for senator. He's determined and will do whatever he can to get me and that includes risking Kayla's life."

"But Nick ... if she dies." Tanner reasons.

"She isn't going to die!" I yell back at him, before understanding his fear. "Let's give it until tomorrow, if there is no improvement, then I will make the necessary arrangements. I can admit her under a fake name and hope she gets better before anyone figures it out." I leave Tanner behind and find Kayla clearly ill and weak. She is sound asleep when I crawl into the bed next to her. Caressing her body closer to me, I kiss her shoulder and up her neck until she wakes. "I was worried about you. Where did you go?" She murmurs.

"I see that, so worried you were sound asleep." I whisper into her ear, with a soft laugh.

"The doctor gave me some medicine. I tried to fight it but ... I was still worried about you ... while I was sleeping." She said burying her burning head into my chest.

"I guess I can forgive you then. But there was no reason to be worried, I was only finishing a card game with the boys."

"Cards? With that smile, I assume you won."

"Oh, Princess, I won big. Real big." I said holding her frail body tight to my chest, determined not to let her go. Now that I have her back, I will protect her at all costs.

~20~
NICK

*T*he doctor warns me again, while I watch Kayla struggle to even breathe. I have no choice, I have to move her to the nearby hospital but I am going to make sure it is a private room and under a false name. I put my own people at her door to guard. Connor isn't dead yet and I'm not taking any chances that he doesn't still have some power left to make one final execution order.

As it turns out, Kayla has pneumonia, the jackass left her freezing and too drugged up to fight it. Her injuries are healing, but the sight of her laid up in that hospital bed makes me wish I hadn't promised Simone that I would let him handle Connor. I assumed he would be dead by now but they are doing a better job than expected keeping him protected. I don't know what they are protecting him for, he isn't ever going to tell them anything. He is better off trying to get bail and shooting himself before his associates get a hold of him. The cops have already raided one associate's warehouse and cleaned him out, but they somehow lost the contents. Luke nearly busted a gut reading that story. I never expected that to happen but the fact that it did only makes Connor that much more of a target. The cops won't protect him much longer, they won't need to if they keep arresting people. Even better, I picked up some new business and I found a warehouse full of narcotics to sell to one my associates for cheap.

Tanner drives me to the hospital on our way back from a meeting and I spend my night talking to Kayla as she fades in and out from the medication. She seems to be getting better, but not fast enough. I have seen too many supposed undercover cops hanging around and it's making me uneasy. My suspicions are confirmed when Ryan stops by with news. Ryan has been my inside man for some time. I have my cleaning business under his name. He runs it by having his people acquire a multitude of information for me. I was able to secure all the government building contracts and allowing my people to clean out the information no one wants me to have. The cleaning lady with her headphones on, pretending to hum a tune is actually recording every conversation in the area. There are ears everywhere and most of them are mine. I wouldn't trust anyone but Ryan to handle them. After I receive his message, I take a quick detour through the hospital and down some stairs before flirting with a nurse so I can follow her through a back employee only door. A couple of nods from some orderlies and I find Ryan in a dark corner outside the building.

"Took you long enough." He said with a smile.

"You couldn't find any place easier to get to?"

"There are cops all over this place." Ryan insists, smiling wider.

"So I have noticed. I have a bad feeling they are waiting on something."

"They are- to get access to Kayla. They are waiting on a judge to give them permission to take over her care- for her own safety. They are coming after you, Nick."

"Greedy bastards. I handed them the biggest bust they ever had and now they … Fuck 'em."

"What are you going to do?" Ryan asked watching the area as I do.

"I was afraid of this. I need you to do something for me. I need you to take some legal documents to my attorney and tell him to get them verified and authorized. Tanner has them. I will have him meet you at the usual place." Ryan nods and gives me his standard sarcastic expression. "What?"

"I haven't gotten to talk to you since you took him down. You have to tell me the moment he knew. Come on, Nick, I am owed it as much as you." Ryan pleads. Quickly, I give him the details he needs and then send him away on a high.

Returning to Kayla is easier said than done. They were waiting for me to leave her so they could block me from getting to her. The more hell I raise, the more cops that show up. No one has any answers or reasons for me to be kept from her. Before I can make my final threat, the district attorney, Spencer Welch, comes strolling in with his smug attitude. "I want this woman moved," He announced.

"Who the fuck do you think you are!" I yell as two cops take hold of me and push me into a wall.

He turns slowly in my direction, "I am now in charge of this woman's care."

"You don't have any right to do that!" I said as he waves a court order at me. Shaking my head, "Leave her where she is, at least. I will leave, but leave her where she is." I asked but he continues to ignore me. "Are you listening to me, you smug bastard? There is no reason to move her! You fucking son of a bitch! I swear ..."

He immediately turns and smiles at me, "Is that a threat? I think that is a threat on the district attorney. Arrest him!" He said and immediately I am thrown to the ground and handcuffed.

As I am pulled back up, I catch sight of Kayla as they begin moving her. "Nick?" She said waking up and becoming more alarmed as she takes in the entire scene. "Nick! Nick, no! What is going on?" I hear her scream for me as they escort me out. Before I can get on the elevator, she somehow manages to leave her bed and comes running to me, holding on to my neck as she tries to hold herself up. "Nick, what happened? Why ..."

Her arm is bleeding after pulling out her IV and she is still extremely weak as she struggles to hold on to me. I lay my head against hers, kissing her as I whisper to her, "It's okay, Princess, I am going to take care of everything. Don't worry." Standing strong, I watch as they pull her away from me and place her back in bed. I jerk away from my escorts and walk out with them on my own, but am still shoved into the back of a patrol car- something I haven't been through since I was arrested for stealing a knife when I was fourteen.

While waiting for my attorney, I have been sitting in a room alone for hours. "How are we, Mr. Jayzon?" The District Attorney said as he walks through the door. "Nothing to say? That's fine. Your girlfriend is in a vulnerable state, so she should be able to tell us all we need to know. We have made sure she isn't given any medication so she can stay awake and talk to us as long as we need her to." He smiles at me. "Unless you would like to be a man and save her from that ordeal?"

"What exactly do you want to know?" I asked curiously.

"I want to know your relationship with Connor Daniels? What kind of business did you deal with together? Why did he let you walk away with Kayla? All these questions are very concerning to me."

"Let me know when my attorney arrives." I said sitting back in my seat.

Tensing up and snarling, Welch slams his fists on the table. "We are going to nail your ass to the wall!" He yells at me. I don't give, not even a little bit. "Fine. You want it this way? Then I will get everything I need to know from Kayla. Your attorney is here, by the way." I leave quickly with my attorney and rush back to the hospital, demanding Kayla be moved back to the room I paid for. Sure enough, I am again face-to-face with the district attorney. "Mr. Jayzon, you are not welcome here."

"Then tell me where Kayla is and I will move her to another hospital." I said.

He laughs at me, "As her temporary guardian, I cannot allow that."

Taking a step into his face, "As her husband, and true legal guardian, I demand it!" My attorney shows the court order verifying and approving my marriage to Kayla. After I confirm with Kayla's doctor, I take her home to finish recovering much to the displeasure of the district attorney.

∾

*W*ithin a few days, Kayla improves and begins to make me crazy asking questions about what happened and how I was able to get her away from Connor. She barely remembers the events and I prefer to keep it that way, especially with the district attorney making it clear he will do whatever possible to talk to her.

I spent most of the day handling some business and left strict orders at the house to keep Kayla on lock-down until I get home. Upon entering the house, I know I am in trouble when Dwayne looks beyond stressed. "That bad, huh?" I asked.

"Nick … that girl is … persistent, I will give her that. But if you ever ask me to baby-sit her again, I would rather you shoot me instead."

"What happened?" I laugh imagining the worst. He tenses up waving his hands at the back door, then upstairs, the phone, the rug for some reason, he shows me the marks on the back of his neck, his leg and then agonizes in the direction of the side door all the while still unable to speak clearly. "What?" I asked confused.

"I don't want to talk about it. I am leaving to go get a drink-several on you. She is all yours. Thank God." He says exiting in a huff.

Once I enter the bedroom I see Kayla sitting up with a terrible pout. "You feel any better?" I asked nearly laughing after seeing Dwayne.

"I'm not talking to you." She said with her arms crossed and looking away from me.

"Why?"

"You know why!"

"Kayla, you're still sick. You need to stay in the house and get better."

"I am not! You are hiding something from me. Don't lie because I know you are."

She's right. Connor's bail was denied, so it is just a matter of time now. Until Connor and his left over men are taken care of, I am not taking any chances that he may have an ally or two who would do him a favor before he dies. Once he's gone, the favor is meaningless and then she can go back to a somewhat normal life. "Can you please appease me a little longer?" She stiffens in a deeper pout. "I bought you some new books." Nothing. "If you're so much better, then prove it to me." As tired as Dwayne looks, she must be nearly a hundred percent, and the way she teased me last night, I am sure she is just as horny as I am. She glances my way but remains silent. "Okay then." I said turning my back on her and putting my jacket in my closet. Within a few minutes I feel her against my back and her hands working down my pants. "Thought you were mad at me?"

"I am but ..." She lets go and I turn around to see her fidgeting.

"But you're horny, aren't you?" I said with a smile pissing her off even more. She stomps her foot and tries unsuccessfully to run from me. "That makes two of us, Princess." I throw her over my shoulder while she giggles and squirms to try to get away from me.

"Nick I am still sick."

"Really? Okay, we will wait then." I put her in bed and walk back towards my closet.

"Nick." I shake my head, ignoring her. "Nick."

"No, Kayla."

"But, Nick, I wasn't being serious. I am better."

"Nope, I am not interested anymore."

"Nick." She throws her shirt at me and I turn around quickly to watch her begin dancing for me, stripping down to nothing, as she teases me back to her. Never has anyone been able to seduce me like her. Her body is amazing, but her sweet seductive eyes bring me to my knees. I sit down enjoying the show that is working its way towards me, tasting her skin whenever she gets near. She strips me down, allowing me to touch and kiss her. Taking my hands, Kayla wraps them around her as she sits down on me with her back facing me. Her ass looks so good moving on me slowly, I become hypnotized by it. She leans back on my chest, taking in my lips and opening her mouth for my tongue to slip easily in next to hers. After massaging her tits, I slip down between her legs and play until her eyes roll, her jaw tightens and she comes strong on me. She is so exhausted, I have to take over. Picking her up, I hold her tight and fuck her hard as she whimpers and moans her pleasures.

When I'm done she leans back and kisses me gently with a smile. "So, you're not mad at me anymore?" I asked playing with her hair and kissing her bare back.

"I didn't say that." She said still smiling.

"How many times will it take before you're not mad at me anymore?"

"I'll let you know when it happens." Laughing, I pick her up and throw her in bed.

"If you can give me a few more days then I will give you whatever you want." I said hovering over her smiling angel face. She seems to look right through me, tracing my face with a single finger reminding me how deeply I feel for her. *It scares the hell out of me.* I should listen to Luke and push her as far away from me as possible but, no matter the warnings, I can't let go of her- not again. I kiss her gently on the lips and it shocks her for some reason.

"I love you, Nick." She said watching my response closely. *Run. Run now! Fucking run, you idiot.* "Do you love me?" *You should have run, dumbass.* Those sweet green eyes hold my focus and I can't do anything but crumble in her arms.

"What do you want me to say, Kayla?" I asked trying to hide my face from her.

"What you feel. I love having sex with you, Nick, but I would love even more to make love with you. To hear you say it. I know you do. Why can't you just say it?"

"If you know it, then why do you have to hear me say it?"

"I guess there is still some doubt in my mind."

"Kayla, I don't even know what it means. Love? It makes no sense to me. I enjoy being with you. I don't want you to leave, but outside that ..." Her hands loosen around my neck and I feel her vibrating underneath me. Looking beneath me I watch her curl into a ball and begin to cry.

"I don't understand, Nick. Why do you do these things for me?

Why do you go out of your way to protect me?" She cries rolling away.

"I don't know. I don't understand anything when it comes to you." She continues to cry and scoots further away from me. "This is ridiculous. We were having a good time … uggghhhh." I get up angry, "You know what I don't understand? Why I have to say I love you? My father said it every day to my mother, but it didn't mean a damn thing! It doesn't mean anything, Kayla. It's just a word! All that should matter is how I treat you." Still she lies there, ignoring me and crying. "Fuck! This is …" Storming back to her, I straighten her out and hover over her until she looks at me. "I love you. I love you Kayla. I hate it, but I do. You drive me absolutely insane but I love you so much that I think about you constantly. Even when you are asleep right next to me, I worry that if I fall asleep that you might not be there when I wake up. Before I found out that Connor took you, I thought you left and I seriously considered hunting you down and bringing you back. Hell, Kayla, I fucking married you!"

"You what?" She asked with her jaw dropped.

Fuck! Might as well tell her now. "On our trip. It wasn't a joke. I am not real sure it is legal here in the States, but yes, I was sober enough to pay the priest to marry us with those two cheap shell rings you bought. You joked about it, but I made it happen and even …." I leave her to go into my closet safe and pull out the small box I have had hidden from her since I bought it. I lay the box in front of her and watch as she opens it to find the diamond ring she looked at in the jewelry store. "I don't know why I bought it. I never had a plan to give it you, but I knew you liked it and so did I." Exhausted by my confession, I close my eyes and let my head drop.

"We're married?" She asked. I slowly look up into her eyes and she looks as though she is about to burst into song. "You married me? You love me so much that you married me without me even knowing it? You bought an engagement ring even? That's kind of insane." She laughs.

"Well, I had been drinking too." I said falling back into the bed rolling my eyes. Kayla takes hold of me and kisses all over my face. "Stop, because now I am mad at you." I said fighting my own smile.

"No. You're my husband and I can do what I want with you." She giggles.

"I should never have said anything." I said enjoying her sweet kisses immensely.

"No, you probably shouldn't have, but it's too late now. So, kiss me and tell me you love me."

"Why should I?"

Kayla leans up and kisses my cheek, nibbling on my ear, "Because unlike our stupid parents, we actually love each other. I won't ever hurt you, Nick, don't hurt me by denying me what you feel for me."

I watch her lie down on top of me and nothing in my life ever made more sense than this, "Don't ever leave me." I said with a shaky voice.

"Never, I promise." She said looking deep into my eyes.

"I love you, Kayla." I said holding her securely in my arms. *I would die for you without question.*

~21~
KAYLA

While Nick is dreaming peacefully, I try to check the internet to see what is going on. Unfortunately, Nick has locked the computers and my cell is nowhere to be found. After finding his keys, I sneak out to find the information on my own. Nothing like an old fashioned newspaper to give me the information I am looking for. Once I have read everything cover to cover, I return to Nick who is none too happy with me. I try to smile innocently when I walk in but his stiff posture remains. "Hi, baby." I said kissing him gently.

"Where have you been?" Nick asked.

Stomping my foot with force, I throw the paper in front of him and show him my worst attitude. "Nick, damn it! You can't shelter me forever! I want to know what's going on!

Nick puts his tea down sighing and takes my hand, "There is no need for any of this attitude ..."

"Connor was murdered in prison? How? How did he even end up in prison? And did you hear how he was murdered?" Nick fights a smile assuring me that he does know. "Nick, it was-"

"What he fucking deserved. And I don't want to hear you say otherwise."

"Why do I get the feeling you had something to do with it?" I asked watching him closely.

"He was in prison, Princess. How could I possibly have anything to do with it?" Nick kisses me tenderly as if I am supposed to believe he is innocent.

"Nick, please tell me what you did. At least tell me that you're going to be okay- that you're ..." I crush myself against his chest, fisting his shirt. "You're not going to be investigated and harassed for this, are you?"

"Nah, the cops are busy sorting out all of Connor's associates and trying to clean up that mess. They don't have time for me right now, even to harass me for no reason. Why do you think I have been here with you so much?"

"Trying to stay out of trouble?" I said wrapping my arms around his neck as he smiles wide.

"Trouble? And when do I ever get into trouble?" Nick winks. "So, do you think you could handle a night out?"

"I would love a night out." I said with excitement.

"There is a charity function tonight that I need to make an appearance at. I would love for you to go with me."

"That sounds perfect, but can I buy something new?" I asked anticipating shopping at my favorite store again.

"Of course. I can drop you off on my way to a short meeting and then pick you up on my way back."

"What kind of meeting?" I asked to his immediate sigh. "It was worth a try." I say with a slight smile.

"Stop trying." He said with no smile at all.

"But maybe I could help you."

"Kayla, I am not going to talk to you about this. I am not going to let you into that part of my life. Don't ask me again." I nod laying my head on his chest with a small sigh.

"Maybe I could help you in some other way, Nick?"

"Like what? You want to manage the club for me again?"

"Maybe. Or, I don't know, maybe I could go to school and learn something more to help. Maybe start a new business- legal, of course."

"You would do that for me? Go to school and suffer through all those classes and books?" Nick leans down to look me in the eyes, smiling.

"For you I would." I smile back.

"For me you will." He laughs. "How about you get all the information together and I will pay the bill? But, you have to make sure you have time for me within all this college mess."

"Oh, Nick! I love you!" I yell jumping into his arms and kissing him passionately.

"I liked it better when you two hated each other. It was more entertaining than this mushy shit all the time." Luke said walking in and crashing in the chair near us.

"Get use to it," I said kissing Nick once more and jumping down to kiss Luke on the head before running off upstairs.

"I prefer the kisses he gets, Kayla." Luke yells.

"Forget it, asshole, you're lucky I allowed that one." Nick laughs, kicking Luke as he passes him.

"Hey! That hurt! Kayla, come and kiss my wound …" I laugh as I watch them wrestle like two little boys. It's nice to see Nick like this, Luke too, they both are so content lately. As I watch them, I wonder if I will ever be as close to Nick as Luke is.

CS80

*N*ick keeps his word and pays for me to go to school. I keep mine, making time for him between taking as many classes I can handle. When my second quarter is nearing its end I have made some new friends. Most of us have several classes together and have already formed study groups to prepare for finals at the end of the quarter. The group consists of Kari, a sweet girl that laughs about everything. I thought about setting her up with Luke since he loves to make people laugh, but I'm not sure how I would explain the numerous amounts of gorgeous women he works with after hours. The other girl is Jesse. She is fun at times, but she doesn't have a filter on her mouth and tends to get into many verbal confrontations. Plus, I am pretty sure she is sleeping with several of her professors for grades. The last person is Scott, a somewhat attractive guy- for a momma's boy. All three of my new friends are well off and have been since birth. With the car Nick bought for me, the expensive designer clothes, and the big house with the great address, my new friends all assume I am much like them. I would tell them otherwise, but where do I start or even end? I am only allowed to say so much and I don't feel comfortable giving away such a key part of myself to people I only just began to know. Once finals are over and we have a couple of weeks off before the next quarter begins, my group decides to go out and celebrate for a much-needed stress relief. Jesse, of course, suggests a party that she knows of. Not feeling comfortable with a campus drink fest, I try to find a way to back out. However, Jesse assures me that it is off campus at a respectable, luxurious home where we will be able to relax comfortably and be catered to like royalty. Curious and needing the stress relief, I decide to go. *Besides, Nick is going to be working late tonight.*

Looking our best, the four of us pile into a limo Scott provides and are driven to a beautiful home on the hill. The security is abundant, the home and party is much the way Jesse described: luxurious and relaxing. Everyone in attendance is enjoying themselves with polite conversations and delicate sips of their drink of choice. I try to make mental notes so I can tell Nick all about the humor I am already seeing in the absurdities of it all. It is only an hour in and I have been offered shoulder massages, various cocktails, and numerous delicacies from around the world. I decline most, since no matter how upscale the environment seems, I know better than to trust appearances. My wary attitude is proven correct when my new friends begin to show signs of obvious drug assisted euphoria. As Kari and Scott drift off into their pleasure filled night, Jesse takes my hand and shows me around. I have fun wandering the massive home with her, talking in detail about the expensive artwork and the priceless heirlooms, all of which are contained in rooms separate from the party. We make ourselves at home in a large room with a pool table and its own bar. We have fun making up our own drink concoctions, playing a revised version of pool, and coming up with new and sexy ways to hit a ball across the table that makes us laugh until we cry. I am enjoying myself immensely when Luke suddenly walks in. Shocked, I jump down and stare at him dumbfounded.

"What are you doing here?" He asked.

"I was invited. What are you doing here?" I asked as Jesse stands next to me checking Luke out blatantly.

"Nick is having a meeting upstairs. I got bored listening to the monotonous bullshit so I thought I would shoot some pool or something." Luke said looking Jesse over to her enjoyment.

"You're welcome to join us." I said as Jesse makes comments about him needing to know how to arch his butt just right or he will lose style points. I laugh, "We haven't been playing a typical game."

"Uh huh. Well, I think I am going to go wander around a little bit. You ladies have fun ... arching you're asses or whatever the hell your doing for points. I will let Nick know you're here." He smiles shaking his head at our giggling and he leaves with little else to say.

"So, Nick is your boyfriend?" Jesse asked.

"He is. I would love for you to meet him." I said feeling good about the idea.

"Sure. I bet he is meeting with my boyfriend, Joseph. He owns this house so you can meet him too." She said scrunching her nose with excitement. "He is so wonderful and he spoils me ridiculously." Jesse runs up to me grabbing my hands, "He is so handsome and he has people bowing down to him to please him. It's amazing how much people respect him. I have never met anyone like him."

"Powerful men do have their appeal."

"So, Nick does well?" She asked with a fleeting interest.

"He does fine." I said simply.

"Well, maybe Joseph can help him out and we can both spend our days shopping instead of worrying about going to school. I tell you, my father is so hell-bent on me becoming someone that he can respect." She said with her chest out and a rich tone. Lying across the pool table, "He is the most lame man I have ever met." Jesse suddenly jumps up, "It drives him crazy that I am dating Joseph, probably because I met him at one of my father's parties." She laughs leaning down to me, "I fucked him in the bathroom while my father was giving a speech. We have been together ever since." With my eyes wide, I laugh shaking my head, "So how did you meet ... Nick, is it?"

I nod, "Ummm..... it's a long story." She sat up, staring at me, and waiting for me to continue. "He dated my sister a long time ago and then we ran into each other a little over a year ago now." Shrugging, "It wasn't a storybook romance or anything but ..."

"But you love him." I nod with a smile. "Well, that is a storybook romance if I ever heard one. But how does your sister fill about you dating her ex?"

Taken aback by her question, I stand speechless and distant as she walks around to face me and try to get my attention. "Uh Bray ... died some time ago." I said turning away and pouring myself another drink. Jesse hugs me from behind and says whatever comes to her mind until I finally force a smile. Ready to go home, I convince Jesse to leave only if I agree to come with her to meet her boyfriend. She guides me upstairs where we are greeted by two younger men, each with a smile too large for me to feel comfortable. I back up instantly looking at Jesse as she walks towards them.

"Kayla, this is Rico Estrella and his friend, Cory. His father is my boyfriend." Jesse said hugging the men stiffly. The two are dressed in designer clothes but wear them in a less than suitable fashion. Their gluttonous attitude creates a disastrous display of custom clothing. Standing afar, I nod with a simple greeting. "We were on our way to see Joseph."

"Dad is in a meeting. We were just in there advising him, he is pretty busy. I don't think he can see you right now, but you're welcome to wait with us. You can see the entire party up here." Rico said waving his hand for us to lead the way to the ornate balcony above everyone. I wait impatiently as Rico and Cory entertain themselves at the expense of the crowd below. I become disgusted when a young woman they believe to be beneath their status doesn't leave after they yell at her too. Jesse holds me back as I fidget in my seat. Since the constant ridicule and laughter seems to be defiantly ignored by the poor woman, Rico pours the contents of his glass down on her head, causing her to scream out in shock. Laughing hysterically, Rico takes hold of the trey of shrimp and sauce with a wink towards his friend. Having enough, I jump up and push the trey back into his face and laugh with pride. Jesse, fighting her own smile, steps in front of me and holds her hand up to Rico as he begins to roar his displeasure. "Get out of my way, slut!" Rico yells slapping her hand out of the way.

"Now, Rico, calm down and give Kayla a chance to apologize properly before you do something you might regret." Jesse said before being pushed aside.

Rico grabs hold of me and pushes me up against a wall, "You better apologize and it better be good. In fact, I suggest you better make it orgasmically good." Rico said rubbing his chest and gripping his belt.

"You're disgusting. I am not going to apologize to two morons who should be whipped with that belt you seem to be so fond of." I said.

"I know what would be a good apology. Why don't you strip naked and stand up on this chair and tell me how much you want me." Rico said proudly as Cory laughs in support. I grab my bag and walk away. I don't get far before they force me into a corner of the hall.

"Rico her boyfriend is here. You don't want to cause any trouble for your father." Jesse pleads with him.

Rico pushes up on me, "Your boyfriend doesn't have anything on me." He breathes repulsively in my face. I laugh causing anger that I didn't prepare for. Rico backhands me across the face and tries to force his way under my clothes. Taking hold of a nearby statue, I leave a mark on his face that bleeds profusely. Before he has a chance to react, I run down the hall into Luke and feel relieved when he faces Rico and Cory with no fear.

"Where you going, fat boy?" Luke said.

"Get out of my way. I am going to finish teaching that bitch a lesson." Rico seethes. Luke rolls his eyes not budging in his position.

Rico dismisses him and takes a lunge for me but falls back on the floor as Luke hits him once and threatens Cory with one finger before he has a chance to help his friend. "You are going to regret that, Son. My father will have your head hung from his wall!" Amused, Luke dismisses him. "I suggest, for your own sake, that you don't touch her again." Luke straightens his suit, "Nick wants you to wait here for him, Kayla. Now I have to get back to work. You boys be good." Shoving Rico's leg out of his way with delight, "Get up, fat boy, before my good mood goes bad." Luke said as he gives me a quick disapproving glance.

Jumping up, Rico takes hold of my arm and drags me to a room where he demands to see his father. Walking in from the next room is a man that possesses a tan that is embedded permanently into his skin which is set off absurdly by his excessively white teeth. Before Rico has a chance to say a word Jesse clings to the man's side, kissing him and hugging him with pleas to spare me from any possible danger. Rico follows with his own pleas of justice. Silencing them both with a sudden hand gesture, he leaves them and walks up to me with a look of clear disapproval. "She is the one that hit me and disrespected me." Rico claims.

"Do you know who I am?" The man asked me. I know better than to answer a question like that. "My name is Joseph Estrella and this is my home. I do not appreciate guests coming in here and disrespecting my son in my own home."

"What I did is defend myself against an overgrown child who has no manners." I blurt out as Jesse cringes at my blunt attitude.

Joseph looks me up and down before forcing me down on the ground roughly. "Apologize to my son." I look up at a confident Rico who stands in front of me but I stay silent. Taking hold of my hair, Rico starts to drag me along the floor.

Jesse runs to Joseph instantly, "Baby, please! I am sure there is something else she can do to make it up to you. She is my friend, Baby. We were having fun together, drinking, playing pool and dancing." Jesse wraps her arms around Joseph's neck tighter to whisper in his ear, "How about I show you a dance Kayla taught me earlier tonight? It's very sexy."

"Hold on!" Joseph yells at Rico as I continue to struggle against him. "How well do you dance?" He leans down to ask me. "If you're that good and you entertain me and my guests well enough, I will consider forgiving you. Yes, I think a performance will be exactly what I need to put me in a better mood." Rico lets me up while Joseph looks me over again with a smile to Jesse's sudden displeasure. "You are quite beautiful. I've changed my mind. Perform for me in private and we will negotiate a much better departure for you."

"The only person she performs for is me." Nick said entering from the next room with Luke at his side. Joseph turns to him, as stunned as everyone else in the room. Nick walks towards us and eyes Joseph with a glare that sets us both back on our heels. "Who hit you, Kayla?" Nick asked controlling the room with ease. I nod in Rico's direction and Nick takes a single breath before beating Rico into a slobbering mess on the floor. He continues the abuse until Rico cries out with apologies. "What did you say?" Nick asked him. Rico struggles to repeat himself as Nick drags him on his knees to my feet. "I don't think she heard you."

Rico, bloodied beyond recognition, looks up to me shaking, "I … I'm."

"LOUDER!" Nick yells startling him into a whimper.

"I'm sorry!" He yells, repeating it until he feels he has satisfied Nick. Joseph motions for Rico and Cory to leave, having one of his men help them to exit more quickly.

Nick walks over to me and rubs his thumb across my swollen cheek with a private, loving appreciation in his eyes. Before I can smile, he turns his back to me, hiding me from Joseph completely. "I don't appreciate you treating my girl like this."

"I am sorry, Nicholas. I had no idea." Joseph straightens up and changes his tone. "It will never happen again and I assure you I will be sending proper apologies to you and Kayla by tomorrow. For now, please let me offer you some food and drink in the parlor." Joseph motions for us to have a seat as servants come in with drinks and food. Nick speaks with Joseph calmly but never looks, touches, or even speaks to me during the rest of our stay. Jesse sits quietly at Joseph's side with no effort to look my way at all. I begin to wonder if she will ever speak to me again. As I gaze in her direction, I watch her look over Nick in what I can only assume is fear. I am sure I have lost a new friend and possibly more. I sit quietly during the rest of our stay, trying to respect Nick and the situation I just put him in. Nick and Joseph quickly move on and forget the previous events, discussing people they both know, and laughing about stories they both know of. At the end of the night, Nick says his goodbyes with a positive tone and Joseph politely kisses my hand before Nick escorts me out. Thankfully, Tanner has the car ready for us as soon as we walk outside.

"Nick ..." I said once he shuts the car door, but he holds up his hand while shaking his head at me. "But ..."

"Don't worry about it, Princess. Everything is fine." He said kissing me on the cheek and putting his arm around me.

"You're not mad at me?" He shakes his head. "But you didn't speak to me ... all I did was go to this party with my friends. It was supposed to be relaxing and nothing more. Jesse and I were hiding from all the craziness and then Rico with his ... and yes, I might have got a little attitude with him, but ..." I look up at Nick as he begins to laugh.

"You might have got a little attitude with him? Might have? That's funny." Nick laughs.

"It's not funny. He was being a jerk."

"I'm sure he was. He is a punk. I rather enjoyed kicking the crap out of him. Thanks for giving me an excuse to do so."

"But you did it in front of his father." Nick merely nods in agreement. "That's it? You're just going to nod like it was nothing?" He glances at me with a pleasing smile. "Nick ... I don't have a clue about how much power you have, do I?" I asked watching as the devil's eyes beam in the moonlight.

~22~
KAYLA

Crawling into our warm, soft bed feels so good after the night I had, but Nick crawls in next to me, caressing my body with desire. "Nick, what are you doing? Don't you think tonight was eventful enough?" I said laughing as he tickles me with strategically placed kisses.

"It's not my fault you showed up at the wrong place at the wrong time. You have a habit of that, by the way, we should discuss that sometime. But first, we need to discuss this business of you calling me your boyfriend." He said kissing me gently on the lips. "I thought I explained to you that we are married and I did buy you an engagement ring that you never wear."

"*Maybe* we got married, I don't know that for sure. I mean I have seen the paperwork but I really have no memory of it and I have nothing to prove it other than some doctored up certificate." Smiling up at him, I lean up and kiss him. "Now, do I, baby? Plus, I feel like the ring really isn't mine since no one actually proposed to me with it."

"I guess I will need to take care of that for you because I care too much about you to have you wandering around with an empty finger and no memory of marrying me." I wrap my arms around his neck and kiss him through my abundant smile. "That's all I have to say, isn't it? That I care or ..." Nick says and kisses me deeply, "that I love you." I nod and he laughs pulling my legs up around him. I watch his eyes concentrate on me as I feel his erection touch me, hit me hard, and finally go deep inside causing me to gasp with satisfaction. "Ohhh, I am so glad classes are over for a little while, I have missed you." He said toying with my lips, holding my body up and into him. "Kayla, I want you to come with me in the morning." I open my eyes as he tastes my lips. "I have a surprise for you." Nick rubs his hand up my thigh and moves into me with a manly thrust. "A wonderful ... big ... surprise for you." He said in tune with my moan.

CROSO

*W*e have been driving all-day it seems like. I didn't know what to pack since Nick said it didn't matter and that we could buy whatever we might need when we got there. I'm trying to be calm and patient, knowing Nick is enjoying watching me become unglued, so I sit quietly playing with my fingers until Tanner stops the car. I jump up at once and look out the window while Nick gets out of the car. I don't recognize anything, not that I can see much since it's so dark. About the only thing I can make out are trees. Nick opens my door and smirks at my questioning expression. This is nothing like I thought it might be. "The woods? You brought me camping or something? I know it was something you said you always wanted to try, but I was hoping you meant for a boy's weekend or something."

He holds his hand out to me laughing. "Come with me please."

"Why? Where are we going? Our ... tent? Maybe a cave?"

"Kayla, please." Nick said taking my hand. He walks me over to the edge of a lake. "Look over there." He said pointing to the other side of the lake. I search hard, squinting until my eyes are about to pop out of my head.

"I don't ..." Suddenly, fireworks shoot up above the tree tops, lighting up the sky. "Nick! It is ... it's ... so beautiful. How did you know that they would ..." I turn and see him on one knee, holding out my diamond ring.

Gasping, I hold my mouth as he smiles. "Run away with me tonight, Kayla, and marry me- legally this time."

Nick planned everything perfectly. We say our vows to each other quietly among the mountains. At the end, he carries me off to a cabin all to ourselves. We barely make time to eat and we never bother getting dressed. The cabin is stocked full of food and I learn that Nick can cook, pancakes, and only pancakes. Our last night of the honeymoon, I lie naked on top of Nick's nude body staring at the stars through the windows while Nick plays with my hair and I hum against his chest. There is nothing in the world I want more right now.

When we return home, Nick carries me through our front door as we both laugh. I think nothing about our onlookers as we enter. Luke and Dwayne wait for Nick in his office coming out to watch us gleefully make our way to our room. He makes love to me again in our bed, where I fall asleep in such bliss that I am surprised by the nightmares that creep into my sweet dreams. I wake up startled, searching for Nick who hasn't come to bed yet. On edge I get up to search for him tiptoeing towards the light from his office, hoping he is alone. When I round the corner however, I find him with Luke.

"Have you lost your DAMN mind?" Luke yells at him.

"What is your problem now?" Nick yells back.

"My problem is you getting your head all messed up with a fucking whore!"

Nick jumps out of his chair and the two meet face-to-face. "She is my wife now and you better get used to it."

"You are going to choose her over me?" Luke asked.

"Why do I have to choose? You're my best friend and she is my wife."

"She is causing you to make stupid mistakes. She is going to cause us to lose everything. We have worked too hard, Nick. Don't let her ruin that!"

"How is she ruining anything? You have a woman you're seeing."

"A woman, then I will have another. I don't let myself get lost in some relationship. Remember, Nick? Remember when you said those words to me? You were right then and I am right now- you know it. Cut her loose, Nick. You need to cut her loose, I know it's hard but clearly the only way to get her out of your system is to kill her. If you need me to do it for you …" Luke reaches for his gun.

Nick turns abruptly and wraps his hand around Luke's neck, "You touch her and I will kill *you*." I back away quietly and run upstairs to bed. No matter how hard I try, I can't get my hands to stop shaking or my mind off what I saw. Before I go to sleep, I get up and grab the knife Nick gave to me and lie down placing it under my pillow. I fall lightly to sleep and easily wake when Nick comes into the room. "Did I wake you?" Nick said. "What's wrong?" He asked noticing my distress.

"Nothing. You scared me is all."

Nick looks down and holds up my hand that grips my knife, "I see that. You might better get some sleep tonight, Princess. You're a little on edge."

"You kind of had me preoccupied the last week." I said still trembling.

"I will leave you alone tonight." He smiles sitting down on the bed next to me, easing his hand around to the center of my back. "I have some business I need to take care of while you get some sleep." He starts to get up but I leap back into his arms with desperation causing Nick to stiffen.

Once I realize there is no hiding my emotions, I pull myself back, still gripping him with clenched fists. "Nick, stay with me. Please stay with me."

"What happened, baby?" He asked.

"I had a bad dream." I said as Nick rubs my back.

"Do you want to tell me about it?" He asked as I shake my head. Nick only waits a few seconds more before he rolls into the bed with me. "Go to sleep. I won't leave, I promise." He says kissing me and holding me tight, "I love you, Kayla."

Over the next few days I try to find a way to talk to Nick about Luke but no words seem to be the right ones. I pay acute attention to Luke whenever he comes around and, though he seems a bit strained around me, he reacts no differently to me than he always has. I begin to think that it is me that is on edge and maybe I was overly tired that night. Maybe … maybe I misunderstood the argument I overheard.

~23~
KAYLA

My day begins with a warm kiss, wandering hands and a whispering desire. Not a bad way to start a day. Nick has a way of knowing how to start a day off flawlessly. If I could only have kept him in bed with me, it would be a much better day. Instead, I have to get ready to meet Jesse for lunch. She called me early today asking if we could talk. I accept only because she says she wants my help with Joseph and not to talk about how awful our night was at the party. Jesse was so excited that she said she will come and get me. It seems odd for her to come all this way when we could meet halfway between her place and mine. However, Jesse barely gives me a chance to say another word before she hangs up and tells me she will see me soon. When she arrives, I am ready to go but she is hell-bent on exploring, asking me to show her around while she wanders deep into my home, as if she is looking for something. Setting my bag aside, I graciously show her around the house and then lead her right back out the front door to her car. She comments on my home with forced appreciation. Our lunch together is light since Jesse's issues are no more than how does she continue accepting all the gifts Joseph is offering, continuing in detail about the expense and quality of each one. Her rambling continues for more than an hour about her new treasures. "So, you two like each other. That's great." I said trying to move along and hopefully escape this lunch with my lunch.

"Yes, it is. I'm sorry about Nick. He sure was moody. I bet you have to put up with a lot from him." She said taking notice of my ring that I have been good so far at hiding. "What's this? Did you marry him?" She asked.

"I did." I said watching her reaction carefully.

"Wow, that's wonderful and it looks like a descent ring too. I can only imagine what you had to do to get him to do that." She said shaking her head.

"Nothing as bad as Rico," I said with a laugh which was only

170

funny to me. Jesse ignores my humor and goes right into all the great things she has going for her until my nausea becomes too much for me. "Umm, Jesse, do you mind if we head back? I am not feeling real well." I interrupt her.

Stunned, she smiles happily, "Sure, sweetie, no problem. Do you need me to stop to get you anything? Should we get you some medicine or something?"

"No, I think I will be fine if I lie down for a little while." She nods and thankfully takes me straight home. Jesse helps me get to bed and makes me a cold pack for my head before she leaves. Her unexpected caring ways make me feel a little better about her, but I still make sure Luke shows her the way out. When I open my eyes, the sun is no longer shining at the edges of my shades and the clock shows the time much later than I would have ever intended on sleeping. Pushing my blanket aside, I get up and go downstairs to see if Nick is home. Nearing his office, I see his light on and I hear voices, neither of which is his. Within a footstep of his door, I hear Jesse giggling. I walk in quickly and see her on the sofa with Luke, nearly in his lap. "Oh, I'm sorry. I thought Nick was home." I said looking awkwardly away.

"He was here, not sure where he went. Do you need him?" Luke said minus his usual sarcastic attitude. I glance his way with a questioning look as he pains an expression silently to me. "Jesse said you weren't feeling well. Are you sure you should be out of bed?" He said. I roll my eyes and sigh walking out with a nod. I fear opening my mouth after seeing this display, I may get sick all over them. I hope, for their sake, they don't have sex on Nick's sofa. I don't even want to think about the words that will come out of his mouth. As it turned out, I didn't have to wait long. Nick enters the office and all I hear is screaming. I wait for some time upstairs, cringing as he walks through the door.

"Are you okay?" I asked to his surprisingly calm demeanor.

"Yes, why?"

"You're not angry about Jesse and Luke?" I tentatively asked.

"I was angry about them screwing in my office but they are going to buy me some new furniture and Jesse is going to do some work for me. So, now, I am in a good mood." Nick said, folding his clothes as he undresses.

"Work for you? Jesse is going to work for you? Doing what?" I ask following him around the room.

"She is in good with Joseph so she is going to help me keep tabs on him."

"She is going to screw Joseph and Luke. That sounds like a good idea to you?"

Nick cups my face in his hand and smiles, "It's not a big deal. Besides, from what she says, Joseph has trouble doing anyone since his heart issues. Apparently, he is not allowed to take his little blue pills until he is cleared from his doctor."

"So what does she do for him then?"

"I don't know and I don't care. As long she feeds me the information that I need, I will keep paying her. Although, maybe she should be paying me for Luke. Not sure her information is going to be as good as what she is getting." He laughs but I am not amused. "Oh, what now?"

"I don't like her working for you."

"She is your friend, isn't she?"

"A friend? Maybe, but she is not Exie. She is not someone I would trust to be working for my husband."

Nick smiles, "I will make sure Luke deals with her. He will enjoy that anyway. But you have to trust me that I will handle her without trying to fuck her." He waits as I struggle to smile back at him. "Besides, it is only you that I love."

I run and jump into his arms, "Okay, baby. Now greet me like a husband is supposed to do when he arrives home." I said, earning the greeting I have been waiting for.

৪৩৪৩

*W*ith classes starting back today, I run out of the house in haste after oversleeping. Having to run into class and take a seat near Jesse. "You don't look so well. Are you still feeling ill?" Jesse asked, feeling my face.

"I am tired for some reason. I think I must be coming down with something, I need to get some vitamins, get in a run, or something to boost my energy level." I said trying to suck it up and get through the day of classes.

Over the next week, I struggle even harder to get up and make it to class. With an upcoming exam for my economics class of which I have barely paid any attention, I begin to get nervous, so I ask Jesse and the others if they are interested in studying together. Thankfully, they are more than willing, however, Jesse suggests studying at my house which isn't something I had even considered. "Is that a problem, Kayla?"

"I don't think so, but I am not sure what Nick has planned for the night. He may ..."

"Oh well, don't worry about it, I talked to him earlier and he is going to be busy working tonight anyway. So see you at your place around seven?" Jesse smiles, walking away before I have a chance to say anything.

Nick is out when my friends arrive. Unfortunately, I haven't been able to reach him to tell him that they are here, only being able to leave him a message that I hope he gets. Sitting around our dining room table, I study my notes as I feel Scott leaning over in my direction and looking down my shirt. *I am too tired to deal with him tonight.* Choosing to ignore him, I continue, answering some of Kari's questions, before I notice Nick standing in the doorway.

"Hi, Nick!" Jesse says with a bright smile.

"Hi, baby," I said getting up and kissing him. "You did get my message, didn't you?" I asked noticing his stern expression.

"I did. It's no problem." He said, kissing me on the cheek. "Who is the geek trying to look down your shirt?" He whispered in my ear as he wraps his arm around my waist.

"Nick, this is Kari, and ... Scott, and you already know Jesse." I said squeezing his hand hoping he will be nice.

"Nice to meet you. Good to see you again, Jesse." He said before kissing me again. I smile feeling relieved that he is going to let it go. "Are you feeling any better?" I nod. "Good. It's been a long day, I am going to go upstairs and get a shower before I finish some business in my office. See you in bed later?" I smile as he squeezes my butt gently.

"Definitely. I love you." I said as he whispers it back, waving to everyone else when he leaves the room. Sitting back down, I notice everyone staring at me, "What?"

Kari leans across the table wide-eyed, "He is so hot! Oh my gosh! You are so lucky. I wish I looked like you, Kayla, so I could find someone like that." She sighs in her seat.

"You are very pretty, Kari. I am sure you do fine on your own." I said.

"I do fine, but I would do so much better if I looked like you. The perfect hair, eyes and body, killer legs and ..."

"Kari, damn. You *really* need to work on your self-esteem. You and

Kayla are not that much different. She just got lucky is all." Jesse said with a forced smile in my direction. "Kayla, where is your rest room?" I give her quick directions and she leaves, prancing away happily.

"She is so jealous of you, that's why she acts that way." Kari said to me. I shake my head, not understanding. "Because everyone thinks you are prettier than she is and she has never had to deal with that before. You're impossible for her to compete with and, boy, does she hate that." Kari returns to her notes, giggling to herself. I glance at Scott who is now checking out my legs. I sigh impatiently and he quickly returns to his notes.

I nearly forget about Jesse as I study. She has been gone for some time and I begin to worry she has taken some sort of drug and has passed out of an overdose in our bathroom. *Nick would love that.* I get up and go look for her, but she is not in the bathroom near us. After searching everywhere downstairs, I begin to head upstairs when Jesse comes walking down with Nick behind her. I eye her as she passes with a smile, "This place is a maze. It took me forever to find a bathroom. Luckily, I ran into Nick for help." She said hanging on his arm as if he is escorting her to the prom. Nick passes me with a quick kiss, releasing Jesse from his arm to go into his office. I watch as she slides her hand down his arm and leisurely across his ass waiting for him to turn to look at her so she can wink. Suddenly, an uneasy feeling hits me and I become instantly ill. I run upstairs and get sick, sinking into a corner of the bathroom with a tight hold around myself.

"Kayla?" Nick said slowly opening the door. "Princess, are you okay?" I shake my head as he pulls my hair back from my face. "I'll tell your friends you are sick and make sure they get home okay. You go ahead and go to bed." He said kissing me on the head before leaving me. I take a quick shower and climb into bed feeling better but unable to sleep. When Nick comes to bed, I turn to him as he puts his arm around me, quickly kisses me, and settles in for the night. Not at all what he suggested earlier. I lean up and kiss him, rubbing my hands over his chest and down past his stomach to fondle him into an erection. Taking hold of my hand, Nick holds me back, "What are you doing?"

"I thought you said you wanted to and-"

"And you're sick. I appreciate the effort but I think we can both get by one night without." He said turning me down for the first time since we have been together.

CRBD

*J*esse is excessively nice these days and Nick has been too busy to give me enough comfort. My mind is going to places I never thought it would ever go. Jesse is over all the time, supposedly coming over to speak to Luke, but I watch her touch Nick and flaunt herself in front of him constantly. She has let her skirt hike up a little too far, leaned into Nick's face with her breasts nearly pressed into his lips and she has made a joke about having both Luke and Nick to herself as the ultimate dream more than once. She thinks I can't hear her in his office, but that's all I can hear- and think about. *Or maybe the bitch does know?*

It is difficult to concentrate, but with my exam occurring in less than twenty minutes, I take a seat in class going through my notes one last time. Jesse suddenly prances over to me and plops down with a glowing smile. I glance up at her but try hard to ignore her, "Trying to get in some last minute studying?" I nod in response. "I probably should. I was up so late last night." She sighs. "Oh, I saw your man last night. I went to that club ... the one I guess you used to work at." I look up as she touches up her lipstick. "He looked good last night. We talked forever. He is so smart and funny too, I would have never thought that about him. He seems so serious all the time."

"Why were you at the club?" I asked.

"Luke asked me to meet him there."

"But Luke was ..." I know he was handling a party last night for the girls so he would have had no time to meet her at the club, but how do I say that without giving away information I am not supposed to even know. "I know he was busy doing something for Nick." I said simply.

She laughs, "I know. Can you believe that? All that planning and I got my nights mixed up. It was fine, though. Luckily Nick was there and kept me entertained until he could leave. He was so nice to take me home. I was not at all in the right state of mind to be driving. He practically had to carry me to bed." She smiles turning around to look at her notes.

I close my notes and somehow manage to find the energy I haven't had in days. Fisting my hands over and over, I imagine choking the hell out of the woman sitting in front of me and I

175

complete my exam in no time, with little effort. With my renewed energy, the answers come to me with ease. I walk out of class and head straight for home. I don't know if I can stand another minute with my so-called friend.

I am home for barely an hour before Jesse walks in with Luke, even though she knows Luke has to leave soon after to make some deposits. So she plops herself in Nick's office, kicking up her heels, and letting her dress slide up her thighs while she giggles and flips her hair in front of him. Taking a step back, I catch my breath before deciding to take the bitch on. I slide my bra off through my sleeve, trade my jeans for boy shorts, and opt to take it a step further by removing my shirt and trading it for my thin tank top to help me with my quest. Walking towards Nick's office, I pull the clip from my hair, grab my book, and lick my lips as I walk in front of his door and drop my book. "Sorry, I didn't mean to startle you." I said meeting Nick's eyes perfectly before bending over to grab my book. "I will be upstairs, baby, if you need anything." I said biting my bottom lip and walking away on my imagined stage with confidence.

"Make yourself at home, Jesse. I am sure Luke will be back soon." Nick said from behind me.

"Where are you going?" Jesse yelled out.

"I have some fucking business to take care of." He said as I hear him running up from behind me. "Where are *you* going?" He asked me throwing me over his shoulder as he races to our room. I helped Nick take care of his business late into the night.

⚜

I have managed to avoid Jesse until our next class, where I barely speak to her as the professor hands out our graded exam papers. I receive my exam and am shocked by the grade. "How did you do?" Jesse asked. "Oh wow, that's not good at all. I don't know how I did it, another 'A', I guess little sleep and barely studying works best for me. Then again, I have always picked things up quickly. I don't know, things just come easy to me. If you need any tutoring, let me know. I know how Nick likes his women smart, you must pretend well for him." She said as I barely hide my groaning displeasure with her. "I tell you what, I will talk to the professor for you. He likes me. Maybe I can talk him into giving you some extra credit work or another exam." She said patting me with encouragement, "Let's get coffee after. Meet you across the street later?" She asked, again not waiting for me to answer before she confirms our date.

After class, I try to speak to the professor but Jesse takes up his time. I know they are talking about me because they keep glancing my way as I wait. Jesse finishes and passes by me with thumbs up, only Professor Rollins walks out of class without talking to me.

"Professor Rollins?" I yell running after him.

"Yes, Mrs. Jayzon, is there a problem?"

"Yes, there is a problem. My paper? You failed me."

"Well, I guess you will have to try harder next time." He said going into his office.

I follow him, still studying my paper in shock, "Professor Rollins, I am not sure what this is about, but I know damn well that I did not deserve this grade."

"Maybe you didn't. So, what do you think we can do about it?" He asked strangely. Sitting casually against the edge of his desk, "Your friend said you would be more than willing to come to an arrangement. You know? To get your grade up?"

"I don't understand." I said taking a step back.

"I thought since you need a better grade and ..." He approaches backing me into a corner. "I have heard that you were one of the best strippers at that club that I can't afford to get into. So maybe we can ..." He takes the back of his hand and floats it down the side of my face. "Maybe you could entertain me for a little while and edge that grade up." I smack him hard and he takes hold of my wrist. "Your grade isn't going to change that way. What's the big deal? If you don't want to fuck, than at least give me a blowjob. Although one will get you a much better grade than the other."

"Don't worry about my grade. I will talk to the Dean instead!" I said reaching for the door.

Angry, he blocks my path, "I don't think you are. You did just attack a professor on campus, so unless you want to get kicked out of school, you will start working on that grade right now!" I step back from him as he takes hold of my arm and starts to unbuckle his pants.

"I would let go of me if I were you, because I guarantee you don't want my husband to see me with a bruise." I said with precise clarity.

"Are you threatening me?" He said changing his overconfident attitude to anger.

"No, I'm warning you. I am not someone you want to fuck with because you will only end up getting yourself killed." I said taking out his erection with my knee and storming out, deciding to end my day before I do something ill-advised. Before I go home angry, I stop by the coffee shop to calm down, although the thought occurs to me that seeing Jesse may cause me to get even angrier. *Nick can't see me this upset though, not when I tell him ... if I tell him.* Twirling the stirrer in my coffee, I drift off to a place far from where I am.

"I knew I was going to run into trouble today." I turn and see Brady smiling from the counter at me. I smirk and turn back around but he still walks over and sits down with me. "I know I am a huge asshole, but I have been going to my asshole classes and they say I am making a lot of progress. They even gave me a ticket for controlling my asshole attitude for sixty days." He pauses with his patent irresistible grin. "I swear, look." He said tossing a ticket on the table.

"This is a movie ticket for the movie Sixty Days, dumbass." I said as he laughs.

"Oh, my bad." He smiles leaning back in his chair. "So, beautiful, are we ever going to be friends again?"

"Friends? Is that what we were?"

"Alright. Then can we start over and be friends? I know I was wrong and you were completely right about me. If it is any consolation, I wouldn't have been able to go through with my inexcusable plan entirely."

"Entirely? What is that suppose to mean?" I ask glancing up from my drink.

"Kayla, you are hard to resist and I am nothing if but only a man. You can't expect me to turn you down if you wanted me to get nasty with you."

I throw a waded up napkin at him as he laughs. "You are not helping your cause, Detective Simone."

"Oh, come on! Now you sound like Jayzon. Don't do that." I smile at him and he takes notice of my hand and shakes his head. "You did marry him? I was hoping that was a sick joke when I heard it."

"I love him." I said watching him make an expression of disgust. "If you want to be friends with me, you can't bad mouth or make awful facial expressions whenever I mention my husband's name." I wait as he smirks in another direction. "So, do you still want to be friends?"

"I guess. I mean, there is a chance you could get divorced at some point." He mumbles.

"We are not off to a good start … *friend*."

Smiling, he sips his coffee and then looks me in the eyes, "So, why are you on this side of town, anyway?"

"Nick is paying for me to go to the college across the street." I said with a smile that shocks me, considering the day I have had.

"How nice of the bastard." He said as I eye him. "Sorry … habit. Wow, that's exciting I bet you're enjoying it!" He sings while I lower my head to look at my swirling drink. "Uh oh. Talk to me. What's going on?"

"I had some trouble at school today."

"Whatever it is, there has to be somebody at school that can help you."

"That would be a good idea except that now I may be kicked out of school." I said as Brady looks at me wide-eyed. "I hit a professor today."

"You? What did he do?" He laughs.

"He wanted me to have sex with him in order to get a better grade."

"Then *he* needs to be kicked off campus, not you. And, you know that, so why are you sitting here looking like the end of the world?"

"Why would they believe me over him? I am …"

"Not the poor, wrong side of the tracks girl anymore. You need to get over that and stop letting people push you around. You have a lot more power than you think, Kayla. Take 'em by the balls and squeeze, honey." I laugh nodding as he smiles. "I can't believe Jayzon hasn't already handled this for you anyway. Hell … how is this professor still alive?" I glance up pressing my lips tight together. Brady chuckles, "So, you are scared tell him."

"I didn't say that! I just don't want to bother him with something so unimportant."

"I am sure he wouldn't find it unimportant. Listen, you don't have to explain it to me but if you need some help, let me know. I may not have your husband's money, but I do have some connections that could make your life a little easier. Not to mention, an attorney friend that would be more than happy to make a call for you to the president of the school and explain the law to him." I smile. "There it is. That's the smile I have been waiting for. Now I know we are friends."

"No, we aren't. Not until you have finished all of your asshole recovery classes and I want to see documentation that you completed every class." I laugh with him until Jesse comes running in all smiles. She kisses my cheek before she sits down and waits to be introduced. "Jesse, this is Detective Simone."

"Brady, nice to meet you." He says shaking Jesse's hand. "Well, it looks like you have some important things to talk about with your friend here so I will catch up with you later. Call me when you get a chance. I like our new friendly arrangement." Brady kisses my cheek with a brotherly messing of my hair before leaving.

"Well, he is cute. I bet Nick doesn't know about him." Jesse said resting on her elbows. "What's wrong? Did things not go well with Professor Rollins?"

"Jesse, he wanted me to have sex with him to get a better grade. Did you tell him I wanted to do that- that I would be willing to do that?" I asked her as she sits back in shock.

"Absolutely NOT! I swear, Kayla, I would never suggest such a thing. All I asked was that he give you a break because you have been so sick lately. I asked if he could find some extra credit work or something. That I was sure that you would be willing to do it."

"Well, he heard the do it part alright, but he said something about me stripping. Did you tell him about that?"

"No, I don't know where he would have heard that unless he overheard us talking or something. Maybe he saw you there once." She said primping in her little pocket mirror.

"We have never talked about it, because I have never said anything to you about it."

She shrugs. "That is strange, Kayla. You better be careful, he may be some kind of a sick stalker or something. I would talk to him again. Maybe at the end of the day when you have more privacy. I will go with you and make sure he stays in line." I glance her way before excusing myself with a sharp tone.

~24~
KAYLA

*W*hile wrestling with myself about calling Brady for help, Nick comes home. "Hi, Princess," he said kissing me with a purr, "Everything okay? You still sick?"

"A little but I think I am getting better." He begins looking at the mail as I battle with what the right thing to do is. All I can think is that Nick is going to kill him and now that I have told Brady about it, the first person they are going to accuse is Nick.

"Are you sure you're okay? You're trembling." He said. I open my mouth but nothing comes out and before I can try again, Luke and Jesse walk in laughing and cuddling each other.

"Nick, let's get this over with. Jesse and I have reservations at that little Italian place on Bertrum Street." Luke said.

"Hold on. I think Kayla has to tell me something." Nick said as everyone in the room looks my way.

"Ummm, no. It's not important." I said backing away.

"It's okay, Kayla, you can tell him. I already told Luke anyway." Jesse said as Luke nods.

"Nick is going to kill that fuck. I can't believe that bastard had the balls to do something like that." Luke said sitting down casually with Jesse.

Nick takes hold of me and looks me in the eyes with concern, "What happened?"

"It sounds worse than it was ..." I said already seeming to apologize for bothering him.

"How can a guy propositioning you for a better grade sound worse than it was?" Luke laughs.

"Who the fuck did that?" Nick snaps as I close my eyes, feeling ill all over again.

"Professor Rollins, he is our economics professor. Asshole gave her a failing grade and then expected her to bend over for him in his office today." Jesse said cuddling with Luke, not realizing the fire she is starting.

"Nick, don't ..." I said gripping his arm.

"Don't what?" He said with darkened eyes.

I caress his hands and try to calm him, "Don't do anything. I can take ..."

"Did you show him your arm?" Jesse said causing both Luke and Nick to stare at me hard.

Nick pulls back my sleeves until he finds a light, bruised handprint. Luke jumps up to see and looks back up at me laughing. "This fuck is dead!"

"No! Nick, let me take care of it. I am going to talk to the Dean, the president of the school and get him fired." I said.

"Fired! You think that's all he deserves?" Nick yells tensing into colors I never like to see. I rush to him caressing him even more to calm down. "What's his full name?" I shake my head. "What's his name, Kayla?"

"Nick, I don't want you doing anything. I don't want you to get into trouble." I plead.

"Oh, Nick won't get into trouble. He knows how to make things happen without anyone seeing or knowing a thing." Luke said proudly.

"Nick, no. I have already said something to Brady. If you go and do ..." I said calmly until Nick stares at me hard. "He stopped by the coffee shop where I was meeting Jesse and we got to talking and it had just happened so ... I was upset and he offered to help."

Backing away from me, "He just happened to be there?" Nick asked. I nod surprised to see him look at me as if I am hiding something from him.

"Oh, Nick, don't be so jealous. I was there it was completely innocent. She couldn't have been there alone with him for more than a few minutes. He said good-bye, kissed her, and left." Jesse said with an innocent smile in my direction.

Nick leans into my face, "Nice kiss, was it?"

I push back, "What is wrong with you? It was a kiss on the cheek- quick and nothing. This should be a conversation between us and not for the whole fucking world to hear!"

"Why not? Apparently the whole fucking world knows about it before your husband does! I want to know this professor's full name and I want you to stay away from Simone. You see him coming, you go the other way. Do you hear me?" He growls at me.

"No, no I won't! And I will be damned if you are going to speak to me this way and think it's okay. I will be friends with whoever I want to and I will handle my own problems. If I need your help, I will let you know." I said stepping away from his snarling expression.

"I am going to take care of this, Kayla. What's the professor's name, Jesse?" Nick asked. I look over at her and shake my head.

"Its ... sorry, Kayla, but I mean you really shouldn't have gone into his office alone like that. It is never a good idea. Especially since he had already been making passes at you and leaving you those disgusting notes. I did ask you to wait for me." Jesse said looking up at Nick sympathetically. "I don't know why she plays those games with people. It really is dangerous." I look at Nick and watch him begin to shake with anger.

"You fucking lying bitch! Get out of my house and don't ever come back!" I yell at her.

"Who the fuck do you think you are, Kayla? I knew you were trouble. You are lucky you are still alive!" Luke yells at me as he closes in on me.

"You don't know what the hell you are doing, Luke. This bitch has done everything she can to weasel her way into this house and push me out. She is using you to get at Nick, you fool!"

Luke waves his hand in my face, "Shut up, Kayla!"

Nick pushes Luke away and leans down to look me directly in the eyes, "I am going to take care of this ..."

"NO! NO, Nick! I swear if you ..." I said watching Nick suddenly eye Luke. I turn to look at him too quickly and become dizzy.

Luke pulls out a gun, "I'll take care of him, Nick."

"NO!" I scream swaying backwards. With a step sideways, I look back up at Nick and collapse.

"Kayla!" Nick yells. My whole body floats away as he calls out to me but I just want him to be quiet and let me close my eyes until the world stops moving. When I open my eyes again, Nick is hovering over me and screaming out orders as he puts me into bed. "Kayla?"

"I'm okay." I mumbled.

"Relax, Kayla, I'm calling the doctor for you." Nick said looking stressed but much calmer than previous. I try to sit up in protest but Nick holds me down. "I said relax." The doctor had Nick ask me a list of questions and decided that he would like to see me first thing in the morning. Before I could even think of protesting the idea, Nick confirmed a time for me and hung up. If not for one of the doctor's questions, I would be a little worried about my so-called illness, but now my reality suddenly seems clear. Thankfully, Nick, in his already ill-tempered mood, hasn't even considered the possibility.

CRWO

*M*y attempt to speak to the Dean about Professor Rollins didn't go as well as I had hoped. I was told that there would have to be an inquiry involving both of us because apparently they can't simply take a student's word for it. I understood their reasoning, but if he isn't off campus soon then my husband will find him and there will be no more Professor Rollins to inquire about. Brady came through for me, and the next day, Professor Rollins is escorted off campus. Every student's grade is reevaluated by his replacement and, without even a discussion, my grade is changed to what I deserve. Everyone whispers all-day long about the rumors of him sleeping with students and giving out grades in return. It seems he has been at this with many of the female student body. Sitting in what was Rollins economics class, is now Professor Leonardo, she is a short, spunky, older lady, and without knowing much more, I am excited to have her. However, one glance around and I know there is at least one person who is not so happy about the new professor. Jesse sits silently stiff in her seat as she stares at her revised grade. I smile at her before I can help myself. A smile she doesn't appreciate.

CRWO

*M*y doctor's appointment was not surprising, but at least the doctor was able to give me some direction on how to feel more like myself. Now all I have to do is tell Nick, which only makes me more nauseous. Despite my unyielding stomach, classes today are comfortable and pleasant. I am more than halfway through the day when I spot the reason why, Jesse heads to her car somberly. Curious, I race towards her, "Jesse, where are you going? I haven't seen you all-day."

"They suspended me- no thanks to you." She said sharply.

"Me, what did I do?"

"You couldn't keep your mouth shut about Professor Rollins. You had to go and make a big deal out of it and now they are going through all my grades and saying that I didn't earn any of them. And that old hag that has taken over for Rollins is hell-bent on having me kicked out." She continues on with revulsion in her voice while I try to manage my laughter.

"Well, Jesse, maybe if you had actually studied and did the work instead of offering favors to get everything you want." I said.

"Are you calling me a whore?" She yells at me but before I can respond she huffs in my face, "If anyone is a whore, it's you. From what I understand, you are one of the best whore's around."

"You don't know what you're talking about." I said waving her off and walking away before I get into it with someone that doesn't matter to me.

"You better be careful, Kayla. Eventually Nick is going to get tired of your tricks and move on to someone new." She yells as I leave her behind.

After my last class is over, I get a call that I am to meet with the president of the school before I leave today. A little nervous about why he, of all people, would be asking to see me, I try to walk into his office with my head up and a proper tone when I greet his assistant. She escorts me into his office, where I wait nervously until he finishes a phone conversation. Upon finishing, he turns to me with an intense expression causing me to sit up straighter than I thought possible.

"Mrs. Jayzon, let me start off by saying your grades are impeccable."

"Thank you, but I don't imagine you called me in here to tell me that." I said wanting him to get to the point.

"No, actually I was informed by a respected booster that you have been soliciting ..." He clears his throat awkwardly. "Well, you have been offering services to students, professors, and a few boosters at the school for money."

"Services? You mean sex? You think I have been prostituting while I am here?" I ask with an angry tone.

"Calm down please. It is certainly not a practice we condone. The accusations along with the recent information I received about your arrest for the similar." He said showing me a copy of my arrest when I was seventeen.

"I was seventeen and trying to get by. And I wasn't prostituting! I was stripping. There were others in the club that were having sex for money, but I wasn't. If you read it, I was cleared of that." I said sitting at the edge of my seat.

"Yes, I see that, but I imagine only because you were under age and considered not responsible." Sitting back in my chair with frustration, I begin to shake with anger. "I think it goes without saying that you will need to leave campus as soon as we are done here and please never return. Obviously, we will return any money due back to you for the remainder of the quarter."

"This is bullshit! I didn't do anything wrong. What right do you have to throw me out of school?" I yell at him.

"This is a private school, Mrs. Jayzon. We are a highly respected private school and we can't have boosters thinking we are allowing your type of ..."

"I AM NOT DOING ANYTHING WRONG!" I yell at him.

"Calm down. There is nothing you can do. It is the school's right to deny whomever they wish on campus, if they feel it threatens the safety of its students. Now, if you ..."

I stand up before he can finish, "No, I don't want to listen to you anymore. You have convicted me based on something I did when I was a kid. Because someone said that I was doing these things. When I accused Professor Rollins of propositioning me for a higher grade, you required me to have a formal inquiry before you would do anything. It took an attorney to call you and let you know he had been dismissed at several other schools for similar behavior before you would even consider throwing him out. But now someone accuses me, and without hesitation, you throw me out? I assume the booster you speak of is Jesse McCreary's father? The same woman who has gone out of her way to sleep with every professor she can for grades? You are taking the word of one booster because of his psycho daughter and probably allowing her back into the school. Why, Mr. Rankin? Why would I need to earn money that way? My husband isn't exactly poor. As you can see, we pay in full every quarter and no loans have ever been taken out. But, apparently, our money isn't good enough for you."

"Mrs. Jayzon, I am sure there is another school that will be interested in accepting your type."

"My type? Exactly what is my type?" I ask with fists drawn.

"You are misquoting me. All I meant to say is that you are not use to this type of school. The students that come here, the majority of them are from fine families and ..."

"You mean you don't have drug addict fathers and alcoholic mothers showing up with other students here? Well, that's no problem, because my parents are dead so they won't be bothering anyone anymore. I mean unless the idea of them bothers you. But then, I imagine the fact that my sister hung herself probably bothers you too. Or, maybe it's because I met my husband stripping at his club? Which part of my life, Mr. Rankin, makes me not the sort of people you want on your campus? Because it is certainly not my straight A's. Or that I graduated high school in less than three years with a 4.2 grade point average. Or that I volunteer to tutor kids at the nearby schools in my off time. I guess in your mind, Mr. Rankin, once a girl is born on the wrong side of the tracks, she will always be on the wrong side." Realizing his mind is already made up, I take my things and walk out of his office. Stupidly, Jesse waits near my car with her arrogant smile. I immediately drop everything and punch her smile right off her face. "Fuck you, bitch!" I yelled at her as she lies on the ground holding her mouth.

Jesse jumps to her feet as a crowd begins to form around us, "You don't deserve him, Kayla!" She yells stopping me in my tracks. I turn catching her emerging smile, "You don't deserve Nick. He deserves someone better than a backstabber." She said. I assume she is referring to my success in getting Rollins removed and therefore causing her entire college stay to be questioned.

"It is not my fault you earned your grades from your knees, Jesse." I said dismissing her ridiculousness.

"At least I didn't betray my own sister." She smirks, "I can't believe anyone would go after their own sister's boyfriend. The man she loved more than anything. So much so that she killed herself over him. Did your jealousy drive her to commit suicide, Kayla?" The slight smile at the edges of her lips doesn't hurt nearly as much as my hardened regret that rushes to the forefront of my heart tearing me apart. Without another word, I get into my car and leave for someplace unknown. A place that I hope can somehow release this pain.

~25~
NICK

*E*ven though Kayla made a desperate attempt to have him removed from the school before I could get to him it didn't take me long to find Rollins. We walked in on the desperation, snapping pictures of some young girls who were under the impression that he was a celebrity photographer which is why they let him dictate their lack of wardrobe. Once the young women were set straight, my boys cleared the way for me to walk in and give Rollins the once over before explaining who I am and what his options are now. Unfortunately for him, he isn't agreeable to any of the options, so I decide for him. "What did you say to me?" I asked him as he grunts and hold his chest out to me.

"I said I rather enjoyed getting a good feel of Kayla. It's too bad for her she didn't get a good feel of me because I am sure she would have enjoyed it. Maybe I will give her a second chance to try me out." Rollins said boastfully before he felt my fist in his mouth. Staggering backwards, he wipes his lip and tries to come at me like a bull. Stepping aside, I get a quick hold of his head by his hair and knock his legs out from under him.

"Tell me again what you are going to say to my wife if you ever see her again?" I asked in my calm voice.

"I'm sorry." He said struggling to release himself from my fists.

"You are one hell of a scumbag with your cameras and erotic magazines. I can only imagine what is on that computer of yours. With all this evidence, I just can't believe that you are really sorry about anything, not someone like you. No, I think the only way to get through to you is taking away your opportunity for a while." Despite his screaming, I let go of him and watch as Luke kicks him onto his back and I take a swing with a nearby bat to his hands. I leave him feeling a little better about my day.

I am not anxious to have this argument with Kayla again but it is done and there is nothing she can do it about now. Pulling up to the house, I don't see her car even though she should have gotten home hours ago. After several hours and even more messages left for her, Kayla is still not home. When Jesse suddenly shows up, I let her in, curious if Kayla might be with her. "What are you doing here?" I asked her looking for Kayla somewhere behind her.

"Is Kayla here?" I shake my head and she smiles wide. "Oh, so we are all alone?" She asked as I roll my eyes and walk away from her. When I turn back around, Jesse has removed her dress and is posing for me in her scantily clad underwear. "I think we both want the same thing, Nick."

"Kayla should be home any minute. If I were you, I wouldn't be here when she gets here- especially dressed like that." I said looking her over once before turning away.

Caressing me, she begins to moan, "You and I could do some great things together. If we combined our forces, we would be unstoppable. Not to mention ..." She eases up on her toes and kisses me, "I will do things to you that will make you beg for me to never leave." She whispered proudly.

"Get away from me." I said wiping myself clean of her.

"Nick, listen to me! I came here to talk to you about becoming partners. If we join forces then we can ..."

"Partners? What the fuck are you talking about?" I yell in frustration still checking the clock wondering where Kayla is.

"I have formed my own corporation and I am willing to combine mine with yours. We would work together to own everything. We can take down Joseph and everyone else."

I laugh, "So Joseph dumped you, huh?"

Stomping forward, "This has nothing to do with my relationship with Joseph. I am out for a better opportunity. Think about it, Nick, with my father's connections, my social standing, and your head for business we could ..."

"We are going to do nothing together. I don't have any interest in working with you, Jesse. I have no reason to."

"But my father ..." She scrambles chasing me around the room.

"I OWN YOUR FATHER!" I roar.

Stepping backwards, she finally understands. "I could make you happy."

"I already am happy- with Kayla." She grips hold of me trying to strip me and herself at the same time, "I don't want you!" I finally yell at her. "I have no interest in you! Do you understand that? Not to partner in business or in bed! The only thing I want from you is to know where my wife is!"

"I have no idea where that whore is!" She screams, jerking away from me.

Sucking in a breath of air, I take hold of her waist and hold her in place, "What the fuck did you do to my wife?" I seethe into her wide eyes.

"I ... I had my father talk to the president and show him the document of her prostitution arrest and let him know about her working the campus for money. She really is no good, Nick, you would be shocked if you knew what all she has been doing." I grip her harder as fire begins to heat up my lungs. "I don't know where she is at! She took off after our argument in the parking lot. She fucking punched me in the mouth! I was luckily able to cover up most of it with makeup ... it's horrible." She grips my hands and presses against my chest as I wait for her to tell me the rest, "Let go of me! I told you I don't know!"

"You are a sick piece of trash." I said, pushing her off me and causing her to stumble backwards into the floor. I call for my guards and leave the room ignoring her screaming at me as they physically escort her away.

Retreating to my office, I call Kayla one more time before I go searching for her. As the phone rings I hear her coming through the door. I run out to her and stop dead in my tracks as she halts me with her expression. "Where have you been?" I asked, wanting to go to her but unsure of why she seems so distant from me.

"I went to see Bray today." She said shockingly. "I need to talk to you."

"I took care of Rollins today. He is even worse than you think." I said as she spins on her heels away from me and clutches her head. "Did you expect me to sit back and do nothing? Let someone hurt my wife and do nothing about it?" I walk over and lean in towards her. "The thought of someone touching you and hurting you ... I don't think you understand what that does to me. I love you so much ..." Kayla spins around and looks up at me with watery eyes.

"Something happened today."

"I know and I will make sure you are back in school tomorrow." I said hoping that will ease the pain that is so obvious in her eyes. "I'm sorry that happened, but Jesse and her father are nothing that I can't handle."

"Nick … I-"

"Don't worry. It will be painless. I just need to make a few calls and everything will be straightened out … just a few calls, Princess."

"Nick!"

"Kayla, Jesse came here tonight and offered herself up to me, but nothing happened and she won't be working for me anymore. I know what she did and she …"

"Nick, please shut up! I have to tell you something." She cries, looking at me in complete fear. "I'm pregnant." I back away from her silently. "Say something."

"What do you want me say? I thought we agreed that we didn't want kids? Damn it, Kayla!" I yell turning away from her and fisting my own hair.

"We did agree, but it happened and … I have decided I want this baby." She said, suddenly standing up strong and defiant.

"You decided. Well, that's great. You decided, so there you go." I laugh sarcastically.

"What is that look for? Do you think I did this on purpose?"

"You tell me, Kayla. You are the one making the decisions."

"That wasn't a decision!"

"Then how, Kayla? How does that happen when we are so careful?"

"I might have missed a few but …"

"Might have missed a few?" Shaking my head with a smile, "That's wonderful. Good job." Kayla punches me as hard as she can but it doesn't even budge me, "Feel better?"

"NO! You are so concerned and can't stand the thought of someone touching me or hurting me but you find it easy to stand there and do just that! You are hurting me horribly- and for what? Because your life isn't going to work out just as you planned it? Because you lost control?"

"It's not about control! It's about being a good father! I don't want to do to a child what my parents did to me! What yours did to you! I am not …"

"You are not your father or your mother, Nick. And I am not either of mine. We love each other and I want nothing more than to share this with you- the only man who has ever made me feel loved and not like a mistake that happiness is wasted on." She steps towards me, touching my chest gently before she lays her head against me sighing exhaustively. "I didn't do it on purpose, but I want this baby. Don't make me feel ashamed for being happy about our baby." I have never felt for anyone the way I feel for her and I want nothing but for her to be happy no matter how I feel. So, despite my fears about being a father, I put my arms around her and hold her on into the night, kissing her, and making her feel as safe as she needs me too.

⊗⊗

I made sure the college had to accept Kayla back and that she would have no further trouble from them. My lawyer was handy in my efforts, but so was my sizable donation. Kayla's first day back at school was a pleasurable one from what I understand. She was treated like a queen and given full apologies from both the president of the school and the board of trustees. Tonight, I am taking her to dinner to celebrate her perfect grades - or so she thinks. Exie has planned a bridal shower for her since we ran off without anyone knowing, as Exie aggressively pointed out to me when I originally protested the idea. After considering her less than optional suggestion, I allowed Exie to close the club on our slowest night, which I insisted upon so she and the other girls could all attend. It will be a surprise for all of them when they show up for work, attending a party that they can still get paid for. With all that has been going on, I think this night is what Kayla needs.

When Kayla sees us pulling into the club, she huffs at me, "Nick, I thought we were going to dinner! You didn't say anything about working too." She complains.

"Give me two minutes. Princess, please? Come in for a second and say hi to Exie." She crosses her arms and looks away from me. "Kayla, come on. I promise two minutes and no longer." With a deep sigh, she slides out of the car and walks in front of me with her arms still crossed.

"It's dark. Why is it so …" She said before the lights flash on and her girls jump out at her, laughing and instantaneously making her up into a bridal mess of decorations. Kayla looks back at me with a huge smile and I feel a lot better. Thankfully, Dwayne meets me there and comes in so I don't have to take part in the craziness. We have a quiet man talk until Luke comes in as if he just spotted Oz at the other end of the yellow brick road. "What is wrong with you?" I said to him.

"Love, Nick. Love is what's wrong."

"You're in love?" I asked with sincere doubt.

"Oh Lord." Dwayne said rolling his eyes.

Luke punches Dwayne in the arm receiving a piercing glare in return, "Don't worry, big guy, one day you will be like Nick and I and find that perfect person."

"I'm married, jackass. Have been for ten years." Dwayne said sighing.

"Really?" Luke asked glancing around the room, seemingly trying to recall. "You mean that fine piece of ass is your wife? How the hell did you get her to marry you? Because she is ..." Luke makes a gesture as Dwayne groans like a bear.

"Please tell me you're not talking about ...?" I asked with little hope in my voice.

Luke's smile diminishes some but returns in an exaggerated style, "You understand, Nick. I know you do. You can't help who you fall in love with. No matter what her flaws are, I love her and we are going to get married." Glancing at Dwayne, we both understand the consequences of this and it isn't going to be good. Before I can say a word, Luke jumps up and orders drinks for us, "Be happy for me, Nick. That's all I am asking from you- my friend, best friend, my brother really when you consider all that we have been through together. There is nothing I want more than for you, of all people, to be happy for me." He said eyeing me with a drink held out to me. I raise my glass and smile, sensing the impending doom of our friendship. "So, what's going on here?" Luke asked watching Kayla and the girls giggling with each other.

"Exie is throwing Kayla a bridal shower." I said.

"A little late, isn't it?" He asked as I give him a quick nod. "I understand all the sexy lingerie and shit, but what's with the teddy bear?" I turn quickly looking at the bear Kayla holds out in front of her with a big smile. "Some sick, twisted sex game you two enjoy?" Turning back around, I glance at both of them but Dwayne knows without me saying a word, "What? What was that look between you two?" Luke asked.

"Kayla is pregnant." I said watching him squirm before finally forcing a smile.

"Congratulations, Nick," Dwayne said.

"Yea, wow ... congratulations. I guess we need another drink." Luke said looking around for someone but finally deciding to get up and get it himself. He returns with several drinks but drinks them all himself. He doesn't smile again until he receives a text and responds back quickly. "You don't mind if Jesse meets me here, do you? I was going to meet her for dinner after I dropped off the payments, but since it is Kayla's bridal shower, Jesse thought it would be a good chance to make amends and give her a gift too."

"Luke, I don't know. They are not anywhere close to friends at this point. I think it would be best for her not to ruin the party." I said to his instant displeasure.

"She isn't going to ruin it. She doesn't even have to join them. She can wait with us and then you can give it to Kayla later, if you want. Or not at all, but take it at least so you don't hurt Jesse's feelings." Luke said as I hide my rolling eyes. *As if I care about hurting that bitch's feelings.* Before I groan too much, Luke runs out the door to let her in. Glancing back at Kayla and the girls, I am thankful they have her too preoccupied to even look our way.

Jesse sits down with us, eyeing me carefully. "Dwayne ... Nick, how are you?" Jesse asked, flashing her new, brightly shining diamond in our faces. I nod in her direction but sip my tea before I say something to the bitch that my friend won't like at all. Dwayne leaves saying he needs to make a call, but I know he can't stand her anymore than I can. Luke gets up to go get her a drink, leaving me alone with her. Before either can get back she is rubbing her foot up my leg. Blocking her from reaching her destination, I push it back to the ground adjusting my position away from her. "So, I guess you haven't decided to take me up on my offer?" She asked.

"Offer? That wasn't an offer that was an insult. Not to mention, I wouldn't fuck you if I thought it would save my dick from falling off." She curls her lip at me and I look for Luke to see how much longer he is going to be. The bitch puts a cigarette in her mouth and I flip it away, "Not in my club."

"It's a strip club, not a health club." She remarks in disgust.

"NOT ... IN ... MY CLUB." I spelled out clearly for her. "Repulsive whore." I mumbled to myself.

"I believe your wife is a whore, if you're looking for one. How many men was she with? I mean, besides the ones you know about. Like the ones she was fucking at that low class place she worked at before here? I can only imagine the disgusting ..." Glaring at Kayla, she chuckles to herself proudly. "Well, I guess if anyone knows her, you do. I mean, she did step over her sister's dead body to get to you. Even Kayla knows she was wrong about that one."

"Say another word about Kayla and I will break your neck right here." I said, eyeing her with malicious intent.

"Such the loyal husband. Never thought someone like you would manage something so moral. Although, I wish we could still be partners- even if it isn't in bed."

"I am not in the habit of helping people up to my level, Jessica." I said, adjusting my sleeves as I sit back in my seat.

"Up to your level? Aren't you full of yourself! You better watch it, Nick. One day you're going to run into someone smarter than you, who will outdo you at your own game." She said with confidence.

"Threatening me now? I wouldn't do that if I were you because you certainly aren't smart enough." I said watching Exie and Kayla walk over to me with odd expressions on their faces.

"Ummm…. Hi." Exie said with a strange giggle. "Ummm… oh my gosh! I can't believe I am doing this." She twisted with a girlish expression. "So, I was wondering if you could help me out and my friends. We are playing a scavenging hunt game and my girl here is getting married and …" Exie said kissing Kayla on the cheek. "Anyway, she has to get so many items on her list tonight to win the game and one of those items is a kiss from a handsome stranger." Understanding the girls joke, I immediately face forward away from them and straighten my curious smile. "So, what do you say? Could you give her a kiss? Oh … on the cheek, of course … I will take care of the rest later." Exie whispered the latter, smacking Kayla on the ass. I nearly laugh but manage to hold off but Exie didn't hold back her laughter-and neither did the other girls roaring with laughter behind us.

Dwayne and Luke return, I glance at them with a serious tone. "I don't kiss on the cheek," I said looking Kayla up and down.

Kayla leans down at my side, "That's alright, Handsome, I wasn't wanting a kiss on the cheek. The cheek on my face anyway. Now, my ass is all yours … that is, if you have the balls to take it." I glance over at her, as she licks her lips lightly and begins to walk away, laughing with all the other girls enjoying their little game.

She should know better than to tease me. I jump up quickly and grab her from behind, throwing her over my shoulder, and carrying her to the back-office. "Nick! No! We don't have time for you … NICHOLAS JAYZON! Don't you fuck on my desk!" Exie yells at me. I open the office door, winking at her, before going in and locking Kayla inside with me.

I sit Kayla down and she backs away from me, "Where are you going? You wanted a kiss, right?"

A blushing smile appears across her face as she shyly plays with the edge of her dress, making me insane. "I guess it would be okay to get a kiss and nothing else. You do understand that I am dedicated to my husband, of course."

"You're not married yet, right?" Eyeing her until she looks into my eyes, I approach her slowly causing her to back into the desk behind her. "Why do you keep backing away from me?" I take hold of her and sit her up on the desk. Breathing against her cheek, I look over her body as she watches my hand edge closer and closer to her bare leg. Waiting for her to look back into my eyes, "So a kiss, huh? How do you want it? Do you want it soft?" I asked brushing my lips across hers. "Or do you want it hard?" I asked gripping her ass suddenly towards me. "I can do it either way. I can do it however you like."

Kayla straightens with a confident smile, "Just a simple kiss will be fine." I forget how immune she is to my usual tactics.

Running my fingers deep into her hair, "I want a little more than a kiss from you." Taking my hand up her dress I feel my way slowly up her thigh, all the while holding her head, and breathing gently against her cheek. "Can I kiss you here?" I asked rubbing her thigh. "What about ... here?" I asked grazing my hand between her legs. Enjoying her soft gasp, I move my hand to her ass and squeeze with a moan against her ear, "This would be nice for me too. You did say I could have it." Just at the right time, she looks into my eyes and I move my hand back between her legs easing it under her panties and down watching her eyes close, "I think you want it here though. I think you want me to taste you here." I said sliding her panties off and kissing her deep on the mouth, helping her lie back on the desk. Spreading her legs, I give her the kiss she really wants and enjoy her frantic gasps for control. Achieving what I want from her, I take my clothes off quickly, slip her dress over her head, and strip her bra with one touch before fondling her full breasts in my hands, kissing her so softly I can barely hold myself back to move her somewhere more suitable. I pick up my beautifully naked wife and carry her to the sofa while she looks into my eyes and holds onto my head with a soft smile.

"I thought you didn't fuck that woman, that debutant, you said ..."

"I didn't fuck her, but you're not her." I reminded her while sliding myself into the wetness I created, feeling her tense around me. Kayla kisses along my neck, rubbing down my chest, my arms, and my back, squeezing my ass down into her with a shaky moan. Pulling her legs up around me, I feel for the place that sends her over the edge and concentrate on it. Pressing down on it, grazing it, sliding over it and over it until she grips me so tight I can hardly move. I kiss her neck, her mouth, waiting for her ... then feeling her. "I love you." Looking into her loving green eyes, I come inside her with a heavy breath, kissing her soft lips with a smile.

Kayla wraps her arms around my neck and holds me against her. "You knew what you were doing the whole time."

"As I recall, you came on to me." I said kissing her nipples with a wicked smile. She cradles me to her chest and I feel so good I don't want to move.

Banging on the door, Exie makes our time alone together short-lived, "You do have your own place to go to! Remember the big house where you can screw anywhere you want? Without bothering other people? Or messing up their things?" She yells at us. Kayla gets dressed quickly and opens the door as soon as I have my pants on. Exie stands with her arms crossed and a sinister glare. "People are waiting for cake. Do you want some?"

"I get cake too?" I asked laughing as Exie focuses on me.

"No. You already had yours." She said, taking Kayla's hand and leaving with her.

I slide my shirt on and walk towards the bathroom noticing something odd: the back door stands open. Suddenly Jesse comes walking through with her cell phone in hand, leaving the door unlocked. "You forgot something." I said, pointing to the lock.

"Oh, so I did," she smiles, waiting for me to walk away. I motion for her to get the lock once again and wait until she does so, sighing exhaustively when she touches my bare chest as she walks by.

I get a strange feeling, an uncomfortable feeling, and walk back into the office to make a call. "Ryan, I need you to do something for me ..." I said as soon as he answers. I explain in detail what I need from him and make sure he understands to act quickly. When I finish, Kayla is at my side and wrapping her arms around me. "Finish your cake?" I asked, pulling her into my arms.

"Everyone was tired and took a piece home. So, I had ours wrapped up too. We can go home and enjoy it together." She said sweetly holding on to me.

"Everybody left?" I asked.

"Everyone but Exie, Dwayne, and Luke … well, Jesse is still here too, I think."

"You think? Did she go outside?"

"Yes, she said she had to get something for me." Kayla watches my expression change. "Why? What's wrong?"

"I don't know yet, but I want you and Exie to go right now." I said rushing her out to the club and stopping Exie from what she is doing. I take hold of them both and rush them towards the door, "Take your car and go home. Don't look back and don't stop- not even for gas." I said as they both begin to panic. As soon as they get to the door, Jesse comes in with a gun to her head being pushed by a group of men behind her.

"Put your hands on your head!" The front man screams at us. Pushing their way in, they corral us into the main area of the club. Dwayne stands up with me and we both walk in front of the girls, while Luke rushes to Jesse's aid and gets taken down to the ground in the process. "Where you going, punk?" The guy yells at him, kicking him, and laughing at him as Luke grimaces with anger. I watch as Jesse glances down at Luke calmly. As they surround us, another man walks in with his head held up too high for the loser that he is. I know of him, Marshal Camsen, a nobody trying desperately to be somebody with a gun.

Marshal walks around, looking at us all, until approaching me with little respect. "Nick Jayzon, I have to tell you, I have admired you for some time. I am so excited to be here in front of you. To have the chance to take you down is truly an honor." He admires my open shirt and looks back at his boys with a laugh, "What's with the new look, though? You trying to make the ladies go that much crazier for you? You're not that sexy, Jayzon." He laughs, taking notice of Kayla behind me. "And you must be Kayla. I have heard a lot about you too." He said with a deep groan. "Baby, I think you and I could make a sweet deal together if you're interested." He said reaching out to take hold of her but I step into him blocking him. "Ooh! Did I touch a nerve?" He walks away, laughing as he picks up the bear that Kayla received as a gift.

Kayla suddenly rushes at him and takes the bear from him, retreating just as quickly behind me. "This is mine." She whispers.

Marshall stares at her hard, "What is so important about that bear, sweetheart?" He starts fumbling through the cards until he comes up on Exie's with a bassinet on the cover. He picks it up as if he just discovered a pot of gold. "Oh, this is too good, too easy. Get the girl." He said ordering his men to take Kayla and forcing me to the ground away from her. Marshal takes hold of Kayla and slides a knife around her stomach, "So, is it a boy or girl, Jayzon?"

"Get the fuck away from her!" I yell, receiving a kick to my back.

"This is what we are going to do. I want you to give me the combination to your office safe and then I want you to let me into your house and give me the combination to your safe there." I lunge towards him and he presses the knife into Kayla enough to cause her to gasp, stopping me dead in my tracks. "If you don't give me what I want, then I will cut your child out of her right now." Marshal rips the bear away from Kayla and has one of his boys rip it into pieces with a knife, while Kayla closes her eyes and looks away heartbroken.

"I'll give you whatever you want, but you let her go." I said.

"I will let her go only when you have done what is asked of you." Marshal said, rubbing his lips along her cheek. "What do you say, Nick? Or maybe you don't want this baby anyway? I don't see you as a family man, maybe I am doing you a favor." He laughs as I look into Kayla's eyes.

Everything suddenly becomes too real for me and my heart pounds its way out of my chest. "I love my child. I am not going to let you hurt my wife or my child." I said to everyone's surprise.

Marshal laughs, "Okay, well, what are you going to do about it?" He waves his hand around like a fool. I glance at Dwayne next to me and wait until he rages into the men in front of us.

Dwayne growls as he attacks, and two other men have to take hold of him from behind. The four men wrestle with him to the best of their abilities. "You better fucking kill me, because I am going to rip your fucking heads off!" He yells.

While Marshal is distracted, I race to him and cold-cock the shit out of him, hitting him twice before he has a chance to realize what's happening. By my third swing, he is falling to the ground and I get in a kick to the jaw before he falls completely. I take hold of Kayla and push her behind me as Marshal's boys stand stunned and stupid with their guns held out at us. Dwayne laughs, as does Luke, who is now mocking the fallen dumbass. Marshall jumps up bleeding profusely, angry, and searching for a way to get back at me as he takes out his gun and shoots the bear, "Hey, Jayzon, this is what is going to happen to that child of yours if you don't stop fucking around and give me what I want." He said shooting the bear again. "Bring the bitch here and I will shoot that fucking kid out of her." He shoots again with a laugh. Suddenly, his men push us down on our knees and they take Kayla out in front of me. Marshal holds the gun near Kayla's stomach, "Bang! Your baby's dead!" He yells laughing.

With a quick glance at the back door, I stare at Marshal hard, "Bang! *You're* dead." I said with a wicked smile. I nod in Dwayne and Luke's direction and move quickly to take hold of Kayla, moving her to safer place while Dwayne pushes Exie under a table. Marshal's expression turns pale as Ryan enters with his men, shooting the fucks that have guns raised, beating the rest into submission before finally killing them mercifully, but leaving me the bleeding fuck on the ground. Ryan tosses me a gun and I aim at Marshal as he begins to curl up into a ball, begging for his life. "Like I said ..." I shoot the fuck in the head, "... you're dead." Kayla runs to my side and I wrap an arm around her, watching as Luke stomps on the guy who laughed at him, clearly, dead - isn't dead enough. Checking for any still alive, I glance around the room before eyeing Jesse, who is suddenly shaking and trembling. "Get rid of them before morning. Change out the entire room and someone better tell me who let them know we were here. Who knew how to get them in here? Who knew Luke was dropping off payments tonight?" Jesse looks at me suddenly as Luke seems to be oblivious.

"Well, it wasn't me!" Jesse yells.

"Nick, come on. She was in the middle of this as much as we were." Luke said rushing to her side.

"Was she? Somebody had to call them to let them know the club was empty except for us. If she is so innocent, then let's see who she dialed last." I said walking towards her.

"I don't have my phone with me." Jesse confessed quickly.

"Is that not what was in your hand when you came in through the back door?" I asked.

"No, you must have been seeing things because I don't have my phone on me. I rushed out here so fast I left it at my condo." She said wrapping her arm around Luke's. I nod and I walk to Marshal, taking his phone out of his pocket, and dialing the last number that called in. Once her bag starts ringing, I don't need to say anything else. Ryan and Dwayne take aim at her as she gets down on her knees.

"Nick! Wait, there has to be an explanation. Jesse would never do this without ..." Luke said.

"Without what? Damn it, Luke! She played you for a fool, Luke! She was using you to get to me! Why can't you fucking see that? She doesn't love you." I continue to yell trying to get through to him. He won't look at her or me, so I walk up to him and hand him a gun, "Drop her." I said, waiting as he battles his emotions. Jesse cries, pleading with him, making it even harder for him, if not impossible. "Leave." I said to him. Looking back at Exie and Kayla, I order them out too but Kayla stubbornly holds her head up and refuses. I assume she is about to try to stop me, but instead she walks in front of Jesse and silently waits with a cold stare against Jesse's watery eyes. Luke looks up at me and takes off out the door with the gun. Looking down at Jesse, I shake my head and take hold of her head, snapping her neck in half. When I look back at Kayla I expect to see a mess, but instead she is strong and controlled. "Let's go home, Princess." I said watching her smile softly with a nod. Kayla's sudden hardness is shocking but comforting to know she can handle this life better than I thought.

છ৪৩

I talked to Exie for hours the next day, making sure she is okay, and that she is good handling the club from here on out. She is a tough woman, convincing me she is ready to carry on as if nothing happened, even reminding me that she remembers it like a bad dream which she believes is all it was, just a dream. After some quick remodeling and some gratitude payments to Exie and my boys, things are back to normal. The only thing that hasn't gotten back to normal is Luke. We haven't seen him since that night. With Luke running wild, I need someone I can trust at my side and I trust no one more than I do Ryan.

Kayla is several months in now, she's showing and causing me to be more cautious about her safety. She is resting at home after a doctor's appointment today. One that she wanted me to go to with her. I wanted to make her happy, but I found an excuse to back out. My guilt got the best of me, so I find out from Exie where she bought the teddy bear for the shower. Apparently, it is similar to the one Kayla wanted as a child and never got. Walking softly into the bedroom as she rests, I kiss her gently on the head and pull a new bear out for her when she opens her eyes.

Kayla jumps up instantly with a bright smile, "Oh, Nick! Thank you." She said hugging the bear.

Lying down next to her, "How was your appointment today, Princess? Everything good?" I asked, prompting her to take out something from her nightstand drawer. I watch her curiously as she turns to me and hands it to me. "What's this?"

"It is our son." She said as I look at the picture, feeling something strange take hold of me.

~26~
NICK

I bought another building and I want to change it into another business I can use to hide money. It has to be a moneymaker and I don't want to compete with my other businesses, so it has to be something different. Wandering the facility, I try to come up with some idea. The place has excellent windows in the front, easy access from the road, and more than enough parking, it could be almost anything but, for some reason, I am at a loss.

"Nick! Kayla has gone into labor!" Tanner suddenly yells with a smile.

For the last few months I have been happy about the prospect of having a son, but I don't think the reality of it all hit me until now. When we reach the door to the hospital, I jump out before the car has a chance to stop and run in a panic to find Kayla. The next few hours are a blur, the events happen so fast, or maybe I am in such a daze trying to comprehend what is going on, that I just don't remember. Taking a seat next to Kayla's bed I watch her nuzzle our son with pride. "Aren't you tired?" I asked.

"Yes, but I am too happy to go to sleep right now." She said, closing her eyes as she kisses his head.

"This coming from the woman that said having to take care of a fish would cause her too much stress." I said.

"Oh yea, I forgot I said that." She said suddenly looking panicked. "Oh, Nick, what if ..."

As soon her eyes widen, I jump up, "Everything is going to be fine. We can hire somebody to help you for as long as you want and I will be there with you too." With a curious smile, Kayla suddenly lifts our son up to me. "What are you doing?"

"If you're going to be there to help me, then you need to learn how to. Right?"

"I meant for moral support ... sexual relief ... massages ...sex." I said with a laugh.

"As great as all that sounds, I think you can do more." I step away from her. "Try, Nick, you have to at least be able to hold him."

"He is very small, Kayla. I don't want to hurt him." I said, hoping she would give up on her quest, but I should have known better. She pulls me to the bed next to her and adjusts my arms before she lays our delicate child in my arms. *He is so warm.* I lift him up into my arms. The moment I look down on him, he opens his eyes to me and instantly he lures me in. "He's perfect." I whispered.

"We have to name him you know. We could name him after his father." Kayla said.

"Nicholas?" I ask to which Kayla nods. "How about Nicholas Aiden Jayzon?" I asked with a smile.

"Aiden? But your middle name is Alexander."

"Aiden is my uncle's name, I was sort of named after him. He was my mother's brother. Alexander was the closest name she could get to his without causing a fight with my father, at least from what I was told." Kayla looks at me obviously preparing numerous questions for me. "He was good to me when I needed it and he is still important to me. If it wasn't for him, I might not be here now. And that's all you're getting." Her frustration is clear but luckily she is too tired to argue with me.

"Aiden it is then." Kayla said, lying back with a peaceful expression and slowly drifting off to sleep.

◌ॐ◌

*I*t has only been a few months since we brought Nicky home, but already it all feels normal. Never would I have ever believed that this would be my life. Today, I am taking Nicky with me, a chance for me to spend time with my son without people watching to see if I turn into a gushing fool. Little do they know, I sneak into his room most every night and wake him up, only to rock him back to sleep. He helps me think, by giving me someone to talk to without me having to worry about giving him too much information. I love Kayla, but I can't tell her about anything I do and Ryan is still learning. Dwayne, on the other hand, is content being told only what he needs to know. It is a lonely world at times. But now- now I have Nicky and he listens to every word and still smiles and laughs when I am done talking. If I had known it would be like this, I would have gotten Kayla pregnant a long time ago.

I am taking Nicky to my new business to show him what he

inspired, a children's gym where he can play safely with other kids and not have to worry about predators coming after him. We open tomorrow but today is our day. Nicky is wide awake and, as always, eager to learn about everything around him. While my guards stand outside, I walk Nicky around, letting him play with whatever he wants to, but all he wants to do is hold onto me. The only thing that catches his attention is a giant stuffed Eeyore. I am not sure if the depressed old donkey is that attractive to him or if he just wants to chew on his ears, but either way, I take him near and let him play. His excitement over the animal is lively, but sure enough the ears are really what he is after. "Nicky, your mother would have my head for letting you chew on that. Good thing she isn't here." I said kissing him until he laughs.

"Can I come in yet?" Tanner said poking his head in through the door, with another gift under his arm.

"Please tell me you didn't buy him something else?" I said waving him over and admiring his new handy work. The impeccably carved rocking horse is gorgeous but a bit too much for Nicky right now.

"Don't you even think of giving me a hard time about spoiling my favorite boy. Besides, I didn't spend a dime and you know it." Tanner said setting the horse down and picking Nicky up, ignoring his fussy attitude about leaving Eeyore. "Oh shush! I am the closest thing to a grandfather you have." Tanner said beaming as he lifts Nicky over his head making him laugh again. "So, you open tomorrow?"

"Yea, should be a nice little celebration. The mayor is coming to help cut the ribbon, as well as my Senator."

"Your Senator?" Tanner asked with a questioning expression.

"I do pay for him, as well as the mayor. The dickheads cost me a small fortune to keep them fat and happy, so they better show up in their best smiles tomorrow."

"Are you bringing Kayla and Nicky?"

"Yes, Kayla is excited and the family together will be a nice picture to boost my image in the community." I said, taking my son back after he whimpers at me.

"Yes, it will be a nice picture for the "feel-good" section of the news but it doesn't explain why you seem to be on edge lately. Is there something I should know?" Tanner asked, knowing me better than anyone.

"No, everything is good. I am not sure why I feel like something is wrong." I said, kissing Nicky gently on his head.

CR80

"*N*ick! This looks amazing. I am shocked at how well you did." Kayla said as we pull up for the opening of the children's gym.

"Well, don't be too shocked. I did have help designing it. I simply came up with the idea." I said, kissing her with a smile. "But, thank you." With Nicky in my arms, I take Kayla by the hand and walk by the line full of mothers waiting to get in with their children.

"Mr. Jayzon!" A lady yells to get my attention. I greet her with a handshake and a smile and she kisses me on the cheek which sparks a whole line of women yelling my name. Kayla's expression is priceless, but I bite my tongue to save myself from sure retaliation.

"Unbelievable. You are even more attractive with a baby in your arms. AND your wife at your side!" Kayla said with a scowl.

"I don't think they saw you, Princess." I nudge her until she smiles. "That's better. Now, be your normal charming self. I need your help making this day go smoothly." After we greet the Mayor and Senator, we pose for pictures before greeting the employees. It all goes smoothly even through the ribbon cutting and welcome speech to everyone. Once all the publicity duties are done, I escort my family right back into the safety of the car and take them home. With a sigh, I wink at Tanner as he drives us away.

CR80

*I*t is late when I show up for my meeting with Joseph Estrella. Nothing out of the ordinary, we have dinner regularly to talk about business and make sure we both have a good understanding of what the other is doing. As normal and routine as it is for me, I still feel like something is off with Estrella lately. Our meeting is at an out-of-the-way restaurant and we both bring backup with us. Trust only goes so far, no matter how long you have worked together. Ryan and Dwayne sit at a table nearby and already Ryan is screwing with Joseph's men. With a single look, he calms back down but I imagine it will be short-lived. After we discuss business, Joseph begins to tell me about some woman he fucked at a party, only to find out later that she had a twin.

"No seriously, Nick, I was so drunk by this point I didn't even notice that they were wearing different dresses. So, when the sister

206

comes up to me, I ... you know, I rubbed myself against her hoping to entice her again, but the bitch turned around and smacked me!" Joseph said smacking the table and laughing out loud.

"You mean, you didn't get to do them both? Oh, Joe, you're letting me down." I said taking a drink of my tea.

"Hey, let me tell you something, I may not have had both sisters but after she slapped me, I had this sweet brunette come up to check on me and she was more than willing to take a ride. The only bad part was- she was the one having the party." He said proudly.

"Why was that bad?"

"Because I was invited by her husband!" He laughed. I laugh respectfully shaking my head. "So, have you had any adventures lately?"

"Nah, no one wants me anymore. I guess I have lost my touch."

"Bullshit! I know you, Nicholas. I have seen the women beating down your door just to suck your dick. Don't tell me you don't have a story or two- probably five just from last night!" I shake my head and refrain from telling my old stories to satisfy him. Joe sits back in his chair with an odd expression on his face, "I saw your new business by the way. A kid's gym? That's something different for you. It looks like it is going to be a huge success. Congratulations on another smart move."

"Thank you, I am excited about it." I said tensing up.

"And Kayla. Wow, looking as good as ever. And a son too? Nice looking family, Nick." He said with an awkward smile. "I ran into Kayla the other day at a coffee shop. She said she attends the college across the street. We had a real nice conversation, I can see why you married her and certainly why you wanted to extend the family name with her. I wish I had chosen someone as well as you did, Nicholas, but who knows- maybe I will get my chance one day."

"What's that suppose to mean?" I asked watching him closely.

"Nothing. I was only saying it looks like you have a real nice family." He barely breathes another breath before I am up and in his face.

"MY FAMILY IS OFF LIMITS! YOU UNDERSTAND ME?" I seethe against his ear, forcing the tip of my gun into his heart. Each of our groups of men jump up with their hands on their guns, but Joseph waves his hand to his guys and sits them back down. I back off and give a slight nod to calm my boys down.

"Fuck, Nick, I was only trying to compliment you." Joe says

pushing tight against my chest. "Please, sit down. I didn't mean anything by it. Hell, I didn't even know you were married until one of my new ... eager boys let me know." Adjusting my jacket back into place, I sit back down still eyeing Joe with an unrelenting glare. With a solemn expression, he rubs his mouth, preparing to say something that I have a feeling I won't like. "I am a good fifteen years or more older than you, Nicholas. I don't know how much longer I have here on earth, but I know one thing our kind of business makes it difficult to let our guard down. It doesn't allow for much romance, although I have tried. You probably know this, but I was married myself a few times and have five kids between the three wives and one maid. After many years dealing with them all, I figured out that I couldn't let myself get attached to them. They leave, Nick, they always leave. If you don't kill the bitch, she will leave. The last fucking whore left me one night and cleaned out all my safes in the process. She had movers come and load up anything that wasn't attached- and still had the balls to sue for alimony. She was damn lucky I didn't have her killed. If it wasn't for the kid, I would have. But then what? I'm supposed to stay home and watch after him? Hire a nanny? I would just wind up screwing the nanny." He laughed. "What I am trying to say, Nick, is enjoy it while you can but be prepared because it is only a matter of time before the bitch is hocking your balls for cash." Joe nods, watching me carefully as I ease my temper down. He continues with his stories while I stay stoned face trying to keep from making things worse than I already have. Joseph is up to something, I can smell his traitorous intent all over him.

~27~
KAYLA

I stopped by the baby store on my way to meet Brady but still he is running late for our friendly date. Before I can think of calling him, I see him waving from across the street and quickly adjust my expression to a disappointed nature as he walks in and sits down.

"I know. I'm late, but I do have a reasonable excuse." He said before quickly ordering some lunch.

"And what excuse is that? You run out of hair gel?" I said as he rolls his eyes at me.

"No. Actually, I woke up late and then decided to stay in bed a little longer today." He smiles as if he wants to tell me something.

"So what's her name?" I asked, laughing as he bounces in his seat.

"I shouldn't tell you. Since we work together, I promised her we would keep it a secret until we know that it's something real for us, but I have to tell someone. She is so amazing. Her name is Lena. She works in the morgue." I gasp with a sour expression. "No- she isn't some freak. She's a coroner. She is the lead examiner and she happened to be on one of my cases when we met. I couldn't get her out of my mind. As soon as I looked into her eyes I had to have her. She said no the first fifteen times I asked her out." My jaw drops as he laughs. "But the sixteenth time, she finally agreed- if we could keep it secret. It's been two months and I am head over heels for this woman. I think she is the one, Kayla."

"I am so happy for you. So, then why can't you tell people now? If it has been two months and both of you seem sure about each other. She does feel the same way, doesn't she?" I asked watching him for any signs of doubt.

"Yes, I mean she tells me she loves me and we spend every night together now. She is very private. I don't know, she has some kind of family issues and doesn't want me to be subjected to them until she is sure they won't scare me off. I am good with whatever their issues are. I mean, as long as Jayzon isn't her brother, how bad can they be?" I laugh as he continues about his new girl, but my mind quickly wanders back to my son.

It is hard to believe how good my life is, despite being married to a criminal. Then again, Nick keeps me so sheltered from all that he does. As far as I know, he is nothing more than an average businessman. At least that's what I tell myself. On occasion, however, life has a way of reminding you of who you really are.

After putting Nicky down for the night, I sit down to read before bed. Nick promised to be home early tonight. "I just have to run a quick errand," he said. I know better but I am anxious for him to get home all the same. As soon as I hear the car, I run to the balcony to greet him but instead watch Nick come in limping and hunched over with his jacket draped over his shoulders. I start to say something to him but notice his grimacing face as he hides in his office. I run down the stairs only to have Dwayne head me off.

"Go upstairs." Dwayne remarks pushing me back to the stairs and out of the way of Tanner who comes running in with two other men. He eyes me quickly but his expression is not what I am use to from him.

No one bothers to stop or answer my questions as they rush to Nick's office. I turn to take a couple of steps up when three other men come rushing in. The drama increases and no matter how hard I try, I can't get anywhere near Nick. Men are scrambling all over our house but one seems to be standing guard on me. He doesn't get too close but he watches my every move and blocks me every time I get up to go in the direction of Nick. "I want to see my husband." I demand.

"It is not a good time right now, Kayla." He said barely looking at me. I have seen him before and even more so recently, but Nick has never introduced us. It almost seems like he is keeping me distant from him.

"Kayla? You speak to me like we are friends, but I have no idea who you are." I said standing tall and waiting for him to look at me.

"My name is Ryan." He said reaching out for me when Nick screams out.

"Let go of me! I want to see him." I yell at him, but Ryan holds tight to me. The more Nick screams out, the more he holds me until I am held tight against his chest and fisting his shirt against my face.

"He is going to be fine, Kayla." He says as Nicky begins to cry out, I run up to him and Ryan follows.

Holding back my fears, I cradle Nicky to my chest trying to comfort him back to sleep while Ryan stands in the doorway watching us. "So, how do you know my husband?" I asked him.

"Long story." Ryan said annoyingly.

"Give me the highlights." I request impatiently.

Ryan smiles, "Nick said you were a handful."

I turn quickly towards him, "He talks to you about me?"

Ryan suddenly straightens his posture, "If you want some privacy, I can shut the door."

"No, I want to ..."

"No, Kayla. No, you don't need to know." I step to him and begin to tell him how it is going to be when he suddenly glares at me. And that's when I know.

Nick's devilish eyes have always been a strong part of him. Even though I fell in love with him, I still see the darkness deep within them- and Ryan is no different. "How come I have never met you before?" I asked.

"I work another area for Nick. We only meet when it's necessary."

"Like when Luke disappeared?" His silence is expected but still irritating as hell. Before I can ask anything else, he leaves me and stands guards at the end of the stairs.

After I put Nicky back down, I go to our room and wait, falling asleep in a chair waiting up for Nick. "Hey, Princess, why don't you try that bed of ours? I hear it's pretty comfortable." I open my eyes to see Nick's weak smile.

I jump up and wrap my arms around him tight. "Oh, Nick, I was so worried. Are you okay?" As soon as the words leave my mouth, I notice the bandages on his body and the sling his arm is in. "Nick! Oh my God!"

"I'm okay, it's nothing." He said dismissing my concern.

"Stop that! Stop babying me and tell me what the hell is going on! I mean it, Nick!" He walks away from me preparing our bed, expecting me to simply let it go. With his back turned, I rip the bandage from his back.

"FUCK!" Nick screams out. He straightens and turns to me with pained anger. "Damn it, Kayla! NO!"

"I swear, Nick, if you don't start talking to me, I will leave you." Nick's expression changes to a level of anger I have never seen from him. The blackness in his eyes swarms to the forefront, forcing me to back away from him. With an uneasy breath, I back slowly towards the door. "I was so worried about you. I love you so much, Nick. I don't know what I would do if something happened to you. All this secrecy is making me crazy, I am so afraid. I am afraid for you, Nick. I am afraid of losing you." I watch him as he slowly walks to me and lays his head against mine.

"Don't leave me. Please. I'm doing everything possible to protect you. Please understand that I will take care of everything, you don't need to be afraid, I am not going to let anything happen to you or Nicky." He said running his fingers through my hair.

"But what about you? Who is protecting you?" I said pulling away from him and holding his pained face in my hands. "I will never love anyone else but you, Nick. It is impossible for me to do so. I can't let anything happen to you."

ᏲᏋᏮ

*T*he energy in the house has changed drastically since Nick's accident. The best I can figure out is that he was attacked by several men. They obviously were sending him a message because they could have easily killed him if they wanted to. What I can't figure out … is how they knew he would be alone or why he was alone.

While Nick is out, I take Nicky and meet Exie for lunch and I couldn't be more excited to be able to talk to someone that might have some clue to what is going on.

"You look tired." Exie said.

"I can hardly sleep I am so worried about him. He sleeps with his gun under his pillow. I don't know, Exie, but something horrible is going on. Have you seen or heard anything?" Her hesitation means she has. "You better tell me. It certainly can't be any worse than what I have imagined."

"I don't know anything really. They have been meeting at the club more regularly lately and they seem to be …" She looks up at me uneasily.

"Tell me."

"It's like they are organizing for a battle." I sit back in my chair, and though I still don't know everything, I feel better having an idea. "There is something else … I overheard Nick talking to someone on the phone. I wasn't trying to listen in but he was in my office and I don't think he expected the call." She looks around nervously before she looks at me again, "I think it was Luke."

"Why do you say that?" I asked.

"It was the way he was talking to him, like he was trying to get him to calm down. He asked to meet whoever it was and then he took off. That was the night it all happened."

"I don't know what to do to help him, Exie."

"That's simple ... nothing. You can't help him, Kayla. He doesn't want you to help him. Whatever is going on you need to stay behind Nick and not try to get in the middle of it. I am sure he knows how to take care of it, he has been doing this for a long time. It's not like before, Kayla, when it was only you going after Nick. There was no one else to worry about but you back then. Now you have Nicky, you have to be there for him. He can't afford to lose both his parents." I look up at her and she bites her lip to try to take back her words but it's too late.

When I get home everything is quiet, so I put Nicky down for a nap and go exploring through the house. Since I moved back in with Nick, I have kept my promise and stayed away from his secrets but now I have to know. The areas that always have been off limits to me are the most inviting. The only place I know not to look is his office, those lock drawers are too obvious and too easily accessible. *There has to be a place in this house that he keeps everything. But where?* My mind traces every line of the house, walking through it almost as if I had built it myself. Once I get to a place that doesn't make sense, I stop and analyze it. Over and over I try to figure out what I have discovered. Not understanding fully why it doesn't make sense, I run upstairs into the spare bedroom and walk into the spacious closet. The giant armoire that sits inside seems all the more mammoth at this moment. I had never thought of it before, even when I once stayed in this room. It seemed normal, although a little too nice for a closet-especially in a spare bedroom closet. The most curious thing about this armoire is the space it takes or rather the space that it blocks. There is missing square footage from this closet and the only thing that could possibly have access is this armoire. Taking it in fully, analyzing every part and piece to it, I start to go through the drawers, the cabinet, feel along the shelves, and ... nothing. Sighing, I step back and decide to feel the edge of the cabinet. The smoothness of the carved wood is beyond excellent craftsmanship, like nothing I had ever seen before. I get down in the floor and look under it noticing a signature. *Aiden Bourghesie. Nick's uncle? Now I know this is where he hides everything. I just have to figure out how.* Tracing the name burned into the wood with my finger, I feel something odd, like a separation in the letters. It is slight but I can feel it along the bottom now that I know where it is. I trace the crack to the edge of the armoire and up its sides searching for where it opens. The armoire sits in a nook with a short ceiling enclosing it fully, only the ceiling seems to be attached somehow. I step back again, taking it all in and the vent above begins to call to me. I run through the house searching for a screw driver. Once I find it, I take off the vent cover and reach in finding a channel that goes down into the armoire. I feel carefully down inside until I find a switch that triggers the armoire to slowly open. I stand back wide-eyed watching as a whole new world opens up to me. The armoire conceals an entire room of about thirty square feet. Within it sits a small built-in desk with a computer, backup drives, and a fireproof safe. It is not connected to any outlet from the house, only a small generator lights the space and powers the computer. There are no outlets and no handwritten information. Opening the laptop, it powers up quickly and lights up with access to every business Nick has or ever had. The businesses are separated into legal and illegal, with notes on deliveries, associates, and every transaction ever performed. In another folder are notes on every person that has ever worked for Nick. He has everything about his dealings written out in detail, even where all his money is, and most importantly, the detailed secrets of every associate that is indebted to help him whenever he needs it.

The last seemingly insignificant folder contains a daily diary of sorts. The last entry was years ago, the year Braylin died. Curious, I scroll to the beginning searching to see if he wrote anything about her. To my surprise, the journal seems to be all about her and me. Things I never knew: the first time he saw me, the cravings he had to see me only to have to deal with Braylin to do so. He wrote in detail about the long nights he spent with her, only to be overjoyed to simply be able to cover me up at night. He writes in agonizing detail his torment fighting himself from needing me, wanting me. Pushing ahead, I search for the time when he left her, searching for a reason. In red letters, I find what I was looking for. Below the last paragraph of the journal is the simple red lettered sentence, *I had to leave her.* I assumed he meant Braylin.

Kayla had nightmares again tonight and, as usual, Braylin didn't hear her at all. I thought nothing about going to check on her, but tonight she touched me. She called out to me. I sat with her for some time because she wouldn't let go of me and, to be honest, I didn't want her to. Feeling her warm body against me made me feel whole for the first time ever. In her sleep she asked me for help and called me her Prince. I told her to come with me and I would rescue her and protect her forever. I thought nothing about it, a private game of sorts but she asked me if I love her. I am not sure why I said it, but I said yes and she said she loves me too. I wanted to take her right then, make love to her like no one else could but ... she doesn't really love me, she doesn't even see me. It was only a dream. For her. The next morning, I tried to explain to Braylin that I couldn't see her anymore. She cried causing me to loathe my very existence and ended up giving into her one more time before leaving her anyway. The worst of it is Kayla looked at me for the first time as I was leaving. I stood there forever. Even now, I have to fight myself from running back there and rescuing her from that mess that she lives in. I think about waiting for Kayla, waiting for her to grow up a little more, maybe then she will see me. Maybe then ... who am I kidding? She will never love me. I have to break this spell she has over me. That's why I had to get away from Braylin- their house, her room, her smell, her sweet lips, even her awful outdated glasses. I had to get away from her before I couldn't hold back any longer and persuaded her or rather cursed her into being with me. I had no other choice.

I had to leave her.

I feel numb reading his thoughts and now truly understanding him- understanding why. Why he does the things he does for me. I put everything back the way I found it and go about my day as I normally would. When Nick comes home, I am not sure whether to run to him or wait for him. I have tried all day to understand how I feel. He used her to get to me and I thought all this time it was me that pushed her but it was the both of us. When Nick walks into the room and smiles at me, I think back to how young he was then and what a man he has grown into being: a husband, a father and the man I have grown to love so deeply. I can't imagine my life without him. Before I can get a word out, I find myself running into his arms and taking in his lips with mine. "I love you, Nick. I love you so much." I said running my hand up the back of his neck and into his hair. Moaning against his lips, I unbutton his shirt and run my hand down into his pants, exciting him instantly. Nick sits me up on the nearby table and jerks my pants off me. He caresses my ass with a moan before he positions himself between my legs.

"You want to fuck right here, Princess?" He smiles, laughing at me as I strip my top off and release my bra. "I guess so." Nick drags my panties down my legs and I wrap my bare legs around his waist. Smiling sheepishly at me, he takes a tight hold of my thighs and pushes deep inside me. He feels so good, I have to lean back, caressing his head against my breasts as he kisses and sucks on each of them. The old wooden table creaks as Nick gets on top of me but quickly goes silent under the heaviness of our bodies. Repeatedly, I feel him slide in deep with such skill, grazing those tender areas that send vibrations all the way to my toes. His soft whispers against my ear asking if I can feel how excited I am making him, how hard he is for me and how good and wet I feel to him. The more he speaks, the more intense the sensations are. I begin to wonder if he could cause me to orgasm simply by speaking to me. Once I release, Nick pulls me off the table and turns me around. Bending me over, he enters me again, taking hold of my hips he doesn't let go until I feel him come inside me, groaning to the last. When we are done, I lean back against his chest holding onto his arms that are wrapped around me. "Is that what you wanted?" He asks between breaths, smiling down at me.

"Do you always give me what I want?" I asked.

"Usually." He said with a quiet laugh.

"What do you want, Nick?" I asked seeming to catch him by surprise.

"I don't think anyone has ever asked me that before."

"Well, now someone is asking."

"I got all I want." He says with a smooth hum.

~28~
KAYLA

During my spare time each day I read Nick's notes on his secret computer, keeping up with what little information he writes these days. I make sure never to say anything or even let on that I know. I'm not sure how Nick would react if he found out but I am sure this secret is best left untold. On top of keeping up with his secrets, I begin preparing myself for more of mine. I bought a gun and have been practicing with it often, my instructor says I am getting good. *Screw good, I am working towards deadly perfect.* In addition to the gun, I feel I need to try to match Nick's skill in taking people down with ease. His quick hands and deadly punches are exciting but I believe it is something I need to learn to do as well. This time when I ask him how he does it, he introduces me to his trainer. With a combination of training, my new instructor is teaching me what I never thought I could possibly do. My days are packed with studying, training, and catching up on all of Nick's past business while I wait for him to update his notes with what is going on now. I finally feel like I have some control over what happens in my life. Nick has done everything, including risk his own life, to protect me, now it is my turn to protect him.

CSEO

Feeling Nick next to me as I drift off to sleep makes my dreams easy and enjoyable. It is so easy to become comfortable when his arm is around me and I can feel him breathing next to me. It has become a necessity I can't live without. I could easily float into a beautiful dream, but when I hear Nicky whimper, I open my eyes and see Luke standing over me with Nicky in his arms. I gasp as he pushes his gun against my forehead. "Don't you fucking move." He said as Nick wakes up. "Hello, Nick."

Nick's wide-eyed expression takes in the situation quickly and leaves his gun hidden under his pillow. "What are you doing here,

Luke?"

"Well, that's simple. You see, I figure you owe me. I mean when I fell for this one's sister, I didn't get mad at you when she preferred you instead. However, I will admit I got a little upset when you dumped her and Connor turned her into a drug addict whore, but not nearly as much as when I offered to help her and she turned me down." Luke huffs a sarcastic chuckle before glancing over at me. "And do you know why she turned me down? Because she still believed she could win Nick back! I mean what a stupid bitch. Kayla, did you know that Nick here was never after your sister ... he was after you."

"I know." I said calmly to Nick's surprise.

"Well, I guess there aren't as many secrets between you two as I thought. However, there is one secret that I am sure he didn't tell you yet." I glimpse Nick as he hardens.

"There is no reason for her to know that, Luke. Why don't you and I get out of here and we can talk?" Nick said, touching my hand beneath the hovering sheet.

Luke laughs, "Ummm... I don't think so. Anyway, so the other night when your husband showed up to meet me, I told him in detail how I killed your sister." I stop breathing watching as Luke calms himself with an easy exhaling breath. "It wasn't as hard as I thought it would be either, considering how long I had admired her. I took the bitch to my car and made sure she understood that Nick here was never interested in her, he was only interested in you. She cried and cried, I thought she would get over him, but when I offered to help her if she was willing to be my girl, do you know what she said?" Luke pushes the gun harder against my head. "Keep calm, Nick, I'm not going to shoot her- yet. Your sister said that neither of us was good enough for you two and she was going to take you and runaway from all of it. I couldn't believe it. I mean, what was she going to do? Work in a broken down diner for the rest of her life? I told her that wasn't going to happen, she was either going to do what I said from now on or she could die. She said she preferred to die. So I fucked her and then choked her with my belt. I tied her up in the bathroom and made it look like she killed herself and Kayla here never woke up once. I watched you sleep trying to figure out the draw he had to you. Knowing how Nick felt about you, I knew I couldn't leave you alive. I mean what kind of friend would I be if I didn't take care of his addiction for him? So, before I left, I turned the gas on in your stove and assumed my work was done. But you didn't pay your bill!" Luke laughs, looking at Nick. "Can you believe it? Apparently within minutes of me turning the gas on, the gas company turned it off. I expected her to be dead the next morning, but instead, I watched her walk out with no problems. I couldn't figure it out. It was days later when I went back to the house and found the notice from the gas company on the door. You are one lucky bitch, Kayla. When you and Nick here got together, I thought he would get you out of his system. Little did I know how in love- how ridiculously obsessed he is with you. It is an amazing feeling, Nick, I will give you that. A powerful one."

"That wasn't love, Luke." Nick said moving too much for Luke's comfort as he twitches at the trigger. Nick puts his hands up and eases back down, "Can I least have my son?"

"No, I am going to make you a deal. I figure you owe me one or I guess it's that I owe you one. I know you don't believe it, but I did love Jesse. Of course she would rather have had you. Hell, she used me to get to you, but I still loved her and you killed her, didn't you?"

"Luke, she was …"

"Answer me!" Luke yelled, causing Nicky to cry.

"Yes. I snapped her neck, but it was as much for you as it was for anyone. She didn't even flinch when they beat you in front of her." Nick said, tensing with every passing second.

"You son of a bitch! Don't bullshit me! You did it for you and your precious wife." With Nicky still crying and reaching for me, Luke handles him roughly, adjusting him to an awkward position and causing him to scream louder. "You choose, Nick. Which one do you love more? Your wife or your son? I will let you keep one- but only one."

"Kill me! Kill me!" I cry trying to reach for Nicky.

"Choose, Nick!" Luke yells even louder.

"I will not choose. You're angry with me. Kill me if I have done you so wrong. Kill me!" Nick yells back at him.

"No, the best way for you to learn is to lose something valuable to you. Either your wife gets a bullet to the head or I am going to break your son's neck. Which will it be, Nick?" I look at Nick struggling to breathe as I try to think of a way out.

"Can I show you something first?" Nick eases out of bed holding his hands up. "I am just going to go over here and get you a key. The key you asked for the other night. I know you're working for Joseph, those were his men that ambushed me at our meeting the other night."

"You were always a smart one, Nick." Luke said with an easy smirk.

"Well, I am sure this is what you want. The key to all my secrets, to all of my money, and to every business deal. All you need to take over everything I have." Nick holds out a key as Luke eases the gun from my head.

"You're going to give up your empire?" Luke asked. "Everything you have worked for? All for them?"

"You said I had to learn by giving up something valuable to me and I choose this. It is all in a storage unit where I have an office, unit number A2592. It is all there, Luke. I will give it all over to you, but you have to give me my son and release Kayla unharmed. We will pack up and leave the house and everything behind." Nick holds out his hand enticing Luke a little more. Luke pulls the gun away from my head and hands Nicky to me before walking slowly towards Nick.

"Okay, Nick, you have a deal but this is my house now you have ten minutes to pack and get the hell out." Luke said as he points his gun at Nick, Luke steps a little closer to Nick with an awkward expression. "You know what though? I can't believe that you will simply walk away from it all. You're too smart, Nick. I can't enjoy it all knowing you're out there somewhere just waiting for me to make a wrong move so you can take it all back. Hell, you know how to get in here without being detected as well as I do. Don't you, Nick? There would be nothing stopping you from sneaking in and killing me in my sleep. So, I think I am going to have to kill you and your family. But, since we have been friends for such a long time, I will do you a favor and kill you first." Luke raises his gun up to Nick with an agonizing sigh. Quickly, I throw the covers over Nicky's head while reaching under Nick's pillow and shoot through it. Luke staggers sideways, staring at me with a shocked expression. Nick disarms Luke as he falls to the ground. I pick up Nicky and stand up to watch Nick hover over Luke with his gun drawn. "What did you tell them, Luke?" Nick yells at him as he fights for breath.

"Nothing. I didn't tell them anything. They are too stupid to take you down. I couldn't help those morons get you no matter how much I hate you. I only wanted to know what it was like to be you, Nick. I wanted to be in love so bad." Luke coughs, holding the blood against his chest as he tries to sit up to Nick. "I don't think you know what it's like living in your shadow all the time. I would have never hurt them, Nick. As much as I hate you … I still love you more than any brother I could have had … I just wanted you to know my pain even if it was only for a few minutes." Luke looks my way with a laugh before facing Nick again. "I expected it to be you, but I guess it is fitting that it was her." He said choking on his own blood and sinking back down to the floor. Luke holds out his hand and Nick takes it until Luke takes his final breath.

Standing up, Nick watches me with a hard breath as I hold onto to Nicky. I walk towards him and he runs to me, wrapping his arms around us. I don't know what to say or if I even need to say anything. Luke knew what he was doing coming here. If Nick didn't kill him, Estrella surely would for betraying his trust … he wanted to die.

~29~
NICK

The war has begun and with every war there will be no winners- only those who remain alive. Ever since my meeting with Joseph, I have had a bad feeling and now I know why. Luke could have easily let them into my house. Coming alone proved that, in the end, he was loyal to me and not Estrella. On top of his loyalty, Luke proved to me that Kayla and Nicky are what's most important to me. All I care about now is getting them away from this, away from the hell that I built and to somewhere safe. I didn't sleep at all the night Luke broke in, I wouldn't even let Nicky sleep anywhere but with Kayla and I. While they slept, I stayed up watching over them and forming a plan to get them out of this. I went through every scenario backwards and forwards, locating the flaws and fixing them, and then running through them again until my plan was flawless. Now, all I have to do is see it through. The next day I begin moving money in several directions and making sure that I appoint one person to handle the most important task, someone that wouldn't dare defy me or break his promise to me. And my brother, Ryan, is that person. Ryan is the most important part of my plan and I am sure he will be hesitant to do as I say once I tell him his entire roll.

I knew about Ryan from the beginning. I wasn't but five when my father started seeing his mother. He visited her often, even after Ryan was born, not that he took to Ryan any more than he did Connor. But, he did have me watch over Ryan while he spent hours with Ryan's mother. I was too young to know the details exactly, but I knew he was my brother and I took care of him, watched over him. He became angry as he got older and rebelled often. Not that I didn't do my fair share of stealing and getting into trouble, but Ryan purposely tried to get caught. I probably would have gotten into more trouble if I hadn't of spent so much time trying to keep him out of it. It just seemed like the more I tried, the more he found to get into. The boy was positively suicidal, he craved our father's attention so desperately. One night he was arrested and the police called the house looking for my father who wasn't interested in helping him, so I did. I went to Harvey and pledged my commitment to him so I could help Ryan and his mother. Harvey was the only choice I had where I could make enough to give them what they needed to get by, they had little left after his mother's medical bills. Soon after his mother died, Ryan came to me pledging his loyalty to me until death. He could have done better, but like Kayla, it was easier to protect him under my guard than someone else's. I gave him a job and taught him as much as I could, all the while making sure to keep our relation a secret and keeping him out of the spotlight. I made sure he never worked for me directly and paid him well for the job he did. In exchange, he was the ears and eyes I needed to let me know who was ready to screw me over and who was too good to be true. He was the one that clued me on the female cops that came after me. Ryan works for our cleaning services, a service no one knows I even have control of. The same service the state government has cleaning their facilities, including the police precincts. He has taken over that business and by working his way from the inside out, he has made long lasting allies. He knows how to take care of his people and he knows how to read them from the moment he makes eye contact. He has come a long way from the troubled kid brother I almost gave up on. I have become successful by strategically placing people that I can trust and luckily I have family that I know will die before they betray me. In this business, you have to have someone you trust watching your back while you look ahead.

☙❧

*D*awson, my so-called protégé- as he so begged to be called, I haven't liked since I saw him whisper in Kayla's ear. So I guess it wasn't a surprise when he hands me an ultimatum from Estrella. The moron has been betraying me and has been helping Estrella for some time, yet has done everything possible to move up in my organization. Luckily, I have closed every door he tried to come through. Now he, with Estrella, wants me to hand all that I have over to him but most importantly, they want my book of secrets. This business is all about money, no matter what people say about power it is still- all about money. The book that in addition, to information on all my businesses, the secrets of every associate of mine, also contains the locations, passwords and keys to all my money. Hand them my book and then I and my family will live. If he hadn't of included me in the living part, I might have believed him or at least wanted to. There is no way he will allow me to walk away alive from this. I could easily battle Estrella, even take him down, but someone else is protecting him. His confidence is too strong and he is boastfully showing his face at big name events. I can't figure out who it is but after seeing intimate pictures of Nicky and Kayla within the message they sent me, I know what I have to do. I have a week to decide or Estrella will issue orders to have us all killed. In response, I send a personal message of my own to Joseph. Wrapped up in red satin and black lace, I send a decorative package of Devil's Berries with a note tempting him to eat up. I know he will find humor in it, at first, but it will surely drive him harder to reach his goal which I'm counting on.

With only a few days left until my supposed impending doom, I stay home and spend as much time as possible with Nicky and Kayla. I know Kayla is nervous even though she won't say anything, Nicky, however, is happy as ever. He is so much fun right now and so loving. He holds onto me tight as he fights his heavy eyes, I cradle him close to my chest one last time before I put him down. "I love you, Nicky. I hope you always know that. I'm doing all this for you and your mother." I lie him down peacefully before leaving and running into Kayla in the hall.

"Doing what exactly?" She asked with arms crossed.

"That was a private conversation."

"A little one-sided, don't you think? Maybe you should try it with someone your own age." I ignore her and go into our room to change. "Nick ..."

"Kayla, let's enjoy our night. We have a nice meal waiting for us downstairs with candles and music. Let's take advantage and talk tomorrow." I said while thinking of what to say to her next.

"You will talk to me tomorrow?" She asked seemingly wanting to enjoy our night as much as I do.

"I will give you the general idea. Will that suffice?"

"It will." She said keeping her eye on me as I smile at her.

"Good. Then get changed and make sure to wear something that's easy to get off." I said with a wink before walking into my closet away from her. It is hard lying to her. It is even harder making sure she believes it. I clean up and put on Kayla's favorite suit before waiting for her in the dining room. She walks into the room, smiling beautifully, and wearing a dress that nearly has me coming out of my pants from the moment I lay eyes on her. "New dress?" I asked, sighing with appreciation.

"I was saving it for a special occasion, it seemed appropriate tonight. You do like red … don't you?"

"My favorite." I said reaching out for her. She moves into my arms and right away stretches up on her toes for my lips. I want to always remember this moment, tasting her lips, feeling her soft skin, caressing her cheek closer to mine, and most of all the fresh, soft scent of her. "Come with me." I said leading her to the middle of the floor and pulling her in close. Taking her hand, I press my lips gently against the side of her face and whisper my intentions for the night into her ear.

"I don't think we have danced together since we went on our first trip together." She said out of the blue.

"No, I'm sorry for that. We should have done it a lot more."

"It's okay. You can make it up to me … I think we are still young enough." She said, smiling up at me.

"Whatever you want, Princess." We dance and kiss for so long that our dinner doesn't look nearly as appealing as it did. We sit down and eat a little before agreeing to leave it behind and take our wine to the bedroom with us. With a glass each, we curl up by the fire. Kayla lies against my chest while I kiss the back of her neck and play with her hair. I want to take my time and make every moment tonight a memorable one but it is becoming increasingly harder to hold back my desire for her.

"Nick, I have an idea I want to talk to you about but I want you to promise that you will listen to me and keep an open mind about it … consider it for Nicky and I." Kayla asks with a crack in her voice.

I ease in closer, kissing the edge of her ear, "I promise. What is it?"

Kayla turns, sitting up, but holding me back as she looks me in the eyes, "Let's runaway- the three of us: you, Nicky and me. We can take enough money to get us by for a long time but leave everything else. Let them have it if they want it. We don't need it. We can be so happy, Nick. I can make you happy."

"I am happy now."

"I mean …"

"I know what you mean, but, Kayla, they are never going to let me leave. They will hunt me down until they find me- hunt us down.

And it will only be that much worse when they do find us."

"Not if they have everything they are after."

I hold her face in my hands so she will look at me, "Yes, they will. They will fear that I will come back and they won't want to be constantly watching their backs waiting for me."

"Nick ... please." She cries suddenly tearing me apart. "We can hide. You know how. I know you do."

"You want to live like that?" I asked her wishing she had never brought it up.

"Yes."

"You want to hide out all the time? Worried about who might be around the corner? Worry about Nicky having to grow up like that?" I asked her shaking my head.

"We will figure it out. You are so smart. Nick. I know you can figure it out. You can figure out exactly what we need to do. Please, Nick." Her teary eyes take hold of me.

"Kayla, I'm not sure you know what you are asking for."

"I do know and I know you can make it happen. Don't say no, Nick. You need to do this for us. You need to do this to protect your son." I try to speak but she fists my shirt and begins to cry, "Please!" She cries over and over.

"Okay. Okay. We will leave tomorrow. Let me make some calls, transfer some money in the afternoon, and we will sneak out tomorrow night." I lift her head from my chest and wipe the tears from her face, "Everything is going to be fine. I don't want you to worry about it anymore. I will take care of everything. All you have to do is pack." Her smile returns as she kisses me through her tears. "Now that we have that settled, let's get back to what we were doing." It takes her a few minutes to regain her composure but eventually she makes her mouth available to me while crossing her leg over mine. Reaching down, I caress her leg and run my hand up her thigh, rubbing it hard as we begin to heat up. Kayla opens my shirt, kisses down my chest, and reaches for my belt looking up at me with a wicked smile that causes me to laugh, but I still move her off me. "No, Princess, this is my night. I want you to dance for me. Seduce me, Kayla, and I will give you what you want."

"Everything I want?" She asked biting her bottom lip in anticipation.

"Don't I always?" Laughing, she gets up and changes the music to a tune she prefers. Sitting back, I watch as she moves provocatively in front of me, stripping her dress off, fondling herself through her bra and panties before easing each of them off. I stop blinking not wanting to miss a thing. Kayla stretches her beautiful legs out in front of me before turning and letting me feel her ass, kissing the places my hands don't touch. Turning again she sits down on me and works me into the hardest of erections, leaning back, and displaying her tits perfectly for me. I grip each of them, sucking and fondling until I can take no more. I drop my hand down low and push my fingers up into her, receiving the moan I was wanting. She moves against them making herself wetter with each pass. My mind is about to explode when I pull her into my arms and carry her to the bed. Spreading her legs out wide, I take a single taste causing her to squirm backwards, so I pull her back down to my mouth and take what I want sending her into a moaning mess. She grips my hair so tight I am sure she is going to pull every hair out of my head if I don't finish her soon. With a final push of my fingers, she comes and I enjoy it until the last before stripping naked and working my way slowly up her body. My dick twitches between her legs, teasing her with every touch it makes. I take one last taste of her tits and find my way inside her, gasping as her body takes hold of me tight. Kayla arches her back and I take full advantage, feeling the tightness inside her until I feel her body quiver and mine tense. Taking hold of my head, she brings me down to her lips, sucking on each while rubbing the back of my head, down my back, and to my ass- squeezing me down into her more. I roll us over and she sits up on me instantly taking control, moving her hips on me, and smiling as I grip the bed frame behind me- groaning out her name. I feel up the front of her, taking hold of the back of her neck, and spinning her back down on the bed, "I love you, Kayla Jayzon." I whispered against her ear as I send us both over the edge. Coming together, groaning, until we are shivering in each other's arms.

CROSO

*T*oday everything changes forever, I sneak out of our bed trying not to wake Kayla. I need to avoid her questions as much as possible. I leave Tanner behind and drive myself to meet Ryan in our secret place. He shows up right on time and I give him the last minute instructions, which he expectedly protests.

"No, Nick!" Ryan yells back at me.

"Don't argue with me, Ryan. You said you would do whatever I asked and this is what I want!" I demanded.

"Are you insane? I can't believe you would give up what you have worked so hard for." He demanded.

"I am not discussing this with you. Either you are going to do this for me or I am going to find someone else that will." I said with no give in my voice. Ryan grumbles for a while but eventually agrees.

With one task down, I check some final notes and make sure my money transfers have been successful before taking care of my son. Nicky is wide awake and ready to go today already. As soon as I enter his room, he reaches out for me. "There's my boy. Daddy is going to feed you today." I look at him as he smiles at me, "Can you say Daddy, Nicky? Say Daddy." He giggles hard as I try to get him to say it at least once. I have been trying for a week but he is no closer than the first day. "I know I am crazy to think you will talk this early." I feed him his breakfast, change him, and play with him as long as I can before Kayla wakes up. She comes into Nicky's room, quietly sneaking up behind me and kissing me and Nicky both.

"I didn't hear you get up." She said.

"I know you didn't, but that's okay." I said with an easy smile.

"Did you take care of everything already?" She asked nervously.

"Most of it. I have a few tasks left to take care of."

"Well, if you are taking care of him, and if you don't mind, I am going to go get ready myself." I nod, kissing her once more before she leaves. Left alone I pick Nicky up, fighting the pain that is creeping in. "I love you so much. Be a good boy, okay? Take care of your mother and do what she says. She is a smart woman and knows what's best for you." My voice cracks and my eyes begin to fill up. All I can do is press my lips hard to his head and hope that he knows I am doing what's best for him. *I have to go before I can't.* I set him down in his crib and walk out with the lump growing in my throat and go to make my last good-bye. Kayla has finished her shower and has clothes draped all over the place as she packs up. "You almost done?"

"I don't know. I am not sure what to take." She said with a giddy anticipation.

"I wouldn't worry about it, you can always buy something new when you get there." I said leaning against the wall to help hold up my shaky legs.

"When ... WE ... get there." She said waiting for me to nod.

"Pack light, it will be easier. Take only what you can't live without." She smiles, prancing around the room with no worries. "I need to go." I said needing to take a deep breath. "I'm going to go now and get the last minute tasks done."

"Okay. Do you want me to pack for you?" She asked, barely acknowledging me as she decides on two different pairs of shoes.

"I already did." I said with a forced smile. She kisses me gently and goes on about her business as if nothing is out of the ordinary. "Kayla, come here." She turns, looking at me sweetly at first but begins to fear my hesitation. "Don't worry. I only want to tell you how much I enjoyed last night with you." Her smile returns as she hugs me, only I don't let go. I kiss her hard and hold her as long as I can. "I love you." I said hiding a tear into her hair.

"I love you too." She said. With one last kiss, I leave them having to carry my unyielding legs forcefully, every step becoming more numb than the last as I walk out the door.

I crash into the backseat of the car, holding my heart so it doesn't explode out of my chest. "Drive! Go!" I yell at Tanner.

"Are you sure this is what you want to do?" He asked hesitating as he glances at the front door.

"I have no other choice. They will never give up. Not until I am dead."

"You're right … not until you are dead," Tanner said. I look up and catch his disapproving glare in the rearview mirror.

~30~
KAYLA

I have been scrambling all day trying to figure out what's important and what isn't. In the end, none of it matters, as long as I have my husband and my son. Changing my focus, I concentrate on Nicky's favorite toys and the special items that Nick has given to me. I have everything ready to go when the sun begins to go down, but Nick still isn't home. I start to get nervous but when the door opens I jump up excitedly and rush to greet Nick- only it isn't Nick. "Ryan?"

"Nick sent me to get you." Ryan said avoiding my eyes.

"He sent you? Why doesn't he come himself?" I asked, stepping away from him slowly.

"He thought ... he thought it would be safer this way."

"Okay, when are we meeting him?" I asked glancing around the immaculately cleaned house.

"Soon. He will send me the information when I let him know I have you safely away." Ryan said walking past me and taking the bags I have packed. He immediately begins packing them into the car while I secure Nicky in the backseat. I glance at Ryan briefly as I sit down next to him and prepare to leave.

Looking back, I watch as my home gets smaller and begin to shake with fear. "Take me back! I changed my mind, I don't want to go." I said but Ryan ignores me, giving me only a glance out of the corner of his eyes. "Did you hear me? I want to go back."

"What about Nick?" Ryan said calmly.

"Call him and tell him to come home."

"I can't do that, Kayla. It's too late anyway. He is already gone." Fearing the worst, I tense up and try to imagine any scenario where Nick would leave ahead of us. After hours of driving, Ryan hands me a note.

"He's not coming is he?" I said fighting my tears.

"He explains everything in the letter ... I hope." Ryan said still avoiding my eyes.

I open the letter and sweep my fingers across his name at the bottom.

Dear Princess,

Never in my life would I have expected to fall for someone so incredible or be blessed to have her love me the way you have. Tell my son I am doing this for you both. You have to get away from me, they won't stop until I am dead and I can't bear the thought that something might happen to either of you. So, I am sending you to a safe place far away from me- far away from this madness that is my life. Ryan will take great care of you and Nicky. I know you have already figured out that he is my brother, he owes me and this is my final favor from him, to make sure you get away safely. You and Nicky mean everything to me, you will never know what this is doing to me. To think of all the ways you used to dream about getting back at me, make me pay, make me suffer, and now I suffer the worst pain I could ever imagine. Run, Kayla, run far away from me, for your own sake and for our son.

I love you always – Nick

To keep from crying out and scaring Nicky I grip Ryan's hand and scream with no voice. *Damn you, Nick!*

⊰⊱

"**K**ayla, are you awake?" Ryan asked shaking me gently. My eyes are still swollen from crying but I am able to sit up and take in the hotel room where we crashed the night before. "We should probably get going."

"Where are we going?" I asked sharply.

"To a place that is already setup for you and Nicky."

"Nick set it up?" I asked still hoping for a possibility of being with him.

"No, I did. He didn't want to know where we were going." I look up at him. "Oh, please don't cry anymore. I don't think I can take it. You think I am happy about this? Because I'm not. I'm going to miss him too."

"And you didn't even have sex with him." I say without thinking.

"Eww, why would you say that? You're disgusting." He said shivering with disgust causing me to laugh. "Come on, get ready so we can go. I would like to get there so I can get this drive over with."

"I need to get a shower. Will you take care of Nicky for me?" I ask as he glances between us.

"What do you want me to do with him? He is sound asleep."

"If he wakes up, change him, feed him, or play with him until I am out of the shower." Ryan looks in Nicky's direction seriously scared. "You will be fine."

"Hurry up." He snaps.

I take my shower and get ready, only to climb back into the car and drive for four more hours. I try to get Ryan to reveal where Nick may have gone, but after many frustrating conversations that only end in arguments, it is clear he has no idea. We arrive in a small town and pull into the driveway of an old Victorian home with a large yard and curious neighbors. The house is already furnished for us and, though a little dusty, cozy. Ryan rushes our bags in and crashes quickly in the sunroom, listening to the rain fall, and drifting off to sleep.

While Ryan is asleep, I take the car out and go to the store with Nicky. It is obvious we don't fit in here. From the moment I walk into the store, people stare at me from every corner. I take notice of the people, trying to take inventory of the proper dress for shopping, but nothing seems that much different. I am not excessively made up, and besides wearing heels with my jeans rather than sneakers I don't see much difference at all. Clearly this is an incredibly small town that isn't welcoming to newcomers. I wonder how long it will take before we aren't "new" anymore. *Not sure I want to stay here long enough to find out.*

When I get back to the house, Ryan comes running out in a panic, "Are you crazy? Where in the hell have you been?" He yells.

"I went to the store to get food, supplies ... you know things we need."

"You couldn't wait until I woke up to do that?" He continues to yell.

"Why does it matter? Am I going to have to be stuck at your side for the rest of my life?"

"No, but until I get a feel for the area and know that you're going to be okay here, then I would like for you to stay where I can keep an eye on you." I sigh walking around him. "Did you just roll your eyes at me?" He yells, wildly causing Nicky to laugh.

"Yes, I did and you better get used to it if you're going to say stupid things." Ryan runs up on me shaking his finger in my face, fighting with his mouth to force out words. "Let me know if you ever come up with a comeback." I said leaving him behind. After I set Nicky down, I check on Ryan who is kicking and flailing like a crazy person talking to himself. It's comical, I have never seen anyone act so frustrated openly. "Bring in the bags while you're out there." He turns with his lips tensed. "Please." I said with a smile.

"UGGGHHH! Nick you owe me big time for this." He raves.

⚬⚬⚬

*A*fter a couple of weeks of being cooped up, Ryan finally agrees to let me get out of the house- although he won't let me go alone. He forces me to go way outside town to a busy area of the nearby city, a place where he says we will blend in easier. *He is determined to make me insane. I am sure of it.* The only consolation is Ryan doesn't seem too happy about having to be here either.

Desperately needing some information about Nick, I think of everything possible to get rid of Ryan so I can call home. I try to make nice with him and invite him to lunch, all the while looking him over for a weakness. "So, when did you know Nick was your brother?" I asked.

"Since birth." He said simply.

Rolling my eyes, "That's a beautiful story, Ryan. You should write a book about it."

"What do you want? He was my older brother."

Shrugging, "A little more detail would be nice. How did you two get along? Did you see each other often?"

Ryan rolls his eyes in my direction with a deep sigh. "Nick was in charge of taking care of me while our Dad enjoyed my mother. The first eight or nine years he always seemed to be around, but then Dad found someone else to spend time with, and Nick got a car so he was always on the go. He would sneak over once in awhile, bringing us ice cream or something- anything in hopes that we would offer to let him stay the night. He hated going home, Mom felt sorry for him, so she would make him up a bed in my room and he would crash. By the next morning, he would be off doing whatever Nick did to get by. It got to where she made a permanent place for him so he could come in at any time of the night. He was a good brother, I guess. Although at the time, I was jealous of him because Dad wanted to spend time with *him* and wanted to be a part of *his* life. The insane part is Nick couldn't stand him. I don't know why I was so jealous of something that made him so miserable. If he was hanging out with friends, Dad would spend all day looking for him and then demand he come home and study or some shit. He was so proud of Nick, he thought he was too smart and too good for the neighborhood they were in- and he was, but nothing Dad did was going to stop him from getting into trouble. My mother, on the other hand, could get him to do anything. She talked him into staying in school several times. He was so smart. He was too smart to be going to that school, it bored him. Everything was too easy for him. As much as I protested having to share my room with him, I did like having him there. It was a nice consolation since Dad was such a dickhead."

"So, you became close growing up? Is that why you are helping him now?" I asked, searching for something I can use to get the information I want.

"That's not the only reason, he helped my mother when she was sick." Ryan stares at me waiting for me to ask but I simply tilt my head and smile. "You're exhausting, do you know that? She had Leukemia. The doctor she was seeing could only do so much, she was miserable and in pain all the time. I didn't have time to do anything but take care of her. One time Nick came to visit her on one of her bad days, I tried to tell him to come back another day but she insisted on seeing him. My mother always liked Nick, treated him like her own. She said she felt sorry for him, but I think it was because he looks a lot like our father- because she knew Nick was no saint. About a week after he left, I got a call that the care facility had an open room waiting for my mother- a private room at that. He never would admit it, but I know it was him. He had started working for that guy, Harvey, doing all his dirty business and that was when it all began. I went to him after my mother passed. He didn't want to let me work for him at first, but then he got this idea to put me somewhere where I could be useful to him. We agreed to keep quiet about being related and I fed him information."

I lean forward curiously, "What kind of information?" Ryan rolls his eyes and turns to watch a pretty girl pass. "Fine. Don't answer me. I will find out anyway though. You know I will."

"Are you finished? I would like to get back before the game comes on."

"Let me go to the bathroom first. You don't mind watching Nicky for me while I'm gone do you?" Ryan looks down at Nicky as

Nicky looks up at him, neither seems excited about the opportunity to get to know each other better. "Thank you." I said running off before either of them can throw a fit. Once I round the corner, I wait for the right person to pass and know I have found him when he looks up at me and blushes. "Hi." I said stopping him, making sure to touch his arm as I take hold of his hand. "My name is April and I was left here by my now ex-boyfriend. He took off with my purse, my money, and my cell phone. Is there any way I could borrow yours to call someone to come get me?" I asked trying to match his shyness.

"Uh, April, right?" I nod. He laughs nervously, "I'm Ralph." He said letting me shake his hand. "You know, I could take you home if you need."

"You are so sweet to offer, but I couldn't put you out like that and … I don't want to come off as ungrateful, but I did just meet you. But, if you let me borrow your phone, I will be happy to leave you my number in it. When I get mine back, maybe we could talk and get to know each other better." I said swaying slowly in place while he watches, seducing him into what I want. He laughs again and happily hands me his phone continuing to watch me. "Thank you, I will be right back." I go into the bathroom before he even realizes what I said. Making a mad dash to a stall, I shut the door and dial the club, knowing someone will answer but hoping Exie is somewhere nearby. A new person answers the phone but luckily is able to get me to Exie quickly.

"OH my God! Are you alright?" She yells into the phone.

"Yes, I was supposed to runaway with Nick, but he sent me away with Ryan instead. I am not sure where he went." I asked frantically.

"I know where he's at … he's here." Exie said.

"WHAT!" I yell.

"Whoa! Easy on the eardrum, sister. Yea, I saw him last night-although he did seem to be saying goodbye before he left. He made sure I understood how to handle the club without him and told me the combination to the safe."

"Open it." I said without thinking.

"What?"

"Open the safe, Exie. Open it now!"

"Okay …oh wow. OH WOW!" She yells.

"You better start talking right now."

"He signed the club over to me. He gave me the club and cash, lots of cash. Why did he do that?" She asked.

"He is still leaving. I have to get back there before he goes."

"Where exactly are you?" She asked.

"I'm not even sure. I am going to wait until Ryan falls asleep tonight and then I am going to take the car to the airport. I will call you when I get there, but you have to come get me."

"I hate being involved in your scheming, Kayla."

"Help me, please!" I begged annoyingly until she gives.

"Okay ... oh, but don't look for my old car, I am sure I am going to be driving a new one within the next couple of hours." She said happily. Laughing, I hang up the phone and run out of the bathroom tossing the phone back to Ralph as I pass, thanking him with half a breath.

"Ready to go?" I asked Ryan with a smile. He gets up, looking at me suspiciously. I pick up Nicky and suddenly realize I am going to have to leave him with Ryan tonight. I stop at the store on the way home and buy Ryan his favorite snacks and beer, having to pretend to be interested in all the same things when he growls at me. As soon as we get home, Ryan gets comfortable watching his game, while I continuously make sure he has a fresh beer. I would slip him something to help him sleep, but I can't have him not hearing Nicky. *This is going to be difficult to pull off.* After I put Nicky to bed, I wait up watching another game with Ryan. *This man is be able to stay up forever.* "I think I am going to go to bed. Are you staying up?" I asked yawning and fluttering my eyes as if they are too heavy to hold open.

"As soon as this game is over." He said barely looking in my direction. Once in my room, I grab my packed bag and throw it out the window. I feel like a kid again, trying to sneak out of the house. But if I don't leave soon, I am never going to get out of here tonight. Tiptoeing out into the living room, I check on Ryan who is starting to doze off. While his eyes are closed, I softly pick up the keys to the car and shove them in my pocket. "What are you doing?" Ryan said sitting up wide awake.

"I think I left something in the car so I was going to go check."

"What did you leave?" He asked.

"The toothpaste I bought today," I said, proud of myself for thinking quickly.

"You didn't buy toothpaste today."

"I did so, you just didn't see it."

Ryan jumps over the sofa and comes at me, quickly throwing me over his shoulder. "You're not going anywhere, Kayla."

"Put me down! You can't hold me here against my will ... it's illegal! I will call the police!" I yell, while kicking and punching him.

"We don't have a phone- or at least you don't." He said as I fight him all the way to my room. "You can have the bag you threw out the window back tomorrow." He throws me on my bed and blocks my exit as I try to run out again.

"Ryan, you don't understand. I have to stop Nick from leaving."

"I told you, he already left." He said huffing in my face.

"No, he didn't! He is still at home and I have to get to him." I said confidently.

"How do you know that?" He asked eyeing me. "Son of a Bitch! Did you fucking call someone?"

"Yes, but I used a stranger's phone."

"WHAT?! Oh well, that is just great! Fuck, Kayla! You may have screwed us here." Ryan stomps off, flailing his hands all around him.

"I did not. Stop overdramatizing."

"Who did you call?" He asked watching me carefully.

"My friend."

"And who is your friend?"

"Exie. She works at the club."

"Nick's club?" He yells.

"Yes." Ryan begins fisting his hair and stomping around groaning. "Would you calm down? I didn't do anything that would jeopardize your plans. Exie wouldn't say anything."

"How do you know? And you know what? It doesn't matter! I am going out of my way to protect you and your son when all you do is give me hell everyday and try to ruin all the work I have done. You are the most ungrateful woman I have ever met." Folding my arms, I force my lips together and stomp away from him. "Don't you walk away from me!"

"You know you should try to be a little more understanding. You did kidnap me from my home and away from my husband."

"Kidnap you? More like I was forced to take you away. Nick is probably grateful to be rid of you!"

"You take that back. You know that is not true!"

Ryan laughs nodding, "Do I? I bet Nick is at home kicking his heels up with a couple of women and loving life right about now. He got rid of you on the cheap." I punch him quickly. "OW!

Motherfucker ...Bitch!"

"Don't yell. My son is asleep."

"You hit me." He grumbles.

"You deserved it, you ass."

"You ...you ..." He said stumbling over his words. I stand tall against him waiting for him to say something else. Ryan holds up his hand pointing at me and shaking his head, "No. No I'm not doing this. No favor is worth this much trouble. I would rather Nick shoot me himself than deal with this."

"Good, then call him and tell him the deal is off." I agreed joyfully.

"I will!" Ryan yells with certainty.

"Do it. Or are you scared? I bet you are. That's it, isn't it? You're scared of Nick." Ryan shakes his finger at me again before turning around and returning to the living room. I follow him quickly as he grabs his cell.

"You think I am going to be in trouble. He is going to be pissed off at you even more little girl."

"I don't care. I'm not scared of him." I said happily.

Ryan dials while cursing me under his breath. He holds the phone to his ear waiting, "Hello! Who is this?" Ryan asked.

"Is it Nick?" I asked, trying to listen, but he holds me back with one hand.

"He is ... a close friend. Why? Where is he?" Ryan turns pale, glancing at me with a serious expression. "When did this happen? Ummm, no. I don't know where she is. No, I haven't seen either in some time. Yes, yes, thank you." Ryan hangs the phone up.

"Who was that? You called Nick, right?" I asked watching him closely. "Who did you call?"

"I called Nick's phone, but he didn't answer." Ryan said with a serious expression.

"Why ... not?" I choked out. Ryan pulls me to him and tries to hug me but I fight him. "No! Why, Ryan ... why?"

"It was the police answering his phone. They are trying to find out where you and Nicky are. Nick's dead, Kayla."

"NO!" I scream as he holds me tight to his chest. "No, Ryan, it has to be a mistake."

"He had it all figured out. He left the house by himself. He was supposed to leave for the airport. Nick figured they would assume that you two would be with him and never think to come looking for you anywhere else, they would spend all their time chasing him down never realizing. He sent Tanner ahead, hoping they would follow him and he could get away undetected. He didn't. They found out he booked a private plane and searched for him until they saw him getting onto the plane. Nick tried to rush the flight, but the plane was badly damaged during the gunfight to take him down. The plane made it up but came right back down and crashed ... no one inside survived. They believe Tanner tipped them off. He has already left the country with quite a bit of money, apparently."

"Maybe he got out- or maybe he..."

"Kayla ..." Ryan holds my face his. "The coroner has already confirmed that Nick was one of the bodies found in the wreckage." He said trying to hold onto me, but all I can do is scream my way into silence. "I'm sorry." He cries, pulling me in close. "I am so sorry." I collapse against him forcing him to pick me up. Ryan puts me to bed, leaving me briefly, before returning with Nicky, who is crying as well. Ryan wraps us up in a blanket and lies down beside me trying to comfort me throughout the night, but all I can do is grieve for my husband.

~31~
KAYLA

*E*very night I go to bed and every night I see Nick. If not for Nicky I'm not sure I would ever bother getting out of bed again. Opening my eyes, I am blinded by the sunlight and quickly jump up and slam the shade back down. *Nicky isn't crying yet and I am not getting up until I hear him.* Closing my eyes I bury my face into the pillow.

"Kayla." Ryan calls out to me. "Kayla!"

"What?" I yell.

"You need to get up. Nicky has been up playing for the last three hours."

"If you're already taking care of him can't you just let me sleep a little longer? I'm not feeling well today." I said burying myself deeper into the bed.

Ryan stomps over and raises my shade, "Get up! I have allowed you to wallow long enough. Nick may be gone, but that doesn't mean you have to chase after him."

"You don't understand."

"I understand plenty and I know if you don't start putting your life back together, you're never going to do it. Nick didn't let me mope around when I lost my mother and I'm not going to let you do it now." Ryan picks me up and puts me in the shower, still clothed, and turns on the water.

"Shit! Damn it, Ryan, it's cold!" I yell at him, hearing him laugh as he leaves the room. I force myself to get cleaned up before walking in on Ryan and Nicky playing. "I'm up. Happy?" I said to Ryan, but alerting Nicky to my presence. His excitement brings a smile to my face and I have to pick him up to hug him.

"I don't know about me, but someone else certainly is. Put your shoes on. I'm taking you out. You need some fresh air- and so do I for that matter."

"Where are we going?"

"Not telling you, it's a surprise." I roll my eyes but put my shoes on anyway. Ryan drives for some time before we arrive at an amusement park. He looks over in my direction and I smile lightly in a silent agreement to try at least. The day begins with a train ride that Nicky is a little unsure about at first, but by the end is clapping with laughter. We walk around mostly eating junk food and nudging each other into passersby. They are not too happy about it but we are having fun. We play some games and take Nicky to the petting zoo where Peggy, the goat, becomes obsessed with Ryan. She follows him everywhere, constantly tugging at his clothes to get his attention. Ryan tries everything to get rid of her: hiding behind me, throwing food in the opposite direction, but Peggy the goat is not giving up. Ryan runs in one direction and she follows. He tries to fake her out but it only makes her more determined. Nicky is laughing hysterically, as is everyone around us, and I don't think I have ever laughed so hard. Ryan finally makes it safely out of the pen, smiling but tired. "That goat is crazy." He said out of breath.

"Crazy for you. You need to dial down the charm a bit, Romeo." I laugh as Ryan lightly bumps my head with his, something we have suddenly begun doing with each other.

"Let's get out of here. I'm exhausted." He says to which I agree and Ryan puts his arm around my shoulders, "You may have to carry me to the car though." I laugh as another couple approaches us.

"That was the funniest thing I have ever seen." The man said. "I have never seen a goat do that."

"I'm not sure what I did to her." Ryan said.

"I think she is in love. She probably doesn't get too many handsome men coming around." The lady said. Ryan blushes and hides a little behind me. "You sure are a lucky woman." She said to me as we walk away, taking me by surprise.

"I think she thinks were married." I said to Ryan.

"What? Really?" Ryan said with a soft laugh. Putting his arm around me, he kisses my cheek, "So, wife, how about we get our boy home?" He laughs, but I have a hard time swallowing it.

೮ॐ౪

*R*yan sits across from me scrolling through his phone for the scores of the games he missed the day before. The questions begin swirling through my head as I look him over. *The problem is that he has features that remind me of Nick- or maybe that isn't a problem. His hair is a lot lighter. Still, he is built ... nicely ... and he has great ... full lips ... STOP!*

What am I thinking? "Ryan, don't you think this situation with us is kind of strange?" I ask.

"What do you mean?" He asked, barely looking my way.

"I mean, we are living together, doing things together like a couple. Are you planning on living with me forever? Don't you want to meet …"

"Hell yes! I don't want to be stuck with you anymore than you want to be stuck with me. As soon as everything settles down and I am sure no one is interested in coming after you, I plan on finding my own place. Do you know how long it has been since I have had sex?"

"I don't care." I said shaking my head and returning to Nicky.

Ryan starts huffing as he reads his phone, "It's been so long, even you are starting to look good to me."

"Hey, you didn't have to say that."

"You heard that?" He said with a cocky smile.

"Ass."

"You're going to talk to me like that in front of you child? Tisk tisk." He said shaking his head at me.

"You called me a lot worse the other night."

"When? You mean when you beamed that ball at my head?" He said waiting for me to respond but all I can do is giggle. "Laugh it up. It fucking hurt." I snap my head around and stare at him. "You tricked me!" He said pointing at me. I hide my smile but catch him looking over at me.

"Well, I only threw the ball because you refused to listen to me."

"You talk constantly, I can't tell when it is important or when it's just crap you're saying just to be saying something." I stare at him harshly with my jaw dropped. "You do! You talk all the time. I walked in on you cleaning up the living room the other day and you were just jabbering away. … At who? I don't know!"

"I didn't see you come in there. You're lying."

"That's because I was sure I didn't want to know what you were talking about. I ducked out before you could see me."

"For your information, I was talking to Nicky. I am trying to teach him words."

"Oh wonderful!" Ryan huffs. Glaring at him, I watch him lean over to Nicky, "Hey, Nicky, here is a word for you to learn. Sssshhhhh." He said as Nicky takes hold of his face and giggles. Ryan continues, laughing with him. "I don't usually like kids but you are alright, Nicky. Kind of cute, too."

"You better like him, he is your nephew." I said watching the reality hit Ryan.

"Yea, I guess he is the only blood I have left." Ryan said before getting up and leaving the room. Sometimes I forget that he lost a brother.

After I put Nicky down for his nap, I find Ryan sitting quietly on the patio. As soon as he sees me, he threatens to get up and leave but I somehow talk him into staying. Slowly, I put him at ease and begin telling him a story about Nick. I tell him about the time I tried to kill Nick and how Meagan ended up trying to shoot me instead. After he laughs at me for some time, he finally admits something to me. He tried to mimic Nick by buying a suit he thought matched one of Nick's, but when he showed up to a meeting with Nick and some others, the stitching of the suit lighted up from the lights of the club and he looked like an Armani patchwork quilt. He said Nick was the only one that didn't laugh, but it was difficult even for him to keep a straight face. Ryan said that was when he realized he had to figure out who he was and not try to be Nick. We spent the rest of the day and on into the night talking about Nick and ourselves. By morning, I woke up lying in his arms in the same place we spent the night talking. It was awkward waking up with him but we managed to look each other in the eyes again after a few days.

છ૪ૅ

*A*fter three weeks straight of rain and storms, even Nicky seems to be going stir crazy in this house. We play games, watch every available movie and count every crack in the ceiling before we end up challenging each other to races around the house: who can run from the kitchen to the top of the stairs first, who can get from the front door to the back door on one leg first, who could balance an egg- walking backwards- or with one eye closed without dropping the egg or falling. That one ended in a tie, I fell and Ryan ran into a wall breaking his egg. We played toss the baby until Nicky had to go to bed. Ryan decided to take this opportunity to check on the news from home.

"Kayla!" Ryan begins yelling for me. I step into the doorway, irked by his yelling for me with Nicky asleep. Ignoring my attitude, he points to the computer screen, "Listen to this. Dawson Reynolds is claiming that Nick agreed that in the event of his death and if no other blood relative can take claim to his estate, then he, Dawson Reynolds, is the rightful heir." Ryan watches as my jaw drops and I rush over to confirm what he is reading.

"How can he claim that?"

"He says he has paperwork that he and Nick both signed so Nick could get Dawson to work for him." Ryan huffs, "He said he managed Nick's money and business assets for him- more than doubling what he had before Mr. Reynolds took over. Yea right! He has gone to a judge and if nothing is claimed within ninety days then everything will be changed over into Dawson's name, including the house. The jerk. I know what he's looking for, he is so desperate to get at Nick's money he will do anything to find Nick's books."

"His books?" I asked curiously.

"Yea, the details of his operations so they can take over everything he had and get at his accounts where he is hiding his money."

"They aren't going to let Dawson have everything, are they?"

"Of course they are. The bank will get more money this way and the state doesn't want to deal with his attorneys forever, it is too much money. It is easier for everyone this way. Besides, outside of you and Nicky, both of whom are presumed to be dead, Nick doesn't have any other living blood relative on record." Ryan said, still shaking his head and cursing under his breath.

I sit down looking up at Ryan, "I know where the books are. I know everything. In fact, I brought it all with me." I said as Ryan's jaw drops to the ground.

He gets up smiling and picks me up spinning me around in circles in his arms, "This is great! We have all the control then, Kayla. They will never find it. They will never have any of it." He smiles overjoyed. "I wish you had told me, but I don't care about that right now. Where did you put them?" I shake my head not knowing what to say. "You're not going to tell me? You trusted me enough to tell me that you have them, but not enough to tell me where you hid them?"

"It is not about trust. It's about keeping the information safe and keeping you safe." I said looking away from his judging eyes.

"Bullshit! Don't tell me then. I don't care." He said walking away from me in a huff.

"Damn it, Nick, come back here!" I yell at him. Ryan stops dead in his tracks.

"I'm not Nick, Kayla! Stop calling me Nick! My name is Ryan!"

"I'm sorry, I can't help it. I look into your eyes and I see him. I am used to arguing with him too." I said, falling against the wall. "If you want to know, I will tell you everything. It is not that I don't want to, it's that I don't feel that I have the right to. Nick didn't exactly tell me about them." I look up into Ryan's eyes, "I searched until I found them. It is all held on a computer and then backed up onto an external drive hidden …"

"In the fireproof safe you demanded we bring?" He asked sighing after I nod. "Well, I guess your snooping paid off this time." Ryan lifts my chin and smiles. "I'm sure Nick would have forgiven you, so I guess I can to." Smiling, I reach out, wrapping my arms around his neck, hugging him tight, and enjoying the feel of him doing the same.

ೕജൈ

$\mathcal{R}$yan never bothers to say a word to me about what I know but he does look at me with obvious questions swirling through his head. I wonder what to say to him as I lie in bed wide awake listening to the storm nearing us. The storm presses hard against the old house, beating it down with threatening winds. Restless, I get up and go check on Nicky and rock him back to sleep when he is awakened by a loud roar blowing through the nearby trees. Dozing off while I rock him, I decide it best to go back to bed. I put Nicky in his crib and shuffle my way in the dark back towards bed.

"Nicky wake up?"

I smile looking into his dark eyes, "Yes, baby, but he is fine. Let's go back to bed." I said, kissing him before I realize where I'm at. I open my eyes wide, watching Ryan stand awkwardly in front of me.

"You thought I was Nick again, didn't you?" He asks while I twist awkwardly in place. "Never mind, I think I already know the answer to that. The weather service said there might be a tornado coming our way. I will keep an eye on the weather by myself, you obviously need to go to bed." Without saying another word, I rush into my room and crash between my covers with embarrassment.

As the storm outside becomes more unruly, Ryan wakes me up and hustles Nicky and I to a safer place in the basement. Nicky eventually falls back asleep while Ryan and I stay awake with uncomfortable glances towards each other. I begin to fall asleep when I hear the back screen door slam open. Ryan and I both jump and I look at him as he halts me from speaking. Settling back into my makeshift bed, I assume it is only the storm but Ryan remains uneasy for some reason. "I locked that door, Kayla." He whispered.

"It could have been broken by the wind." I said as he shakes his head. Ryan pulls out his gun and moves us further into a dark corner. I begin to think he is worried for nothing when we hear footsteps above us. Gasping, I step back into the wall as Ryan shields us. My heart beats so loudly I think I can hear it over our breathing. When the basement door starts to creep open, I grip Ryan's shirt and hold him back from running out to meet whoever it is. A large dark figure eases down the stairs with exceptional care. I want to close my eyes, but I also want to run and get my gun, but I can't do either. Ryan raises his gun and waits as the figure takes the last step off the staircase. Suddenly, the loud roar of the thunder breaks to a bright lightening strike, lighting up the room.

"Ryan?"

"Dwayne?" Ryan yells out.

"Oh shit, you scared the hell out of me son." Dwayne said putting his gun up and sitting down on the stairs. Breathing again, I step out of the dark following Ryan.

"What the hell are you doing here?" Ryan asked.

"Looking for you. You guys need to get out of here. Estrella is looking for you and I am sure he is right on my heels." Dwayne said taking out his phone. "Hey, yea. In the basement." He said before hanging up. "Reggie and I have been searching for a couple of weeks for you." He said as Reginald heads downstairs soaking wet, nodding towards both of us. "You guys remember Reginald Blackstone, don't you? He used to work for Connor until Nick hired him away. Like I was saying, you guys need to get out of here now. There is a video of you being chased by a goat that went viral. It wouldn't have been a big deal, but the video expert also recorded Kayla a few times during your ... whatever it was you were doing with that goat." Dwayne said watching Ryan raise his arms above his head frustrated.

"What are we supposed to do now?" I asked, watching Ryan for a solution. "Ryan?"

"I don't know. It was easy to relocate you when they weren't looking for me but now ... FUCK!" Ryan yelled, waking Nicky. I huff trying to calm him back to sleep. "Sorry. Listen, Kayla, they are not going to give up until they have Nick's books." He says as I glare at him.

"It wouldn't matter. Estrella wants Kayla. He is obsessed with her." Dwayne said.

"Me? Why?" I asked.

"Reggie has been working for him and has been privy to some important information. That's how we knew to come get you. We have been working with each other since Nick died. I have been trying to find Nick's books before they do so I can destroy them, but I can't find anything so they must have them already." Dwayne said. "Reggie has been waiting for Estrella or Dawson to screw up and say something about them, but instead all he hears is Estrella yelling about wanting Kayla. He clearly has a thing for her and wants to romance her or some shit. I don't know. Either way, it isn't just Nick's books he's after." Dwayne glances at Reggie and he nods silently.

"Well, this is great. Nick went to all that trouble to hide you and Estrella was after you the whole time. I have no idea what to do." Ryan said.

As the three boys stand around and debate it with each other, I come up with a plan of my own. "Take me back." They all three stare at me silently. "Take me back home, I want to take claim to what is rightfully mine." The three faces stare at me, dumbfounded. "The way I see it, I'm in charge now, boys and from now on, what I say goes. And I say we take down Estrella and Dawson and take back what is ours." I work my way to the center of the three men and boldly take my claim, "For Nick."

~32~
KAYLA

*E*very Sunday Joseph Estrella has brunch on the patio of his favorite restaurant. He never strays from the place or the time. He comes in the door with his bright white smile and an air of complete confidence. He doesn't think to look twice at the tables around him as he sits, folding his napkin perfectly in his lap, and taking a sip of the drink that already awaits him. His guards stand back thinking nothing of the patrons that eat their meals with proper manners and polite conversations. Joseph takes in the view from the patio with pride, smiling joyfully, before he reaches for his glass again, only this time his eyes open wide. "Good afternoon, Joseph." I said, raising my glass from a table in front of him. Joseph sits back in his chair with a slight smile but obviously curious about our chance meeting. To put his questions to rest, I walk to him and take a seat at his table once he offers it to me like a gentleman. "I hear you have been looking for me?"

Joseph hesitates before responding, "I was worried about your well-being and I wanted to make sure you and your son were alright."

"Well, no reason to worry. We are both doing fine- outside my husband's death of course."

"Of course, I am sorry to hear about Nicholas. I was quite astonished when I heard the news."

"I am sure you were." I said watching him closely.

"I assume you are here to see to Nicholas's interests." I smile with a slight nod. "Well, I like a savvy businesswoman, so I will be willing to make you a fair offer for it all." Joseph said taking out his checkbook and pen.

"Oh, I am not here to sell you anything, Mr. Estrella." Joseph sits back with an inquisitive smile. "No, I'm here to offer you an opportunity."

"You're here to offer *me* an opportunity? Well, I have to say I am curious." Joseph leans towards me, placing his hand on my leg. "I can only imagine that this offer leads to something good for both of us."

Removing his hand from my leg, I lean into him, "I don't think you understand my intentions Mr. Estrella. I'm not here to try to get into your bed. I'm here to allow you to peacefully hand everything you own over to me." I said sitting up in my chair and taking a sip of my tea.

After sitting quiet for some time, Joseph sits up straight in his chair with a light chuckle, "And why, sweetheart, would I ever *willing* hand anything over to you?"

"Because, Joseph, I am going to take it whether you give it to me or not. It is your choice on how I do it." With a fleeting smile, I breathe in deep and exhale his death warrant in his ear before leaving with my guards at my side.

CREW

Since arriving home, I have been so busy that this part of the plan never bothered me- until now. I glance up at Ryan and take a deep breath before walking through the doors. We walk into the coroner's office and request to see the person in charge. "Can I help you?" A woman comes out with a puzzled expression.

"I am Kayla Jayzon and I am here to claim my husband" I said with a sudden shakiness.

"Jayzon?" She questioned fiddling with her glasses and looking down at her paperwork.

"His name was Nicholas Jayzon."

"I know who he is, I am just surprised to see you. I was told no one would be claiming him. Not knowing, we went ahead with his cremation. It has been awhile since ..." She said still seemingly nervous that I am going to make a fuss of some sort.

"I would still like to ..."I gulped.

"Ummm, okay. Let me get the paperwork for you. He isn't here, obviously, but we can process the request to have him delivered directly to you ... if you want."

"Yes, thank you ..." I said looking at her name tag. "Ms. Chambers."

"Lena, call me Lena." She smiled at me.

"Thank you, Lena." I said happy to have this part over with. I sign all the necessary paperwork to have my husband returned to me and leave to begin planning his funeral service.

CRITICAL

*D*ressed all in black and standing near a decorative urn that holds the ashes of my husband, reality hits me hard. The weakness in my legs, blurred vision, and a great need to tell everyone who greets me to fuck off and leave me the hell alone is all supposed to be normal. Person after person comes in telling me how sorry they are but I know none of them care about Nick. Their presence here only means they are interested in seeing if I pick up the pieces and take over where Nick left off- a good sign for our plan, but an annoyance to me right now. However, it is not nearly as annoying as the large number of women showing up crying all over the pictures of Nick I have sitting out. *If I take out one of them right now, no one would blame me. Especially the screeching slut in the back.*

The room is filling up and it is almost time to begin when I notice a familiar face in the back. She stands near a dark corner, trying to hide behind her dark sunglasses seemingly to be more interested in the people attending than that of Nick. Curious, I make sure to greet her since she hasn't bothered to try to greet me. "Ms. Chambers, right?" I asked her as she suddenly notices me standing next to her.

"Oh … yes. Mrs. Jayzon, I am so sorry for your loss, I hope you don't mind me being here?" She asked glancing around at everyone but me.

"Please … call me Kayla. And no, I don't mind. Did you know Nick?" I asked trying to hold onto Nicky who is intent on getting to this woman.

"Please call me Lena. Do you mind if I hold him for a second?" She asked taking Nicky and hugging him as if he were her own. Nicky rarely allows anyone he doesn't know to hold him and he doesn't make a fuss to get to them. *Who is this woman?*

"So you know Nicky too?" I asked, watching him smile at her.

With a stunned expression, she hands Nicky back to me. "Oh, no. He must sense that I like kids. Children they have a great sense about people."

Taking Nicky back I eye her up and down, "How again did you say you knew my husband?"

"We met when we were kids … he was like a little brother to me. Dealing with his … well, it brought back some nice memories and I felt compelled to come." Lena glances in my direction uncomfortably. "Maybe it was a bad idea. I am sorry to …"

"No, please stay. I would like to talk to you later. Learning some stories from Nick's childhood might be nice to hear." I start to walk away and then remember something, "Do you know Detective Simone? Brady Simone?" She smiles nervously and that's all I need to answer my question. *Damn you, Brady, using your own girlfriend to spy on me.* I walk away from her and take my seat.

After Dwayne and a few other close friends speak, there are requests from others to have a chance to speak as well. I am astonished at how many people want to take the opportunity to say something about Nick. The self-centered pricks went on forever but at least keep me from crying. It takes me awhile to realize that they are buttering me up, hoping I won't give up any of their secrets. This is a new position for me- the position of control and power and I'm not sure if I can get use to it or not. I crave a familiar hand. To protect his identity, Ryan sits safely in the back. Luckily, Exie is able to come and sit with me. She takes my hand with a sympathetic expression. The service comes to a close with a prayer by the minister. He begins talking about Nick's journey and how we are grateful to have at least had the opportunity to share our lives with him while he was here. No matter how wrong that feels, I am still numb to everything around me except Nicky. Nicky begins squirming and whimpering in my lap until I have to sit him in the empty chair next to me, but he continues trying to get me to look at something behind us, pointing and whining, louder and louder. I try to ignore him but he becomes even more persistent. "Daddy!" He yells suddenly speaking his first words. The entire room stops breathing, watching my reaction. "Daddy! Daddy!" Nicky begins clapping and jumping excitedly. I reach out to take him, but my hands are shaking so badly, I am afraid to pick him up.

"I'll get him," Exie said racing Nicky out of the room as he becomes hysterical.

Left alone, I feel the need to look for someone- anyone- but all I can see are blurry stares. "Kayla, are you okay?" Dwayne said.

Grateful for a familiar face, I grip hold of him and whimper, "No." Dwayne quickly escorts me out of the room and as soon we reach a safe place out of sight and out of earshot of everyone, I break down crying hysterically on Dwayne's shoulder. Curling up in bed, I release the tension that has been building since the start of this day and let go of the pain I have held onto so desperately in order to go on. "Nick … Nick, you said you would never leave me. You promised, Nick!" I cry out. A comforting hand slowly pulls me close, "Nick?"

"No … Ryan."

"I'm sorry. I ruined everything. I tried, Ryan, but I …"

"It's okay. This is even better. You look like the weak, grieving widow like we wanted. Besides, no one would have expected for you to have acted much differently. Hell, I nearly fell out of my chair." Ryan pushes my hair from my face and kisses my head, "It is going to be okay."

Ryan stays with me until the doctor comes and gives me something to calm me down. The medicine helps me fall asleep peacefully, sleeping soundly for the first time in awhile. Instead of the nightmares that have typically forced their way in on me lately, tonight is soothing and comfortable. I can almost feel Nick next to me. This is our room, our bed, and no other place could make me feel him more. I know he is here. Believing it to be true, I reach out for him, "Nick." *I know he's here and I have to make him stay.* "I love you, Nick." Suddenly, I can feel my cheek heat up from his breath, "Kiss me," I whispered. "Kiss me." The want is becoming too much, "A Prince is suppose to kiss the one he loves, to save her." His presence becomes stronger and I feel his lips touch mine tenderly. Quickly, I reach out and take hold of him before he can leave me again. "Don't leave me, I need you. I want you." I run my bare leg up his, finding his hand and sliding it up my thigh, kissing his lips and face. "Make love to me."

"No, Kayla." He whispered.

I smile, "I know you want to. I want you, Nick, I want to feel you inside me. I want to feel secure in your arms again."

"Kayla, I love you but you need to go on without me." I shake my head. "Why did you come back here, Kayla?"

"I want to kill him." I said defiantly.

"That's not why. Why, Kayla?"

Gasping, I pull him close and cry against his cheek. "Oh, Nick, you can't be gone. You can't be. You promised you would never leave me. You promised to take care of me." I try to speak more but all I can do is cry.

"Oh, Kayla, I'm sorry. I'm so sorry but they were going to get me eventually and it is better that you didn't see it happen. I want you to move on. Forget about me." He said trying to slide away from me.

"NO! No, Nick! Don't you leave me, you owe me. You owe me the life I was supposed to have ... remember? You have to stay with me because you owe me."

"I will always be with you. I love you. I would do anything for you, but I can't come back."

"Then make love to me. You can do that, you're right here." I said sliding my top off, pushing my panties down my legs, and opening my eyes slightly to see his dark eyes staring back at me. "I ... love ... you." I whispered slowly, nearly losing my breath seeing his eyes again.

"Close your eyes, Kayla. I don't want you waking up before we are done." He said running his hand down my face as I close my eyes. His warm lips press softly against mine, he takes hold of my body as he lets me feel all of his. His hand follows his lips down my neck and to my breasts where I feel his tongue vibrate with his moan against the hardness of my nipples. Reaching deep down his back, I hold his heated moans against my navel ... my thigh, "Don't open your eyes, Kayla, or I will go away." I nod and he moves into me, pushing inside me with a gasping groan. Taking hold of the bed frame behind me, I arch my back pushing into him more. He moves slowly, caressing my body with every motion, kissing me with every moan. "How do you feel?" He whispered against my ear.

"Incredible. Don't stop. You feel so good. I love how you feel, how you smell ... and ohhh ... how you hold me. You do everything right, Nick." He pulls my legs up around him, takes hold of my ass, and jerks my hips up into him. Working into me with purpose, he sends me backwards deep into my pillow, wreathing and moaning for him. With one last charge of excitement, I let go and come with a heavy moan while Nick holds tight to me. I begin to feel him leave me, "Nick?"

"Close your eyes, Kayla. Don't worry, I'm still here." He kisses me again, laying me back down and holding me tight. "I love you, Princess."

~33~
KAYLA

*A*lone, I wake up to a bright sun. I slept perfectly and my dreams of Nick now give me a reason to look forward to my dreams every night. Hearing Nicky cry, I jump up and find my clothes on the ground by the bed. *Wow, that was some dream.* Still a little lightheaded, I sit down for a second before trying again.

"Kayla, are you ... whoa. Sorry" Ryan said barging into the room.

"Don't you know how to knock?" I yell at him.

Ryan fights a smile as he looks away from me. "I said I was sorry. What are you doing naked anyway? I put you to bed fully clothed."

"I took some off as soon as you left and then ... I'm not sure, I must have gotten hot."

"Uh huh. Hot. I bet." He said sarcastically.

I glare at him as he snickers obnoxiously. "What do you want anyway?"

"I came to see if you heard Nicky, I didn't know if I should get him or not." He said vibrating as he holds back his laughter.

"Well, why don't you go ahead while I get dressed rather than standing there being an ass?"

"Okay. Oh, and, Kayla, ... your panties are over there." He said pointing to them hanging off the side of the chest. "You must have been smoking hot." He laughed.

"Get out!" I yelled throwing a pillow at him. I rush to get dressed and make Nicky's breakfast before Ryan has a chance to come down with him. I take Nicky from him as soon as he enters the room, ignoring his annoying smile. All through breakfast he watches me but I continue to ignore him.

Ryan leans across the table at me, "Kayla?" I look away from him. "Kayla." Huffing, I look over at him and his stupid smile. "I wanted to ask you something."

"What is it?" I asked impatiently.

"Was it good?" He asked with a cocky smile.

"Was what good?"

"You know ... your hot night." He laughs.

"Best sex I have ever had, jerk!" I huffed.

"Really? Wow. Maybe you can teach me something." He continued to laugh.

"Ryan, why would I have sex with you when I can enjoy myself so much more alone?" I smile forcefully.

"Ouch. Okay then, but let me know if you change your mind- or, you know, if you need new batteries or something."

"You are so annoying sometimes." I said growling at him.

"Oh, but you are such a joy." He said sitting back in his chair, rolling his eyes.

"Ass," I whispered.

"Bitch," he whispered back.

"Uggghhh," I stomped startling Nicky.

"See what you did? It's all right, Nicky. Mommy has anger issues but I think we can get her some help for that."

"Don't you have somewhere to be?" I asked him.

"As a matter of fact, I do. Thanks for the lovely breakfast, but next time I prefer some eggs rather than squished apricots and bananas." He said glancing at the label of Nicky's baby food. "Have a good day, dear." I fake a smile for him and go on about my day.

०३८०

*T*oday I am meeting with clients, establishing my new role. I begin nervously. Lionel, the man Ryan hired to drive me, is not helping me much either. Tanner would at least talk to me, tell me some stupid story that had no relevance to anything to take my mind off of my troubles. I try to learn more about him. To break the ice, I tell him a joke. He doesn't laugh, he doesn't even smile. He simply nods and comments on how funny it is before he put up the window between us. We are not off to the best of starts.

The first client I meet with is giving us the most trouble. He feeds us crucial information when we need to find special items for other clients. Banister Auckland handles all the items coming through customs, some of which may be drugs, but usually its priceless artwork, cars, jewelry- just about everything you could imagine comes through him. We need him and he knows it. Auckland is demanding to be paid what he had been with Nick, only stating numbers that are nowhere near what he was making. The fool somehow believes that I would come here unprepared. During his rants I sit back and wait for him to calm which makes him angrier. Auckland rages and spouts off crazy demands but, in the end, states that if he doesn't get them he is going to work with Estrella and Dawson. I had a feeling this is what he was going to do and I'm prepared and confident, which shocks him, throwing him slightly off his plan. I stand with a simple sigh as he watches me slide my gloves on. "Let me tell you something, Mr. Auckland," I said leaning down into his face. "You either take this deal or nothing- and- by nothing- I mean I will tear you apart and feed you to my dogs." He is taken aback at first but then begins to laugh at me. I stand back from him and laugh as I take out the knife Nick gave me and then plunge it down into his hand. "How about we start with this finger here?" I asked. Unrelenting from the pressure, I push down into his hand.

Screaming, "You fucking bitch!"

"That's right! Now tell everyone you know this bitch is taking over!" After my negotiation, Auckland agrees that I am right about everything and assures me that he will be happy to help me in any way he can. One thing I learned from Nick is there are times for negotiation and there are times to be heard.

∞

*M*y next day begins the same way. This morning, though, I bring Lionel a couple of muffins. He almost smiles but I still can't get him to talk to me. However, it does take him a few seconds longer to put up the window between us. Today's clients are less frustrating for some reason. I assume it is because Dwayne and Ryan are standing at my back, looking ever so intimidating.

Another day starting similarly to the two prior, but with a slight change- chocolate chip cookies that no one can resist. I bounce out handing my nicely decorative bag to Lionel with a cheerful smile as he opens the car door for me. "How is your day so far, Lionel?" I asked.

"Fine, Ma'am."

Frustrated, I wait to get in the car until I can think of something, "Lionel, do you not like me?"

"I like you fine, Ma'am." He said motioning me into the car.

"Then why is it you won't hardly speak a word to me?" I ask as he sighs.

"Mr. Ryan said I shouldn't encourage you to speak too much because of your illness."

"My illness?" I asked.

"Yes, your brain disease that affects your ability to make sense after speaking for long periods of time." He said waving me in to the car.

That son of a bitch! "I do not have a disease." I said forcefully.

"Then your jokes are you making sense?" He asked curiously.

"Funny, Lionel. Keep it up and I'm not bringing you cookies tomorrow." I said sliding into the car.

"Yes, Ma'am." He said with a smile.

My last day of client meetings and I have saved our political connections for last. I have some trouble at first, but once I start clearly noting their flaws and secrets the decision is easy for them. All except for one who thinks he is going to threaten me. While Dwayne and Ryan wait outside, this asshole thinks he has the upper hand and takes advantage.

"You know Nick always had the best taste in women and you are one his finest I do believe." He said, pushing me up against a wall and looking me over. "I tell you what, I will give you what you want for the same price. But now I want a free fuck for every deal. What do you say, Kayla?" I smile as he gets excited. "Yea, you like that, don't you?" He asked rubbing against me.

"No, not really." I said knocking his hand away from my waist and elbowing him in the face, sending him down into the floor. I press my spiked heel down deep into his crotch, enjoying his screams. Dwayne and Ryan rush in with guns drawn. "I got it." I said simply.

"No shit." Ryan said, nodding towards Dwayne.

"You have three seconds to apologize." I said waiting for him to stop crying about the pain. "Three ... two ..."

"I'm SORRY! SORRY! I was wrong, whatever you want!"

"Good enough, I guess." I pull my heel out and kneel down to him, "You should respect women more. You never know when one might cut off your little weenie there. I tell you what if you do well for me then I will see about getting one of my girls to teach you all you need to know about women. It will be quite enjoyable for you. Probably not so much for her, but that's the downside of the job sometimes. Otherwise, I will personally hunt you down and jerk you off until your dick falls off- and I do mean that literally. What do you say?" He nods still clutching his crotch with both hands. "Good, I am so happy we could come to a reasonable agreement." I said walking out happily.

CR&O

*W*hen I get home, I walk into the house and dance with excitement until Ryan comes running in, wrapping his arms around me, "You were amazing today! Amazing, Kayla!"

"It felt so good but I couldn't have done it without you and Dwayne standing with me." I said taking the glass of wine from his hand.

"No, you would have been fine without us. Your strength is beyond anything I have ever seen." He said looking me over in awe.

"Strength? That's right, I owe you." I said, punching him.

"Ow! What the hell was that for?" He said rubbing his arm.

Glaring at him, "Lionel told me what you said to him ..." Ryan looks as if he knows nothing of what I am taking about. "My speaking disease?" He suddenly begins laughing hysterically. "Not funny at all. I thought the man hated me. I baked him muffins and cookies to get him to talk to me." Ryan laughs harder forcing me to hit him again.

"Ow! Come on! That's hilarious." Ignoring him, I cross my arms and turn away from him. He reaches out to me and kisses my cheek. "You're cute when you're angry. But, you might want to be careful, you don't want to aggravate your condition." He laughs.

I turn around quickly watching him run, "Damn it, Nick!" I yell towards him, immediately regretting it.

Ryan's good mood dwindles quickly. He walks over to me, and takes hold of my face, "I'm not Nick, Kayla!"

"I know."

"I don't think you do. I have seen you watching me. Looking at me as if I can fill his place. That's not why I am here. Nick is gone, Kayla. He is gone and I am here. When this is all over, he isn't going to come back. There is only going to be me. Are you going to be able to deal with that?" Ryan asked breaking me with every second that I stare into his eyes.

"I know all that. It slipped. I am used to saying his name when I am ..." I tensed, trying to break free of him.

"No, you listen to me. I promised Nick I would take care of you and I am going to make sure I keep that promise, but I am not going to be his replacement. I know you are still grieving for him and I am okay with that, but if you think you can ever look at me and not see him … I would like to try to make you happy too." Ryan kisses my cheek but lingers along my lips and brushes against them softly. "I want to kiss you so bad it is driving me insane." His lips stay within an easy distance. All I have to do is take hold of them. I move slightly and he makes the move for me, taking my lips within his, caressing me softly, and holding me close. I run my hand up his chest, feeling his muscles, tasting his lips, and enjoying the closeness. Opening my eyes, I look into his and, for an instant, I see Nick and moan. He stops suddenly, "One day you're going to see me. And only me!" He lets go of me with obvious frustration, kicking one of Nicky's toys out of his way as he leaves the room.

Seeking comfort, I go into Nicky's room and find him already becoming cranky from the yelling. I pick him up from his bed and notice a new stuffed animal that he holds close to him. "Where did you get this? What is this? A donkey?" I hold him up and see his name engraved on his hind end, "Eeyore." Nicky frustratingly takes him back with a whimper. "Okay, he's yours. Damn you're cranky tonight. You have been sleeping for hours. What has gotten into you today?" Rocking him back to sleep, I think of Ryan and all that he has done for us and wonder if I could ever see myself giving into him. It feels so good in his arms, but I wonder if it is because I miss Nick so much or if I feel something for Ryan. As I rock Nicky, I admire the rocking horse sitting beautifully across the room and wonder where Nick bought such an expertly crafted piece. Nick did have a love for well crafted wood furniture. I wonder if he bought it … *or didn't buy it?* I put Nicky and Eeyore back to bed and take a closer look at the rocking horse. Hidden beneath the horses mane is a signature, Aiden Bourghesie. *Nick made me believe his uncle was dead. Why would he do that? What was he hiding?* Rushing to my room, I search for the key that Nick offered to Luke but cannot find it. *A2325, that was it, I know it.* I am his wife, I should be entitled to what is in there- key or no key.

~34~
KAYLA

*L*ionel drives me to the storage facility that I once visited with Nick. I hope this is the right one. Walking into the office, I greet a solemn manager that has little interest in helping me. "Hi, my husband ... I mean, my late husband, had a storage unit here but I am unable to find the key. Can you help me out, by chance?"

"Name?" He asked with a long-drawn-out sigh.

"Jayzon. Nicholas Jayzon." I said trying to see onto his computer screen before he turns it away from me.

"Nope, no Jayzon." He said dismissing me with a disinterested glare.

"I know it's here." I said as he shrugs chewing his gum with a slow draw. Thinking for a second, "try Aiden Bourghesie." I said having to return a stiff glare back to the bothered man.

Sighing impatiently he types in his computer, "His wife has already been here and paid the fees for the next year." The man said.

"I am his wife. I know I haven't been here and I certainly haven't paid any fees." I said as he stares blankly at me. "There has to be a mistake?"

"Lady, I don't know what to tell you. The fees have been paid so there isn't much I can do to help you unless you have a key. Come back when the fees aren't paid and I will be glad to hand it over to you- for a price." He said.

"How about, for a price, you let me in and find something interesting to distract you for a while?" I asked waiting for his interest to peak. I take out my wallet and start laying down hundred dollar bills until his eyes twitch. "So, do you think you have something that might hold your interest for half hour?"

"It takes fifteen minutes to cook my meal. In fifteen minutes, exactly, I will be back here to watch my monitors for any suspicious activity." He said, beeping me in before I have a chance to leave.

Rushing out to Lionel, I have him help with locating the storage unit which I find at the end of the aisle. Standing in front of the unit,

I take out my gun and aim.

"Whoa! What are you doing?" Lionel yells. Before I can answer, he gets a giant bolt cutter out of the trunk and snaps the lock in half. He smirks at me as he gets back into the car.

I raise the door and find clothes, shoes, money and jewelry, all of which belongs to Nick. In the back, I find personal items and childhood items. There are several boxes of pictures of Nick and his father, his mother, and miscellaneous pictures of friends and family. I search quickly to find anything on his uncle, reading as best I can the barely legible handwriting on each photo. I find a picture of Nick and Ryan, when they were both young and adorable. They have their arms around each other's shoulder and smile as if they were forced to do so. This one says my brother and the ones following were all of Ryan growing up with his mother and some including Nick. Then, there is another of Nick and a girl, she is hugging him while planting a heavy kiss on his cheek as he looks disgusted. She is taller than he and seems to be older, but the writing is tough to read. I assume she is some neighborhood girl or a girlfriend, but the caption seems to say differently. Struggling to read the writing, I continue to search for another and find a college graduation picture. I don't have to decipher the name because I know her. "Lena's graduation." On the back is a handwritten note from her to Nick, reading simply, love you always, Lena. Running out of time, I take out a new lock and put it on the storage door. *I think Lena Chambers and I need to have a conversation.*

☙❦❧

*T*his week has been successful. We have managed to put a sizable dent into Joseph Estrella, making it even harder for him to do business- but it was only a week ago that he put a sizable dent in to our business. I believe we are close to succeeding in our revenge against Estrella, but the process has increased his desperation to get to me. Ryan has demanded that I stay home or be closely guarded when I do leave. However, I need to talk to Lena and I can't have a bunch of guards around listening in on my conversation or drawing attention to her. There is something about this woman that doesn't fit and if she knows anything about Nick, then maybe she knows where I can find his uncle. At least tell me her true relationship with Nick and why my son seems to know her so well. I know Lena has been seeing Brady, so I waited until I knew he was working to ensure that she would be home alone. Her quiet, charming house is friendly and peaceful with its beautiful gardens. When she answers the door, she forces a smile and holds tight to the door, "I think we need to talk." I said to her, holding my hand against the door.

"This isn't a good time, Kayla." She said still trying to hold me back from entering her home.

I pull out the picture of her and hold it up, "I need an explanation to why my son knows you and how you know my husband and I am not leaving here until I get it." She motions for me to come in.

"You shouldn't have come here. My relationship with Nick is nothing for you to worry about." Lena said with her arms crossed, looking at me disapprovingly.

"Who said I was worried?"

"Kayla, Nick and I are good friends. Nothing more." She said with a sweet smile.

"You mean were?"

"What?" She asked confused.

"You said ... *are* ... good friends. You meant *were* good friends ... right?" I asked watching her become staggered. Letting my nitpicking ways go, I glance around the room studying who she is, "Did you and Nick meet in school?" She nods. "And you never dated?" She shakes her head looking away from me, squinting my eyes I watch her move around the room quickly, straightening it up. "Did you have company?" I asked noticing the two glasses she picked up.

"You know, I don't appreciate being questioned like a suspect of some kind. I was your husband's friend-nothing more. I would meet with him for lunch once and awhile and sometimes he would bring Nicky with him. I am sorry Nick never told you, but considering how you're acting right now I can see why he didn't."

Tired of her games, I walk up to her with clear intent, "you're hiding something and I know it. You better tell me what it is and you better tell me now!" I yell at her with clenched fists.

"Back off, Kayla!" She said eying me down with darkening eyes. I step back, wide-eyed, "I would like for you to go now." She holds the door open for me and stares hard at me with her blackened eyes. Without another word, I leave her and make my way back home in a daze. Before I can make it home, I get a text from Ryan and I assume I have been caught doing what I was specifically told not to do.

Instead he requests for me to meet him at Hannigan's wharf so he can show me something. I drive to the strange place and wait as I get a call.

"Kayla, where are you?" Ryan yells at me.

"I'm at Hannigan's wharf, where you said to meet you." I said frustrated.

"Where I said? Get out of there! Somebody stole my phone, Kayla. I don't know who you're meeting with, but it is not me." I start the car, back up and glance around quickly looking for anyone suspicious. "I'm on my way!" Ryan yelled hanging up before I can say another word. I speed out from where I am and run right into another car that blocks me quickly. I grab for my bag looking for my gun as a man gets out and rushes to the side of my car. Before I know it, he has crashed through my window and is dragging me out of the car. I nail him once in the jaw when I realize it's Dawson.

"Get the fuck away from me!" I yell at him kicking him again and again. Suddenly, I feel a blow to my head and fall over waiting for the ringing to stop. I try to fight another man off me when Dawson paralyzes me with a taser.

"Get her bag and check the rest of the car for anything we might need. What are you coming here for, Kayla?" I groan struggling against him as he ties my hands. "Joseph is going to be so happy to see you, especially since you are going to give us Nick's books, right?"

"Fuck you!" I said

"I wouldn't speak to me that way, Kayla, I am, after all, the one holding your life in my hands right now. How about you and I take a walk?" He drags me to my feet and forces me down a path, "You see, I think they are here somewhere and I think you are going to tell me where they are." He said tasering me again and laughing as I crumble against him. "Hurts, huh? Well, I could stop. Just tell me where his books are!" I stay silent, "Very well. Let's try something else." He picks me up off the ground and bends me over an old picnic table.

"No!" I yell struggling against him as he pushes me down and rips at my clothes.

"I know you have been after me since we first met. Since you will soon be Joseph's, I should probably get some while I can." He said before I can get in a good kick and push him backwards. I manage to free my hands and run down the dock with Dawson chasing after me. I notice a boat off in the distance and decide that's my only hope at this point. Jumping into the ice-cold water I swim as fast as I can. Dawson jumps in after me, still weak from his taser I cannot outswim him. Dawson takes hold of me and continuously pushes me under water while I try to fight him. "Wayne! Wayne, get your ass down here and help me!" He yells as the other man comes running down the path. "Finally!" As I choke on the water in my lungs he pulls me out and throws me onto the dock. "What the fuck? How….? Put your gun down or I will kill her right now!" Dawson yells as I try to crawl away from him. He grabs hold of the back of my head and tries to pull me up but drops me onto the hard surface of the dock as he stumbles backwards. My head spins, my heart pounds, and I begin to lose focus as the yelling increases around me. "I'm warning you! Stay back!" Dawson grabs hold of me again but suddenly, I hear a gun go off and Dawson releases his grip on me, screaming. When another shot rings out, Dawson falls to his knees next to me. "Please! Please! I had no choice. You have to understand! Joseph would have killed me. He …."

"Fuck you!" I hear someone growl. Another shot rings out and Dawson falls backwards off the dock, gurgling his last breaths as he sinks into the water.

Holding my head, I sit up trying to focus as the dark figure comes near me, "You got here quick. You must have driven like a madman." I said as I watch him walk towards me. I swallow hard as he slowly comes into the moonlight, "Nick?"

Made in the USA
Lexington, KY
04 May 2012